STAR TREK
NEW FRONTIER

No Limits

No Limits

Edited by Peter David

Associate Editor: Keith R.A. DeCandido

**Based on STAR TREK: THE NEXT GENERATION®
created by Gene Roddenberry**

POCKET BOOKS

New York   London   Toronto   Sydney   Singapore   Xenex

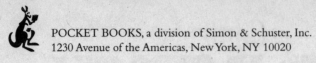

POCKET BOOKS, a division of Simon & Schuster, Inc.
1230 Avenue of the Americas, New York, NY 10020

STAR TREK is a Registered Trademark of Paramount Pictures.

This book is published by Pocket Books,
a division of Simon & Schuster, Inc.,
under exclusive license from Paramount Pictures.

Library of Congress Cataloging-in-Publication Data

Star Trek : New Frontier, no limits / edited by Peter David ; associate editor, Keith R.A.
DeCandido.
    p. cm.
  "Based on Star trek: the next generation created by Gene Roddenberry."
  ISBN: 0-7434-7707-3
    1. Interplanetary voyages—Fiction. 2. Space ships—Fiction. 3. Science fiction,
American. 4. Star Trek fiction. I. David, Peter (Peter Allen) II. DeCandido, Keith R.A. III.
Roddenberry, Gene.

PS648.S3S6589 2003
813'.0876208—dc22   2003060159

First Pocket Books trade paperback edition October 2003

10 9 8 7 6 5 4 3 2 1

For information regarding special discounts for bulk purchases,
please contact Simon & Schuster Special Sales at 1-800-456-6798
or business@simonandschuster.com

Contents

Introduction

Peter David

When John Ordover suggested the idea of a *New Frontier* short story anthology, my first reaction was one of keen interest.

This promptly gave way to panic. Not the running-around, sky-is-falling, woe-is-me type of panic, or at least no more so than one sees on any given day from me. This was more subdued panic.

It's not as if I'm unused to sharing characters. Most of my comic book work has taken place in shared universes, as I've watched characters whom I was overseeing in particular titles show up elsewhere. The problem is, frequently they're talking and acting in ways that seemed just flat-out wrong to me. But I've learned to accept that and live with it because, bottom line, they're not my characters.

In a sense, neither are the crews of the *Excalibur* and *Trident*. The copyright page sure doesn't say "Copyright © Peter David." Some have previous lives on television, and those I've conceptualized are officially owned by others.

Nevertheless, in contemplating this anthology, I realized just how possessive of them I've become. I've written more words about them—their hopes, dreams, relationships, aspirations, and adventures—than any other novel denizens I've thought up. I've seen them through birth, marriage, pregnancies, death, and everything in between. The thought of turning the reins that are guiding my literary children over to other writers was anathema to me. I wasn't fighting the notion kicking and screaming, but I approached the endeavor with a singular lack of enthusiasm.

That, however, was before we really started to get into it. Before associate editor Keith DeCandido (or as reviewers refer to him, "the next Peter David," which is nice because that means my kids can hit *him* up for college tuition) put out the call for story proposals to a select group of authors. The proposals and ideas came fast and furious, and rather than feel threatened and unnerved by the process, I quickly discovered that it gave *New Frontier* a sense of validation.

For starters, it wasn't as if every writer said, "I want Calhoun!" Instead different people zeroed in on their own preferences about whom they wanted to write. It gave a real indication of the breadth of interest that *New Frontier* had for its readers, that no one character was the single favorite of everyone.

Second, it was nice to see that so many people whose work I respected (not to mention whose company I enjoyed) were *New Frontier* enthusiasts. I'm not saying that "regular" fans are an undemanding audience. Far from it. But other writers are an extremely formidable bunch, because they're always second-guessing the narrative or aware of all the mechanics that go into producing the story. So if *this* bunch was interested enough to want to play in the *New Frontier* universe, that was proof of something. I'm not sure exactly of what, but it was a good thing.

Third, it helped that certain parameters were drawn. I was skittish over the idea of having stories set in "current" *New Frontier* continuity, because I was worried over the logistical nightmare of how so many visions might impact on the ongoing narrative. We could, of course, just do an anthology of meaningless "They Go to a Planet and Stuff Happens and Then They Leave" stories, but what would have been the point? If we were to do the first *Trek* anthology based on a non-TV series *Trek* universe, we had to do something more special than that. It was at that point we decided to go backward instead of forward. All the characters have rich, detailed histories that have been hinted at in some way, shape, or form. Some have been catalysts for entire stories (McHenry, for instance), while others have yet to be explored. Feeling this was fertile ground, the writers were set loose on the characters' backgrounds, free to set stories in some of the most emotional and challenging periods in our heroes' lives before they joined the *Excalibur.* (The single exception is the oft' mentioned, but never-told-until-now tale of Calhoun and Shelby's honeymoon-from-hell, written by yours truly. When you make the rules, you get to break them.)

Did I spell out what all the stories should be? Lord, no; I'm not *that* organized. In several instances I suggested specific time periods in which to set stories. And one tale originated entirely from my saying, "Gee, wouldn't it be cool if we had a story where . . ." The vast majority of endeavors, however, are entirely the invention of the individual writers. But I vetted them all, commented on them all, had changes made where needed, and oversaw the whole thing.

I'm emphasizing this not out of a compulsion for self-aggrandizement, but because when the anthology was announced on my website, a sizable number of readers instantly expressed reservations. They claimed the attraction of *New Frontier* for them was the uniformity of vision in the world conceived by John Ordover and myself. I've been the sole writer, and they were uncertain over the idea of suddenly bringing in over a dozen new voices to the mix.

So I want to take this opportunity to assure anyone who is furtively reading this intro in a bookstore trying to make up his or her mind, or anyone who has already plunked down the money and is hoping it was well spent, that our lineup of writers has done a sensational job in taking us back to before it all began. That they have presented key moments in our characters' lives as well as, if not better than, even the most ardent *New Frontier* fan could possibly have hoped.

If anything, *New Frontier* is elevated by this anthology. It's one thing when a single writer produces a body of work. But when talented writers want to jump into the pool and splash about, suddenly it becomes more than just a series of books. It becomes a true universe, a nice bit of mythos building, of different creators saying, "This is a particular piece of the universe that appeals to me. Come share it."

Shout-outs go once again to: Keith DeCandido, associate editor supreme; John Ordover, whose idea *New Frontier* was; Kathleen David, my wife and a superb editor in her own right; Glenn Hauman and Bob Greenberger, who expressed early interest and were fonts of ideas; Paula Block at Paramount, one of the most eminently reasonable "powers that be" in the world; Bill Mumy, from whom I copped the all-purpose profanity "Grozit"; and, ultimately, you the readership. *New Frontier* was in abeyance for a while as the popularity of *Sir Apropos of Nothing* changed a one-shot novel into a three-book deal. There are limits to what even I can turn out in a year. But we're back now, and we thank you for your patience and your continued support.

Peter David
Long Island, New York
June 2003

MACKENZIE CALHOUN
Loose Ends

Dayton Ward

After the *U.S.S. Grissom*'s mission to Anzibar, which ended with Captain Norman Kenyon's death and Commander Mackenzie Calhoun resigning from Starfleet in disgust, Calhoun, the future captain of the *U.S.S. Excalibur*, roamed the galaxy, getting into no small degree of trouble. After one particular incident, Admiral Alynna Nechayev bailed Calhoun out in exchange for conscripting him to do occasional covert missions on behalf of Starfleet Intelligence—all unofficial, of course. "Loose Ends" takes place during that time in Calhoun's life between Starfleet tenures, and also shortly after the *Star Trek: The Next Generation* episode "The *Pegasus*."

Dayton Ward

Dayton Ward got his start in professional writing by placing stories in each of the first three *Star Trek: Strange New Worlds* anthologies. He is the author of the *Star Trek* novel *In the Name of Honor* and the science fiction novel *The Last World War*, and with Kevin Dilmore he has written several *Star Trek: S.C.E.* adventures, a story for the upcoming *Star Trek: Tales of the Dominion War* anthology, and a pair of upcoming *Star Trek: The Next Generation* novels. Though he currently lives in Kansas City with his wife Michi, Dayton is a Florida native and still maintains a torrid long-distance romance with his beloved Tampa Bay Buccaneers. You can contact Dayton and learn more about his writing at www.daytonward.com.

The Romulan threw Calhoun into the brig.

He fell to the deck, rolling at the last second to avoid serious injury. Sitting up on the floor of the detention cell, he regarded the Romulan smiling at him from outside the brig as the centurion tossed a small satchel with Calhoun's personal belongings on the cell's small bunk.

"On your feet," another Romulan said as he entered the cell, carrying what Calhoun recognized as a standard-issue medikit. Extracting a tricorder, the Romulan doctor activated the device and pointed it in Calhoun's direction, no doubt searching for any illicit weapons or other items hidden on his person.

Take as long as you like, Calhoun thought.

"That will be all for now, Centurion," a new voice said, and Calhoun looked up to see two more Romulans staring back at him. One was dark-skinned, and even without the uniform insignia designating him as this ship's commander, Calhoun recognized Sirol instantly.

With the cell's forcefield now activated, Sirol waited for the guard to exit the room and the doors to close behind him before he said, "You are quite a long way from your home, Xenexian. From what I have heard, very few of your people elect to leave their home planet." The commander's voice possessed a pleasant, almost lyrical quality, yet Calhoun still detected the suspicion behind the words.

Standing next to Sirol, the other Romulan was examining a padd he carried in his right hand. "According to our sources, he is a former Starfleet officer who apparently left the service in disgrace, and since then has been known to take on various jobs, many of them of dubious legality, for the right price." Reviewing the padd again, he added, "My people have completed their inspection of the spy's vessel and turned up nothing. If he has anything of value to justify us not killing him, we have yet to find it."

Calhoun saw the first hint of a smile curling the corners of Sirol's mouth. "And his claims of working as a smuggler? What of those, Major Taelus?"

"I believe the line between smuggler and spy to be very thin, Commander," the other Romulan replied. "It is a distinction I waste little time making. His cargo holds are empty, and given that he has trespassed into our space from the Federation side of the border, I see no reason to belabor the point."

From the uniform insignia, Calhoun recognized that Taelus was an agent of the Tal Shiar, an organization feared throughout the Romulan Empire. So far this agent's behavior was consistent with the normal methods employed by the Empire's elite secret police. That much had been demonstrated even as Calhoun was escorted through the ship. He noted how members of the *Terix*'s crew moved with deliberate purpose to clear a path for them, avoiding eye contact with Taelus and doing everything to avoid drawing his attention.

"If he is a spy," Sirol said, "then you will have plenty of time to interrogate him once our current mission is completed."

"That is another point of concern," Taelus replied. "The timing of his arrival strikes me as decidedly convenient. Considering the cargo we carry for the Praetor, we cannot be too careful."

Sirol turned to Calhoun. "Why were you trespassing in Romulan space?"

"Like I said," Calhoun replied, "I'm a freelancer. I've been running arms and other supplies for various Maquis cells for about a year now. I'm sure your real spies have been keeping you up to date on that state of affairs."

Described by many as nothing more than a ragtag group of renegades, the Maquis had been wreaking havoc along the Federation-Cardassian border in recent months in defiance of the oppression and cruelty many of them had suffered at the hands of the Cardassians. Among their growing numbers were sympathizers who had renounced Federation citizenships and taken up arms to support their comrades. Black marketers throughout the quadrant had quickly seen the situation's profit potential, and the providing of weapons, food, medical supplies, and other equipment for the various resistance cells had become a clandestine industry unto itself.

"And you're buying weaponry from a Romulan contact?" Taelus asked, making no effort to hide his disdain and distrust. "From whom?" When Calhoun said nothing after several seconds, Taelus stepped closer to the forcefield. "You will answer my questions, Xenexian, I promise you."

Calhoun smiled at the expected threat. "You need to work on your temper, Major. It can blind you in a dangerous situation if you lose control of it."

Beside him, the Romulan doctor finally finished his examination and deactivated his scanner. "He is free of disease or other contaminants, Commander, and I've found nothing hidden on his person or among his clothing or possessions." He indicated the innocuous collection of items emptied from Calhoun's pockets and the pouch on his belt.

"Thank you, Dr. Arnata," Sirol replied. He pointed to the scar on Calhoun's face. "Considering the advanced nature of modern medical technology, particularly that belonging to the Federation, I have to wonder why you choose to retain such an unsightly blemish."

"It's a reminder to never let my guard down," Calhoun replied. "Hard to forget when you look at it in the mirror every day."

Reaching for Calhoun's left arm, Arnata pushed the sleeve of the loose-fitting tan shirt up to his elbow, revealing another thick, puckered scar running half the length of his forearm. "Is this one also a reminder?"

"Yes, that things aren't always what they appear to be." Leaning closer to Arnata, Calhoun added, "That's good advice, you know."

The doctor snorted derisively, but any comment he might have made was forgotten as the ship's intercom blared to life.

"Commander Sirol, this is the bridge. Internal sensors have detected several systems activating aboard the smuggler's ship. We are reading a buildup in its warp core."

Alarm washed over the faces of the Romulans, and Calhoun stood fast as Sirol stepped so close to the cell that he nearly made contact with the forcefield. "What have you done?" When Calhoun said nothing, the commander tapped his communicator pendant. "This is Sirol. Get that ship out of my landing bay immediately."

The voice from the bridge responded, "Commander, we have already attempted to do so, but it has activated a tractor beam and used it to secure itself to the deck plating. Its deflector shields are also raised, preventing us from approaching the vessel."

"What can this spy possibly be doing from inside his cell?" Taelus asked, his voice incredulous.

"I'm brokering a deal," Calhoun replied before exploding into motion.

He lunged across the cell and seized Arnata from behind, wrapping a forearm around his throat and twisting the doctor's left arm up and behind his back. Arnata screamed at the painful attack as Calhoun maneuvered him toward the cell entrance.

Taelus leapt forward, drawing his disruptor from its holster at his waist. "Release him!" he shouted as he reached for the panel controlling the force-field. He was reacting instinctively, just as Calhoun had hoped he would.

"Wait!" he heard Sirol shout. Perhaps, in an instant of clarity, he had understood what Calhoun was doing.

By then it was too late.

The forcefield blinked and dissolved as Taelus leveled his disruptor at Calhoun, but the Xenexian had already moved Arnata in front of him to block the major's aim. Then Calhoun shoved the doctor forward and into Taelus, and both Romulans were forced off balance and heaved into the nearby bulkhead. The agent's arms came up as he slipped and fell to the deck, and Calhoun grabbed for Taelus's disruptor, wrenching it free of the major's grip.

"Stop right there!" Calhoun shouted as he saw Sirol moving for the door. The Romulan froze in his tracks, by which time Calhoun had the disruptor and was aiming it at him.

"Sound the alarm!" Taelus hissed as he and Arnata scrambled to extricate themselves from the tangle of their arms and legs, but Sirol would never reach his communicator before Calhoun stopped him. There was no way to alert the guard still waiting just outside.

After relieving the three Romulans of their communicators and weapons, Calhoun waved the disruptor's muzzle toward the cell, motioning Taelus and Arnata into the small room. Once they were inside he keyed the control panel and the forcefield flared back into existence.

Turning his attention back to Sirol, Calhoun noted how the commander seemed to be studying him with equal parts astonishment and admiration. "An ingenious, if rather foolhardy, tactic," Sirol said. "What do you want?"

Calhoun allowed himself a small smile. "It's really very simple. You have weapons and other supplies I need. Give me what I want, or else I'll destroy your ship."

"You cannot be serious," Sirol said, a challenge in his tone.

By way of reply, alert klaxons sounded and the voice from the intercom spoke again.

"Commander, the vessel's warp core is continuing to increase its energy output. We believe it is on a buildup to detonation!"

"It will continue to build for several more minutes," Calhoun said, "at which time my ship's computer will wait for a command from me to overload. Do I sound serious now?"

Sirol said nothing for several seconds, and Calhoun could not really blame him for the shock he must be feeling. After all, it was quite uncommon for a single man, working alone, to incapacitate a warbird of the Romulan fleet. The very idea should have been preposterous.

As long as you buy it for the time being.

Holding up Sirol's communicator, Calhoun said, "Your science officer should be receiving a set of instructions at his station on the bridge right about now. They call for a detail of five crewmen to begin transferring weapons and equipment I've specified to my ship's cargo hold."

"All of this, just to obtain supplies?" Sirol asked, his voice a strangled whisper.

Calhoun shrugged. "Desperate times, Commander. I also want you to order the rest of your crew to confine themselves to the cargo holds on the lowest levels. I don't want anyone in the corridors when we leave here. Follow my instructions and you have my word that no harm will come to your crew. If you don't, you have my word that I'll blow this ship straight to hell."

He could almost see the commander's mind racing even as Sirol accepted the communicator and issued the appropriate orders, searching for some method to counter the attack on his ship. His options were few, Calhoun knew, except perhaps ordering the destruction of the ship itself.

"Thank you, Commander," Calhoun said as Sirol completed issuing his orders and handed back the communicator. "This will all be over soon."

"You dare to extort from us?" Taelus snarled from inside the cell. "I will carve your heart from your chest with a cook's dulled blade, Xenexian." Naked fury laced every word, and so palpable was the hatred in the agent's eyes that Calhoun thought he might actually try to push through the forcefield.

Instead of replying, Calhoun turned his attention to the tricorder he had confiscated from Dr. Arnata. It took only a moment to remember how to operate the device before he entered a series of commands and the unit's scan functions engaged. The tricorder took only a few seconds to lock on to the object he was seeking.

Okay, he mused as the tricorder showed him the location of the top-secret phased-cloaking device. *Now I just have to get to it.*

"Do you really expect to succeed here?" Sirol demanded as they walked down the otherwise empty corridor.

Glancing down at the tricorder to verify their position, Calhoun said,

"So long as you and your crew do as I ask, everything will be fine, I promise you."

He had waited nearly ten minutes for the *Terix*'s crew to migrate to the ship's cargo section. At his direction, Sirol had then instructed the computer to seal all hatches leading to those areas and verify that the entire complement had complied with their commander's orders. Satisfied that everything was in place the way he wanted it, Calhoun had taken Sirol from the detention center and set out through the corridors of the ship.

The pair reached a turbolift and Calhoun motioned Sirol inside. *Almost there,* he thought as he directed the car to descend nine levels.

"Whoever you are," Sirol said, "you're not a simple smuggler. You are obviously here for something, and it's not weapons for the Maquis."

The turbolift slowed to a halt and the doors opened, and Calhoun aimed one of his two confiscated disruptors down the corridor. It surprised him to find the passageway empty, as he held no illusions that members of the ship's complement would refrain from deploying some kind of response to his unorthodox attack. After all, there was no real way to prevent the more industrious among the crew from escaping if they decided to test the limits of their incarceration.

The only question was: When would whatever scheme they came up with be put into play? Calhoun had programmed his tricorder to alert him if any of the cargo-bay hatches were tampered with or if anyone was approaching his position, but that was as far as he could concern himself with possible reprisals. For now, he had no choice but to focus on his mission and hope he could carry it out quickly.

Handing Sirol his communicator, he said, "Order the computer to seal off access to this deck, and allow only you to rescind that order." It was an additional measure of protection, but not a foolproof one, he knew. Determined pursuers would be able to circumvent the computer's directives. They might even cut through hatches with their weapons, but that would take time. Calhoun had no problem with that, as such delays would keep the crew in check.

"Thank you for confirming my suspicions," Sirol said as they proceeded down the corridor. "You're obviously here for the phase-cloaking device, and considering how secret the project was, that means you must be a Starfleet operative."

He was bound to guess, Calhoun thought. *It's not as though he's a fool.* Though the façade created so painstakingly for him by Starfleet Intelligence was designed to withstand even detailed background checks, Calhoun had not really expected it to hold up once he put the most daring part of his plan into motion.

Only days had passed since the Starship *Enterprise* had encountered the *Terix* in the Devolin system while searching for the *U.S.S. Pegasus,* a prototype vessel presumed destroyed twelve years earlier while testing classified experimental equipment. Chief among those tests was that of a cloaking device that could alter the structure of a ship, making it able to pass through normal matter. A revolutionary development in the concept of cloaking technology, the device was also a clear violation of the Treaty of Algeron, the peace accord signed by both the Federation and the Romulan Empire decades ago.

Something had happened during the experiment, whether as a fault in the system's design or owing to the interference of *Pegasus* crew members trying to shut down the device. The result sent the ship drifting through space in a phased state until it arrived in the asteroid field surrounding the Devolin system. As the vessel was passing through one of the larger asteroids, the cloak failed and the *Pegasus* returned to its normal molecular state. Most of the ship integrated with the solid rock of the asteroid's interior, killing the crew.

When the Romulans discovered the existence of the ship and its cloaking device years later, only the actions of Jean-Luc Picard, the *Enterprise*'s captain and Calhoun's friend, prevented the eruption of a full-blown interstellar incident between the Empire and the Federation. After a lengthy private meeting with Sirol on the *Enterprise,* Picard surrendered the device to the Romulan commander.

It was a gesture that was already being seized by diplomats on both sides of the border as a stepping-stone toward improved political relations between the two governments. However, there were those in the Starfleet community, particularly in the intelligence branch, who were galled at the idea of such a decisive strategic advantage delivered to their enemy on a silver platter.

Which was why Calhoun had been sent in.

His mission parameters had always called for the *Terix* to intercept his ship, and to do so before it could transfer its precious cargo to a Romulan base or other vessel. Insuring that he came across the border in the right area so that Sirol's vessel would be the one sent to pick him up had been a marvelous feat of logistical coordination between Starfleet Intelligence and one of their double agents working deep inside the Romulan military.

Calhoun had always found it fascinating how easily entities of opposing governments could come together for less than noble purposes, yet never actually trust each other long enough to pursue anything resembling lasting peace. He would have liked to learn more about the logistics of this mission, but he suspected that Admiral Alynna Nechayev, his Starfleet benefactor and the one who gave him his assignments, would be as tight-lipped as always with the details. As she had since he had started working directly for her as a deep-cover "specialist," Nechayev had given him only the parameters for the operation, as well as the requisite equipment and other accessories, and left the specifics to him.

He could only hope that Nechayev's report about Sirol, based largely on observations submitted by Picard following the incident, was as accurate as the rest of the intelligence she had compiled for this mission.

Tempted simply to tell Sirol the truth about his mission right now, Calhoun instead said, "Since I'm going to require your cooperation to accomplish my mission, Commander, I'll tell you everything when the time is right." He had taken Sirol from the detention center under the guise of using him as cover in the event the crew attempted retaliation, but in truth, he needed the commander in order to complete his assignment quickly.

Turning a corner, they arrived at a pair of heavy doors set into the bulkhead at the end of the corridor. Unlike other hatches they had passed, this one bore no signage indicating what might lie beyond it. They stepped closer and Calhoun studied the security panel controlling the door, set into the wall to the right of the entrance.

"This is a secure storage area," Sirol explained. "We use it for sensitive or high-value cargo that requires additional protective measures. Ordinarily this door would be guarded by two centurions."

Calhoun nodded. "I know, which is another reason why I had you order the crew to the cargo bays. I assume your voice authorization is required to gain entry?" He already knew the answer to the question, of course.

Nodding, the commander said, "Yes, but do you really expect me to assist you?"

"There's always the alternative," Calhoun said, letting the rest of the sentence trail away. Both men knew what he meant, anyway.

Sighing in apparent resignation, Sirol turned to the security panel and issued a verbal command string in his native language. A status light on the panel changed color and the doors parted, revealing a dimly lighted room beyond.

Calhoun's tricorder told him the chamber was unoccupied, but he took no chances as he stepped through the doorway, examining the entire room from left to right. The muzzle of his disruptor aimed wherever he looked, but he saw no one.

Once they both were inside, Calhoun closed and sealed the door and keyed the lights. The increased illumination revealed several dozen storage containers of various shapes, sizes, and colors. Stepping farther into the room, he saw that one of the containers was of a type used aboard Federation starships, its markings indicating that it had come from the *Enterprise.*

"Here we are," he said, more to himself than to Sirol, as he tapped a command into the small padd on the container's side. The distinctive sounds of vacuum seals releasing echoed in the room, and after a moment Calhoun was able to open the access door set into the container's side and get his first look at its contents.

Cylindrical in shape, the cloaking device stood perhaps a meter in height, with several optical cables extending from its top. Though it was dormant, Calhoun had read Picard's report on the device's operation and could almost sense the power it was capable of generating. This single piece of equipment had altered the molecular structure of the *Enterprise* and allowed it to pass through a dense asteroid as though it were nothing more than air. He knew that to whoever controlled it, the tactical value of the device would be staggering.

"I do not understand," Sirol said. "Why was Captain Picard allowed to surrender it, only to have you retrieve it now?"

The time had come, Calhoun decided, to lay all of his cards on the table, so to speak. If his mission were to have any chance at success, it would start with Sirol. Would he act like a typical Romulan officer, with contempt and suspicion, or did he really possess whatever other qualities Picard had evidently seen during his meetings with him?

There's only one way to find out.

"I'm not here to retrieve it," he said after a moment. "My orders are to destroy it, in a manner of speaking."

Sirol's brow wrinkled in confusion. "Picard sent you?"

"Not exactly," Calhoun replied. "Though he's the reason I'm here, and why I've gone to great pains to isolate you with this thing here and now."

Pointing to the cloaking device, Sirol said, "By giving it to us, Captain Picard avoided a potentially disastrous situation between our peoples. I commend him for seeking out a solution that did not involve violence."

"I agree," Calhoun replied, "but he caused a lot of problems for the people in power when he did it, even though it was the right thing to do." While Picard's actions had engendered a series of tenuous, if embarrassing, diplomatic inroads, to many at Starfleet they had also flown in the face of military necessity. "He reported afterward that he met with you in private, and that the two of you discussed destroying the device then and there."

"That is true," Sirol replied, "but my orders were quite clear on the matter. I am to surrender it to the Tal Shiar when they arrive. Despite your captain's gesture of good faith, I fear my people will exploit this turn of events for political and military gain."

Calhoun nodded. "That's why I'm here." He indicated the device with one hand. "My orders are to destroy that thing and tie up any other loose ends." He paused a moment before adding, "The catch is that it's supposed to look like an accident."

This is it, he thought, several seconds passing as Sirol regarded him with an unreadable expression. They had arrived at the crucial turning point, Calhoun knew, when the Romulan commander would decide if he was going to help him.

"An accident," Sirol repeated, nodding. "Interesting. Such a development, particularly if it occurs while the device is in our possession, would do much to preserve the positive outcome Picard created when he surrendered it in the first place."

Studying the cloaking device, Calhoun shook his head in disgust. He knew that several people in the corridors of power at Starfleet Headquarters were anxiously awaiting the outcome of this operation, with the hope that he would preserve yet another of their dirty little secrets. "To be honest, I don't care about any of that. I'm just here to destroy that thing, and to do it in a way that leaves Picard free of blame."

Sirol's right eyebrow arched at that. "Is that one of your mission parameters?"

"My own addendum," Calhoun replied. He believed he had known the *Enterprise* captain long enough to understand his beliefs and values. Jean-Luc Picard did not blindly follow orders or regulations if they violated what he believed to be right. That sense of morality had put him in direct conflict with his superiors, placing his career at risk in order to uphold the Treaty of Algeron and the peace it protected between the Federation and the Romulans. "Picard did a good thing, maybe even averted a war by doing it, and I'll be damned if I let a bunch of politicians and other brands of idiot waste that effort. He seemed to think you're a man of similar convictions."

Negotiating with an adversary was not something that came easily to Mackenzie Calhoun. In all his years battling the Danteri, the brutal, warlike race that had plunged his home planet into oppression and slavery, he had rarely viewed his enemies with anything other than scorn. For the most part, he regarded the Romulans in the same manner, but Sirol had already shown himself to be of a different breed. Yes, the commander was shrewd and calculating in fine Romulan fashion, yet he possessed an intangible quality that Calhoun instinctively wanted to trust. Calhoun had also always had a kind of "sixth sense" whenever danger reared its head. That sense was staying quiet right now.

Reaching a decision, he calmly flipped the disruptor around in his hand and held it, handgrip first, to Sirol. "For both our sakes, I hope Picard was right." Despite the confidence in his choice and the fact that he had a second disruptor tucked in his belt, he still tensed as the commander took the weapon from him and examined it for a moment. Sirol, however, calmly returned the disruptor to the holster at his waist.

"Obviously, you require my assistance for this to be successful," Sirol said. He shook his head, and Calhoun got the sense that the commander was weighing the consequences of his next action. "I have experienced my share of battle, so the thought of forestalling more conflict, if even for a short time, appeals to me." Glowering at Calhoun, he added, "But understand that I cannot permit any danger to my ship or crew."

"That was always the plan," Calhoun replied. Kneeling down, he grasped the heel of his left boot and twisted it until it swung away from the bottom of his foot. The action exposed a small cavity from which he extracted a small, cylindrical object. He twisted the cylinder and pulled it apart to reveal a Federation-standard isolinear data chip.

"How did you hide that from Dr. Arnata?" Sirol asked.

Smiling, Calhoun said, "Spy toys, Commander. The cylinder houses a small dampening field generator that renders it invisible to most scans. I took a chance that you wouldn't subject me to much more than a basic tricorder sweep when I came aboard."

"I have to wonder what else the doctor missed." Sirol indicated the chip. "What does it do?"

Stepping closer to the cloaking device, Calhoun opened an access panel on the unit's side and examined a bank of computer interface ports. He took a moment to recall his instructions for installing the chip before replying, "It's designed to interact with the cloak's existing embedded systems, while at the same time being indistinguishable from the rest of the software."

He saw that other chips already occupied some of the slots, and a quick tricorder scan told him which chips had to be reconfigured to make room for the new one. "The first time it's activated without a proper security code, it will initiate an overload of its primary power source."

"Simple, yet elegant," Sirol conceded. "With the possibility of weeks passing before the device is tested aboard a Romulan vessel, there will be little reason to suspect deliberate duplicity on Captain Picard's part." Nodding in approval, he asked, "This is something created just for this mission?"

Calhoun shook his head. "The procedure was part of the device's original development, but the software was never installed into this prototype. Even those members of the *Pegasus* crew involved with its testing didn't know about it. Perhaps if they had, they might have avoided what happened to them."

He inserted the chip into the slot he had selected and it snapped into place. It was somehow interesting to him that he was, in a way, completing the original construction of the cloaking device that had begun more than twelve years earlier.

"And it won't harm anyone?" Sirol asked.

Calhoun shook his head as he ran a final scan with the tricorder to confirm that his modifications were correct before replying. "No, though I'm told there will be some ancillary damage to whatever systems it's joined to."

Finished with his alterations, Calhoun rose and handed Sirol his communicator. "Request a status update on the delivery of the supplies to my vessel, please." When he saw the confused look on the commander's face he added, "I'm afraid I'll have to leave with all of that matériel, to maintain the illusion, you understand."

Before Sirol could carry out the request, he and Calhoun were startled by the sound of the hatch seals deactivating. The doors parted to reveal Taelus, flanked by two centurions whose uniforms also bore the insignia of the Tal Shiar. All three Romulans carried disruptors.

"Greetings, spy," Taelus said. Turning to Sirol, he added, "And to his accomplice." He held up his disruptor for emphasis. "Please, do not move."

Despite the shock at being caught off guard, Calhoun schooled his features to avoid revealing his surprise. How the hell had they gotten here undetected? His tricorder had never alerted him to their approach.

As if reading his mind, Taelus retrieved a small device clipped to his belt and held it up for Calhoun to see. "A sensor mask. You are not the only one with special tools at your disposal, after all." Calhoun heard a click as the agent pressed a control, after which his tricorder immediately emitted the shrill proximity alert signal he had set up. He stabbed a finger at the device in disgust, silencing the alarm.

Should have seen that coming, he chastised himself. *I must be losing my touch.*

His two escorts remaining at the door, Taelus stepped into the room, focusing his attention on Sirol. "You do realize that this is all your doing, Commander? If you had simply taken that Federation ship into custody when this all began, there would be no residual mess for me to clean up."

"It was a valid option in the beginning," Sirol countered, "and one I honestly considered. However, when the full facts of the matter were revealed, the risk of inciting an interstellar incident made such action untenable. Surely even you can see that." Glaring at the agent, he added, "Besides, I acted well within my discretion as commander of this vessel."

A thin, sinister smile creased the subcommander's features. "But now it can be argued that your leniency was born out of disloyalty and contempt for the people you have sworn to serve."

Calhoun could already see where Taelus was leading with this even as the agent turned to him.

"For a fleeting moment I actually believed you were a mere smuggler," the major said, "a deranged if not incredibly fearless one at that. Did you really think my agents or I would stand by while you did whatever you wanted?" Waving to the ceiling, he said, "Everything the two of you discussed has been recorded, and will be most helpful when I submit my report."

"Do you honestly expect anyone to believe such a report?" Sirol asked, aghast. "I have pledged an oath to the Praetor just as you have. How does working to prevent a war contradict that pledge?"

"The safety of the Empire is the prime concern of the Tal Shiar, and your actions here today are a direct threat to that security. That is what your superiors will be told, and that is what they will believe, traitor." Looking to Calhoun, Taelus added, "In that regard, I must also thank you, Xenexian. By herding the ship's crew into the cargo areas like so many sheep, you have given them the opportunity to demonstrate their cowardice. That shortcoming will also be addressed at the appropriate time."

Snorting at that, Calhoun said, "The same old story, isn't it? You say you're here to protect the people, but you do it through oppression and by instilling terror in their hearts. That makes them easier to control, doesn't it?" He could feel the fingers of his right hand twitching, aching to reach for the disruptor stuck in his belt, yet he willed his hand to remain still.

Not yet.

"I will not be questioned or judged by you, spy," Taelus replied, swinging his disruptor to aim at Calhoun. "The sole reason you remain alive is so that you and the commander can be tried in a very public court. Your Starfleet-sponsored espionage and treason will be revealed to all, after which you will be found guilty and executed as a fitting punctuation to the rampant hypocrisy that is Federation diplomacy." Then the agent smiled abruptly, as if an amusing thought had just occurred to him. "Tell me, why did you not destroy the device outright? You went to all this trouble, created such an elaborate charade, simply to install a computer chip?"

"They don't give the exciting assignments to rookies," Calhoun deadpanned. Shrugging, he added, "It seemed kind of silly to just sneak aboard disguised as a Romulan, even though I hear you people fall for that one all the time."

Calhoun saw Taelus's jaw torque in response to the verbal jab, and the major's fingers squirmed around his disruptor's handgrip. "Take caution in your tone, spy. I really only need one of you, and in truth Sirol would provide the better example."

"It seems to me that I'm dead, anyway," Calhoun replied, "so it might as well be now."

His hand was almost a blur as he drew the disruptor and fired.

The shot was wild, screaming over Taelus's left shoulder, but it was enough to make the agent duck to avoid being hit. He leapt toward the door and his two subordinates likewise dodged for cover as Calhoun's second volley hit the control pad next to the entrance. The doors immediately began to close and the Romulans had to scramble to get out of the way. Taelus was nearly crushed between the heavy metal hatches but fell backward into the corridor before they sealed shut, trapping the other two agents inside the room.

One of the Romulans fired as he tried to regain his feet but the shot went high, hitting the wall above and behind Calhoun. Ignoring the attack, Calhoun aimed and returned fire, striking the Romulan in the chest.

More fire erupted in the room even as the agent collapsed, and it took Calhoun an extra instant to realize it was coming from his right. Sirol had drawn his own weapon and fired, catching the second agent in the leg and spinning him into a nearby bulkhead. Calhoun added a second shot and the Romulan dropped unconscious to the deck.

"Are you all right?" Sirol asked.

Dashing across the room to retrieve the fallen Romulans' disruptors,

Calhoun tossed one to the commander. "Fair enough, but we can't stay here. How many more agents does Taelus have on board?"

"Two," Sirol replied. "They were most likely dispatched to the bridge to communicate our situation to their superiors, but Taelus will surely be calling on them to help him now."

A hissing sound began somewhere behind them and Calhoun turned in search of the source but saw nothing. "What's that?" He activated his tricorder and had an answer a moment later. "The oxygen is being pulled from the room." Taelus had decided against another direct confrontation, choosing instead to simply incapacitate or even kill him and Sirol before trying to reenter the room. "We have to get out of here."

Searching for another exit, Calhoun's eyes fell on the cloaking device.

His plan for the unit's covert destruction was a wash, of course. Taelus would insure that the device was properly examined before any testing was performed, knowing to look for the self-destruct program Calhoun had installed. The mission would be exposed as an embarrassment to Starfleet, with Picard's efforts at maintaining the peace between the Federation and the Empire squandered. There was no way to imagine the ultimate consequences if the device was allowed to remain in Romulan hands.

With practiced ease and without another thought, Calhoun thumbed his disruptor's power setting to maximum, aimed, and pressed the firing stud.

Energy exploded from the weapon and enveloped the cloaking device. It was obliterated, taking with it every shameful secret and senseless death surrounding it for more than twelve years.

"Good riddance," he said. *Damn Nechayev and her crazy schemes.*

Turning his back on what little debris remained of the device to survey their limited escape options, Calhoun realized he was already beginning to feel the initial effects of oxygen deficiency. If they were going to get out of this, it would have to be in the next minute or two. "Is there another way out of here?"

"No," Sirol said, indicating the lone door. "The main purpose of the room precludes multiple points of entry, after all. None of the ship's maintenance shafts connect here, and the ventilation ducts are not large enough to crawl through." Shaking his head, he added, "This part of the ship is also equipped with transport inhibitors."

Calhoun's gaze settled on the sealed hatch, their only way out of the room. "Looks like it's back the way we came."

Sirol said, "The door is sealed. We will not be able to cut through it in time."

"That's okay," Calhoun said as he reached for his left arm. "I have one more trick up my sleeve." Pushing back the material of his shirt, he exposed his forearm and the large, nasty scar there. He dug under the skin with his fingernails, and the scar peeled away to reveal unmarred flesh underneath. "It's a fake," he said when he saw Sirol's astonished look, "designed to fool even a medical scan." He pointed to the other cargo containers stacked haphazardly behind them. "Find some cover."

Stars danced in his vision as Calhoun reached for the hatch, pushing the artificial scar into the seam joining the doors. Composed of *Qo'legh*, a highly volatile chemical compound and an able explosive even when used in small quantities, it was extremely difficult to detect and was a favored weapon of Klingon Imperial Intelligence. Calhoun had occasionally found uses for the explosive during past missions, and he figured that the amount of the chemical saturating the simulated tissue would be more than enough to blast through the heavy metal of the door.

If it's not, you're dead.

"Duck," he said as he lumbered for the cargo container Sirol had selected for cover. Forcing his eyes to focus long enough to sight on the door with his disruptor, Calhoun fired one more time.

Even though he covered his ears, the blast was deafening in the enclosed room as the door exploded and heated air washed over them. Smoke quickly filled the room, but Calhoun also sensed the inrush of fresh oxygen and greedily gulped air into his lungs. He could already feel the effects of deprivation beginning to fade as he pulled himself to his feet.

Charging into the smoke-filled corridor with a disruptor in each hand, he searched for targets. Shrapnel from the destroyed doors littered the passageway, and lying among the debris was the unmoving body of a Romulan, one Calhoun did not recognize.

"One of Taelus's men," Sirol said as he stepped out of the room, also brandishing a pair of disruptors. It was obvious that the agent was dead, caught unaware when the door blew.

Forgetting the dead Romulan, Calhoun moved forward. The smoke was clearing in the corridor and it was easier to see another body lying on the cluttered deck. He saw that the second agent had survived the blast but the injuries to his chest and arms prevented him from being a threat any longer.

That left only Taelus.

Calhoun saw him, lying in the shadows near an intersection in the corridor, the second before the major fired.

White heat exploded in his shoulder, spinning him off balance and pushing him into the bulkhead. He dropped the weapon in his right hand as he reached for his wounded arm. Pain racked his body, and it was an effort even to hold on to his remaining disruptor as he slid to the floor.

"Drop your weapon," a weak voice rasped from up the corridor. Obviously, Taelus had also been caught in the explosion, close enough to be wounded but far enough away to avoid lethal harm. The disruptor in the major's hand was shaking, but Calhoun doubted he could bring his own weapon up fast enough to get a shot off before Taelus fired.

"Wait, Taelus," Sirol said from behind him, "it doesn't have to end like this. You need medical treatment. Let me call for help."

"No . . . time for that," Taelus said, the words coming between ragged gasps for breath. "My duty . . . is to . . . the Praetor. Must . . ." The words trailed off, but his intention was clear. Calhoun tried to raise his weapon in defense even as the agent struggled to pull himself to a sitting position.

Energy erupted once more in the corridor and Calhoun flinched as the disruptor bolt hurled past him to strike Taelus in the chest. The Romulan simply buckled under the onslaught, falling lifeless to the deck.

Calhoun looked up as Sirol knelt beside him, leaning closer to inspect his injured shoulder. "It is not serious," he said. "Dr. Arnata will be able to treat that easily."

Unable to help the small chuckle escaping his lips, Calhoun said, "Are you sure he'll want to? I'm still a spy, after all."

Watching as a pair of Romulan centurions loaded the last storage container into his ship's cargo hold, Calhoun shook his head.

"What am I going to do with all of this?"

Standing at the entrance to the hold, his hands clasped behind his back, Sirol dismissed the two subordinates after they had finished their task. Once they had gone, he entered the storage area. "You mean you do not have a plan for the supplies as part of your cover story?"

"To be honest? No." Calhoun laughed at that as he rubbed his right shoulder, which still itched after Dr. Arnata had healed the injury inflicted by Taelus's disruptor. "I didn't really expect to get this far." Slapping the nearby bulkhead, he added, "I didn't even have to blow up my only ride home. It's not my fault I'm better at this than even my boss gives me credit for." He hoped he would be able to see Nechayev's face when she read his final report for this assignment.

"We will be in position for you to depart within the hour," Sirol said.

"You should be able to cross into the Neutral Zone and back into Federation space with little trouble."

"I don't anticipate any problems," Calhoun replied. "After all, you only caught me because I wanted you to." He smiled mischievously at that, but it faded a moment later. Nodding in the direction of the cargo-bay hatch, Calhoun said, "Are you sure you can trust your people to keep quiet about this?"

"Absolutely," Sirol said without hesitation. "My officers are handling the details of disseminating a proper cover story to the rest of the crew. As for those who do know the truth, I trust them with my life, as well as to remain silent on a matter in the best interests of the Empire. My crew follows me out of respect, Mr. Calhoun, not because they fear retribution but because they know I will treat them fairly at all times."

Calhoun could appreciate the sentiment. Having led men in battle many times during his life, he had discovered long ago that to be truly successful, a leader had to extend the same level of trust that he expected from those he commanded. He suspected Sirol had learned the same lesson early in his career as well.

"Do you think your superiors will buy your story?" he asked. "I imagine many questions will be raised about what happened here today."

Sirol nodded. "It would not be the first time that ambition was the undoing of a younger officer. My report will show that Taelus, eager to demonstrate the power of the new cloaking technology, was unable to wait for more experienced engineers to inspect the device and certify it safe for testing. While examining it, he accidentally triggered the hidden self-destruct protocol and was killed in the resulting explosion. He will not be missed."

Tempted to ask about the story that would explain the other Tal Shiar agents' fates, Calhoun instead thought better of it. The less he knew about Romulan internal politics, the happier he would be.

"If you feel that the investigations might not go in your favor," he said, "I have authorization to offer you asylum in Federation space." Nechayev had believed from the beginning that Sirol could be convinced to assist with the cloak's destruction, as well as to accept an invitation to defect to the Federation as reward for his efforts. While his instincts had proven the admiral correct on the first score, Calhoun himself was not so sure about the second.

Sirol confirmed his suspicions.

"It is a tempting offer, Mr. Calhoun, but I am a creature of duty. My place is here, with my crew. If there is one positive aspect about this situation, it is them." Sighing in acceptance, he added, "This matter is far from over, after all, and the Tal Shiar's investigation will be lengthy and thorough. By standing with me, my crew has placed themselves at great risk, and it would be disloyal of me to abandon them for the relative safety offered by asylum. I hope you understand."

"Loyalty is one thing I most certainly understand, Commander," Calhoun said.

If there was one loose end about this entire affair that was worth resolving, it was the one not directly related to the mission at all. Instead, it was the matter that had hung over Calhoun's head for years, since Picard had recommended him and supported him for entry into Starfleet. Calhoun had never, in his own opinion at least, found a way to repay the debt he felt he owed the captain.

He had not undertaken this assignment out of some burning desire to preserve the peace between two governments. The politics of the situation did not concern him, nor did he care about any of the people who had created the embarrassing mess he had been sent to clean up.

When it came right down to it, he had accepted the mission out of loyalty to a friend. As far as Calhoun was concerned, so long as the spirit of Jean-Luc Picard's intentions remained intact, everyone else involved in this ridiculous situation could all go straight to hell.

A futile wish, Calhoun knew. *After all, they will only stay there until they call on me again.*

ELIZABETH SHELBY
All That Glisters . . .

Loren L. Coleman

Elizabeth Shelby's career path has taken her from the head of Borg Tactical to the bridge of the Starship *Enterprise,* from first officer on the *Chekov* and the *Excalibur* to captain of the *Exeter* and the *Trident.* But all journeys begin with a single step—"All that Glisters . . ." goes back to Shelby's tenure on the *U.S.S. Yosemite* as an engineer trying to find her way onto the command track, telling a story that takes place about nine months prior to the *Star Trek: The Next Generation* episode "The Best of Both Worlds."

Loren L. Coleman

Loren L. Coleman has been writing fiction professionally since 1994. His fourteenth novel is due to be published at the end of 2003, as is his two-part *Star Trek: Starfleet Corps of Engineers* eBook. He lives in the Pacific Northwest with his wife Heather, three children, three Siamese cats who believe they are children, and a confused dog who believes he can herd both children and cats.

All that glisters is not gold.
—William Shakespeare, *The Merchant of Venice,* Act II, Scene 6

From the door to her quarters, Lieutenant Elizabeth Shelby threw her commendation across the room. The electronic padd sailed through the air in a flat spin, thumped into the middle of her bed, and bounced once before fetching up against the stiff roll of Rigelian memory cotton that she used as a pillow.

Her door whispered closed.

Shelby's pro forma smile slipped wearily away and her hands balled up into fists. *For this outstanding service and dedication . . .* Strong words. Great, even. So why did she let them get to her every time? With fifteen minutes' grace before her team assembled in transporter room one, she decided to brave the enemy's door. She tugged at the hem of her gold tunic, squaring up her uniform. Then, with a deep breath, she stepped up to the replicator.

The replicator was the enemy. It was evil. From its memory buffers came chocolate. Sweets.

Caffeine.

Shelby leaned in to rest her forehead against the cool metal skirting as she deliberated her choices. Here, at least, she was free to chart her own course. Mostly. "Double *raktajino,*" she said, ordering the strong Klingon coffee. "Laced with chocolate and peppermint." If she satisfied any more vices in a single drink, Starfleet would probably classify it as illegal.

A hum of resequenced energy heralded the arrival of a thermal-insulated mug. She picked it up, warming both hands around the mug's tall, metal sides. A waft of strong coffee and chocolate mint assailed her, but she resisted the urge to drink too fast. *Raktajino* was best served at near scalding. She sipped carefully, blowing a veil of steam from the top. Heaven. She should find a quiet seat and enjoy the moment, and not worry about the rest.

But like a comet circling its star, Shelby was drawn back to the padd Captain Blackswan had handed her. She dropped down onto the bed, pinned her mug between one hand and the side of her leg, and fished over the device. From within the picture on her bedside table, her parents watched, smiling with confidence. Shelby avoided their holographic stares. Instead, she glanced again to the padd's selected text. Amber letters glowed on the small, dark screen. Everything she needed to see in one short display:

U.S.S. *Yosemite,* NCC–19002, Stardate 43095.1
did help the U.S.S. Yosemite *surpass all expectations. For this outstanding service and dedication to the field of engineering, Captain Patricia Blackswan does hereby commend Lieutenant Shelby and recommend her for promotion at the earliest possible*

She could scroll back up, to read the list of accomplishments Captain Blackswan had so meticulously logged. Or down, for more glowing recommendations to be appended to her personnel file—for her next captain to read and wonder why a Starfleet officer with such glowing reviews had moved through six vessels in eight years. But this was the meat.

No mention of her leadership abilities.

No recommendation for command.

Shelby flicked one polished nail at the screen, tapping the glowing power-off icon, which shut down the padd's display. A quick glance bedside. Her parents in spotless dress uniforms of red and black and each with the boxed pips of admiral's rank. In this picture, mom had just made vice-admiral. They smiled their approval. They always did.

Then again, they had smiled approval over her brief engagement to Mackenzie Calhoun, and look how well *that* had turned out. . . .

One of the first things Shelby noted after beaming down was that nature had barely begun to reclaim the devastation visited on Science Outpost D5. It had been over a year since the complete loss of the Federation's outpost here. Her team saw it nearly as the original investigating crew must have. As though a giant hand had reached down to the planet's surface and scooped up every living body, building, and artifact.

They had beamed down near the center of the concave depression, three kilometers wide and almost perfectly circular on the perimeter. Its depth sank down to approximately two hundred meters—she would have Chief Jodd Pako take precise measurements. The ravaged ground still showed striations in the clay, although weather and erosion had begun to blur the lines a little. A small, stagnant lake, little better than a pond, pooled over the bottom of the basin, and some stunted vegetation crowded around the brackish waters. A few hardy plants claimed footholds along the sloping sides, but it would be years before softer, soil-loving vegetation returned.

And her first scan of the area showed some residual energy traces still lingering after all this time. That was good.

"Spread out and take readings," Shelby commanded her away team. The handful of engineers and science specialists picked their way over rocks and stretches of mushy clay, instruments out, samples being taken. "Chief, get me physical baselines on the entire area."

"You got it," the Iotian said, his nasal voice distant as he buried his gaze into a tricorder. Belatedly he added, "Lieutenant."

Better than "sweetheart," Shelby decided. The Iotian tried hard, but as adaptive and imitative as he was, he had yet to shed all of his culture's rough social skills.

Shelby tapped on her personal recorder. "Engineer's log, supplemental. Initial evaluation of Science Outpost D5 shows no obvious trace signatures previously unrecorded. We are in the process of conducting a detailed survey."

Which they would compare with the earlier surveys, and surveys taken at a Romulan outpost that had suffered a similar fate, looking for anything that had been missed. With their updated data pool, the *Yosemite*'s crew would then compare and contrast the D5 data with detailed files provided specifically by Starfleet for this operation. They weren't being told what to look for, what Starfleet wanted them to prove, which was as frustrating for her team as it was challenging. And with the ship-to-ship grapevine carrying rumors that Starfleet was looking for someone (or some one*s*) with solid engineering experience, a fast-track candidate, there was no little buzz among her people that this was some kind of test. An engineer's *Kobayashi Maru*.

"I see no scarring that would indicate destruction by weapons fire," Shelby continued her official log entry. "Scans show negative for any known energy footprint, including all variations on known Romulan technology." All in keeping with initial reports.

"Lieutenant," Ensign Davidson called out. "We looking for anything in particular?"

How to answer that? "You'll know it when you see it," she said. "In the meantime, soak up everything you can for the data pool. Information is never wasted, Ensign."

"Yes, Lieutenant."

Not that she expected to find anything new. The initial responding team had come from the *Enterprise*. It wasn't likely they had missed anything.

But if they had . . .

Shelby combed her fingers back through her ash blond curls. She tested the mineral scent of the air, as if she might sniff out what was hidden. What would have kept the *Enterprise* from discovering a crucial clue to the outpost's fate? She pulled up the data on her tricorder, looking over the initial findings. There. Their chief engineer reported high-spectrum flux, which in itself could be considered an unusual footprint. Maybe individualistic enough to track to a source.

"It could also be interference," Shelby whispered aloud.

Ensign Rocha was close enough to overhear. "What was that, Lieutenant?" the earth-sciences specialist asked. Her blue uniform was already streaked with rusty-brown clay.

"HSF." This time Shelby spoke up for everyone to hear. "The *Enterprise* reported high-spectrum flux. Look for any trace signals that might have been masked by HSF."

Davidson looked askance at her. "How are we supposed to guess what *might* be masked by HSF?"

Shelby couldn't answer that. It was something you had to feel your way toward. For the young ensign's benefit, though, she shrugged and said again, "You'll know it when you see it."

She set herself to work.

But when she found it, she still couldn't help wondering how much more she was cementing her career in engineering and sciences.

Freshened from a hot shower and change of uniform, Shelby exited the turbolift with a crisp, purposeful stride. Shift change was over and engineering had settled into the easy silence of the evening watch. The entire space smelled slightly of ozone, common on most engineering decks. She checked the logs out of habit as she passed by a wall-mounted command station, double-checking crew assignments and the maintenance schedule.

She felt eyes on her; the members of her away team who now waited around the *Yosemite*'s largest workstation. They could wait. Attention to detail was part of what made her an exceptional engineer. That, and thinking outside the box, as she had just proven down on D5.

It also, in her weighty opinion, made her exceptionally qualified for command, though chief engineer on the *Yosemite* was the best she had risen to as yet.

As yet. Twenty-nine and on the cusp of being promoted to lieutenant commander. Command was in her future—had to be; it just wasn't here yet. What did she expect of herself?

Everything.

Still, in her lighter moments she had to admit that her career would be enviable from any of a dozen different viewpoints: from the perspective of the cadets she had graduated with out of Starfleet Academy, from the perspective of maybe even the engineers working around her on the *Yosemite*. The thought made her smile, which made a few of the younger officers visibly nervous. Shelby? The Shellfish? Smiling?

Well, she wasn't aboard the *Yosemite* to make friends. She was here to learn and to try and convince Captain Blackswan to recommend her for command. A recommendation she had failed to get so far. That was enough to erase the smile from her face.

"What have we got?" she asked, spearing Chief Pako with her opening question.

The Iotian had a knack for organization. "New?" he asked. "Most of our data conforms to the regular degradation of trace signals and energy patterns recorded in the initial survey." He ran down the entire list, from the most obvious entries to the ones that had taken her team hours to prove. "Only the one new trace you discovered appears to be of original origin."

It was a low-end quantum signature. Might be nothing. Background noise. Then again . . .

Rocha tried a tentative smile. "Polishing your boots for that posting at Starfleet yet, Lieutenant?" Twellum, the Delbian transporter and tractor specialist and the only other alien on her team, found this amusing. His chuckle sounded like a soft flute.

"No interest," Shelby said in clipped tones.

Davidson started. "You're kidding, right?" Though Shelby doubted any of them had ever known her to kid. "I mean, it's Starfleet Command."

Earth-based and with little to no opportunity for command experience. Shelby wasn't immune to the rumors; she had checked up on what a posting like that meant to an engineer. The chance to work on incredible new systems, maybe help develop the next warp-core advancement, or on a special-projects team like the Starfleet Corps of Engineers. All well and good if your mind was completely into the toys, and not the tactics that went with them.

"I have other things on my mind right now," Shelby said, which was true. "Like what we can make of the data comparison, first and foremost." It was, in fact, neither. Though it was in the top two.

Davidson had been assigned to do the initial run-through. "Nothing," he said in disappointment. He had a nervous habit of tapping his teeth with his fingers as he thought. "Nothing obvious, anyway."

"The computer is only as smart as our questions," Shelby reminded him. "Let's get to work."

Davidson's pronouncement held up for the better part of two hours, though, and Shelby quickly saw why. The data sent to the *Yosemite* had been sterilized. There was no record of the mission, the ship, the place of encounter. Raw data flooded the display in page after page of sensor readings, mostly to do with power signatures, tractor-beam displacement, and phase differentials. But there was no context whatsoever. Some of it could be inferred—the obvious contest between shields and phasers, the push and pull of starship tractors dueling with each other. It was a battle. But what a space battle had to do with the vanished outpost, Shelby could not begin to guess.

They found some similar cases of high-spectrum flux, but nothing that proved conclusive. Of course, there was no quantum reading like the one Shelby had found. No one had thought to look for it, or it was masked behind the HSF interference.

"This is ridiculous." Shelby finally surrendered, resting forward with tight fists knuckle-down on the workstation's glassy surface. "If Starfleet wants a real analysis, why not give us real data?"

"A question you can certainly put into your report," Patricia Blackswan, the *Yosemite*'s captain, told her, stepping into the engineering work area. The woman was short and compact, of a similar build to Shelby, with straight, raven black hair and a dusky complexion that still told of her Native American bloodline. "But I wouldn't recommend it."

"Captain." Shelby stiffened to a semblance of attention, though it wasn't mandated by the informal setting. Only the tall Delbian seemed to remain relaxed in the presence of their captain. The Delbian always looked relaxed, though, a skill Shelby secretly envied at times.

"I've kept up on your progress," Blackswan informed the team, stepping up to the workstation and reading the layout with a practiced eye. "Good work getting behind the high-spectrum flux, Lieutenant. We'll have to copy the *Enterprise* on your discovery."

"Thank you, Captain. I wish we had better news to report on the comparative analysis with Starfleet's data files."

"You haven't found any definite ties. That is something in itself."

"Nah," Chief Pako said dismissively, his mind still buried in the analysis, "it's nothin'. The doll's right. We're shootin' in the dark here."

Blackswan did not run a strict ship, but she did require basic decorum. Before the captain could upbraid the Iotian, though, Shelby stepped in to shelter the oblivious engineer behind one shoulder. "My people are working hard, Captain. If there is anything here, we'll find it."

The captain nodded. "I'm certain you will." She drew the chief engineer aside with a pointed glance toward the archway that led back to the turbolifts. Both women dropped their voices a notch, though Shelby thought the Delbian could still hear them, judging from the way the tall alien twitched.

"Don't think I don't know that my commendation upset you," Blackswan said softly. Not in apology, though. The captain rarely, if ever, had to apologize.

"The commendation was a glowing review of my service aboard this vessel," Shelby said. *If incomplete,* she did not say.

Blackswan nodded as if she had heard the unspoken comment as well. "Sometimes those are the hardest to take. Just don't let your personal feelings interfere with your analysis of the data."

"My personal feelings never interfere with my analysis."

"Spoken like a true engineer."

And not like a commander? Shelby choked back a sigh of frustration. "Captain," she said, in acknowledgment if not in agreement. "It *would* help if we had access to Starfleet's original data."

"You have everything Starfleet sent. Use the data as given, Lieutenant."

"The data is nearly useless. I can't do my job with what I've been given, sir." She shook her head. "I need context. Reading between the lines is the one thing we excel at over the computers."

Blackswan almost looked like she would relent. Then, "So read between them, Elizabeth. Starfleet has its reasons for scrubbing the data clean, but what you *infer* from that data is completely up to you."

Shelby nodded brusquely. "Yes, Captain."

Blackswan took her leave with a nod and a sharp turn on one heel. Shelby waited for her captain's footsteps to recede, sure that her own voice would not travel so far, and then turned back to her team.

"Get back in there and run all the comparatives again. Try some free thinking and see if you can match up anything. I don't believe Starfleet is wasting our time here, looking for proof positive that the two are *not* related. They are. We need to see how and why."

"Unless it *is* a test," Davidson said. "No right answer."

Rocha nodded. *"Kobayashi Maru."*

"I'm not buying," Shelby snapped. "Anyway, you've got nothing to sell. Get to work. I'll be on the auxiliary terminal in the next space."

"Just so we don't duplicate our efforts," the Delbian said, "what will you be looking for, Lieutenant?"

Shelby shrugged. "Answers."

Captains might have to take data as given, but Shelby's duties right now were as an engineer. And one of the first maxims of being an engineer was to question everything.

Even Starfleet.

Easier said than done.

"Damn overachieving technicians," Shelby muttered aloud after another hour of searching and sifting through data. Whoever at Starfleet had been in charge of sterilizing the data, they'd done a damn fine job. Not one marker was left to indicate the ship or station involved. No stellar phenomena that could be easily catalogued and matched in stellar cartography. And all time stamps had been cut down to give only hour and minute, no dates. The intelligence could be from last month, last year, or in the last decade.

The empty mugs from two scalding *raktajino*s (sans mint this time) stood at ease on the edge of the workstation. Absently, Shelby carried them back to the nearest replicator, letting her brain relax over the mundane cleaning duties. Her team was still at work in the other room, although Rocha was into her off time now and had an early watch tomorrow. The sciences ensign couldn't be kept on task much longer.

Neither, likely, could Shelby.

Too much data, she decided, depositing the mugs into the replicator and sequencing them back into pure energy. She needed help.

"All right," she said, stopping her team in the middle of what might have been their third analysis, maybe their fifth. "We're setting aside the D5 surveys for now and we're digging into the Starfleet files."

"What do you think we'll find there?" Davidson asked, flicking his teeth.

"That's what I want you to tell me. Chief, recheck all the time stamps.

Order the data as best you can, and while you are at it cross-check with known operations recorded in the computer. Rocha, pull out anything not starship-related. Davidson, you do the same *for* starship data. You two have early duty tomorrow, so another hour and then break for the night."

"What about me?" the Delbian asked.

"Twellum, you are on anomalies. Some of those power signatures I saw in there looked way out of proportion to Federation systems. Isolate and identify, if you can. I'll be doing some similar work, so we'll cross-check with each other as needed."

Shelby was used to being the brightest star, ready with the answer. Always had been, since her early days in the Academy and as she raced through her first assignments with a meteoric flash. This time, though, it was Rocha who made the first discovery. Working with Pako, Rocha pulled an entire set of sensor readings out of the data stream that had nothing to do with starship functions and everything in common with some of the readings they had taken today on D5.

"There is no indication of what they were measuring," she said, showing the team. "But there is similar HSF interference, and they used shielded gamma pulses to take surface readings, not unlike what we did from orbit before beaming down."

"Coincidence?" Shelby asked, rubbing at an ache in the back of her neck.

"Maybe. High-spectrum flux is not uncommon in areas where large energy signatures have overlapped. Shielded gamma pulses are a standard high-orbit sweep when the atmosphere shows even mild ionization. Still . . ."

"Still," Shelby agreed. Both went back to work.

So if Starfleet had an idea who or what did this to the D5 outpost, of course they would sanitize the data. Especially if it was the Romulans. Colonies along the Neutral Zone would panic. Militias might decide to make a few preemptive strikes against Romulan targets. Containment would be important.

But how to tell where this happened? To whom? Federation starships were most often identified by the tags inserted into sensor data. Also by personal log entries and patrol zones. By transmission codes, warp energy signatures, and at times by weapons configuration if the vessel was outfitted with anything not-quite-standard.

Configuration.

Configuration.

Something about that rattled around inside Shelby's head. Something useful. She relaxed and let her mind spin off into free thinking, a feat not too difficult considering the late hour. Then she had it! Diagnostic configurations!

Starfleet vessels calibrated sensors and weapons according to a set of prepared standards, but there was a variance, and those variances could be as unique as any warp-engine signature. Shelby pulled the shield data, sensor guides, and phaser emissions from the files, filtering them through the computer to glean the specs by which they had been calibrated. She didn't get them all, but she got enough to make a comparison. Of course, that would only help if the vessel was one the *Yosemite* had come into contact with and had similar information on. A long shot, but she programmed it into the computer anyway.

And got a match in less than ten seconds.

Shelby was more inclined to doubt the results, pulled up so fast when there must have been thousands of points to match and compare for probability. Then she saw the registry.

NCC-1701-D. *U.S.S. Enterprise.* In System J-25 on Stardate 42761.3.

The variances matched those from the initial survey data of D5.

That's when the rest of the data fell into place, and Shelby felt her strength hit an all-time low as a prickly sensation slowly crawled over the back of her neck. Reports of the *Enterprise*'s last big encounter were still circulating through official and unofficial channels. A new threat to the Federation. Or, maybe, only newly *known*.

"Chief," she said, voice cracking just a bit as her throat tightened up. "Chief, run what you have organized against any reports from the *Enterprise*. Put whatever timeline you have established against verbal reports of their encounter two . . . three months ago." *Be wrong. Be wrong.*

"Dead-on match, sweet . . . uh, Lieutenant."

Shelby nodded slowly as the rest of the team straightened to stiff attention, realizing just what data they had been working with this day. It wasn't much of a game anymore, and it certainly wasn't a test.

It was the Borg.

Which made their comparative analysis all but impossible, though impossible was gaining ground fast.

Shelby hadn't expected sleep to come easily the night before, and she'd been right. As she lay awake on her bed, the roll of Rigelian memory cotton cradling her head, all she could think about was how to give Starfleet what it wanted. How to prove that D5's outpost had been attacked by the Borg. If the Borg had come through this quadrant last year, and if they were coming back now that the *Enterprise* had stirred them, they could be closer than anyone thought.

Not a pleasant thought to sleep on.

Of course, in the morning the problem remained, and Shelby still didn't see a way to solve it. They knew next to nothing about the Borg, especially when compared with their age-old enemies the Romulans, or even with the Ferengi or Cardassians.

The Borg represented a threat on a scale the Federation had never faced, and Shelby knew she had more to contribute than a simple data analysis. Yet it looked more and more certain that at best (if the rumors held true) she'd end up tucked away in some lab at Starfleet, and at worst she'd be heading for the chief-engineer position on a larger starship already with a full complement of command-level officers. Trapped by her natural gifts. Overlooked as the pressure forced Starfleet to sacrifice career paths for the expedient gathering of intelligence.

Outstanding service and dedication. That's what they expected of her.

It was all that she knew how to give.

Her family's admirality greeted her in the morning, as always. Mother and father, resplendent in the red uniforms of command, ready to meet the universe head-on so long as they had each other. Their support meant everything to Shelby, and she would never think to indulge her own career over the needs of Starfleet.

She showered and prepared herself for a new day, then selected a fresh gold uniform from her closet. Her rank insignia attached to the collar, she brushed her fingers over the two golden pips. Then she put all thoughts of promotion, of command, of someday having a red uniform in her closet instead of gold, out of her mind. Today she had a tough challenge ahead of her, and personal needs would not figure into her plans.

Plans that involved her entire team. She stopped in to see Captain Blackswan first thing, to personally update her CO on everything she had discovered the evening before. Then, securing permission from the captain, Shelby pulled Rocha and Davidson off duty and ordered replacements to fill in for them. Twellum and Jodd Pako were already back to work on their own, and quickly grabbed fresh beverages as the team gathered around the common workstation.

"This is too much," she admitted, first thing. "We don't know enough about the Borg, and what we do know quite frankly scares the hell out of me. But, what we have is all we get to work with. Now, how do we handle it? How do we prove, or conclusively deny, that the Borg are responsible for our lost outpost at D5?"

"Mostly," Rocha began, "we have two different encounters. The *Enterprise* did analyze a second planetside site, presumably where the Borg had attacked everything and everyone there, but it isn't helpful in our case."

Twellum nodded, turning it into a half-bow. "We're trying to compare starship combat data to a planetside survey. They do not have enough commonalities for a frame of reference." His voice was high and reedy this morning. From stress? Lack of sleep? Shelby wasn't sure. Aliens were just so . . . alien. And the Borg more so.

"Then we have to find a frame of reference," Shelby ordered them. She paused, looked them over one by one. "Davidson, you are the Borg."

"What did I ever do to you?"

"Cut it. You're the Borg and you're going to scoop up the outpost. How?"

Davidson flicked his teeth, thought about the data provided in the military reports from the *Enterprise*. It was sketchy, Shelby knew. "Tractor beam?" he finally asked. "They operate on a scale we don't normally approach. Big freaking vessels. And they used one—a tractor beam, I mean—on the *Enterprise* when they cut into her hull."

It was the most obvious answer. They checked sensor data on the Borg tractors against residuals first encountered on D5. There wasn't enough data.

Frustrated, Shelby snapped, "Rocha?"

"Well, it's not likely, but has anyone considered physical means?"

"Impractical," Twellum said. "Borg are too advanced." He held up one long, skinny arm. "And I've already considered transporters," he said to the chief engineer. "The Crystalline Entity used a kind of large-scale matter-to-energy conversion to strip-mine entire planets. It is possible the Borg beamed up the outpost, and materialized it later in whole or part."

"Or simply assimilated it as raw data," Shelby considered. "Worth a look."

It was also worth a bit more to the harried engineer, who felt a spark of something warm deep inside. *This is what it is like to command,* she knew suddenly. *Bring others in at the peak of their talent, direct them, and engineer a solution to a problem.* Maybe she did not necessarily need to wear the red to take advantage of those abilities.

It gave her a surge of hope as the team tore into the computer files, trying to prove their theory, which had taken a huge leap away from merely trying to match up data to serious tactical considerations with regard to the Borg. Shelby barely noticed when one of her team members pressed a steaming *raktajino* into her hands, flavored heavily with chocolate and peppermint.

"Not enough information," she finally decided. "Dammit. Nice theory, though. We save that one for the formal report. Starfleet will want to look into it more."

"Look into what more?" Captain Blackswan asked, making another of her casual visits to engineering. If she felt the intensity of the room, the charge that had taken hold of the team since this morning, she did not comment on it. Shelby brought the captain up to date, including the theories being pounded back and forth. "Don't let me interrupt," she said. She carried her own beverage, an Orion tea that Shelby had tried once and (privately) compared to grass clippings. Blackswan took up station near the door, supervising.

"Okay," Shelby said, turning to Jodd Pako. The Iotian had watched the last bit of byplay with some interest, but then had stuck his face back into the display on which he had looped through over and over again a small segment of the *Enterprise*'s run-in with the Borg. "Chief, you are the Borg now."

"I've been assimilated?" His nasal twang made the word sound like a slang term for murder. In a way it was.

"Yeah, Chief. You are Borg."

"*We* are the Borg," the Iotian said deadpan, with an eerie lifelessness. "You will join us and learn to service the Borg."

No one spoke for a few painful heartbeats, no doubt thinking, as Shelby was, of the voice recordings taken from the *Enterprise*'s encounter.

"O-kay." Davidson sidestepped away from the Iotian. "That's as close as I ever want to be to one of *those.*"

Shelby spent a stern glance on the younger ensign. "Davidson, you are the outpost spokesman. Twellum, handle your stuff. Rocha, life sciences. I'm tactical."

The four engineers each readied what might be a line of defense against Pako, whose fingers flew over the workstation controls to bat aside defenses in the same way the Borg ship had brushed aside nearly all efforts by the *Enterprise*. It took considerable restraint for Shelby not to counter some of his more basic moves, or to declare limited victories when an assault she formulated might—might!—have injured a Borg vessel. She let Pako have his head, deciding for himself what worked and what didn't. With nearly unlimited power reserves, there wasn't much they could do that a Borg vessel couldn't counter in the end.

But it was when she noticed Pako repeating the same tactics the third time through that she halted the free-form simulation.

"Why?" she asked. "Why not come at us with a different combination of resources?"

The chief shrugged, an exaggerated gesture that used most of his upper body. "Because they didn't do that against the *Enterprise*. We . . . Borg . . . cannot be denied in the end."

"Interesting idea," Rocha said. "Can a collective consciousness truly innovate?"

"No," Shelby decided. "They grow by assimilating other cultures, new technology. Innovation would be frowned upon as individualistic."

"So they adapt, but do not innovate," Blackswan said, interested now. "Can you use that?"

Shelby smiled. Her team had come through, and she held the last piece in hand. "We can," she said. "It gives us everything we need to prove what happened on D5." She looked at her team, who were all now outside the box, but maybe just not quite as far as her. "The Borg must have diagnostic configurations too," she explained. "Want to bet they don't have near as many variances?"

The *Yosemite*'s bridge seemed more crowded than usual to Shelby. One additional person was all it took, though, if it was the right person. Especially if it was a Starfleet admiral.

J.P. Hanson was a short bulldog of a man who carried his years in Starfleet around with him like duranium armor. He had a careworn face and dark diamond cutters for eyes. He also had a way of putting the ship's captain at her ease, while everyone around Patricia Blackswan jumped to their duties to help keep up the ship's reputation. The admiral and captain spoke like old friends, hardly paying attention to any of the crew around them. He referred to Captain Blackswan only as "Patricia." Coming from him, it seemed high praise rather than inappropriate familiarity.

Shelby stood awkwardly by, staffing one of the bridge engineering stations, feeling in the admiral's presence the same confidence that greeted her every morning and watched over her every night. He had barely noticed her, except for the introduction made by the captain and to commend her on the report her team had developed. Hanson had ordered the *U.S.S. Mel-*

bourne out to D5 to be on hand personally, to witness the final proof, positive or negative, regarding the test.

There wasn't much to it. The *Yosemite*'s main dish had been modified to simulate a smaller version of the Borg tractor, using the same phase differentials and subspace variances recorded by the *Enterprise*'s scans. Also, Twellum had managed to rig a cargo transporter to simulate Borg pattern signatures, though their shield-penetrating capability was far beyond Federation technology. Their two best working theories, about to be put to the test.

"Lieutenant Shelby, commence test procedure one," Blackswan ordered.

"Yes, Captain." She tapped the console screen, and the preprogrammed test series used the modified tractor beam to grapple up a section of mountainside from D5. "Beam engaged," she read from the panel, "and released. Ready for second test."

"At your command, Lieutenant."

A second set, this time more complicated and run by Twellum in the lower cargo bay. "Energize," she said, passing the order along.

When Twellum let her know that the transport was complete, Shelby relaxed. All that was left now was a thumbs-up or thumbs-down. Yes or no. And then dealing with the consequences. Engineers rarely dealt with consequences. "We'll have data in a few moments, Admiral, Captain. Ensigns Davidson and Rocha were standing by to sample for our low-end quantum footprint."

"Fascinating work," Hanson said to the captain, eyes on the main viewscreen, on which D5 turned slowly, oblivious of the Starfleet testing. "You've got a good crew, Patricia."

"And then some, Admiral."

Davidson was first, his scratchy voice relayed directly over the bridge coms. Shelby imagined him down there on the planet, flicking his teeth as the data finally came back. "Lieutenant, we have no—zero—high-spectrum flux. Whatever caused it, it wasn't the tractor itself. Maybe some related part of the Borg systems."

A related part . . . That meant—

"Your low-end quantum footprint is right in front of me, Lieutenant. Call it proof positive."

"Times two," Rocha followed up before anyone had the chance to thank Davidson or remark on the findings. "Same thing on the transporter site. We can't prove *how* they did it, Lieutenant. But I think this is beyond coincidence now. They did it."

Admiral Hanson slapped the arm of his chair. Not in victory, but in certainty. Shelby knew the feeling. Proving a Borg incursion did not leave much room for the thrill of a job well done. Instead, a chill shook its way down her spine as she imagined a repeat of D5 on any of a hundred Federation planets. On Earth itself.

"Fine work, Patricia." Admiral Hanson was up on his feet, full of energy and restless. "I'll want to get your test results in front of teams back at Starfleet Tactical right away, to see what they can do with it. If nothing else, though, we can close the file on D5."

Captain Blackswan had followed the admiral to her feet, and accompanied him to the turbolift door. "I'll see you back to the *Melbourne*," she said.

"No. No need. You have a ship to run and I want repeated tests conducted as soon as possible." He looked curiously at a padd handed him by the captain a moment, then said, "Yes, of course," and encoded his signature over the readout before stepping up to the turbolift.

Captain Blackswan came right over to Shelby, who was verifying all data as it came back from Rocha and Davidson. Down in engineering, Chief Pako would already be tearing it apart, running comparisons, and adding to the ship's library on the Borg. "We've got a lot to do," she said to the captain. "Where would you like me to start?"

Patricia Blackswan handed over the padd. "With this."

The amber-lit screen held everything she needed to know:

U.S.S. Yosemite, NCC–19002, Stardate 43117.2
Effective immediately, Lieutenant Elizabeth Paula Shelby is advanced to the rank of lieutenant commander. She is to complete all duties pursuant to her current station, but report to Starfleet Tactical no later than Stardate 43328.8.

It was authorized by the thumbprint of Admiral J.P. Hanson.

"Tactical?" Shelby nearly stammered the duty station. "Not engineering?"

Blackswan smiled thinly. "As formidable as your talents are, Commander, they would be wasted as an engineer."

"But the command-grade test. I haven't taken it."

"That is at my discretion, and from what I saw in engineering, I'd say you passed." Blackswan glanced toward the turbolift, after the departed admiral. "That, and maybe a great deal more."

Tactical. Command. Shelby had all but given up on that dream, deciding to blend her desire for command and gifts in engineering here on the *Yosemite*. To have it come after all, and now . . . Now she would be able to embrace her engineering skills, and make them part of her ability to command. "It's really happening, folks."

Blackswan nodded, and clapped her chief engineer on the shoulder. "Don't forget to put your team in for commendations, Commander. But first, go find a new uniform. Gold looks good on you, but you are due for a change."

Yes, Shelby considered. She supposed that she was.

ZAK KEBRON
Waiting for G'Doh
or
How I Learned to Stop Moving and Hate People

David Mack

The first Brikar in Starfleet, Zak Kebron met his future *Excalibur* crewmates Soleta and Mark McHenry while attending Starfleet Academy. The trio went on to different postings after graduating, and Kebron found himself assigned to security on the *U.S.S. Ranger*. "Waiting for G'Doh" takes place during the first year after Kebron's graduation from the Academy and assignment to that ship.

David Mack

David Mack is a writer whose work spans multiple media, from books and television to comic books and computer games. His credits include two episodes of the TV series *Star Trek: Deep Space Nine* and, more recently, the critically acclaimed and best-selling two-part eBook *Star Trek: S.C.E.: Wildfire.* Mack currently resides in New York City, where he is hard at work on a pair of *Star Trek: The Next Generation* novels.

Captain Yuri Danilov, commanding officer of the Starship *Ranger*, sat and looked at his reflection on the pristine, mirror-perfect black surface of his crescent-shaped desk. His face was full and round, and his chin had lately been doubled by the unfortunate combination of advancing age and the sedentary lifestyle of a starship captain saddled with an overachieving first officer who commanded all the away missions.

On the other side of his desk sat Lieutenant Commander Raka, his serious-looking young Trill chief of security, who drummed his fingers on Danilov's desk. Danilov had named Raka security chief last month, after the *Ranger*'s former security chief—with no warning whatsoever—retired, married a nice Bajoran woman, and began a new career in aquatic farming.

"He's late," Raka said. Danilov checked the chronometer. Ensign Kebron's orders were to report here to Danilov's ready room at 1330 hours. It was 1329 hours and ten seconds. Raka was the sort of person who believed that if one wasn't early for an appointment, one was late. Danilov sighed and reached for his coffee, then saw a tremor ripple disturb the surface of his French roast.

Danilov felt the vibration through the floor. The items on his ready-room shelves trembled, settled for a split second, then were shaken again. *Thud. Thud. Thud.*

The captain sipped his coffee and watched the chronometer. At precisely 1330 hours his door chime sounded.

"Enter," he said. The door swished open to reveal what at first looked like a hastily erected stone barricade dressed in a Starfleet uniform. Danilov blinked, then realized that, through the narrow doorway, he could see the ensign only from the chin down. He noted that both of the man's shoulders were beyond the outer edges of the doorframe.

The enormous young officer stooped, turned sideways, and inched his way into the ready room, his every step vibrating the deck. Danilov noted that Kebron wore a gravity compensator on his uniform belt—for all the good that it did.

After nearly fifty-five years in Starfleet, Danilov had seen his share of impressive sights. Regardless, he still was awed by the sheer presence of the young Brikar who snapped to attention in front of him and caused a minor earthquake as he did so. "Ensign Zak Kebron reporting, Captain."

"At ease, Ensign," Danilov said. After several seconds, he realized that Kebron remained motionless in front of his desk. "That means you can relax."

"I did," Kebron said.

Danilov blinked, then opened Kebron's service record on his desk console. The young Brikar had joined the security detail of the *Ranger* less than two months ago, which made the reason for this meeting all the more puzzling to the captain.

"I see you've asked Lieutenant Commander Raka for a transfer out of security," Danilov said as he scrolled through the information on the screen. Kebron stood in front of the desk, silent and grim as a golem. Danilov waited for him to respond, then realized that he hadn't actually asked the ensign a question. "Please tell me why."

"Security seems . . ." Kebron paused and looked at Raka before he finished: "Limited."

"But it was the specialty you trained for at the Academy," Danilov said. "Why train for a job you didn't want to do?"

"No one ever asked me," Kebron said.

"What options would you like to consider?" Raka asked.

"Astrometrics," Kebron said. "Maybe engineering."

An incredulous look passed between Raka and Danilov, who both then looked back at Kebron. "Well, I'm sure Commander Krueger will miss you on future away missions," Danilov said. "But before we process your transfer, Starfleet Security has one more mission for you." Danilov nodded to Raka.

The Trill security chief turned his chair toward Kebron. "Ensign, are you familiar with the planet Iban?"

"Neutral," Kebron said. "M-class. Four-point-two billion mixed humanoids. Located between the Federation and Cardassia." Kebron paused, then added, as an afterthought, "Mostly harmless."

"Correct," Raka said. "We're sending you there." The security chief picked up a padd from the captain's desk and handed it to Kebron. The tiny Starfleet display device seemed to vanish into Kebron's massive palm.

"Starfleet Intelligence has learned that a Federation bureaucrat named Erril G'Doh has been selling military and scientific secrets to the Cardassians," Raka said. "G'Doh is scheduled to meet his Cardassian contact tomorrow morning in a public park in the middle of the planet's capital city, to hand off an unspecified number of data chips. When he does, you're going to be there to take them both into custody until agents from Starfleet Intelligence arrive."

Kebron studied the information on the padd. Danilov was amazed that the Brikar could work the padd's controls without pulverizing the device. Though Kebron's expression seemed never to change, Danilov sensed that the ensign was puzzled.

"Won't they notice me? I'm . . . conspicuous."

"You'll be undercover," Raka said.

Kebron stared blankly at Raka for several seconds. "Undercover? Me? How?"

"As a park statue," Danilov said, beating Raka to the punch line. "You'll be concealed inside a polymer shell crafted to look exactly like the statue under which G'Doh and his contact plan to meet. You'll be swapped in with a transporter."

"Most important," Raka added, "the shell will conceal your life signs from G'Doh's tricorder. He's become extra cautious since spotting a Starfleet Intelligence operative tailing him last month. SI also has reason to suspect that G'Doh's contact can identify most of their field agents in this sector, so they need to keep all other Starfleet personnel out of the park. When G'Doh hands over the data chips to his contact, you'll grab them and be beamed out."

Kebron looked at Danilov, then back at Raka. He handed the padd back to Raka. "Will this take long?"

"You leave immediately," Raka said. "We have just enough time to get you to Iban via high-warp transport, and swap you for the statue, before G'Doh and his contact meet. They tell me you'll be back here in less than two days."

Kebron was silent for a moment; then he said, "I understand." Danilov stood up. He was about to extend his hand to shake Kebron's, then looked at the Brikar's massive fist and thought better of it. "Good luck, Ensign," he said with a courteous nod, then watched all his office furnishings quake as Kebron turned and lumbered out of his ready room.

Kebron made the jaunt to Iban via high-warp transport in just over sixteen hours. He had spent most of the trip asleep.

After arriving on Iban, he'd been fitted for the polymer shell that

Starfleet Intelligence had created in advance of his arrival. As soon as the technicians had begun fitting pieces of the shell around his legs, they had begged him not to move, lest he shatter the brittle polymer.

That, of course, was the key to the plan: When it came time for him to grab G'Doh and his accomplice, Kebron would simply flex his muscles, shatter the shell, and seize the spies.

The officer in charge of the operation was Lieutenant Commander Sotak, a gaunt and weathered-looking humanoid man with webbed fingers. Sotak briefed Kebron as the technicians sealed the young Brikar inside the shell, stopping short of his face.

"You won't be able to speak to us while you're in the shell," Sotak said. "We'll communicate with you through a pair of encrypted transceivers. We'll implant them near your ears before we encase your head."

"You did put in breathing holes, right?" Kebron said. Sotak looked at the grotesquely detailed minotaur headpiece, which was suspended from a harness attached to tracks on the ceiling.

"We weren't told that'd be a requirement," Sotak said. "I hope that's not a problem." Kebron was still crafting the perfect sarcastic reply when Sotak's poker face broke and revealed a grin. He patted Kebron's shoulder.

"Just kidding. We took care of it, you'll be fine." Sotak took out a tricorder and scanned the lower half of the shell.

"Question," Kebron said.

"Shoot," Sotak said. He adjusted the tricorder's settings.

"Why a statue?" Kebron asked. "Why not a hologram?" Sotak chuckled and shook his head.

"G'Doh would detect a hologram's energy signature a kilometer away," Sotak said. He turned off the tricorder. Kebron eyed the web-fingered man with suspicion.

"Why me?" Kebron said. "Why not a regular agent?" Sotak put away his tricorder and looked Kebron in the eye.

"Because G'Doh and his accomplice will probably be armed, and whoever we put out there is going to be all alone with them for up to twenty seconds before we can beam them out," Sotak said. "We need someone who can hold two suspects and not worry about getting shot at point-blank range. And that brings us to you." Sotak motioned to the technicians. "Okay, let's finish up. We have to make the swap in twenty minutes." He nodded to Kebron. "Good luck, Ensign."

"Whatever," Kebron said.

The technicians—two human men who appeared to be twins, a Vulcan woman with a helmet of hair shaped to an unflattering point in the middle of her forehead, a young Orion man who looked barely old enough to shave, and a Bolian woman with a dramatically pronounced cranial ridge—snapped into action. They moved the headpiece into place above him and began lowering it. As it met the shell that surrounded his massive torso, the binary resin on the headpiece and the body segment fused the two elements into a single, unbroken shell.

The artisans congratulated one another on their fine work and exited together. The Bolian woman was the last one out. She turned off the lights and closed the door behind her.

Kebron stood in the darkened room, entombed in a polymer shell and forbidden to move or to speak.

You've got to be kidding me, he thought. *Tell me they didn't just leave me here. The least they could do is put on some music, or a newsfeed.* Kebron sighed. *Where does Starfleet get these people? The Starfleet Corps of Engineers' special top-secret sculpture division?*

A sickening notion occurred to him. *What if there is no assignment? What if this is just some kind of bizarre prank by McHenry?* He quickly exonerated his Academy friend. *No, not his style,* Kebron assured himself. *Not abstract enough.* Kebron also reminded himself that Ensign Mark McHenry was at least forty-one light-years away, piloting the Starship *Valentina.*

Before he could focus further paranoid suspicions on anyone else, Kebron was beamed to the park.

Kebron materialized inside the statue alcove, which was recessed into a natural-rock cliff face at the south end of the oval-shaped park. He was on top of the broad statue base, elevated several feet above ground level. Directly in front of and below him was an empty bench. The bench had a wrought-iron frame that supported rough wooden planks coated in peeling, weather-beaten white paint that had grayed with antiquity.

Beyond the bench was a smooth, paved pedestrian path that curved around the park perimeter and intersected with several other paved walkways, which meandered in undulating shapes beneath the drooping boughs of a variety of trees, most of them flowering with sweetly fragrant blossoms in a variety of colors.

On the other side of the path in front of Kebron was a large, meticulously maintained Zen rock garden. In the center of the pristine arrangement of white marble chips and jutting black basaltic rocks was a serene, burbling pond.

Inside the pond's crystal-clear waters swam a quartet of koi, a particular breed of carp first bred on Earth in the nation of Japan for domestic ponds. Kebron had seen fish much like these in several similar ponds on the Starfleet Academy campus.

Kebron carefully scanned the park from west to east and familiarized himself with its layout. It was just before dawn. The chill of night vanished as the sky shifted quickly from the last traces of indigo to the washed-out flare of sunrise. The park came alive with the chipper chirps of birdsong.

Far from Kebron, at the north end of the park, one of the automated gates slid open. Half a second later, a jogger, a young humanoid man, turned and bounded through the open gate into the park. The man circled the park four times, then exited through the east gate and continued away, past the planetary parliament building.

Within an hour, the city was awake. The park teemed with bird-watchers, joggers, and people who apparently had nowhere better to be first thing in the morning. Kebron observed their comings and goings with mild curiosity, but he devoted his concentration to waiting for the spy G'Doh and his unnamed Cardassian handler to reveal themselves.

Minutes later, a flock of orange-and-white birds fluttered noisily to a landing on his shoulders and head.

Before Kebron could delude himself with some Vulcanesque "infinite diversity" claptrap about the beauty of life's many forms, the flock festooned his pristine polymer shell with excrement. He thought the stench seemed unusually powerful until he realized that the dirty squabs squatting on his head had deposited their cloacal products on the statue's face, beneath his breathing vents.

Kebron wanted to shout a string of Brikar obscenities to disperse the feathered pests, but he remembered at the last moment that if he spoke he would crack the polymer shell that hid him from his quarry.

While the birds went on marking their territory, Kebron stifled a deep growl and silently concocted no fewer than a dozen recipes that all entailed roasting small birds alive over white-hot coals.

Several hours later, Kebron began to suspect that something was amiss. By his estimation it was late afternoon, yet the sun had barely risen more than a few degrees above the horizon. The picnickers had departed, leaving the park mostly empty. An Atrean man played an uninspired game of fetch with his huge, long-furred dog on a broad knoll in the middle of the park.

Kebron's com transceiver crackled to life, painfully loud: *"Ensign Kebron, this is Lieutenant Commander Sotak."*

Aside from the transceiver's output being magnified by its proximity to his ear, Kebron could tell from the distortion that someone had left it turned up to full volume. Unfortunately, there was no way to adjust it or to tell Sotak to lower the gain on his own transmission without blowing his cover. He winced as Sotak's squawking voice drilled a hole through his brain.

"We've had a minor delay," Sotak said.

No kidding, Kebron thought.

"The meeting's still on for today, but we're not sure of the exact time. We need you to hold position until further notice," Sotak said.

Kebron was ready to chalk up the delay to a run-of-the-mill snag until Sotak added one final comment: *"By the way, I'm sure this was covered in your mission briefing, but I just want to remind you that one day on Iban lasts sixty-four-point-one standard Federation hours. So hang in there. Sotak out."*

No, Kebron noted glumly, *that wasn't in the briefing.*

Kebron passed the next few hours observing the Atrean man playing fetch with his dog, and trying to discern a pattern in the severely curtailed meanderings of the koi in their pond.

"New reports just came in," Sotak said. His voice, rendered shrill by the distorted transceivers, was like a nail being hammered through Kebron's eardrum. *"We've confirmed that G'Doh is making the drop in the next few hours. Stay sharp."*

The day had grown sunny and hot, and the park was packed with a new wave of visitors. Beyond the park perimeter, a nonstop flow of hovercars and shuttlecraft arrived and departed from the main entrance of Iban's parliament building.

Staring at traffic was mind-numbingly boring, but Kebron preferred it to witnessing the revolting public display of affection that had, for the past two hours, been transpiring on the bench in front of him. He assumed that either the young couple had nowhere else to go or they wanted to show off.

The Brikar envied the park visitors who, when they rounded the curve to this isolated bend in the park and saw the near-pornographic wrestling match on the bench, had been able to avert their eyes and walk away.

Kebron, who often was repulsed by humanoids' frenzied pursuit of such fevered liaisons, couldn't even close his eyes, lest he fail to see the conspicuously absent traitor, G'Doh. So he focused his attention past the sweaty, moaning couple on the bench and took solace in the quiet dignity of the koi pond.

Fish never embarrass anyone like this, he thought. *They mind their own business. They're quiet. They don't run away.*

The birds that perched on his shoulders and head relieved themselves in unison, as if in response to some silent cue. The couple on the bench carried on, oblivious of both Kebron's presence and his plight. The young Brikar realized then what he liked best about fish, as a life-form: *They're clean.*

The Iban sun was at midheaven, shining down on the capital city. *If it's high noon,* Kebron thought, *this must be Thursday.*

Commander Sotak's voice squawked in his ear.

"I know this must be frustrating for you," Sotak said.

The transceivers had developed a slight feedback loop, and Kebron was quickly growing accustomed to the high-pitched ringing tone that now haunted his every conscious moment.

"Our sources indicate the meeting is about to start," Sotak said. *"You'll be out of there before the park closes."* Kebron did not believe a word Sotak said. The shadows that Kebron had watched shorten from morning until noon had long since lengthened and stretched away in the opposite direction.

In the middle of the park, the Atrean man threw a stick. His shaggy dog retrieved the stick. The Atrean threw the stick again, and again, and again, to the dog's unending delight.

Kebron tuned out the cooing of the despicable flying feces machines that had made his head and shoulders their home. Only the perfect tranquility of the koi pond spared the innocent citizens of Iban the rampage of a Brikar pushed beyond the fragile edge of his sanity.

He had taken the liberty of naming the four fish, since no one else seemed to have bothered. The even-tempered one he dubbed Vladimir, and he named the melancholy but proud one Estragon. The serenely inscrutable one he called Sam, and the aggressive one was now known to him as Pozzo.

By narrowing his vision until all he saw was the bliss of the koi pond, Kebron was able to endure Sotak's latest vague excuse for the failure of G'Doh to appear.

A few hours later, the park gates slid closed.

"We've learned that G'Doh and his contact intend to meet tonight, while the

park is closed," Sotak said. Kebron recalled every parentage-disparaging ob-scenity in the Brikar language.

The park was illuminated by dozens of antique glow-globe lamps along its walkways. Elegant towers of duranium and transparent aluminum sur-rounding the park darkened one window at a time, until only a scattered pattern of lighted offices remained. Overhead, Iban's twin moons slowly made their joint transit of the night sky.

The yelp of a dog caught Kebron's attention. His eyes pierced the dark-ness. In the middle of the park, on the knoll, the Atrean man had concealed himself beneath some shrubbery and huddled with his pet against the chilly night air.

Doesn't this guy have a home? Kebron wondered. *How can such an advanced society still have people living on the streets?* Kebron despised elitist thinking, but he was certain that such a state of affairs would never be ignored on a Federation world.

During the night, he made up names for constellations he had never seen before, and he witnessed a hovercar accident outside the park's north gate. What he did not see, however, was any sign of G'Doh or his accomplice.

The sun rose again—thirty-two hours, two minutes, and eleven seconds after it had set. Moments later the park gates slid open, the humanoid jog-ger loped into the park, and the Atrean and his dog resumed their game of fetch. Within an hour of sunrise, the park once again bustled with visitors.

"Sotak to Kebron." Kebron clenched his jaw in response to the all-too-familiar jabbing pain that the faulty transceiver caused in his ears. *"I have some, uh . . . interesting news,"* Sotak said over the com.

Please let him be brief, Kebron prayed. From beyond the east wall of the park, he heard the high-pitched whine of six medium-sized official shuttles approaching the parliament building from the south.

"We just received word that, um. . . ." Sotak paused. He sounded ex-tremely embarrassed. Outside the park's east gate, the shuttles descended in unison. The park visitors stopped to gawk at the arrival of some local celebrity politician. *"It seems that, um, G'Doh was arrested on Deneva by Starfleet Security."*

Kebron hoped he had heard Sotak incorrectly. *Did he just say* Deneva? *Tell me he didn't just say Deneva.*

"Apparently, they, uh . . . took him into custody two days ago."

Kebron imagined what Sotak would look like after he finished making origami out of him.

In front of the parliament building, the shuttles landed. Their gull-wing doors opened with a low hiss. Two dozen bodyguards piled out of the shuttles and flanked a lone dignitary as he climbed the steps of the parliament building.

In the middle of the park, the Atrean man dropped his stick and whistled for his dog. The canine galloped toward him, its tongue dangling from the side of its mouth.

"Obviously, we don't want to make a scene by beaming you out while the park is full," Sotak said, *"especially since the Iban government doesn't even know we're here."*

The dog lurched to a stop next to its Atrean master, who knelt beside the shaggy animal and placed a hand on its back.

He's never petted that dog once, Kebron realized. *And if he's a homeless person, why doesn't he beg for food or money?*

Kebron scrutinized the Atrean, whose attention was fixed on the politician ascending the parliament steps.

"Just be patient," Sotak said, his volume-distorted voice scrambling Kebron's already overtaxed auditory nerve. *"We'll beam you out tonight after the park closes."*

The Atrean grabbed a fistful of fur on the dog's back and pulled it upward. Instead of tearing out a clump of fur, he lifted away a fake-fur drapery to reveal a compact, collapsible plasma rifle strapped to the animal's shorn flank. The Atrean plucked it from its holster. With fast, expertly smooth motions, he extended its shoulder stock and targeting sight, then lifted the weapon to his shoulder.

Kebron leaped forward and exploded from his shell.

The enormous Brikar hit the ground with an earthshaking impact. Everyone in the park turned instantly toward him. A few hundred people screamed.

Kebron swatted a tree out of his way and marched in a straight line toward the Atrean sniper.

"Drop your weapon!" Kebron shouted. His voice boomed over the screeches of terrified civilians. The Atrean aimed his rifle at Kebron and fired. The plasma burst scorched Kebron's uniform but failed to stop his approach.

Across the street, the Iban dignitary's bodyguards hustled their client inside the parliament building to safety. Three squads of local police charged into the park through the east, west, and north gates.

The Atrean made a run for it. Kebron plodded after him.

The sniper dodged a crossfire of police blaster shots as he ran from one part of the park to another seeking an escape route, but he found them all blocked. He stumbled into a dead-end path that terminated at the south cliff wall, and turned to see Kebron behind him.

Kebron, eyes gleaming with menace, shambled toward the Atrean, who fired blast after blast of charged plasma at him. Kebron wasn't injured by the blasts, but he grew irritated as the charged plasma burned away what was left of his uniform.

He reached out, grabbed the plasma rifle, and mangled it. The Atrean sank to his knees and cowered on the ground, shrinking in terror from the gigantic, nude Brikar towering over him. Kebron nabbed the sniper and lifted him off the ground, then heard footfalls behind him. He turned to see a dozen Iban police, their weapons aimed at the Atrean.

"He's all yours," Kebron said as he tossed the Atrean to the cops.

The officer in charge stared at Kebron. "Who *are* you?" he said. "What are you *doing* here?"

"I'm Zak Kebron," the Brikar security officer said, "and this has been the longest day of my life."

Captain Danilov sat at his desk in his ready room aboard the *Ranger,* reading Kebron's mission report with raised eyebrows. Kebron stood at attention on the other side of his desk.

Lieutenant Commander Raka stood next to Kebron. The Trill security chief wore a disapproving scowl but had said nothing since the Brikar had entered the ready room.

Danilov looked up at Kebron, then shook his head and resumed reading. Finally, he turned off his viewscreen. He rubbed his eyes for a moment, then looked up at the ensign.

"Sotak wants me to reprimand you for disobeying his order to remain undercover," Danilov said. "On the other hand, Iban's Prime Minister Niad wants to honor you with a parade for saving his life. Frankly, I'm torn."

"I'd prefer the reprimand," Kebron said.

"Consider it done," Danilov said. "We're lucky the Iban government believed you were there to stop the assassin, instead of on a covert Starfleet mission. You do grasp the importance of the chain of command, don't you, Ensign?"

"Yes, sir," Kebron said. "But I would do the same thing again."

Raka arched his left eyebrow and glared at Kebron, who stared back and loomed above the slender Trill man.

"And why is that, Ensign?" Raka said.

"Saving lives is more important than saving face."

Raka held his ground for a moment; then the corners of his mouth turned slightly upward.

"Spoken like a true security officer," Raka said. "I assume that's why you've withdrawn your transfer request?"

"Transfer request?" Kebron said.

Raka blinked. "The one you asked for before you—"

"Never requested a transfer," Kebron said ominously. Raka leaned backward, away from the hulking Brikar, and glanced at the captain.

"Of course you didn't," Danilov said. "I'm sure the commander must be thinking of someone else. . . . Now what's this about you requisitioning half a dozen live fish from Earth?"

"Koi. They're soothing," Kebron said. A few seconds later he added, "And they're clean."

"Mm-hmm," Danilov said. "Bit large to keep as pets aboard a starship, don't you think?"

"I don't have furniture," Kebron said. "Wastes space." Danilov scratched his chin pensively. He picked up his mug of coffee and leaned forward as he took a sip of the scathing beverage and swallowed.

"Tell you what," he said. "Start off with something a bit easier to manage—goldfish, let's say—and see how that goes, *before* we gut your quarters. Sound acceptable?"

Kebron considered the captain's proposal for a moment before he replied, "Okay. Goldfish."

Danilov nodded. "All right, then. I'll have Commander Krueger take care of it." He reclined his chair and took another sip of coffee. "Dismissed, Ensign."

Kebron turned and lumbered out of the ready room. His every step sent shudders through the deck. As he stooped and turned sideways to shimmy out the door to the bridge, his last step toppled the books on a shelf next to the door. The leather-bound tome at the end tumbled to the deck with a leaden thump as the door swished shut behind Kebron.

Danilov listened as the enormous ensign's thudding steps receded. He looked at Raka, who rolled his eyes and shook his head. "You look unhappy, Commander," Danilov said.

"Four days ago I was sorry to lose him," Raka said. "Now I'm worried I might not be able to control him. He's strong, tough, *and* smart, but stubborn. I'd hate to see him ruin a promising career before it gets started."

Danilov chuckled. "I wouldn't worry about his career," the captain said. "He's idealistic, eccentric, and has a head like a rock. What's more, he exhibits selective memory and he's capable of not moving for days at a time." Danilov sighed. "If you ask me, I'd say he's on a fast track to the admiralty."

ROBIN LEFLER
Lefler's Logs

Robert Greenberger

During her days at Starfleet Academy and as an engineer on the *U.S.S. Enterprise,* Robin Lefler was known for her "Lefler's Laws." Those laws, and much of Robin's personality, grew out of her odd experiences growing up the child of Charles Lefler and his wife Morgan—a woman who is much more than she seems. "Lefler's Logs" takes us through the childhood of the future operations officer of the *U.S.S. Excalibur.*

Robert Greenberger

Robert Greenberger is a senior editor at DC Comics in their collected-editions department. Additionally, he has extensive writing credits ranging from non-fiction books for young adults to a smattering of original fiction to lots of *Star Trek*. In 2004 he will contribute to *Star Trek: Tales of the Dominion War* and pen two *Star Trek: The Next Generation* novels, *A Time to Love* and *A Time to Hate*. His *Star Trek: S.C.E.* eBooks, *Past Life* and *Buying Time*, are both available for download. Foolish mortal, he is a lifelong Mets fan. He makes his home in Connecticut with his wife Deb and children Kate and Robbie.

LEFLER'S LOG, Stardate 31345.3

We're on Tantalus, wherever that is. It's kinda weird since it's always so dark. Daddy says we won't be here for long since the plasma studies are scheduled for only a month or two. He keeps trying to explain what plasma is and all I think is that it sounds like a gooey sauce to go over my chicken.

The people who live here have been pretty strange, not at all like the ones at Starbase 42. Here, they keep to themselves and I haven't seen a single kid since we set up our new home a few days ago.

Mr. Consadine lives next door to us but we only see him in the building lobby, never on our floor. He wears big coats and I think he's stealing. I keep trying to peek inside his coat—they're all gray or brown—and see what's there but no luck yet. Tomorrow I will talk with Ms. Wis'noki and see what she knows. So far, she's the only one who's been nice and gave me a cookie the day we moved in. It was the tangiest cookie I've ever had, fizzling on my tongue, and watching me eat it made Mom giggle.

LEFLER'S LOG, Stardate 31393.7

Alice. Cheshire. Those are our new names. We decided this after she read the book to me. Mom, that is Alice, likes my smile and says coming home to see my seven-year-old smile is worth putting up with life on Tantalus.

Dad says it'll take some getting used to, calling us Alice and Cheshire, but we told him those were names just for us. He put on a big frown but I think he was playing with us.

I wish I had someone here to play with but there don't seem to be any kids in the building. Instead, I'm looking at all the people in here, figuring out who they really are and why none have kids my age.

LEFLER'S LOG, Stardate 31443.8

Okay, I think he's stealing chips. Dad says they're isolinear chips, and he brings them home to work on away from the lab. But I never see him bring any back. Mr. Consadine must be a spy, maybe for the Klingons. Dad thinks I'm being silly and won't let me contact Starfleet. So, I'll just keep making notes and see what happens. Mom says if I'm right, I can make Daddy buy me a new dress. I think I'd like one just like the one Mom wore last night to the big holiday party. It was all red and shimmery and she wore her hair loose so it was full and curly, making her prettier than usual. Dad kept hugging her as they got ready. They left ten minutes late. I got to stay behind and watch some new vids they downloaded at the lab.

LEFLER'S LOG, Stardate 31448.6

Ms. Wis'noki must be in on it.

This morning, as I was leaving for school, I saw her sneak out of Mr. Consadine's apartment. She was still wearing her bathrobe and she bunched the front up in her hands, like she was taking out the chips he steals from the lab. So, they're in on it together. If I can prove they're both spies, I bet I can get two dresses!

LEFLER'S LOG, Supplemental

Dad laughed a lot when I told him about Ms. Wis'noki being a spy. He sat me down and tried to explain that sometimes adults visit one another and have sleepovers. That made me kind of sad because I can't remember the last time I had a sleepover with anyone. It had to have been before Starbase 42, so I guess that makes it Coridan. It would have been with LaShaundra. She was nice and now that I think of her, I miss her.

It's a good thing I have this tricorder Alice gave me for my birthday two years ago. I didn't really know how to use it then—heck, I was only five. But she says I use it as well as a starship officer. That got me to thinking about starships and how much fun it must be to live on one ship traveling from star to star with everyone. Visiting the new planets is nice, but it's just Dad, Mom, and me and sometimes I'd like to have a friend to share this with when they're at work.

LEFLER'S LOG, Stardate 31653.7

This place is haunted. I've been hearing weird noises ever since we settled in and I was the only one who noticed. Just like when I found out Mr. Consadine was stealing chips. Well, Dad finally looked into that, I think just to shut me up. He turns out not to be a spy. Darn. He really does design work on isolinear chips. I just never see him go to work so I never see him carry them back out of the apartment.

Anyway, I can hear the noises between the walls. They're low thuds without a rhythm. And they happen day or night. I can't figure out what the spirits want. Wait, there's one now! It came from the hallway so I'm moving carefully out of my room, trying to follow it.

Dad's been teaching me about this method—scientific method he calls it. I have to record my observations and take good notes, he said. The sound is coming from the wall, not near the vent or the light panel. It's low, below my knees but not at the floor. The sound is deep and lasts maybe two seconds. I can't understand why I'm the only one who hears it. I'm putting my ear next to the wall to listen closer. Maybe it's not haunted, but something is trying to dig its way out.

LEFLER'S LOG, Supplemental

Alice couldn't stop herself from laughing so I'm mad at her. She found me in my closet, behind my protective wall of luggage and packing crates.

That sound was really loud this time, probably because I had my ear on the wall. And this time there were two thumps! I thought for sure whatever was haunting the building was coming out of the wall. I heard a story once about an alien being buried on another world and he punched and punched and punched his way out of his deep prison even though it took him a thousand years.

If they could bury some monster on one world, they could do it again.

When I explained my thinking to Mom, she put me in her lap and laughed again. It made me so mad, I tried to get away. She just held me tight and whispered in my ear. She said that only happened once and it happened a long time ago and on a planet nowhere near here.

Mom still didn't know what I heard so I made her promise to have Dad find out.

LEFLER'S LOG, Stardate 31610.7

I'm mad. Turns out Dad found my evil spirit. It was something in the heating system starting to fail. The building's owner was happy I discovered the problem before it got serious so he took my family to dinner tonight. They let me have whatever I wanted so I asked for King Crab. I remember hearing about that somewhere and the owner had never seen one.

It was huge and I loved every mouthful.

Mom thinks I could be a detective when I grow up because I'm very observant. That's something I never thought of and will consider.

But only if detectives can travel on starships.

LEFLER'S LOG, Stardate 32854.6

The ship left orbit an hour ago and I just stopped crying. I feel bad and not at all ready to come out of my room. It's really small and cramped but it's mine and I'm just not ready to get out. So I thought I'd dig out the old tricorder.

Rimbor was a rough world for Mom and Dad but we spent a year there this time, the longest I remember being anywhere. They were conducting research at a new science institute and it was a one-year assignment. We knew when we arrived that's how long it would be and I hoped to make friends this time. I didn't expect Mom—

No. I'm not ready to talk about Mom yet. I want to talk about my friend.

His name is Whis. Well, that's what I call him. He's an Andorian and isn't exactly a he, he says, and the proper name is just too long to always get right. I stopped trying to pronounce it when he kept laughing when I tripped on the third—no fourth—syllable. His mom—he calls her his *zhavey*—was in Starfleet, assigned to security at the same place, so we saw a lot of each other.

Whis showed me how to find ways into the building that his mom was trying to protect. He thought it was pretty funny that he could do better than her but he never told her about any of it. Had that been me, I would have made notes with the tricorder and showed my mom.

We did a lot of stuff together like go for long hikes in the hills that surrounded the city. They formed a ring and the natives built this city hoping the natural formations would protect it from raiders. Rimbor is a rough world, filled with people angry over some war that ended a century ago that made no one happy. I never did understand what it was all about. Dad said it was about land, like most every other war, and I guess he's right.

So anyway, Whis showed me his favorite trails and then we set out to find new ones. There was one I liked that took us to a stream where we could swim in the warm months. The air is nice and toasty warm for about three months and we went there a lot to swim and splash. I showed him how to skip stones, something Dad taught me.

It's funny, but I think about our time on Rimbor and I remember spending more time with Dad than ever before. He was there for school shows and met with the teachers. We played cards a lot and he let me try some of his novels but I didn't like them too much. They were mostly histories of different alien worlds and were thick and boring. I much prefer the stories about explorers or the *Pegasus Tales.*

I guess I should talk about Mom.

Mom went away while we were on the planet. She just wasn't there one morning when I came out for breakfast. She had never missed breakfast before and Dad was there, mixing up the oatmeal. His is less lumpy than Mom's which is kind of nice. Anyway, he kept me going, talking about my school and his studies, and it wasn't until Mom skipped dinner as well that I figured out something was wrong.

She stayed away four days and when she returned she was bright and cheerful as usual, but wouldn't tell me what's going on. I wondered if Starfleet sent her on special assignment. That's one good reason for not knowing.

I checked my logs and Mom stayed with us exactly three months before going off again. Dad seemed sad about it but kept me distracted and I see now that he was forcing the smile. After a few days, he told me she had been abducted. My first thought was that her secret mission turned out well and she was a captured by someone angry at her. I told Whis about it and he asked why would anyone want a plasma specialist? He just shrugged his antennae and wouldn't even mention it to his *zhavey.* When I asked Dad, his answer didn't really sound right.

Maybe she discovered something and got kidnapped. I've been hearing a lot about the Cardassians—they sound pretty nasty so maybe they took Mom. I'll never know, I guess. She returned, just like the last time, and never told me a thing. She didn't seem as happy to be back this time, though.

I guess I should have looked over the last year's entries a lot sooner. It's like doing research, something I've gotten to like. I can see Mom staying out later here and there, then the absences. Never a word if she was on a secret mission or was captured or anything.

Here's something from the first time she returned. She seemed happy and everything seemed normal. Mom called me Cheshire, like she always did. But the second time she returned, she kept to her room a lot. I'd bring her tea after dinner and sit on the bed and try to amuse her.

I told her that if she was going to keep going away, I'd have to help Dad run the house. To do that, I needed rules, like the ones they had for me. She looked at me with great interest, for a change, and asked what the first rule would be.

"You can only count on yourself."

She was silent for a while and I thought she'd be mad at me. Instead, she just sipped her tea and gave me a small smile. But, she encouraged me to do more.

I guess she knew she'd be away again, because three weeks later she was gone for a month. Just like before.

I began to wonder if Mom was doing something more than study plasma, which I still can't quite understand.

Anyway, I'm going to stay in the cabin by myself until I stop missing Rimbor and Whis and maybe until I can figure out why Mom got so sad during the last year.

LEFLER'S LOG, Stardate 33678.2

I'm confused.

We just got home from our camping trip and the weirdest thing happened. I thought things would be great by moving back to Earth. We hadn't been here since I was born and I don't remember the place at all. Yesterday, we went to New Jersey, part of North America, and went camping by the shore. It was soft and warm and we flew a kite and did some boating. The water was calm and we just paddled around, just the three of us.

Mom had been home six straight months without being kidnapped again. Dad keeps telling me people keep nabbing her because she's so brilliant. Well, I know she's brilliant, but she's just a plasma scientist. It's not like she's found the cure to a disease or has figured out a safe time-travel plan. It's just energy. Lots of people know about energy.

Since this nonsense started a few years ago, Mom just vanishes for days or weeks at a shot, and Dad and I have to make do. He seems sad all the time, even when she's around, but she seems even sadder.

I've been trying for years now to keep her happy and it isn't working. Maybe for a day or even an hour, but it's never enough. I bring home great grades, if I do say so myself, and she just nods. I do fancy art projects and she won't even come to the exhibitions. When we're home, she sits and reads or combs the net for information, bringing her work home I guess.

It's gotten that each time she magically reappears, her first question is what new rule I've come up. The last time, I told her they weren't rules. They were my laws. She delights in them, I think, and they've been coming easier and easier. I'm up to sixteen of them and I wonder how many more times she'll go away. Sixteen and I'm only nine, if this keeps up how many rules will I have?

Like I was saying, we went camping. Dad told some pretty scroggy ghost stories while he roasted some fish. Mom sipped some wine and had a far-away look in her eyes but she did help make some sort of fruit-filled pie that got toasted over the fire. It was kind of neat; I didn't know she could do that.

We had gotten into our sleeping bags and gone to sleep. I awoke with Mom's hand on my mouth. She gestured for me to follow her outside. Without a word, we went hiking a bit, going up a hill. At its top, she pointed and we were overlooking the water. It looked so still, with the crescent moon perfectly reflected on its surface. Her hands were on my shoulders and after a time, they tightened. And then they relaxed. This repeated a few times until finally, she turned me around and led me back to the camp. She zipped me in and returned to her own sleeping bag.

Not a word. No idea why we went for the hike. The view was pretty nice, but I'm not sure it was worth getting up in the middle of the night.

Mom is gone again. It's time for another law. Number seventeen. "When all else fails, do it yourself."

LEFLER'S LOG, Stardate 359487.1

What exactly is a diary? It can be anything. Most people use one to write down their important thoughts and experiences, and others write really personal stuff about boyfriends and other people. I've been keeping these log entries since I was seven, five years ago, and it's all the former. There aren't any boys, let alone friends.

I carefully download the entries to isolinear chips, which I keep in a wooden box Mom brought me from a bazaar when we lived on Rimbor. I miss Whis. He wrote me a few times but I haven't heard from him in two years so I guess he's got his own life now.

Starfleet started some new warp engine experiments and needed Mom and Dad's expertise. We've been at Starbase 179 for a few months now and it's nice enough but I still want us posted to a starship. Mom arranged for me to tour the *Saratoga* when it docked here recently. It was filled with activity, and everyone looked so amazing in their uniforms. The ship was thrumming, purring like a cat, and it felt filled with life. It just fueled my desire to grow up and be on my own.

It's probably good I feel this way since I think I'm going to be alone soon enough. Mom and Dad have been fighting again. I thought that ended when we left Utopia Planitia. Shows what I know. Dad has finally had his fill with Mom's moods and disappearances. Good for him. He stopped trying to convince me she was kidnapped when we were on Earth. That camping trip changed everything. Mom isn't sick, at least not physically. Dad says she's been depressed and she's stopped trying to laugh that off. She won't admit to it but I can't imagine what else the problem is.

Mom doesn't even smile anymore. She works late hours and so far, it seems her work hasn't suffered. Just me. I want to talk to my mother, shop with her and do things that we're expected to do. I just want a normal life and she's denying it to me.

Dad suffers. I suffer. Mom suffers. We don't even do things together except sometimes eat a meal. It might be better if I had some true friends, but we all come and go on starbases or planets so I have friends, but not the true deep ones I've read about. Maybe, just maybe, if I had two consecutive years somewhere, that would change. But no, we get a new posting and I pack up my learning discs and clothes—and of course you, dear tricorder—and move away. Not a single friend I've made on any of these places keeps in touch. We exchange a few notes and then one of us stops. I'm as bad as they are so I've caused my own pain. I should know better, but I make the mistake and then time passes and it feels wrong to finally write.

LEFLER'S LOG, Stardate 37592.4

Well, I wanted my two years somewhere and here it is our second anniversary at Starbase 212. It's a big rock with great tunnels connecting the buildings. Mom called it a habitrail after we beamed aboard and she had to explain it to me and Dad both. I've never had a pet; Dad always said it was just too much trouble given how often we move about. Would have been nice, but hey, I have you, my trusty tricorder. We've been together just over nine years so you're my best friend.

Life is so weird and little surprises happen when you least expect them. Especially when all my friends are involved. At school, there was a plumbing leak and we were standing on the steps, talking. We were pushing each other around but didn't really mean it. Then, when I least expected it, Jamey pushed me really hard and I went flying across the asphalt. I landed in this big puddle and got absolutely soaked. But it was worth it to see them all coming toward me with really concerned expressions on their faces. It made me feel like I belonged somewhere. About five minutes later, we were all laughing about it. Even though my hip was aching, I was having fun.

I'm not sure getting drenched and calling it fun is right. It certainly isn't fun at home. Mother and Dad barely speak to one another and he seems more bothered by it than she is. In fact, she seems more withdrawn, almost like a Vulcan, keeping things bottled up. I can't even remember the last time I saw her smile. Dad's been starting to keep later hours so I see them both in the morning and that's it. They go to the labs and I go to school.

Jamey was the first one to say hi and we've gotten closer with time. She's from Deneb and her parents are actually in a support position so they move a lot less often. She's been here four years and I've actually heard her call this rock home. Wonder if I'll do that if we stay.

LEFLER'S LOG, Stardate 38548.3

Giancarlo kissed me. Kissed *me!*

We were in the lab doing a chem project when he just leaned over and planted one on me. His lips were soft, a little salty. I've kind of liked him and even thought about asking him to the dance next month. But this came from nowhere.

I think I kissed back. It happened so fast.

I'm not sure what all this means. We're lab partners and I've known him five months, ever since he arrived. It's odd not being the newest one somewhere and I'm starting to feel like a veteran. He likes parrises squares and is good at archery but struggles with literature. He hates poetry, like me; but also hates the music I like.

Anyway, when I pulled back, he smiled and I wanted to melt. It was a sweet smile, one I haven't seen on him before, and I like it. A lot. I took a good long look at him, his soft brown hair coming just over his ears and the piece that drops in front of his right eye. The small scar on the left earlobe. His eyes are deep brown, like dark chocolate, and I just stared at them for a while.

He looked back at me, smiling, and we were quiet. It went on like that for a bit until finally he looked at the experiment and got back to work. And he never said a word. I was left wondering what that was all about and, as time passed, and he still didn't say anything, I started to get mad at him.

When class ended, we went into the hall and he looked ready to say something. And I just kept on going. When I got to my next class, one without him, I hated myself for not talking to him. He's cute and I do like him. But why didn't he say something? Why'd he kiss me today?

I wish Jamey were here. But no, she stayed on 212 and I got to move to another rock. Haven't heard from her since my fifteenth birthday. Been here awhile and still have no one close. So, I decided to wait until I got home and figured I'd try and talk to Mother about it. We don't talk about guys and stuff; I'm usually busy trying to cheer her up so I keep my problems to myself. Sometimes I can talk to Dad about things, but I doubt he'd want to hear about Giancarlo kissing me.

Sure enough, I got home and the apartment was empty. Typically despite Mother's work hours being over the same as school. She said she did this so we could be together but she almost immediately started working late, taking on extra assignments. Not even a note on the net. I made a snack and got to my work, hoping she'd turn up for dinner.

I did try and work but couldn't focus on the Andorian poets. It just made me think of Whis. History was about Federation founding worlds, usually interesting, but all I kept thinking about was the kiss. It was soft. I dreamt about kissing him in the rain. At a park, under a tree. In the rain. It sounds so romantic. I wondered about touching him and him touching me and how far I'd let him get. Other couples have formed this year and one couple already had their wedding. I know, it sounds weird, but that's how they do things on Gemaris V. They were thirteen and had been betrothed shortly after birth. It was kind of sweet—even though they looked too young to me.

I didn't think I'd be coupled this year. Guess I haven't thought much about it. I read about romance a lot in my books but it's not something Mother talks about. When she talks at all, it's about plans and the future, my future. She makes it sound like she'll be a plasma specialist until she dies. If she loves it, I guess that works. Dad has talked about retiring and doing a lot of sailing. We haven't really sailed since that camping trip and I know he misses it. Especially on a rock like this, without a lot of good lakes for boats. Anyway, I think about Dad wanting to retire and sail and Mother wanting to still work. I can't imagine how they'd be happy doing different things. They spend so much time apart; I also can't imagine why they're still together.

It's past midnight and Mother is just getting home. I should be asleep but I've been so pumped, so full of excitement and with no one to share it with it feels like I could go nova. Dad could tell I was fidgety but I deflected his questions and just went on about the experiment, not mentioning Giancarlo at all. It's like I'm keeping him to myself. I can't really sleep, since I keep thinking about him, his lips, and wanting to tell Mother. She should look in on me and we can chat, even though it's late.

Wait, she's going straight to her room, not even looking in on me. Why tonight of all nights? What's happening to her? Is she going to leave Dad?

LEFLER'S LOG, Stardate 40777.4

We haven't camped in years and I think it's great Mom and Dad were making an effort. We even went back to the New Jersey shore and stayed at the same campground. It's perfect late-summer weather and I got to do some water-skiing, haven't done that in ages. Most of our postings have been on worlds with precious little water so this is heaven!

Dad said we deserved this time together. Mother seems more alert and lively than usual but it's Dad who is not being responsive. Sure, he likes the sailing, but he doesn't seem . . . connected to Mother. Something is going on and of course I have no idea what it is and when I think about it, it drives me to nova.

LEFLER'S LOG, Stardate 40778.4

Something's weird.

I feel hungover, which is crazy. All I've drunk tonight is lemonade and that was hours ago. I'm in my tent, in my sleeping bag, and still, I feel exhausted, my tongue thick, my head fuzzy.

"Oh, baby," I hear Mother's voice in my head. It's like she said it moments ago, but she's nowhere in sight.

My heart's been thumping at warp speed since I woke up, a tendril of panic in my mind. There are echoes of a dream and I close my eyes. Me and Mom, somewhere bright, somewhere wrong. I don't know where.

I slowly got out of my bag and left the tent, finding Mom and Dad in their tent. Exactly where they should be. But it feels wrong. The world started to tilt on me so I went back to my tent and tried to go back to sleep.

Just as I began to drift off, my dream returned.

"Oh, my poor mother. Mom, I love you, and nothing you've done is so terrible that I'll stop loving you for a single instant, ever, and you can't make me hate you or wish I'd never been born, you can't ma . . ."

Where did that come from?

LEFLER'S LOG, Stardate 40879.4

It must have been our fight.

That's all I keep thinking about. I have no idea what we fought about, but it was something huge and I can't remember. But it must have affected Mother as much as me.

I'm to blame.

Dad and I were approached by the park ranger and he had that certain look on his face. Dad stopped moving and stood like a statue as the ranger said sensors showed Mom's shuttle having crashed into the Atlantic.

Earlier, we came back from the boardwalk and Mom said she had to take care of something, but neither of us imagined it meant leaving the campsite. And then word came that the shuttle crashed. It was found but Mother was not.

"No body," Dad repeated to himself, almost like a mantra.

He thinks she disappeared again. Normally, her absences have been timed to clean break points in her work. Dad caught on to that about four years ago so he's been checking and the pattern has fit each and every period of vanishing. Except now.

When we returned home tonight there was a holo on my desk. Without even touching it, I knew it was from Mom. Sure enough, it was a portrait of Mom. She's leaning against one huge rock, wet from the surf, all grays and browns. It makes a stunning backdrop for her as she leans on it in a white shirt with a high collar, so it frames her face. I have the computer zoom and I study her eyes. I can't remember the last time they weren't filled with sadness. But here, they're clear. There's life in them, also a rare sight. I continue to study them as I sit on my bed, putting some distance between me and the screen.

And there was a message, her tone fairly matter-of-fact. She said she had to see relatives, but not why. Then she added something odd. "There's a doctor named Pointer. When you're ready, you may want to pay him a visit. Just to talk. He's very good and comes with my highest recommendation."

I checked the details and he's a psychiatrist. Why on Earth would Mother have needed a psychiatrist? A marriage counselor perhaps, but when did this all start? I realize I'm the Cheshire cat, the mysterious one, but it's Mother who had all the family secrets. Have I ever really known her?

It's the same sort of distance I've been feeling for a while. Mom and Dad stopped even pretending to be together after we got home. They may both be plasma specialists, but work on different projects, in different complexes, on different parts of the planet. They cross paths in the apartment and share the same room but that's kind of it. We'll all shuffle through the kitchen but Mom will just replicate some coffee and head out the door. Dad at least has breakfast with me, but we seem to run out of things to talk about fast.

He seems sad, but in a different way than Mom. If I wanted to be a writer, I certainly have lots of degrees of depression, sadness, and misery to work with. However, I don't want to write, I want to be an engineer. They get to solve problems . . . and fix things. Lots of opportunities for engineers on starships so I'm applying to Starfleet Academy. It'll be tough, but worth it.

LEFLER'S LOG, Stardate 40910.6

Dad's a mess. I've been trying to help him with things like shopping. He doesn't seem to eat when I'm not around, and I'm scared about what'll happen when I start at the Academy. Starfleet has been really good about his leave of absence and leaving him alone.

I know, it's been ages since I made a log entry, I'm sorry. But, talking to my trusty tricorder just doesn't seem a priority when your family is falling apart.

The local authorities don't think Mom is alive. There's no evidence of her body. I've been talking to them, since Dad keeps to himself. Mom's listed as missing but they presume she's dead so the lab is reassigning her work and have terminated her access codes and passwords. I asked for her personal belongings and two days later they said they couldn't find any to send back.

Dad's been dreading this day, and anticipating it. When he used to tell me she was kidnapped, I imagined her putting up quite a fight with her nails leaving deep scars on her captors. She'd scheme and plot her escape, desperate to come home to me. But every time she returned, she just seemed sad. Withdrawn more than happy and I'd work my butt off to make her happy with me. I didn't want to ever give her reason to leave me.

I've been playing back some of my log entries, trying to see what I might have done to drive her away—or what the fight was about. I always got sad when we left postings since it meant leaving behind friends time and again, but that doesn't seem like the cause. She and Dad seemed happy enough, at first. We did stuff together and I can't recall her ever really getting mad at me. Disappointed a lot, I guess, but I probably deserved it, too.

I still can't help but think that being part of the family contributed to Mom's leaving. It could be why she never wanted to bring me, except maybe that one time. Still haven't figured that one out. But she continued to come and go, driving me crazy and making Dad an unhappy man.

And never again will she want me. Forty-five laws were created to amuse her, keep her interested in me. And now she's gone and it looks to be for good. Alive? Dead? Will we ever know? I think she's dead and gone for good. Suicide is as likely a possibility as anything given her bouts of depression.

"Life isn't always fair." There, my final law.

LEFLER'S LOG, Stardate 41153.7

I've been lax again, I know. I'm a lousy *dangib* and should be a better correspondent. If for nothing else, it's because they all keep logs in Starfleet. If I intend to be an officer and an engineer I need to get back into the habit.

Here I am, ready to leave home for good, ready for the Academy. I couldn't have made it this far without you, tricorder. You're an out-of-date model but have been with me from the beginning and know me better than anyone does, even Dad. I learned how to analyze and interpret the readings from this, thanks to Mother and Dad. You let me double-check the scans when Mom vanished.

Dad's back to work but not happy with it and I can't blame him. He's been a real solid support during all this. Not once did he let me stop trying for the Academy even though it meant he'd be on his own. He says I deserve my chance at happiness, and I have to admit, I agree. Dad has been my home, not a planet or posting but him. He's never once left me, never once gave me reason to believe Mom left because of anything I said and did. He even credited me for her staying with us for as long as she did.

Like that helps.

That's my final log entry for now. Maybe for good. I'll probably need to start recording on Academy equipment, but you're coming along. You know too much to fall into someone else's hands.

Lefler's Logs . . . end recording.

MORGAN PRIMUS
Alice, on the Edge of Night

Ilsa J. Bick

Robin Lefler believed that her mother Morgan died when she was a teenager, before the *U.S.S. Excalibur* discovered her alive and well on the world of Ahmista some ten years later. "Alice, on the Edge of Night" brings us back to the days prior to Robin losing her mother and what led Morgan to her fateful decision.

Ilsa J. Bick

Ilsa J. Bick is a child, adolescent, and forensic psychiatrist, and a latecomer to fiction. Still, she's done okay. Her story "A Ribbon for Rosie" won Grand Prize in *Star Trek: Strange New Worlds II*, and "Shadows, in the Dark" took Second Prize in *Strange New Worlds IV*. Her novelette "The Quality of Wetness" (Second Prize) appeared in *Writers of the Future*, Vol. XVI. Her work has appeared, among other places, in SCIFI.COM, *Challenging Destiny*, and *Talebones*. Her short story "Strawberry Fields" was recently published in *Beyond the Last Star* (edited by Sherwood Smith). Her *Star Trek The Lost Era* novel *Well of Souls*, the first full-length adventure of Captain Rachel Garrett and the *U.S.S. Enterprise*-C, will be out very shortly from Pocket Books. She lives in Wisconsin, with her husband, two children, three cats, and other assorted vermin.

Now: Labor Day—Monday, September 2, 2363

There's a Klingon saying: Today is a good day to die. Morgan Primus has seen a lot of good days and tried a lot of good ways. She stopped trying for about five years. Then, a couple of months ago, she tried with an antique plasma pistol, but all she got was a visit to the emergency room—care of the police—and a nosy psychiatrist.

Still, today's another damn fine day to die.

The shuttle's cabin smells like warm cotton candy. Morgan's skin still tingles from the September sun, and she scratches the right side of her neck where the seawater's dried, leaving a crust of itchy salt. Her muscles are rubbery from running in sand, and there's grit on her tongue. The end of summer and Robin's childhood: It's been good, this last day.

But nothing good lasts. I should never have told Charles because now he thinks I'm a freak, a monster. Morgan's eyes burn, and her instruments waver as if she peers through a window into the rain. *Dr. Pointer's wrong. Love isn't enough.* And as for Pointer, the look on his face when she used the phaser— her sharp nails bite into her palms; her flesh rips and there's a brief flicker of pain—even he's repelled.

I'm like Alice, only I can't get out of the mirror.

Morgan looks at her hands and sees that her cells have begun their tireless ritual of mending together. In another minute—or maybe three, she stopped counting centuries ago—there won't even be a scar. She carries nothing except memories that fade and blur. Even Robin, her little Cheshire cat, will grow up and move away, and then Morgan will be alone again.

Not if I can help it. Her hand moves to her console. Go to warp, and they'll rocket past Venus and Mercury before hurtling into the sun. A bright flash, a flare of unbearable heat—and then nothing but cold, black, merciful oblivion. Robin never has to know.

Morgan looks into space, and because the cabin lights are dim and they're approaching Venus's dark side, Morgan sees herself reflected in a black void. For a wild, insane moment, it looks to Morgan as if someone's scissored the fabric of space in a perfect circle, cutting away the stars to reveal nothing but the utter darkness on the far side beyond space, a limbo she's inhabited all the long days of her life: Alice, in the mirror, on the knife edge of night.

"Alice, and her Cheshire cat," she says, out loud, and laughs. "I'm mad, you're mad, we're all mad here."

Then she hears a small soft sigh like the formless cry of a young child, and her blood freezes. *No, she can't be awake, I gave her the drugs, she isn't supposed to know. . . .*

"Mom?" Robin's voice is dreamy with sleep, and Morgan's throat constricts in a sharp pang of tenderness and despair. "Mom, what . . . what are you doing?"

Dr. Kevin Pointer stands at one end of a long hotel corridor that smells of recycled Wyndham air and oranges. (In his dreams—green nightmares that spit him from sleep—the corridor is thick with the sickly sweet stench of bloated, decayed bodies, and he moves in slow motion, the nightmares cutting off as if hacked by a guillotine, just as he wraps his hands around Ellen's throat.) The hall is so quiet he hears the tiny pops and crackles in his knees as he shifts his weight from one foot to the other. At both ends of the corridor, there are identical rectangular mirrors trimmed with gold scrollwork, and Pointer sees himself—his wheat brown hair and the white oval of his face peppered with black stubble—hemmed by an endless cascade of smaller worlds, staggering off into infinity.

Like Morgan Primus: *I'm Alice, in that mirror, and I can't get out. . . .*

Ellen's in Room 421. Third down from the left. Pointer's head feels as huge and empty as it did when the investigator showed him the surveillance tape, and Pointer saw how Ellen laughed with that other, nameless man, and touched his arm in an intimate way that made the feeling leak out of Pointer's body like runny chalk on a wet sidewalk. When the investigator handed him the passkey crystal and beam-in coordinates, Pointer realized that he really hadn't wanted to know at all. Best, maybe, for Ellen simply to have stayed gone, a missing period at the end of the last sentence.

They'll jerk awake, or maybe they're making love, but I'll kill them both because—my darling, treacherous Ellen—Morgan was right. Sometimes love isn't enough, and I'm so tired of the pain, I'm sick to death of loving you.

The door is an antique, with a brass latch. Pointer tugs the passkey crystal from his left jacket pocket, and the phaser from his right. Then he inserts the passkey; there's a tiny scraping *snick* of crystal against metal. When the small red light winks green, he depresses the latch and pushes. The door swings in with a faint squeal of hinges.

"Ellen," he says, stepping into a darkness edged with the grief of a single short summer. His thumb flicks the phaser to kill. "Darling, it's me."

Then: Memorial Day Weekend—Friday, May 24, 2363

"And why a plasma pistol?" Pointer asked.

"It was handy."

"And that's why you chose to shoot yourself in the chest? Because the pistol was handy?"

The woman on the gurney leveled a gaze at Pointer with eyes that were blacker than a crow's wing and matched the color of her shoulder-length hair. She wore a jade green hospital gown that ended at her knees, hospital slippers, and no socks. "Well, that's a different question. You asked about the pistol, I told you. But why my chest, and not my head . . . beats me. I guess I wanted to see what might happen. Couldn't very well do that if I blew my head off."

She sounded as if she thought he was extremely stupid, and Pointer felt like throttling the woman until her eyeballs squirted out of their sockets like wet watermelon seeds. Just his luck to be stuck seeing some smart-ass patient on the Friday before Memorial Day when he'd planned to be as far away from Hartford Hospital as possible—with Ellen, at their Maine-shingle cottage on Isle au Haut.

The getaway wasn't romantic, but they'd made a commitment to work at the marriage. Their relationship had degenerated into sniping asides and barbed silences that pricked and bit until Pointer thought it miraculous his heart worked at all. But they would try, one last time. Except his communicator had gone off, and he'd read the keen disappointment in Ellen's eyes, a silent message that screamed: *You're doing it again, Kevin, you're never here and even when you are, you're not, your mind is always with those crazy people and their problems.* It did no good to tell her that he had little control over patients. The great paradox: Psychiatrists were the keepers of secrets, and patients *kept* secrets from psychiatrists—little things like planning a suicide.

When he'd kissed Ellen good-bye, she'd given him a cheek colder than marble. What stunned and then saddened him was this didn't hurt as much as it used to. Instead, he experienced a seismic tremor of rage so intense he wanted to beat Ellen's head with a brick. But he didn't, and Ellen's face dissolved as the transporter beam whisked him from a tranquil Maine pinewood and dropped him into the middle of a noisy downtown emergency room in Hartford, Connecticut.

Now Pointer suppressed a sigh. "You had doubts? Last time I checked, plasma pistols go boom, people's guts go splat."

"Aren't you supposed to be sympathetic?"

"Just stating facts."

The woman, Morgan—she wouldn't give a last name—laughed. A shock of black hair had fallen into her eyes, and she flipped it aside with a surprisingly girlish gesture. "There are *facts*, Doctor, and then there are the ways one *states* the facts."

"Fair enough." *And I've had enough.* Or, possibly, he was thinking of Ellen because he had this sudden, awful premonition: *Ellen's gone.*

Pivoting on his heel, he went to the door and began keying in his exit code. "Look, all I know is you tried to kill yourself, only you botched it. Or maybe you didn't mean it, I don't know. Anyway, you play with pistols and people get, well, a little upset. Then doctors like *me* get to talk to people like *you* about why you want to raise such a fuss. The downside is you don't get to leave until I'm convinced you're not going to hurt yourself. So you'll sit here until you stop playing games. And if you don't like it, try killing yourself more quietly, so no one calls the cops."

She spoke just as the door slid open. "Done that."

No, Pointer thought wearily, *please, just let me go.* But he took a step back, and the door hissed shut. "Done what?"

"Trying where no one will hear. In space, on another planet. Different years, different times. Knives, jumping, hanging." She gave him a bemused smile. "I'm still here."

Lying through her teeth. The emergency-room report indicated that Morgan had no scars of any kind, no evidence of past trauma. Plus, Morgan had used an antique plasma pistol with a spent charge, and this belied her intent. A person who really wanted to die succeeded. "And why do you think that is?"

"I don't know." She threw him a frank look. "You don't like me very much."

"My emotions are none of your business."

"But mine are yours?"

"You know they are. Whether or not I like myself is not your concern. All I ask, Morgan, is that you trust me enough to tell the truth."

"And how would you know if I did?"

"A last name is a good start."

"Primus."

"Well, Morgan Primus," said Pointer, not believing this was her last name for one second, because that had been way too easy, "why aren't you in the Federation database?"

"Because not everyone comes from a Federation planet. And as for trusting that I won't try to kill myself again in the very near future," she said, forestalling his next question, "you have my word."

"Oh, that's worth a lot."

Morgan chuckled. "You're all right. You don't pull punches. That's good. Now, you going to let me go?"

In the end, they compromised. Morgan would come and see him. After he'd talked to the nurses and written his orders, Pointer returned with a data chip that held his office address and com identification.

"My office," he said. "Tuesday, one o'clock. I'm at the Institute of Living, on Washington. You can't miss it: red brick walls, a lot of trees. Just come. Talk. It can't hurt. And leave your com ID before you go, so I can reach you."

"Fine," said Morgan, her response so automatic that Pointer suspected the com ID would be a fake. But there was nothing he could do about that either. Patients had to want help. He wasn't God.

He was at the door when Morgan said, "I didn't say it, you know."

Pointer turned, his hand on the jamb. "What?"

"That you didn't like yourself. I didn't say that." Morgan aimed an index finger. "You did."

When Pointer beamed back to Maine, Ellen was gone. There was a message. Ellen thought a separation would be good, she'd be in touch, take care, blah, blah, blah. Pointer listened to her message a few times. Then he left the cottage and picked his way over rocks to the beach. He listened to black water slap stones. There was no moon, and the night was overcast, so there were no stars either. That was all right.

Tuesday: One o'clock came and went. Morgan didn't show up. Pointer wasn't surprised. Her com ID was phony, and that didn't surprise him, either.

The next day melted into the day after, and then the next. Patients came and went, and Ellen didn't call. Pointer forgot about Morgan Primus. He beamed to Maine every night, hoping against hope. And he dreamed green, awful nightmares of love and revenge.

Two weeks later, Pointer's companel buzzed. He hesitated, annoyed. It was six, and he wanted to go home. (Why was obscure. He never stayed indoors but roamed the beach half the night.)

The com buzzed again. Sighing, he punched up the channel, his mind already riffling through excuses to keep the call short. So Pointer wasn't prepared when he saw that the caller was Morgan.

"Tomorrow at six," she said, without preamble.

Pointer recovered enough to say, "Sorry, I don't work after six."

"That's the time I have."

"Come at five."

"Six. Take it, or leave it."

All his instincts screamed to leave it. Instead, he said, "Maybe. I don't make any promises."

"That's fine, Doctor." Morgan smiled. "Neither do I."

He fully expected her to cancel, so he wasn't surprised the next afternoon when he peeked into his waiting room at three minutes before six and saw only empty chairs. *I knew it,* he thought as he circled back to his desk and jammed his padd, filled with patient records, into his pocket. *I just knew she wouldn't show.*

His companel buzzed, and his eyes flicked to the time: two minutes to six. Morgan Primus. Had to be. Probably wanted another time. *Ask away, sweetheart*—he gave the com a vicious jab—*ask until you're bluer in the face than a Bolian.*

His companel winked, and Ellen's face shimmered into focus.

The sight of her took his breath away, and suddenly his knees were weak and he had to sit down. "Ellen," he managed, "my God, where . . . ?"

"Hello, Kevin," she said. Ellen's oval face was white and pinched, and the hard edge to her jaw that he'd come to associate with her disappointment and anger were softer. There were purple smudges beneath her dark brown eyes.

"I . . . I don't know why I called, exactly, just," her tongue flicked over her lips, "I just wanted you to know that . . . I'm all right. But I need time to think. Time to be away from you, us."

"Ellen." Pointer's voice was strangled. "Ellen, please, come home. . . ."

"No." Ellen's eyes shifted to somewhere offscreen, then back. "It's better I stay away."

She's not alone. "No, it's not. Look, can we meet? You choose the spot, and I'll be there. . . ."

Again, that hesitation, that brief jerk of her eyes up and away, and

Pointer's heart almost exploded with grief and fury. *She's with someone else; my God, I love her so much, I'm going to kill her. . . .*

The soft chime of his outer door sounded, and Pointer glanced at his chronometer: six, on the dot. *Christ. Morgan.*

Then Ellen surprised him. She nodded. "All right—if you come now. I have the beam-in coordinates."

Pointer's heart sank. "I . . . Ellen, can we meet in an hour? Half an hour? I have—"

"God," she said, making the word sound ugly. The hard edges reappeared, and her eyes seemed to retreat and disappear into the sockets of her skull. "Nothing changes. What do I have to do, Kevin? Why aren't *I* important enough?"

"You *are*. Ellen, be fair. You disappear, and then you expect me to drop everything . . ." He stopped, sucked in a breath. "Please, Ellen, please, I'm begging you. I don't have a choice."

"Yes, you do. You keep choosing *them.*"

Pointer felt desperate. Trapped. "Ellen, I *have* to see this patient. She's very disturbed, and this might be my only chance. But then I can . . ."

Her hand reached for the disconnect. "Don't bother. Patients always *have* come first."

"Ellen! Wait!" Pointer grabbed the companel with both hands as if to hold her in place. "Ellen!"

But the screen went dead.

Pointer wasted five minutes trying to get CommCent to trace the call. (They couldn't.) Then Pointer went to get Morgan. She mentioned he was ten minutes late; he didn't bother explaining.

The next morning, Pointer called an investigator.

Now . . .

"Mom?" Robin's voice is dreamy with sleep, and drug. "Mom, what are you doing?"

Morgan's heart flutters, and she swallows, hard. *I watched her drink that lemonade, how can she be awake?* Morgan plasters on a smile and turns to her daughter, who is curled in the copilot's chair.

"What are you doing up? Go back to sleep, Ches," Morgan says, grateful she's had the foresight to reroute helm and navigational controls so that Robin's systems remain black.

Robin's eyelids shutter in a slow, heavy blink, and Morgan can see that the girl's eyes are a little crossed—a side effect of the amnestic agent in

Robin's lemonade cocktail that included a sedative-hypnotic. The amnestic's overkill; after all, when they burn up, there won't be anything to remember, will there? But, in a past identity, Morgan worked as a surgical nurse, and she knows a lot about anesthesia. Amnestics send patients into a twilight state, teetering between sleep and wakefulness, from which they emerge with no memory of events that occurred during the surgery, or for an hour or two before and after.

"Whersh . . . ?" Robin's voice is slurry, and then she giggles, a bubbly sound. "I feel drunk. So where're we going?" *Showhershswegoan?*

"Saturn. Don't you remember?" (Morgan knows Robin doesn't.) "You wanted to see the Academy training facility, only you conked out. . . ."

"No," Robin says, trying to push out of her slump, but the drugs have made her awkward, and her hands slip on slick trivinyl. She falls back against her chair.

"Oh," Robin says, cupping her forehead in her right hand. Now her voice sounds young, like a child's. "Mom, I don't feel very well."

"All that sun," says Morgan, keeping her tone light and cheery. "All that running around. Fresh air does that. Go back to sleep, Ches. I'll wake you when there's something to see."

Robin licks her lips. "Thirsty." *Shershty.*

Got to put her out. Morgan unbuckles. "There's more of that lemonade. That'll hit the spot, Ches."

Morgan hurries aft, trying to remember where she's stowed the thermos. The drink was supposed to knock Robin out, and if Morgan can't get her back to sleep soon, she'll have to turn around.

Because I don't want her to know. Morgan riffles through the medical kit where she's stowed the hypospray vials of the various drugs she's pilfered. She hesitates, then jams a vial of amnestic mixed with a sedative-hypnotic into an empty hypo. *If she won't drink, then I'll pump her full of drugs. I want her out, dreaming good dreams.*

Shoving the hypo into a back pocket, she spies the thermos wedged behind a tension spanner. Tugging it free, she turns, already talking. "Here we go, here . . ."

Her voice trails away.

Somehow, Robin is in the pilot's chair, and Morgan can tell by the set of her shoulders and back that, even through a drug-induced fog, Robin knows.

"Ches," Morgan says. Her blood hammers in her temples. "I . . ."

"Oh, my God," Robin says. Slowly, she swivels around. Her red-rimmed eyes are wide. "Mother, my God, what are you *doing?*"

★   ★   ★

The hotel room is small and dim but not dark. Enough light fans from a bedside lamp for Pointer to make out a lounge chair and an ottoman, a small desk with a companel, a straight-back wooden chair with green striped fabric—and the bed. King-sized. Unmade; three pillows humped along a wooden headboard; a floral quilt puddled on the floor; the apricot sheets mussed and a cord of brown blanket twined like a string of chocolate licorice. A lump, with the vague contours of a body, on the far side.

Pointer's phaser hand trembles. "Ellen," he whispers, and then clears his throat. He steadies his aim and calls again. "Ellen!"

Two feet from the bed he realizes that the lump is Ellen's clothing. The bed is empty. Pointer brings his face close to the tousled sheets and smells Ellen: an intoxicating mix of sweaty musk and jasmine.

It's then that Pointer becomes aware of a low sizzle, like grease on a hot griddle, and his eyes rake the darkness until he makes out a thin stripe of orange light seeping beneath a door. *Bathroom. They're taking a shower.* The image of Ellen's wet body under another man's hands sends a shock wave of rage surging through Pointer. Before this instant, he wasn't sure, but now he knows, without question. He'll kill them, and then himself. But before he does, he needs Ellen to understand, to know *why* she's driven him to this moment where reality's fractured, and his life's snapped in two. And maybe, just maybe, Pointer wants Ellen to beg for her life because, dammit, she owes him for all love's pain.

Pointer crosses to the other side of the bed, the one nearest the lamp and night table. Angling the chair so he faces the closed bathroom door, Pointer arranges himself in the chair, his hand with the phaser resting on his lap. He'll be the first and last thing Ellen will see.

An array of items on the night table catches his attention, and for an instant the items are so incongruous he can't place them. Then his brain ticks off the items, one by one. A slim, butter-colored ivory case, with a stylized sea done in scrimshaw. Three—no, *four* squat hypospray cartridges arrayed, like an assortment of antique saltcellars, beside an empty hypospray jet.

Pointer's brow furrows. What is Ellen doing with drugs? Pointer plucks up a vial and angles it into the light. He recognizes it immediately: phenylpromazine, a potent antipsychotic. And besides the antipsychotic, there's a vial of duraxalamine, a sedative; another contains a neuromuscular paralytic; and the fourth is filled with a strong barbiturate. All the vials have his office stamp.

My God, she stole them. There's enough here to kill a herd of Cartagan elephants.

Replacing the vials, Pointer picks up the slim ivory case. The case is heavier than he expects. There's a stamp on one side: a four-leaf clover and the word EDGEWELL beneath, done in red-brown scrimshaw. Odd. He thinks, at first, it must be some antique pencil case—until he sees a metallic prong jutting from one end, a hinge, and a thin strip of bright, square-backed metal nestled between ivory spacers. Pointer uses the side of his right thumb to depress the tang. He feels the metal catch, hesitate, then glide free. Pointer's breath hisses through his teeth as the sweeping blade of a straight razor pops up.

The square-backed, untarnished blade flashes in the light. The blade's tip is scalloped, and Pointer puts his left thumb to the beveled edge. The blade is so sharp he doesn't realize he's cut himself until red blood bubbles, staining the blade. Pointer gasps, as much from pain as sudden realization.

The drugs. A straight razor. His fury evanesces like fog under a blazing hot sun. *No, no, no! Ellen, what are you* doing?

And then there's Morgan's voice: *I wanted to see if she would bleed. I wanted to see if she would heal.*

Only then does Pointer realize that the sound of water drumming in the shower has ceased. Dumbly, he looks over at the bathroom door. His mind shouts for him to go to his wife and shake her and hold her close, but he's too shocked to move or utter a sound. Instead, he sits, an open straight razor in his right hand, a drizzle of blood spattering onto his trousers from the cut on his left thumb.

The bathroom door—it has a crystal knob—opens; scented steam billows out; and then there is Ellen, backlit and naked, emerging from the fragrant mist as if materializing from the depths of a half-forgotten dream.

She starts, and he sees shock then dismay in her eyes. Her gaze flicks to the razor, the vials. And, finally, the phaser.

"Oh, Kevin," she says. "Did you come to kill me, too?"

Then: Mid-August, 2345

Robin was four months old. Morgan and the baby were staying at the beach house. Charles was away on assignment for Starfleet but would join them in a few days.

Morgan had noticed nothing unusual about Robin. The baby ate; she slept; she smiled on time. To all appearances, Robin was normal. But what if Morgan and Robin were the same, two peas in a pod, sharing the same secret? Morgan couldn't remember when she became aware that she was one-of-a-kind. Rambling over the heaths, tending to the sheep, doing needlework—casting her mind back over the centuries, Morgan couldn't recall if she ever skinned her knee, or cut her lip, or stuck her finger with the point of a needle. Likely, she did, only she mended so quickly, her secret was safe—even from her until she became more self-aware.

Morgan designed an experiment. She took Robin from her midday bath and placed her, still moist and warm, on a fluffy white towel spread upon a changing table. The window on the far wall was open, and a crisp sea breeze that smelled of salt fluttered a pair of gauzy yellow curtains. Watching the curtains snap and dance, Robin's brown eyes sparkled, and her pudgy, pink fists wheeled with delight.

Robin's nails needed trimming. Catching Robin's left hand, Morgan snipped. She trimmed all of Robin's nails, on both hands, into perfect crescent moons. And then, after just a single instant's hesitation, Morgan nipped off the very tip—the tiniest sliver—of Robin's right index finger.

There was a moment when everything was totally still, and Morgan felt horror ice her veins. *What are you doing, are you crazy?* Robin hadn't felt the pain just yet and so was still cooing, her chubby little face wreathed in smiles. And then Robin's eyes darkened first with astonishment, and then confused shock and pain, and Morgan's blood roared like hot lava through her veins as the baby wailed.

"It's okay, sweetie, it's okay," Morgan said, hanging on to Robin's right hand as the baby flailed. Bright red blood welled up from the cut and then dribbled down the side of Robin's finger like a tear. Morgan daubed it away. "Sssh, sssh, it'll be fine, sweetie, just let Mommy see . . ."

Eventually, the blood slowed. Stopped. Robin's cries subsided into watery hiccups, but Morgan didn't let go. Instead, she stared at the cut, half-afraid nothing would happen, and hoping with all her might that something would. *Because then I won't be the only one.*

After five minutes, the snipped finger was still fleshy and raw. After fifteen, when nothing had changed, Morgan went to get ointment and a pressure bandage. When she took Robin's hand again, the baby watched her with wary eyes.

And a few days later, when Charles saw the bandage, Morgan told him that it was just an accident, and nothing more.

Tuesday: August 27, 2363
"And why did you do that?" asked Pointer. They were in his second-floor office in the red brick and cedar-shingled Whitehall Building on the grounds of the Institute of Living, a very old psychiatric hospital in exis-

tence since Dickens's day. The building had no turbolifts, just stairs and doors with real knobs. (Pointer thought the lack of amenities a damn nuisance.) Pointer sat in his accustomed spot: a high-backed black leather swivel chair with matching ottoman, a gift from Ellen when he'd been appointed to the institute's staff.

"I told you," Morgan said. She stood at his office's single window, looking at a view Pointer knew well: an ancient ginkgo, thirty meters high and twenty-five around. "I wanted to see if she would bleed. No, that's not right. I wanted to see if she would *heal.*"

"You had doubts?" Pointer's tone was neutral, but his mind cast over various diagnostic possibilities. Three months had passed, with nothing from Ellen. But Morgan came faithfully—Tuesdays and Thursdays at 6:00 P.M., after all the regular staff was gone. Pointer knew Morgan was married and had a nearly grown daughter, but he didn't know the girl's name (Morgan refused to tell him). He sensed that the marriage was in trouble and the husband away a good deal. Or maybe Morgan was; she'd hinted that she left the family for weeks at a time and mentioned abduction once or twice. But abduction was absurd: just one more manifestation of the woman's instability.

And this talk about the daughter—Pointer gnawed on the inside of his cheek—damn worrisome. Morgan couldn't see the girl as an individual, couldn't call her by *name* but insisted upon a private nickname: Ches, after the Cheshire cat in *Alice's Adventures in Wonderland.* What was it the cat said? Something about everyone being mad, and that Alice must also be mad or else she'd never have tripped into Wonderland to begin with.

My God, nicknaming a child after a cat in a madhouse. Poor kid's lucky to be alive.

Pointer thought it a wonder Morgan hadn't killed first her child, then herself: a murder-suicide. When a depressed mother was suicidal, she saw murdering her child as something done out of love, because she couldn't conceive that the child wasn't in as much pain as she was, or couldn't bear the idea of leaving the child behind in a cruel, heartless universe.

But without evidence of a plan and intent, I can't do a damn thing but sit here and listen and see if I can break through.

That was the trouble, wasn't it? Breaking through? Pointer found it maddening, getting only bits and pieces of the complicated jigsaw puzzle that was Morgan's psyche. He felt trapped and helpless and then reflected that, just maybe, that was how Morgan felt, too.

He waited for Morgan to answer his question, but she didn't. She stood with her back to him, and that mane of hair spilling over her shoulders like a shroud of black velvet.

What the hell, I've got to risk it. Worst-case scenario is she doesn't come back, and then I won't be responsible anymore. "Morgan, have you ever tried to kill your daughter?"

Morgan stiffened as if Pointer had jabbed her in the small of the back. Her head swiveled, and she looked over her shoulder with those huge, black, unblinking eyes. "And if I have?"

"I'd like to hear about it," said Pointer calmly, even as his heart battered his ribs.

"And after that?"

"Doesn't that depend on what you say?"

"Questions answered with questions. A psychiatrist's specialty." Morgan's lips parted in a soundless laugh. She turned her gaze back out the window and then, as if in afterthought, pressed the palms of both hands against the glass, like a child looking in at candy her parents won't buy. "Once, before she was born. We were at the beach. This was in March. I was eight months pregnant. One night, I decided to go for a swim."

"To drown yourself?"

"Yes. I'd been feeling . . . black. So I slipped out of bed, stripped, and went out, buck-naked. The tide was coming in and it was damn cold. No moon, so all I could see was the smudge of the beach—it's very rocky there and I remember that because the waves stirred rocks around my ankles— and all this black water."

"Had you left a note?"

"For Charles?" Morgan sounded faintly surprised. "No."

"Why not?"

Morgan lifted one shoulder then let it fall. "I didn't have anything to say, and he wouldn't have understood, anyway. Hell, if he knew the truth, he'd be the first person to push me in. The waves were high, and the water was so cold my skin burned. The baby was sleeping. But then when the water reached my waist, all of a sudden, my belly moved. I *felt* the baby scrambling away from the cold. I remember standing there, dumbstruck, because it had never occurred to me that the baby might have an opinion about things."

This, Pointer thought, was a good sign. "So you were reminded of your separateness."

"I guess you could say that." Morgan's eyes were faraway looking at the memory. "I had liked being pregnant because I was never alone. But then there she was, and she wanted to live, so I decided to try things her way."

This was what Pointer had been waiting for: an opportunity to reinforce the idea that the daughter had an identity and a life separate from her mother. "Morgan, let's go back to that moment when you hurt your baby daughter. You said you wanted to see if she would heal. Morgan, she's not a monster. Everyone bleeds, and everyone heals."

"Some heal faster than others."

"That's your depression talking. You're wounded, Morgan. You've been in mental hell for years, and your depression's tricked you into believing that things will never change."

"But that's just it. I *don't* change, Doctor. Ever."

"That's because change is painful. But change doesn't have to be radical. You could make a very small change that might help a great deal."

"What, medicine?" Morgan made the idea sound ridiculous. "Believe me, I know all about medicine."

"Yes, but that wasn't all I had in mind. See, Morgan, I think what's happening is that your daughter's gotten to the point in her life where she's ready to strike out on her own. Only that means she leaves you behind, and you believe that will hurt so much, you'll never heal. It's very important for you to maintain the fantasy of being inseparable, so you never have to be alone again. And I think that the reason you've tried to kill yourself again, now, is because your daughter's growing up. The hardest thing for a mother to understand is that it's her *job* to become obsolete. Mothers *have* to be left, and that means they have to *be* there *to* be left. If you kill yourself, Morgan, your daughter will be trapped by a moment in time, wondering why love wasn't enough."

"Love." Morgan hit the window with her forehead, once, twice. Not hard enough to shatter but enough so Pointer heard the dull, muted thud of Morgan's skull against glass. "Love isn't enough."

No, no, no. Pointer's skin crawled with anxiety. He got to his feet. "Morgan, please. Stop."

"You don't understand," Morgan said, her voice clogged with emotion. *Thud.* "You're such an antique, looking back to memories for meaning. But memories fade, Doctor, just like my Ches and her sweet smile, and I'm Alice, only I can't get out of the mirror." *Thud.*

"Morgan, I understand how painful this is for you."

"No, you don't. No one understands," and now Pointer knew that she was crying. "Not you, not Charles."

"You said that before," said Pointer, trying to keep calm even though his insides twisted and churned. "You said that if he knew the truth about you, he'd think you were a monster. Morgan, just because you think your depression is a terrible thing doesn't mean that negates love . . ."

"God, stop *talking* to me about *love!*" And then Morgan brought her head down, hard. There was a sharp crack, and Pointer saw a cobweb of splintered glass bloom upon the windowpane. The window didn't shatter, and after an instant of stunned disbelief, Pointer bounded across the room and grabbed Morgan by the arm. But she was strong, and with a wild cry, she whipped her arm free. Pointer staggered back on his heels. Morgan fled and stood in a far corner, her face toward the wall.

Pointer didn't try to touch her again, all too aware that the building was empty and he was on his own. He dragged in a calming breath and blew out. "Morgan, are you hurt? Let me . . ."

"Just a minute," Morgan said. She kept her back to him, her black hair tented over her shoulders, her hands cupped over her face.

Pointer's eyes drifted to the window. Morgan had hit hard enough to leave a concave indentation, like a meteor strike. *My God, if she hasn't split her forehead open, she'll have a hell of a bruise.* "Morgan. Please, let me help you."

Morgan's hands dropped, and she turned, a slow motion pirouette. Her cheeks were stained with tears, but no blood.

Then Pointer squinted, and his brow crinkled. *No bruise either, but . . . she hit hard enough to crack the glass . . .*

"You can't help," Morgan said. "I don't even know if I can help myself anymore."

Pointer blinked back to attention. "Morgan, if you won't let *me* help, then let your husband try. Let him know what's happening."

"Why?"

"Because he's your husband, and you owe him that much," said Pointer, and he couldn't help it, but his thoughts flew to Ellen, whom he'd loved with all his might. His throat balled with emotion, and when he continued, he knew he was speaking for himself as much as for Morgan: "His love is all he has to give, and that has to be enough for the black times because, in the end, love is all we have."

Her dark eyes were liquid with tears, and Pointer thought that, for a moment, she would simply leave. But then Morgan drew in a shuddery breath.

"All right," she said. "We'll do it your way. God knows why. Maybe I'm still human enough to hope. But I'll talk to Charles. Then, we'll see. I don't make any promises."

Relief coursed through him. "You'll see, Morgan. The people who love you won't leave, and neither will I. Whatever happens, I'm here for you."

"You can't know that." Morgan regarded him with large, sad eyes. "Doctor, you said mothers are there to be left. Well, this is the first time I've been a mother. But I'm always left."

Much later when Morgan had gone (he couldn't hold her; she wasn't suicidal and she promised to come back with her husband, on Thursday), Pointer's companel bleated.

Dammit, Morgan tried again, he thought, dread wrapping its fingers around his heart and squeezing. *Psychiatrists keep the secrets, and patients keep secrets from their psychiatrists.*

But the call wasn't about Morgan and another suicide attempt. Pointer listened as the investigator said that he thought he'd have something definite on Ellen probably the Friday before Labor Day, maybe Thursday, and could he come by? Numb now with apprehension, Pointer gave him a time for right after Morgan's session, on Thursday. Then he punched off and went to stare through a spider's web of cracked glass at that ancient tree.

And that's when it hit him. *Still human enough,* Morgan had said. What did that mean? And *I'm always left.*

He realized it now; he'd missed the emphasis. Not on *always.* On *left:* as in, *last.*

Now . . .

The hush in the cabin is so complete Morgan hears her blood thundering in her ears.

"Mom?" Robin's voice wavers and then gets stronger, as if she's fighting to stay conscious. "Are you going to tell me? And don't," she swallows again as if she doesn't have enough spit to make her mouth move properly, "don't *lie* . . . we're not . . . on course for Saturn. We're . . . you . . . you've plotted course for . . . for the *sun.*"

Morgan's grasping the thermos of lemonade so tightly her fingers cramp. She forces them to relax and then places the thermos on the flight deck. *Hypo,* she thinks, her right hand inching toward her back pocket. *It's the only way.*

"Mom?"

"Robin, what are you talking about?" Morgan gives a false, light laugh. "Ches, you're so tired your eyes are playing tricks. Now, come on, get back in the copilot's chair, and let me . . ."

Robin lifts her chin in defiance. She's still slurring but she only stumbles a little. "Don't . . . don't talk to me like I'm . . . some *kid*. The computer doesn't lie, and I don't know what's going on, but," Robin makes a move to turn around, "I'm going to plot a course back to Earth and . . ."

But Morgan is already moving, erasing the distance between them in three long strides, the hypo in her right hand. Robin senses her coming; she half-turns and raises her right arm to deflect the blow, but the drugs have tamped her reflexes, and she's too slow. Still, she manages to knock the hypo away, and it clatters to the deck. Morgan grabs Robin's right arm, but Robin's left hand scrambles over the console.

"Mother," Robin gasps, as Morgan, who is much stronger and not drugged, plants her elbow in her daughter's chest and pins her to the chair. "Mother, stop!"

But Morgan doesn't pay attention. Her fingers fly over the controls, and in another second, there's an infinitesimal lurch as the engines jump to full impulse.

The shuttle hurtles toward the sun.

Thursday: August 29, 2363

Things had gotten worse. Pointer read Morgan's face before she'd uttered a word, and knew.

"And then?" he asked.

"And then, nothing," said Morgan. She'd come alone. She stood by the window, her usual spot. She hadn't commented on the glass having been replaced, and neither she nor Pointer alluded to the incident in the previous session.

"You mean, he said absolutely *nothing?*"

"Not exactly. I told him when we got into bed that night. I thought that would be the best place, away from Ro . . . Ches. I talked. He listened, but I could tell from the look on his face. He thought I was crazy."

Pointer frowned. He supposed that a husband might initially react that way, but his experience was that, after the initial shock, spouses were eager to help. He would've done the same for Ellen, if she'd given him half a chance. "What did you say?"

"The truth: about how I'm always left."

"And he didn't offer to help, wasn't worried?"

Morgan gave a bleak laugh. "Oh, I think he's worried all right, especially after I showed him how serious I am. How real this is."

A cold fist bunched in Pointer's chest. *Oh, no, God, please, not again.* "Morgan, did you . . . ?"

"Try again?" Morgan pivoted on her heels so she was facing him now. "Yes, I did."

Pointer's gaze skittered over her arms and throat, but he didn't see any marks. *Hypos, or maybe she tried to bash her head against the wall or window, like she did here.* Pointer didn't put anything past Morgan, and now his mind was busy working over his available options. She *had* been suicidal. She'd tried once that he'd documented, twice by her admission. Maybe he could convince a judge, get her committed to a hospital. . . .

"What did you do, Morgan?"

Morgan drilled him with a look. "This," she said, and pulled a hand phaser from her pocket.

Pointer's breath died in his throat, and for the first time in his life, he felt real, personal fear. *Oh, my God, she's going to kill us both.* "Morgan," he said, his voice almost a wheeze. "Morgan, put down the phaser."

"No," she said, and then in one fluid movement, she turned the phaser to her chest.

"Morgan!" Pointer shouted, breaking out of his paralysis. He launched himself from his chair, diving for the phaser. "Morgan, *stop!*"

"See you in a bit," said Morgan, and fired.

He hit her—not soon enough. There was a high sizzle-crackle of phaser fire, a brilliant flash, and then their bodies collided. Pointer felt them crashing against the far wall, and the impact knocked the wind from his lungs with a grunt. For a brief instant, his vision blackened, and he had to work to remember how to breathe. Finally, his burning lungs pulled in a breath, then another.

"Morgan." Pointer coughed, clambered to all fours, sucking in air like a winded horse. "Morgan."

Morgan lay, unmoving, on her right side. Her black hair fanned over the floor, hiding her face.

Oh, God. Pointer crawled to Morgan's limp form. The stench of ozone and charred meat hit his nostrils. He saw that she must have died instantly; the fingers of her right hand clutched the phaser in a cadaveric spasm, and when he rolled her over, he saw that her lips peeled back from her teeth in a rictus smile of death. A black flower of burned fabric had blossomed over her left breast.

"Oh, God," he gasped, his stomach bottoming out. "Oh, God, oh, God."

Somehow, he was on his feet, staggering back to his desk. *Have to call in an EMT crew by transporter*—his thoughts clattered around his skull, like a stack of plates knocked askew. He was shaking so badly, he miskeyed the emergency frequency. He cursed. *My fault,* he thought, forcing his fingers to cooperate. *This is all my fault.*

And then Morgan moaned.

Pointer froze, his index finger poised over his companel. His jaw fell open, but no sound came.

Morgan moaned again. Then she moved.

Pointer's eyes bulged. He watched in stunned disbelief as Morgan Primus twitched and moaned and came to life a millimeter at a time, like a discarded marionette whose strings have been repaired.

She propped herself up on her arms, and then slid her body up the wall until she rested with her back against it. Her chest convulsed as she dragged in a ragged breath; the black, burned fabric rose over her left breast bloomed, contracted. With a sluggish gesture, she pushed her hair out of her eyes and took one tottering step.

Pointer couldn't help it. He screamed in horror.

"You see?" Morgan was panting, but she managed a slow, sad smile. "Now you think I'm a monster, too."

Now . . .

"Mother!" Robin screams. She's flailing, but Morgan has her by both wrists now. "Mother, please, no!"

"I'm sorry, Ches." Tears stream over Morgan's cheeks, and she's desperate to get the hypo and put Robin to sleep, but the hypo's just out of reach and she can't risk letting Robin go. "Trust me, please, baby, just a little longer, just a few more minutes, and then we'll both be at peace."

"Mom." Robin's eyes bug and she stares at her mother as if seeing her for the first time. "Mom, please, what's wrong, why are you doing this, I don't want to die . . ."

Yes, I'm a monster. There's no comfort in the thought, just a grim certitude. Morgan's got an iron grip around her daughter's wrists with one hand and now she pats the deck until she feels the cool metal of the hypo. *Better this way.*

The cabin fills with a sudden blistering burst of golden light so intense it seems liquid. Robin gasps, blinks against the glare. Then the shuttle's polarizing filters snap into place, but Morgan knows. They've shot out from behind Mercury's shadow, and if she looked now, she'd see the sun, burning brighter than the fires of hell.

Soon, Morgan thinks, *soon, and then I can rest and love can't hurt me anymore.*

And maybe her face changes, because Robin stops struggling. They are so close Morgan sees Robin's eyes jerk back and forth as if her daughter's trying to peer into Morgan's soul.

"Mother," Robin whispers, and Morgan sees love and something close to compassion brimming in her daughter's eyes. "Oh, my poor mother. Mom, I love you, and nothing you've done is so terrible that I'll stop loving you for a single instant, ever, and you can't make me hate you or wish I'd never been born, you can't ma . . ."

A hiss, and Robin stiffens, chokes. Her eyes roll back into her skull, and she sags.

"Oh, baby," says Morgan, catching her daughter in her arms. The empty hypo falls from her limp fingers. She eases her daughter back into the pilot's chair. "Oh, Ches."

Pointer's voice, in her head: *In the end, love is all we have.*

"Oh, my poor little girl." Morgan keys in her final commands. "My love has to be enough."

"Is that what you came for?" asks Ellen. She is naked and so beautiful that it hurts Pointer to look. She nods at the phaser. "Did you come to kill me?"

Pointer stares, stupidly, at the weapon. He remembers standing there, listening to the soft shush of Morgan's shoes as she walked to the door of his office, the click of the latch catching as she left. And then he'd come out of his stupor and dashed after her, but when he yanked open the door, he'd seen only the quizzical face of the investigator, and no Morgan. Pointer had stammered out an excuse, ducked back into his office, with its heavy, oily odor of cooked meat and charcoal, and slid the phaser into his pocket. Then he'd invited the investigator in, and if the man noticed the stink, he didn't let on. And then Pointer had seen the tape, and his shock turned to fury and rage.

"Yes," Pointer says, looking into Ellen's eyes. "No. I . . . don't know. Yes, I came to kill us both. And him."

Her face is calm. "There is no *him*, Kevin. There was, but I . . . I couldn't go through with it, and I sent him away."

"And these?" With his bad hand, Pointer gestures at the hypospray, the drugs. The razor. Droplets of his blood patter onto the night table.

"Oh, Kevin, you've hurt yourself."

"No," says Pointer. "I mean, yes, but . . . Ellen, my God, I *love* you, only there's so much pain, and I can't stand it anymore. It has to end, somehow, and only we have the power to heal each other, don't you see?"

"No." Ellen moves to the bed and tweezes the sheet free. She wraps it around herself before sitting on the edge of the bed. "I don't. I can't."

Pointer's left thumb throbs with every wild beat of his heart. "I don't accept that," he says, and he feels like he's coming awake from a long and continuous bad dream. "Ellen, I love you enough to . . . to kill you. *Die* with you. And that's crazy." He gives a bleak laugh. "It's the great paradox. I keep the secrets, and you hold the key to my life, because if you die, Ellen, I'll die with you. Maybe not my body, but I will die anyway, a piece at a time. God, *Ellen,*" and now Pointer can feel the hot sting of tears behind his eyes. *"Why?"*

"I don't know. Reasons that aren't reasons, I guess." Ellen shakes her head. Her head's bowed, and her brown hair hangs in wet strands, like waterlogged rope. Her restless fingers pick at the sheet, working and twisting. "I feel . . . black. Dying seems the only way. I thought it would be better . . . for you. Me. I just wouldn't have to think anymore, and if I can't think, then I won't hurt. In time, you'd forget, move on."

"No," says Pointer. He moves from the chair; the phaser slips, unnoticed, to the floor. He kneels before his wife. "I'd be stuck in time, at this moment, forever, wondering what I could have done differently. You'd be gone, Ellen, but you'd always be in my heart and soul, a wound that would never heal. Please." Tears leak from the corners of his eyes. "Please, let me help and . . . Ellen, help . . . I need . . . please, please help me."

Burying his face in her lap, he weeps, out loud, in a way he hasn't since he was a boy.

Tuesday: October 15, 2363

Hands in his pockets, Pointer stood at his office window, looking out at the institute's grounds. The days were getting shorter; here it was only a little before six, and already the shadows of the trees were like long black fingers inked on the grass. Fall was close, and the ginkgo's leaves had turned bright yellow, the setting sun making them glow like tiny gold fans. Up in Maine, they'd had their first frost, and this had driven away the tourists. But that was good, because it gave him and Ellen plenty of privacy, and time and space to heal.

Pointer rubbed the first finger and thumb of his left hand together, an unconscious gesture. He felt the slight raised ridge of scar left from the straight razor. He could have had the scar removed, but he hadn't.

There can't be love without pain, he thought, *and it's good to remember that, under the pain, the love's always there.*

He was startled out of his reverie by the chime of his outer door. A patient? Now? The only patient he'd ever had who came after hours on a Tuesday . . .

"Morgan," he whispered. After that horrible afternoon, Morgan had never returned. He thought that she hadn't died; she'd proven that her body wouldn't let her. But still he'd wondered if she'd found some way, and that made the guilt almost too much to bear. And to think that he'd once wished Ellen to simply vanish. Now he knew that not knowing was an endless torture that condemned the living to a single moment in time.

Alice, in the mirror. But now, if she was *back* . . .

Taking the distance to his outer door in two long strides, he pushed open the door. "Mo . . ."

A young woman—no more than eighteen, Pointer guessed—looked up. She had rich, chestnut brown hair that was tucked up in a bun, and she wore a uniform that Pointer recognized as one of those worn by Starfleet cadets. But what caught Pointer's interest was her eyes: so deep brown, they were almost black.

"Are you Dr. Pointer?" she asked. She stood, and Pointer saw that she clutched a slim brass holotube in her hands.

Pointer nodded. "Yes. But my office hours are over for the day. If you'd like an appointment, I'd be happy to . . ."

"I don't know what I want." A tentative smile flickered on and off the woman's lips, and for an instant, Pointer saw a ghost of someone else lurking just behind the woman's eyes. "That is . . . well, I've been putting this off and . . . oh, hell," she sighed. "I probably sound crazy."

Pointer thought it best not to observe that most of his patients did, and he understood. He'd gone a little crazy himself. "How can I help?"

"I don't know," she said. She pulled herself straighter. "Look, I've been dithering about this for a couple of months, but I just can't put it off anymore. My mother's shuttle crashed in the Atlantic right after Labor Day."

"I'm sorry."

"Me, too," she said, without irony. "We'd had a really good day, just before. I remember the boardwalk and the beach. Only she and I had a big fight; I don't remember exactly what it was about. For some reason, my memory's kind of fuzzy. The doctors said it's probably post-traumatic, like I'm blocking it out. Anyway, Mom said in her message, the one she left, that she was sorry, but she had to see relatives. Only they found her shuttle in the Atlantic, off the coast of New Jersey. No body, so it's been kind of hard to reach closure, you know? But it's like she knew something was going to happen, because the next day, I got this." She held up the holo-tube. "Turns out she'd made it the night before."

"May I see?"

"Sure," she said, handing him the tube.

Pointer held the cylinder to his right eye, his thumb flicking the tiny projector to life. There was an imperceptible hum, and the tube vibrated beneath his fingers, and a fractal image glowed then coalesced. In the next instant, Pointer went rigid with shock.

The face and the figure of the holographic portrait belonged to Morgan Primus.

I'm Alice, in the mirror. Stunned, Pointer watched as the tiny portrait pirouetted upon its invisible axis. *The way she turned after she broke the glass and I saw that there was nothing, no cut, no bruise. Because she always heals, and she's always left.*

The girl was speaking again. "In her message, she said that when I was ready, I should come talk to you. That maybe," her voice faltered, and he heard the pain, "you could he . . . help me get . . . get past this."

Pointer flicked off the holotube. Morgan's image fizzled and the tube went black.

He looked down at Morgan's daughter. "What's your name?"

"Well, my mom used to call me Ches, after the cat in Wonderland." And then she tried a wobbly smile, and this nearly broke Pointer's heart because Morgan had been right: Her Ches's smile was so very sweet. "But my name's Robin. Robin Lefler."

Not Primus. The significance of the name Morgan had chosen—*the first, the only*—wasn't lost on him.

"I'm so glad to meet you, Robin," he said.

"Yeah." Robin smeared a tear from her cheek. "You're a psychiatrist." When Pointer nodded, she continued, "And my mother saw you."

"Yes."

"Can you tell me what she . . . ?"

But Pointer was already shaking his head. *Psychiatrists are the keepers of secrets.* "No, I'm so sorry," he said, gently, and meant it. "I'm not trying to be cruel, but your mother had *her* life, and you have *yours*, Robin. You have your whole life, and I'd like to hear about it."

He held the door open for her. "Please, come in, and let's talk, and let's see what comes up."

SOLETA
Revelations

Keith R.A. DeCandido

After graduating Starfleet Academy alongside fellow future *Excalibur* crewmates Zak Kebron and Mark McHenry, Soleta was assigned to the *U.S.S. Aldrin*, accompanied by fellow graduates Worf and Tania Tobias. "Revelations" takes place about a year into that posting.

Keith R.A. DeCandido

In a review of his two-book *Star Trek* series *The Brave and the Bold*, *Cinescape* referred to Keith R.A. DeCandido as "the second coming of Peter David," which adds a touch of irony to his involvement in this anthology (not to mention prompting Peter to fob off tuition responsibilities for his children onto Keith in his introduction to this volume). Keith's other *Trek* work includes the novels *Diplomatic Implausibility*, *Demons of Air and Darkness*, and *The Art of the Impossible*; short stories in *What Lay Beyond*, *Prophecy and Change*, and the upcoming *Tales of the Dominion War*; the comic book miniseries *Perchance to Dream*; and several eBooks for the *Starfleet Corps of Engineers* series. Keith is also the author of the upcoming *Star Trek: I.K.S. Gorkon* novels, a series focusing entirely on Klingons, and has written fiction in the universes of *Buffy the Vampire Slayer*, *Gene Roddenberry's Andromeda*, *Farscape*, and many more, with his first original novel, *Dragon Precinct*, due in 2004. Keith, who lives in New York City with fellow author Terri Osborne and two silly cats, is now off to write more *Trek* fiction, having just learned how much college tuitions have gone up since he graduated in 1990. Find out too much about Keith at his Web site at DeCandido.net.

Stardate 39022.5

"Mind if I ask you a question, Ensign?"

Soleta looked up from her tricorder, turned to the security guard, and said, "I believe you just have."

The guard, a broad-shouldered human named Chan Pak, had a flat face, with features that seemed to have been intended for a head a quarter of the size of his actual cranium, resulting in wide cheeks and a massive jaw.

He laughed at the Vulcan woman's response to his query, a piercing sound that made Soleta's ears hurt. "Y'know, they warned me about you."

Why is it that humans always feel the need to credit a nebulous "they" for so much? "Of what did this warning consist, Mr. Pak?"

"They say that you Vulcans are all pedantic."

Soleta finished her scan. "Do they?"

"You don't agree?"

Closing her tricorder, Soleta said, "I have met many Vulcans who were not especially pedantic."

Again, Pak laughed. Soleta felt constrained to move back a few decimeters to avoid further wear and tear on her eardrums. "Fair enough. Anyhow, I wanted to ask about that pin in your hair."

"Feel free."

Soleta knew that it would save time and trouble if she simply went ahead and explained the pin, but she decided, in a fit of something like pique, to live up to the guard's characterization of her species.

A third braying laugh. Until encountering non-Vulcans at Starfleet Academy, Soleta, as a Vulcan, had never comprehended why any language would need more than one word for "laugh." Now, though, she understood. Chan Pak's particular version of the action was best classified as a "guffaw."

"Fine. Ensign, what is the significance of that pin in your hair?"

Her hand unconsciously moved to the pin that secured her thick, long black hair. "It belonged to my mother. She passed it on to me when I left for Starfleet Academy. The symbol is the cornerstone of Vulcan philosophy."

" 'Thou shalt always be pedantic'?"

Soleta was tempted to reply in the affirmative. "No. It best translates into English as 'infinite diversity in infinite combinations.' Since humans have a predilection for abbreviations that rivals my people's tendency toward pedantry, it has been simplified to 'IDIC.' "

"Oh, so *that's* what that means. I'd heard it before, but I never knew what it stood for." Pak scratched his expansive jaw with one massive finger. The guard's hands were unusually large, even for his already-prodigious two-point-three-meter height. "I figured it was the Vulcan word for your planet or something."

"The Vulcan word for our planet is 'Vulcan.' To call it otherwise would be illogical."

Pak frowned. "Humans call their planet Earth."

"I do not believe that anyone has ever accused your species of being logical."

The frown became a grin. "Good point, well made."

They were standing in one of the control rooms of an outpost that once had the designation T-22. Located on Kalandra Minor, it had been a frontier outpost in the early days of the Federation, intended as a jumping-off point for colonization. Unfortunately, the bulk of the worlds beyond T-22 proved unsuitable for one reason or another. Federation expansion went in different directions, and the outpost was eventually decommissioned a century ago.

Now, however, the Cardassian Union—in their continued aggressive expansion that had been going on for the past four decades—was moving into the area of space the planet occupied. Given the Federation's continued hostilities with the Cardassians, Starfleet Command felt it might not be a bad idea to make Outpost T-22 a going concern again.

To that end, a team from the *U.S.S. Aldrin,* an *Oberth*-class ship, was sent to the surface of Kalandra Minor to evaluate the outpost and see if it could be salvaged and/or upgraded, or if it needed to be scrapped and rebuilt entirely. While the team—led by the *Aldrin's* second officer, Lieutenant Ashanté Shimura—performed that evaluation, the *Aldrin* itself was patrolling the sector to make sure that the Cardassian incursion into this sector wasn't farther along than intelligence reports indicated. The ship would return in three days to pick them up and return to Starbase 375 with a report.

The away team consisted of Shimura; five enlisted engineers, under the command of Ensign Tania Tobias (her first command situation, though Shimura was there to back her up as necessary); half a dozen security guards, including Pak, led by Deputy Chief of Security Wheeler; the ship's conn officer, Ensign Worf, who was there to gain away-team experience; and three science officers, Soleta among them.

Kalandra Minor was a relatively small planet that was mostly covered in oceans laced with an acidic compound that made the liquid fatal to most humanoid races. Indeed, the risks inherent in maintaining an outpost on a planet that was eighty percent covered in a lethal substance was one of the contributing factors to it being decommissioned. One of the landmasses was a four-square-kilometer island, on which sat fifteen buildings, composing Outpost T-22. At present, Soleta was assigned to the small structure that housed the enivronmental controls. Among T-22's manifold functions was to be as storage for goods en route to those colonies that never actually materialized, and the controls here maintained those storage facilities.

Soleta tapped her combadge. "Soleta to Shimura."

"Go ahead, Ensign."

"I have completed my examination. For a two-century-old environmental-control console that has been left unmaintained for one century, it is in remarkable condition."

"Meaning?"

"Meaning, it should be abandoned and replaced with a modern unit as soon as possible. What is remarkable is that it has not fallen to pieces. It should be moved to a museum as an example of the soundness of Starfleet structural engineering practices of the twenty-second and twenty-third centuries."

Shimura laughed, though hers was a much more pleasant sound than that of Pak. Soleta stifled an urge to tell Pak to emulate it. *"I'll make a note of your recommendation, Ensign. Return to the main base. Most of the other teams are making similar reports. About the only thing that's actually working are the defensive and security protocols—and even so, they're still a hundred years out of date."*

"That is not entirely surprising."

"No, but it may mean we sit on our thumbs for three days until the Aldrin *comes back."*

"Quite possibly. Soleta out."

"Wow."

Soleta turned to the security guard. " 'Wow'?"

"Well, I thought for *sure* that you'd make some kind of comment about how illogical it would be to sit on your thumbs."

"And why would I say such an *idiotic* thing, Mr. Pak?" Soleta snapped.

Pak recoiled as if he'd been punched in his immense jaw. "I'm—I'm sorry, Ensign, I didn't mean anything by it. I was just making conversation."

"*Were* you? A piece of advice, Mr. Pak: Do not always listen to what *they* say. I have found—"

Whatever it was that Soleta had found was cut off by the sound of an explosion.

"*Away team, report to the main building now!*" That was Shimura's voice, coming over both Soleta's and Pak's combadges. More explosions could be heard through the tiny speakers. "*Worf, raise shields! Tobias, identify that thing!*"

The phaser rifle that had been slung over Pak's shoulder was now firmly in the guard's oversized hands. "C'mon, Ensign."

Without waiting to see if she was behind him, Pak ran for the exit to the small structure. Soleta followed, easily keeping up with the taller human's massive strides, and admonished herself for losing her temper the way she did. It was frustrating—she had always worked so hard to maintain the Vulcan disciplines, yet she lost control so easily. Others, who made far less effort than she, were able to keep their emotions in check so well, they almost lived up to other species' stereotypes of Vulcans' robotic behavior. But for Soleta, it was always as if there were a volcano waiting to erupt in her heart.

She supposed that was why she had always gotten along with Worf, the first Klingon in Starfleet. She and Worf, along with Tobias and two other classmates, had formed a study group and stuck together throughout their four years at the Academy. Worf—as a Klingon growing up among much more fragile humans—had to learn to keep his passions under control. In a way it was much more difficult for him, as Vulcans had had millennia to perfect the techniques for suppressing their emotions, where Worf had no cultural precedent to follow. Indeed, the very idea of suppressing emotions was anathema to most Klingons, but it was necessary for Worf to survive.

Still, both of them had largely succeeded. *Aside from moments like I just had with Pak. But those moments have become more common of late. . . .*

The ground shook. Soleta did not lose her footing; nor did Pak. She looked up to see that some kind of disruptor fire was striking a shield barrier—and the barrier was not holding up well. She could not see where the shots were coming from, though she did recognize the weapon type as either Klingon or Breen.

Or Romulan, she added, though that was unlikely, all things considered. The Romulan Star Empire closed its borders after the Tomed Incident five decades ago, though there had been occasional rumblings from them in the time since—mostly directed at the Klingon Empire. *But this is far from either Empire's sphere of influence.*

She and Pak entered the main control room. Shimura stood with Tobias, Worf, and two more security guards. The two ensigns were seated at the old-fashioned consoles, with their toggle switches and blinking lights. Worf was the picture of calm intensity, sitting ramrod-straight in his chair, the gold Klingon sash he wore over his red-and-black uniform bunching up a bit at the shoulder. Tobias was the opposite—her blond hair was tousled and she looked more apprehensive than she had during finals week of their last year at the Academy.

Shimura stood behind them, one hand resting on the back of each of the ensigns' chairs. Her smooth almond skin seemed to be pulled tight over her high cheekbones. The two guards stood behind her, phaser rifles at the ready. Pak took up position next to them, while Soleta moved to stand just to the left of Shimura.

The large viewscreen in front of the trio showed a tactical display, with a circle labeled UNIDENTIFIED VESSEL flying in a fairly standard attack pattern: Fly down toward the outpost, level off and do a strafing run on the outpost, fly back upward, circle around, and start again.

"Can we get any kind of reading?" Shimura asked.

"No," Worf said. "Sensors are unable to determine the ship's configuration."

So it is a ship attacking, Soleta thought. That was the most logical deduction from the disruptor blasts she and Pak had seen on their way here.

The ground shook once more. Worf looked up at the ceiling, then at Shimura. "Shields will not maintain integrity for much longer."

"I'm amazed they've held up this long," Tobias said through gritted teeth. "These shields are older than dirt."

Soleta turned to Pak. "Don't worry, I don't plan to comment on how illogical it would be to classify the shields as being of a greater age than the ground beneath our feet."

Pak scowled at her. "I wasn't going to, Ensign." Soleta noted the all-business tone, and regretted her outburst. During the relative downtime of the outpost investigation, Pak was attempting to be friendly, albeit some-what clumsily, but now that there was a crisis he was all business.

As I should be. She opened her tricorder and used it to scan the area im-mediately above, on the theory that her top-of-the-line tricorder was more sensitive than T-22's century-old sensors. After a moment, it told her some-thing surprising. "Sir, the vessel attacking us is a Romulan transport vessel, probably *Golgaroth* class."

Worf rose from his chair, his hand going to his phaser. "Romulan?"

"Mind your post, Ensign," Shimura snapped. "What the hell are Romu-lans doing here?"

"Shooting at us," Balbuena, one of the security guards, muttered.

"The *Golgaroth* class is a civilian design, Lieutenant," Soleta said. "It also dates back to a time when we had better intelligence on the Romulan Empire, and is therefore likely to be at least fifty years old. I would guess that this is not an official engagement of their military. The ship can theo-retically hold up to fifteen passengers, but I am only reading two life signs."

Three of the engineers came running in. One of them, a human woman named Mattacks, said, "Phaser banks are completely dead, sir, the torpedo bays are empty, and the firing system's offline."

The ground shook with another impact. "Shields are down to fifteen percent," Tobias said, sounding frantic. Soleta could see a rivulet of sweat running down her forehead from her blond hair. "Another shot, and we're dead."

However, Mattacks wasn't finished. "But we've got an ion cannon in perfect working order."

Soleta frowned. Shimura noticed this. "Something wrong, Ensign?"

"An ion cannon would be consistent with the construction date of this outpost, Lieutenant. However, I question the description of it as in 'perfect working order,' given that the weapon's very unrealiability is what led to its falling out of common usage."

"Maybe, Ensign," Mattacks said with a grin, "but it beats a kick in the head."

"Speaking of which," Tobias said, "we're about to get kicked in the head. They're coming in for another pass."

Worf pointed at one set of controls at his station. "Are these the ion-cannon controls?"

Sounding surprised that Worf deduced this on his own, Mattacks said, "Uh, yeah—yeah, that's it." Soleta almost smiled at that—Worf's aptitude for weapons systems was impressive, though not something that had come up much in his time as a conn officer on the *Aldrin*. His range of study had been broad at the Academy, preparing him for both the command track he was currently on or for a career in security, at which Soleta suspected he would be more comfortable.

"Fire when ready, Mr. Worf," Shimura said.

"Yes, *sir.*" The young Klingon spoke with uncharacteristic enthusiasm.

The ground shook much harder from the firing of the ion cannon than from the Romulan barrage. Sparks flew from the console, blowing Worf and the chair in which he sat—as well as Shimura, who was standing behind him—backward.

"Worf!" Tobias cried.

"I am all right. See to the lieutenant."

Soleta, however, was already doing so. Shimura had burns on her forehead and cheek and was unconscious. She looked up at Pak and the two next to him. "We need to take her to the infirmary."

"Afraid not," said a voice from the doorway. Soleta turned to see the squat, bulky form of Tynan Wheeler, the *Aldrin*'s deputy security chief, who had entered along with one other security guard. "The infirmary was trashed on that last shot when the shields went down. Janzen, DeBacco, Cuirle, Lieutenant Ordoñez, and Ensign T'a'a'y'r were all in there when it went up."

Everyone except Soleta and Worf looked up in shock at that. Janzen and DeBacco were two of the engineers; Cuirle was a security guard; Ordoñez and T'a'a'y'r were the other members of Soleta's science team.

Tobias ran back to her console and peered into the old-fashioned sensor hood, blue light shining on her face. "Dammit, confirmed. They fired just as the ion cannon hit them. The Romulan ship *has* gone down, but they took out the infirmary and two of the barracks. And both shields and the ion cannon are fried."

Soleta turned to Tobias. "What are your orders, Ensign?"

Tobias whirled around, her blond hair bouncing with the action. Her face was still covered in sweat. *"My* orders?"

"With Lieutenant Shimura unconscious and both Lieutenant Ordoñez and Ensign T'a'a'y'r dead, that only leaves you, me, and Ensign Worf as ranking officers. You are in command of the engineering team, which is the primary component of this away team, therefore logic dictates that you should be the one to take command for as long as the lieutenant is incapacitated."

"Uh, right. Okay." Tobias took a moment to compose herself—a moment more than she probably should have, in Soleta's opinion, but this was hardly an expected turn of events—and then looked at the Klingon. "Ensign Worf, you will lead the damage-control team. Assess our situation, see if the shields can be repaired, and try to fix the ion cannon."

"Aye, sir," Worf said with a curt nod. He gave another nod to Mattacks and the other engineers, who fanned out.

To Wheeler, she said, "Chief, search the wreckage of the Romulan ship for survivors."

"What if we find some?"

Tobias hesitated. Soleta jumped in. "Lieutenant Shimura indicated that security protocols were still intact. That means the brigs are working."

Wheeler nodded. "Yeah, and they're still in one piece."

"All right, then, bring any prisoners there," Tobias said.

"Yes, sir." Wheeler led Pak and the others out.

"Soleta, try to keep Lieutenant Shimura comfortable. There's a first-aid kit in here somewhere."

"Of course, Ensign." She scanned the room for the material that would be found in such a kit, and quickly found it located under one of the secondary consoles. *Standard placement.*

"And Soleta?"

The ensign turned to look at her former classmate. "Yes, Tania?"

"Thanks a *lot.* " Smiling grimly, Tobias turned back to the console.

Soleta did not bother pointing out that her actions were wholly logical. It wouldn't do to come across as pedantic, after all. . . .

Tania Tobias sat dolefully looking at the console. She felt guilty every time she touched one of the ancient controls, convinced that the museum guard would yell at her not to touch the exhibits. *But no*, she thought, *these are all real, working components. Well, some of them are, anyhow.*

To her continued annoyance, many of the colored lights were not lit, meaning they were dead, or were lit with red rather than green illumination, meaning they were not working properly.

Helluva first command.

A deep, booming, yet gentle voice said, "Tania."

Tobias turned around to see Worf and Soleta standing side by side. For a moment, she imagined that they were back at the Academy getting ready for a class, along with Zak Kebron and Mark McHenry. But no, they weren't cadets anymore. They had the single pips indicating their status as commissioned officers in Starfleet, not mere plebes, and they wore the uniforms of command red (Worf), sciences blue (Soleta), and operations gold (herself), not the plain red-and-white of cadets. *People are dead and injured. No, this is as real as it gets.*

More than ever, she just wanted to collapse in Worf's arms and have herself a good cry. But officers didn't do that, and she had long since lost the opportunity to tell Worf how she felt. She doubted that he viewed her as anything other than a friend. Not that it was easy to tell how Worf felt. Ever since his and K'Ehleyr's rather nasty breakup, he had gotten more withdrawn and stony, if that were possible.

Taking a deep breath through her nose and exhaling it in a burst through her mouth, Tobias said, "Report."

"Communications are completely inoperable. The subspace transmitter and receiver were both destroyed in the final attack."

"Damn."

Soleta's right eyebrow raised. "I assume Lieutenant Shimura sent a distress call when the Romulans first attacked."

"Of course," Worf said.

"But we don't know if anyone replied to it," Tobias added, "or even heard it. Nothing's salvageable?"

"Mattacks and her team are attempting to do so now, but she was not optimistic."

Tobias slumped her shoulders, then straightened. *Dammit, I'm in command. I need to look like it.* True, it was just Worf and Soleta—if there was anyone who would let her off the hook for not being completely spit-and-polish, it would be these two. *Though,* she mused, *they probably would be disappointed.* She decided that that would be even worse, and forced herself to keep her best command face on. *Assuming I even have one.*

She turned to Soleta. "How is Lieutenant Shimura?"

"Not good. The tricorder readings indicate a subdural hematoma. It is possible that a skilled surgeon might be able to treat this problem with the limited supplies we have available. It is quite impossible for anyone presently on this planet to do so—unless one of the Romulans in that transport is a doctor."

"Unlikely," Worf said with a sneer. "And even if one was, I would not trust such a creature to operate on the lieutenant."

Tobias almost physically recoiled from the bile in Worf's tone. She knew, of course, that Worf was the only survivor of the massacre on Khitomer by Romulan forces, which claimed his parents' lives. Her own father had been the chief engineer of the *U.S.S. Intrepid*, the vessel that rescued him. And she had certainly seen Worf angry in the five-plus years they'd known each other. However, the level of pure hatred he was giving off now was palpable.

"That would be unwise," Soleta said dryly.

"Let's just hope the *Aldrin* heard our distress signal and is heading back," Tobias said ruefully.

"Even if they are," Soleta said, "the soonest we can expect them is in twenty-three hours, four minutes, assuming they followed a standard search pattern and received the distress call when the attack began, and then proceeded back to Kalandra Minor at maximum warp."

Worf asked, "Can you keep Lieutenant Shimura alive until then?"

"It is beyond my means to keep her alive, Worf," Soleta said with as much incredulity as she was ever likely to display publicly. "I can keep her comfortable indefinitely, until the hematoma becomes serious enough to endanger her life. Then she will die."

An idea suddenly struck Tobias. "What about the Romulan ship?"

"What about it?" Worf asked.

"If you are inquiring as to whether or not they might have medical equipment that would aid us," Soleta said, "it is unlikely. *Golgaroth*-class vessels were not equipped with sickbays or dispensaries—the best we could hope for is a medikit similar to the one we have, and it would only be equipped for Romulans and perhaps Remans and other Romulan subject species. It is unlikely to be of any use for treating a human."

"And even if it did," came a voice from the doorway, "it wouldn't be intact."

Tobias turned to see Wheeler enter the building, blood staining the part of his uniform over his left shoulder. Behind him, Sookdeo was carrying Balbuena in a firefighter's carry—Balbuena was covered in burns.

"What happened?" she asked even as Worf went to assist Sookdeo in setting Balbuena down next to Shimura on the far side of the room. Tobias wondered where Pak and Melnyk were.

Wheeler looked like a spring about to uncoil. His teeth were practically clenched as he gave his report. "The Rom ship was completely trashed. There's nothing in there we can use—not even the comm systems. Unfortunately, its passengers *weren't* trashed, and neither were their disruptors." The deputy chief shook his head and looked away. "They vaporized Melnyk, and Balbuena and I took a couple of glancing hits."

Balbuena looked like she'd taken considerably more than that, but Tobias said nothing.

"One of them got away, but we captured the other one. Pak's keeping an eye on him in the brig."

Soleta walked over to Tobias. "Balbuena has several burns of varying degrees. I can do little for her here. Like Lieutenant Shimura, she needs either a trained physician or the *Aldrin*'s sickbay—preferably both." She ran her tricorder over Wheeler. "You, Chief, need a microsuture and a dermal regenerator, and you'll be fine."

"I'll handle it myself," Wheeler said, teeth still clenched. "Where's the medikit?"

"That would be illogical," Soleta said.

"I don't give a damn about logic right now, Ensign. Those bastards killed several of my people. I can lick my own damn wounds."

To Tobias's surprise, Soleta snapped. "Forget logic, then, Chief—that would be incredibly stupid. You have a shoulder wound. You would have to treat it one-handed, which would be awkward at best."

Quickly, Tobias added, "At least have Sookdeo do it." She gave the guard in question a quick look, and he quickly grabbed the medikit off the floor and approached Wheeler with it.

"Fine, whatever," Wheeler muttered. "But we need to get out after that other one. We found half a dozen crates in the wreckage. Most of them were just as trashed as the ship, but they had labels and manifests that were from all over the place. Cardassian, Lissepian, Asfar Qatala, a bunch I didn't recognize—I'm thinking smugglers."

"That would explain their presence so far from Romulan space," Worf said.

"As well as their use of an old, civilian-issue vessel," Soleta added.

Tobias bit her lower lip. "Mr. Wheeler's right—we need to find the other one."

Worf scowled. "If we are to conduct a proper search, we must utilize all remaining personnel."

Wheeler nodded, shaking off Sookdeo, who was putting the finishing touches on his shoulder. "The ensign's right. I think it's safe to say that these guys have been using this planet as a base of operations. Probably got pissed that we horned in on their territory. That means we're going to need a search party of at least eight—and since there are only nine of us left . . ."

Again, Tobias bit her lip. Normally, this would be a job for security, but their numbers had been cut in half. She remembered enough of her tactical training at the Academy to know that, in this terrain, four two-person search parties was the most efficient way to search the island.

"All right," she said. She thought a moment. *Three security guards, three engineers—best to double them up.* "Chief, you and Mattacks go north. Sookdeo, take chuLor and head west. Have Pak take Schechter east. Worf and I will handle the south. Soleta, you stay here and keep an eye on Balbuena and Lieutenant Shimura."

"Someone needs to guard the prisoner," Worf said emphatically. "He *cannot* be allowed to escape."

Wheeler said, "Worf's right."

"I will guard the prisoner," Soleta said. "If Shimura or Balbuena's condition deteriorates, there is quite literally nothing I can do. However, I can guard the prisoner, and also interrogate him."

Disdainfully, Wheeler asked, "What the hell do *you* know about interrogation, Ensign?"

"I know that it is best conducted in a dispassionate, logical manner, and that I am the best candidate for such a task."

"No, those of us with *training* are best suited."

Soleta raised an eyebrow. "As I recall, Chief, your exact words a few minutes ago were, 'I don't give a damn about logic right now, Ensign. Those bastards killed several of my people.' Hardly the statement of an objective interrogator."

Wheeler moved closer to Soleta so that he was staring right down at her. "So what're you gonna do, tell him he's stupid and hope he cracks?"

Speaking with a violent fury that Tobias would have sooner expected from Worf, Soleta said, "Chief, remove yourself from my immediate vicinity, or I will show you how painful a Vulcan neck pinch is on someone with an injured shoulder."

"That's enough!" Tobias yelled. "Soleta's right, we need someone to interrogate the prisoner, and I'd rather all three security personnel were involved in the search. Does the brig have a monitoring station?"

It took Wheeler a moment to realize that she had addressed the question to him, busy as he was staring daggers at Soleta. "Yeah—yeah, there's one."

"Good. Soleta, keep it trained on this room so you can monitor Shimura and Balbuena." Tobias stared at Wheeler, whose gaze remained fixed on Soleta. "Is there any particular reason why you're still standing here, Chief?"

Wheeler shook his head, as if coming out of a trance. "Uh, no, sir."

"You've got your orders. Move it."

Quickly, Wheeler departed, Sookdeo right on his heels. *Well, if that isn't my command face, it was obviously good enough,* Tobias thought with satisfaction.

Then she turned to Soleta and Worf and let the command face fall. "You know, I keep waiting for an instructor to walk in and say, 'Computer, end simulation.' "

In a tone as gentle as her words to Wheeler were harsh, Soleta said, "This is why we went through those simulations, Tania."

"I know." She exhaled a long breath. "C'mon, let's do this."

Soleta felt a pang of shame as she entered the brig. Pak was already there, along with Schechter from engineering. They departed to commence their search for the other Romulan, leaving Soleta alone with the prisoner.

The structure included a small workstation with an old-fashioned viewer protruding upward from the computer console, and three cells framed by forcefield generators. The cells included modest toilet facilities and an uncomfortable-looking bench.

In one of them sat a Romulan.

Soleta's pang of shame was because she lied to Tobias. *Pak's "they" would insist that Vulcans never lie, of course—but what kind of a pedants would we be if we did not?* She did not wish to interrogate the Romulan because she was best qualified for the job, or because logic dictated that she be the one to do so, though those were both true.

No, she wished to interrogate the Romulan because she'd never seen one before.

What she saw in the middle of the three brigs now was a sight she never imagined: a Vulcan with a vicious, nasty smile on his face.

He wasn't Vulcan, of course, but one could not discern that upon first glance, any more than one could tell a human from a Betazoid on first glance.

Except for that smile. The smile branded him as a Romulan, for Soleta could not believe that even the most undisciplined of Vulcans, one who had utterly discarded the teachings of Surak and the ways of logic, would ever be capable of so contemptible a smile.

"Well well well," the Romulan said. "A Vulcan. A pretty one, too. And young, based on that single pip on your collar. Pretty young Vulcan—very nice, yes. You're much prettier than that human bitch I had to teach a lesson to. Yes, that one."

This last was added as Soleta activated the viewer and programmed it to transmit from the main base, specifically Balbuena and Shimura's prone forms. She also placed her tricorder on the workstation and set it to record everything that went on in the room. The brig's security system was doing likewise, but her tricorder was of more recent vintage, and therefore more likely to provide a useful recording.

"She shot at me. I don't like it when women shoot at me. Women are meant to be subject to men's whims, after all."

"If you are endeavoring to get an emotional reaction out of me, you are bound to fail."

"You think so, do you?" The Romulan laughed at that. It was a vile sound that made Soleta nostalgic for Pak. "I may change your mind about that."

"Unlikely."

The Romulan leaned back on the bench, resting the top of his head against the wall. "I assume you're not here to provide me with entertainment, Ensign—which is a pity, as I suspect you'd be *very* entertaining—so you may as well get to it. You want to know who I am and what I'm doing here, yes?"

"And why you fired on this outpost."

Grinning, the Romulan said, "Oh, that's easy. We fired on you because you were trespassing on our property."

Soleta raised an eyebrow. "This is a Federation outpost."

"Correction: an *abandoned* Federation outpost. You people haven't come anywhere near this place in a hundred years. So it's ours by any reasonable interpretation of interstellar salvage law." He leaned forward. "You know, I must say, I prefer this version of the Starfleet uniform over that maroon atrocity you people wore for so long. This skintight look is *much* more flattering—especially on you. Admittedly, it doesn't leave much to the imagination, but I prefer reality to imagination in any case. Now I know *exactly* what to expect when I have you."

The Romulan continued to speak in a natural tone of voice, not varying in the slightest when he modulated from his discourse on salvage rights to his positive opinion of Soleta's physical form. She asked, "Do you truly imagine that you will get that opportunity?"

"V'Ret is still free. We've been avoiding Starfleet for sixty years, I can't see that changing now."

Soleta allowed herself the tiniest of smiles. "I would say that your vision is limited."

Again, he laughed. It was no more pleasant the second time. "Oh, very good! And here I was worried!"

"About what?"

"Do you know what we say on Romulus about Vulcans?"

"I am quite sure that I do not."

Rising from the bench, the Romulan said, "That the sundering of our people from yours came about because we found you so insufferably boring. But you are not in the least bit boring, Ensign."

Soleta turned to look at the monitor for a moment, then turned back. "You said your comrade's name was V'Ret. What is yours?"

"Rajari."

"You provide this information with surprising ease."

Shrugging, Rajari said, "It's of little consequence. Besides, I want you to scream my name when you—"

"You are *pathetic*," Soleta said suddenly.

Rajari's eyes widened. "Oho, what's this? Is that a bit of vitriol I see seeping through the cracks of that Surakian façade?"

Tamping down the anger that built in that inner volcano of hers, Soleta said, "Hardly."

"Oh, you can't fool me, Ensign." He walked right up to the edge of the forcefield, a few wisps of his black-and-gray hair rising and moving toward the field from the static electricity. "There's a monster lurking in your heart, just like in every Vulcan. You may have spent centuries trying to bury it, but it's there. You'd be much better off letting it loose."

Considering that she'd spent a lifetime burying it, Soleta was hardly likely to take that advice. The conversation was, however, providing fascinating insights into the Romulan psyche.

Sadly, that was not her purpose here. "What is your business on this planet?"

"Ah, back to the dull interrogator." Rajari started to pace the cell. "Such a pity this forcefield is here. The first thing I'd do, of course, is remove that hairpin and let your hair down. You have lovely hair, Ensign. Although, I must say, I like the pin, too—it reminds me of someone."

Soleta's eyebrow raised. "An IDIC symbol reminds you of a person?"

"No, the hairpin itself, actually. You see, while I am the first Romulan you've ever encountered—and don't try to deny it, Ensign. Even through your attempt at a cool exterior, I could see the eagerness in your eyes. 'One of our evil cousins has been captured! I can study him!' " He shook his head and continued pacing; given the cell's small dimensions, he turned around quite a bit. "Vulcans. In any case, while I am your first Romulan, you are hardly my first Vulcan. You're not even my first Vulcan woman wearing an IDIC pin in her hair. The other one was this magnificent woman on Cor Coroli IX." Scratching his left ear, he looked pensive for a moment, staring at the side wall as if it would provide insight. "That must have been, oh, twenty, twenty-five years ago now. No, twenty-five— definitely, it was right after we stole that Klingon shuttle. V'Ret was off on some other mission, and I was in a one-person ship that crashed on Cor Coroli. It was a small Vulcan colony, only a few hundred people on it." He laughed sadistically and resumed his pacing. "There was this scientist who came to my aid after the crash, a gray-eyed beauty named T'Pas. She had a pin in her hair just like yours, with that silly symbol on it. I removed it, of course, along with her clothing. She put up a fight, but it was to no avail. Men are superior to women, after all, and Romulans are superior to Vulcans. Most don't appreciate how weak Vulcans are, since their strength is greater than most, but strength without passion is no strength at all." He grinned. "And I had plenty of passion. So did she, eventually." Turning to look back at Soleta, he finished, "I can assure you, I succeeded in getting an emotional reaction out of *her*."

Soleta—who was born to T'Pas of the Cor Coroli IX colony two and a half decades previous—stared into the eyes of the man on the other side of the forcefield.

Eyes that were the same deep black as her own.

T'Pas, as Rajari had already noted, had gray eyes, as had Soleta's maternal grandmother; her maternal grandfather had green eyes. T'Pas's husband, Volak, had brown eyes, as had both his own parents. Soleta had never met a relative with such black eyes as her own. She had also never given it much thought, assuming to have inherited them from a relative of whose eye color she was unaware. Having grown up on Cor Coroli, she had met very few members of her family in any event.

A rage beyond anything Soleta had ever felt in her life, even as a child before she had been old enough to know the mental disciplines that all Vulcan children were taught, started to build within her. Reaching deep down within the recesses of her being, Soleta summoned all the years of discipline, of training, of experience in suppressing the emotions that were always far closer to the surface than her teachers seemed to think they should have been, in order to keep her reaction to this news from showing on her person.

Somehow, she managed to simply raise an eyebrow and keep her voice controlled as she said, "Indeed?"

Rajari threw his head back and laughed. "Perfect! Exactly the reaction I expected! I describe the brutal rape of one of your people, and all you can do is that damn thing with your eyebrows. Do they teach that at schools on

Vulcan, I wonder?" He sat back down on the bench. "No matter. You obviously aren't interested in turning this forcefield off, so I have nothing more to say."

On the contrary. I want very much to turn the forcefield off, so I can beat you until my fists are green with your blood.

"Besides," he added, now lying down on the bench and closing his eyes (*his black eyes, his eyes that he passed on to the daughter he didn't even realize he had, his daughter who was standing right there in front of him*), "V'Ret will likely kill you all off and free me in short order."

Knowing it was a violation of her orders, she turned and left the brig. She could not stand to be in the same room as him—not and still restrain herself from killing him.

All these years, thinking my own discipline was lacking, when in fact it was him. *Romulan passion—an inheritance from my father, along with my mysterious black eyes.*

Questions flooded her mind. *Why did my parents not tell me of this? Why did Mother go through with the pregnancy?*

Most critical of all: *What do I do now?*

Starfleet regulations required that its personnel report their full heritage, particularly if a member of a hostile species was in that heritage. Though the Romulans had kept their borders closed for over fifty years, they definitely fell into the category of "hostile" where the Federation was concerned.

But revealing her parentage now—assuming it was true; a call home would verify it, since she doubted her parents would deny it if she confronted them directly—would have dire consequences.

Indeed, it had consequences already. As time went on, Soleta had found her control deteriorating. She had assumed it to be the by-product of living among so many emotional beings, but what if it wasn't that? *What if it is simply my father's birthright asserting itself?*

And even if it isn't, what happens when the wrong person gets on my bad side? What happens the next time someone asks me about Vulcans as Pak did—or challenges my logic in as aggressive a manner as Wheeler—and I cannot control my emotions?

Suddenly, Soleta felt very alone. For the first time in her career—in her life—she did not know what to do.

Tania Tobias watched as Worf took the point. They were heading up an incline that, according to the outpost's maps, would lead to a cliff. The dirt-

and-grass path they now took was lined on either side by trees, and looked like it had been used as a walkway once but allowed to grow over with disuse. It would've reminded Tobias of some forests she'd been to back on Earth, but for the leaves and grass being bright yellow and the tree bark being a russety red.

Worf stopped walking as they came to the end of the road. They stood before a sheer forty-meter drop into the heavily acidic ocean. Tobias could hear waves breaking on the rocks below, and she shuddered. Even being caught in the spray of those waves would burn the skin off a human.

She walked up beside Worf, brushing her blond hair out of her face as the wind changed so that it was blowing from behind her. She wished she'd had the forethought to secure her hair before they left, but it wasn't windy back at the main base.

"Something is wrong," Worf said while peering at his tricorder.

"What is it?" she asked.

"The wind has shifted. I can smell several avians in the trees about six meters to our right—but they are not registering on the tricorder at all."

Tobias knew that Klingons had superior olfactory senses—Worf said it aided in hunting, though Tobias never understood why any post-industrial society would engage in such an activity—but it had never occurred to her to put it to practical use like this before. "So if the tricorder's not picking them up, it means there's something nearby that's masking life-form readings."

"Yes. We should—"

Worf's words were cut off by the Romulan who leapt out from behind one of the red-barked, yellow-leafed trees and tackled him. "A Klingon and a human with brains. What're the odds?" the Romulan said after punching Worf in the face following the tackle.

Tobias unholstered her phaser, but the Romulan was unbelievably fast, and knocked it out of her hands before she could fire. It clattered off one of the trees and ricocheted beyond her reach. The Romulan then grabbed her in a choke hold, which she proceeded to break easily with a move she'd learned in her first year at the Academy.

She faced off against the Romulan, who grinned. "Not bad for a slow human."

He lunged at her, and she dodged out of the way, ever mindful of the nearby cliff. *Have to maneuver him away from it.*

A phaser blast on stun then struck the Romulan in the side. The Romulan stumbled—

—but did not fall down. Tobias stared wide-eyed at the Romulan for half a second—

—which was all he needed to grab her and put a disruptor muzzle to her neck.

They were now standing right at the cliff's edge. Worf was still lying on the ground, yellow grass stains on his black-and-red uniform, holding his phaser at them.

"That's enough, Klingon. Make one more move, and the human dies."

"If anything happens to her, you will die, Romulan." Worf spoke with as much venom as Tobias had ever heard from him.

"And if I let her go, you'll still try to kill me."

"Definitely," Worf said. "You are a Romulan *petaQ*, and I will not rest until you are exterminated."

"Now now, what did *I* ever do to you, Klingon?"

"Your people are the detritus of the galaxy." Worf got to his feet, his tone growing even harsher, his phaser never wavering. "You were responsible for the massacre of my family."

"I suppose it's possible," the Romulan said pensively. "I've killed many Klingons in my time. It's not difficult—you lot tend to lead with your chins. In any case, you can't hurt me. And if you don't lower the phaser, I'll shoot this human."

"Go ahead."

Tobias felt the blood drain from her face. *What is he doing?* Worf had to be bluffing, she thought, even as she could hear his deep voice proclaiming that Klingons never bluffed. But this man had already proven that he had no compunctions about killing them with the attack on the base, and now that he'd leapt from the trees . . .

Then Tobias realized *why* Worf said what he said, and elbowed the Romulan in the stomach.

As expected, he doubled over, his finger spasming on his disruptor's firing button, and nothing happening. *Because if his disruptor had power, he'd have shot us from under cover instead of a frontal assault. Good deduction, Worf.*

Tobias ran to Worf's side. He still held his phaser on the Romulan, who was still at the cliff's edge, clutching his stomach. "Fine, you saw through my ruse," he said in a strained voice, tossing his powerless disruptor off to the side. "But the same field that masks my life signs also is proof against *your* weapon. So what's it to be, Klingon?"

"Your death." Worf then shot the ground at the Romulan's feet.

The brown dirt and yellow grass burned away from the amber beam of the phaser, causing the Romulan to stumble backward. He pinwheeled his arms in an attempt to regain a balance that had suddenly been taken from him.

Tobias ran to grab him, to try to save him, wondering what the hell Worf was thinking, even as the Romulan fell over the cliff. But she was too late.

The Romulan didn't scream until after he hit the water.

Turning and facing her friend with a fury she had never felt before, she asked, "Worf—what the *hell* did you just *do?*"

"Cleaned up the galaxy by eliminating one more Romulan."

With that, he turned and headed back down the pathway.

As it turned out, the *Aldrin* had heard T-22's initial distress signal, and returned to Kalandra Minor at maximum warp, arriving exactly twenty-three hours and four minutes from the time Soleta had given her prediction. The ensign tried to take solace in the fact that her Vulcan training had gone that far, at least.

Shimura and Balbuena were both brought to sickbay in time to be healed, the former just barely, the latter with a somewhat longer recovery period. Upon awakening, Shimura recommended that all surviving members of the away team receive commendations and the dead ones receive posthumous honors.

Rajari—who was somewhat devastated at the news of V'Ret's untimely death in the acid oceans of Kalandra Minor—was transferred to the *Aldrin* brig. After the memorial service for her six deceased crewmates, Soleta went to visit Rajari, but found herself unable to say anything. The Romulan just laughed at her, and then she left.

Then she contacted her parents on Vulcan on a secure channel. The conversation was very calm and rational and logical, and Soleta managed not to scream as T'Pas and Volak confirmed that Soleta was indeed the result of the rape committed by Rajari. Not screaming took more willpower than Soleta knew she had, particularly when Mother asked if they would want her to testify to the rape. Soleta managed to calmly assure her that it wouldn't be necessary to reveal this information, as Rajari's firing on a Federation outpost and killing Starfleet personnel—not to mention assorted outstanding warrants dating back some sixty years—would be more than sufficient to keep him locked up for the rest of his natural life.

Soleta did not ask why they went ahead with having her after the rape. She thought that if she did, it would shred the tattered remains of her self-control.

Right after she signed off with her parents, she composed her request for a leave of absence from Starfleet.

The door chime rang in the middle of that. "Come," she said automatically, not really wanting to see anyone, but unable to contrive an excuse to keep anyone out.

It was Tania. "Soleta, can I talk to you for a second?"

"About what?"

"Worf."

Soleta raised an eyebrow. "I have told you in the past, Tania, if you wish to let him know your true feelings—"

"No, it's not that," Tobias said with a wave of her hand.

She then told Soleta about what happened on Kalandra Minor, and what Worf did to V'Ret.

"Worf was true to his nature," Soleta said. "Klingons are firm believers in vengeance, and he sees Romulans as responsible for the death of his family. It's a blood debt."

"That's sick."

Tania Tobias was a good person, and someone with whom Soleta had shared many adventures, and with whom she was proud to serve. But enough was enough.

"It's who he is," Soleta said angrily. "If you care for him as much as you claim to, then you must accept that. If you don't, then it's past time you got over your tiresome infatuation and got on with your life."

Tobias recoiled as if she'd been struck—not surprising, since Soleta was feeling an overwhelming urge to strike her. "Soleta, what's gotten into you?"

My father. "Nothing, Tania. Nothing at all. I'm merely trying to convey that what you saw on Kalandra Minor was Worf as he truly is." *And me as I truly am.*

"People can change, Soleta," Tobias said defensively. "We don't have to be slaves to our 'nature.'" With that, she turned and left Soleta's quarters.

If only I believed that.

She finished composing the LOA request.

SI CWAN
Turning Point

Josepha Sherman

Years before the fall of the Thallonian Empire, and his role as unofficial ambassador aiding the crew of the *Excalibur* and *Trident* in Sector 221G, Si Cwan was a member of the empire's royal family, living a life of privilege—some might say excessive privilege. "Turning Point" takes place shortly after the birth of Cwan's younger sister Kalinda.

Josepha Sherman

Josepha Sherman is a fantasy novelist, freelance editor, and folklorist, whose latest titles include *Son of Darkness* (Roc Books), the folklore title *Merlin's Kin* (August House), and, together with Susan Shwartz, two *Star Trek* novels, *Vulcan's Forge* and *Vulcan's Heart*. She has also written for the educational market on everything from Bill Gates to the workings of the human ear. Forthcoming titles include *Mythology for Storytellers* (M.E. Sharpe) and the *Star Trek: Vulcan's Soul* trilogy (also with Shwartz). Visit her at www.JosephaSherman.com.

" 'Wan!" The tiny child, bright in her red and gold baby dress, pulled away from her nursemaid and tottered her unsteady way over to where young Prince Si Cwan knelt in the palace nursery. " 'Wan!"

My sister, he thought with a surge of warmth he felt for no one else, *so small, so innocent, so happy. My lovely little sister.*

He held out his hands to her, and Kalinda *almost* made it all the way to him without falling. Landing on her bottom, she sat and looked up at him with a wide, two-toothed grin.

"Come here, little one," he said, and scooped her up, smiling to hear her giggle. "Ooof! You're putting on weight."

He might be sixteen, nearly his royal father's height (though nowhere near his bulk and not yet bearing royal tattoos), but damned if he was going to give up the chance to play with Kalinda. His sister, his only sibling, the one innocent bit of life at court, and the only one in the court who didn't want anything from him but his love.

"And you've got that, Kalinda. I'm never going to let anything hurt you, you know that, don't you? No one's ever going to hurt you. Now, think you can say 'brother'?"

"B'o'er."

"Good start!"

The nursemaid, a good, solid commoner named . . . Si Cwan realized he didn't know her name. Anyhow, she was sitting back on her heels, smiling with pleasure at the prince's affection for her small charge. Then suddenly alarm flared in the woman's eyes and she went flat in adoration.

"Now, isn't this a delightful picture?" a cold voice said.

Father.

"My son and heir makes quite a charming nursemaid. Perhaps he has found his true calling."

With a silent sigh, Si Cwan handed Kalinda back to the nursemaid. The little girl gave a wail of disapproval, and Si Cwan told her, "Hush, now. Behave. You are a princess, after all."

" 'Wan!"

Resolutely ignoring that plaintive cry, Si Cwan got to his feet, giving his father the reverence of prince-to-emperor. The emperor was in full hunting gear, soft gorrick-leather boots, trousers, tunic. Si Cwan realized with a pang that there had been a royal hunt—and his father hadn't even bothered to tell him.

"Father, I—"

"What? The hunt? You were not missed. Now, leave this nonsense and practice your fighting skills. Prove to me that you truly are my son and not some trick played on me by your mother."

Only by fiercely clenching his fists till they ached did Si Cwan keep from a suicidal attack. "My mother was your honored wife, Father. She did not betray you."

"Ah, at least the boy shows *some* spark of fire. Now, leave me."

Gladly.

It was a beautiful day, the kind sung about by the poets, with blue sky, soft breezes, wari-birds zooming by like streaks of red flame, and the royal gold flowers in full, sweet bloom—Si Cwan had to laugh as he looked around the white-walled roof garden of his father's estate. Difficult to stay angry or dejected just now. You couldn't ask for a more perfect day for fighting!

Maybe Zoran didn't think so, having just been knocked back on his rump. Zoran Si Verdin right now was clearly refusing to move.

"Come on, Zoran, get up."

His friend, panting, lying back on his elbows, quirked an eyebrow at him. For the barest instant, Zoran's eyes were not those of a friend.

No, Si Cwan told himself. *Don't spoil this part of the day, too.* He must have imagined that coldness. "Come on," he insisted. "I didn't hit you *that* hard."

He held out a hand. Zoran took it with a grunt. "You think you *could* hit that hard?"

"Hah. Think? I know!"

"Yeah, sure. Like this!"

As soon as he was back on his feet, Zoran lunged right into an attack. The two youngsters grappled, lips curled back in fierce grins. Si Cwan felt Zoran trying to lock his leg with a foot to pull him down, and twisted, trying in turn to get Zoran off balance. He had him—whoops! No, he didn't!

Zoran broke off so suddenly that Si Cwan was the one off balance. He staggered, trying to recover, hopping on one foot.

"Graceful," Zoran drawled, stepping back out of the way.

"It's deliberate."

"Su-u-u-re it is."

"Don't get it?" Si Cwan paused on one foot. "It's my imitation of the digbi-bird, you know . . ." He took two hopping steps forward, flapping his arms, mimicking that long-legged marsh bird, and Zoran snickered. "And then," Si Cwan finished sweetly, "when it finishes its stalk, it strikes, like *this!*"

His stiffened arm stabbed out, hitting Zoran square on the chest. Si Cwan knew very well what such a blow could do, and deliberately pulled its force, hardly wanting to kill his friend. Even so, Zoran stumbled back with an indignant "Ow! Dammit, Si Cwan—"

"I didn't really hurt you . . . did I?"

He took a wary step forward—and Zoran pounced. Laughing, they began their wrestling anew.

"Is *this* how you waste your time?" a voice asked, cold and cruel as the edge of a blade.

Father again. So much for the lovely day.

Zoran was already sinking to one knee in wise reverence, head down. Si Cwan, of course, remained on his feet, as befitted the emperor's son, but once again lowered his head in proper prince-to-emperor respect.

Ah yes, Father. Like a war icon as always.

Just now, the man looked like a tall, muscular statue of red stone, no longer in hunting gear but draped in the glittering regal robes of green and gold. Si Cwan began, "We were—"

"I know what you were doing. *Playing!*"

"But—we were—"

"Be still! I gave you an order to practice your fighting skills. This play-sparring teaches nothing!"

Si Cwan saw the chill contempt in his father's dark eyes—twin flat stones—and bit back the rest of what he'd been going to say. There was no reasoning with the emperor when the man was in this mood. When he was convinced yet again, despite everything that Si Cwan had done and still did to disprove it, that his son and heir was—weak.

Curse it, Father, I am not weak! I don't know what else to do to prove myself to you! I'm not about to turn regicide, no matter what you might think, or—no matter how much I love my sweet little baby sister—turn into a—a nursemaid for her!

The last time that the emperor had gotten the idea into his head that his son was weak . . . Si Cwan grit his teeth, remembering what he didn't really want to remember. That last time had meant a trip to—*well, be honest, Si Cwan told himself, call it what it really is, not the Place of Gentle Correction but the royal torture chamber.*

Difficult to forget that dark underground realm, richly hung with velvet draperies and elegantly carved with images of avenging spirits. A somber, beautiful, hideous place. As if what happened there was theater, not torture—or maybe, considering what he'd already seen of this court, the two weren't so far apart at that.

There, Si Cwan had reluctantly watched political prisoners questioned. There, he had been forced by his father to wield the implements, knowing all the while it was as good as his life to resist. . . . He'd gotten through the ordeal only by shutting down his mind completely and refusing to accept what he was doing—no, what he was being made to do. Even so, he'd dreamed of the experience for nights on end—the worst of it being that in a royal court, even his nightmares were spied upon, discussed and reported to his father. He kept seeing the victim's eyes staring up at him, in them not so much anguish as the simple question *Why?*

Why, indeed?

And now—bah! Never mind what had happened then. Here and now, it was bad enough that his father was in one of his "Si Cwan is a weakling" moods. It was worse that a gaggle of courtiers was standing at the usual politic distance behind the emperor, watching every move of this parental drama with hungry eyes. They'd be gossiping about this encounter for days. Si Cwan felt his muscles tense at the sight of all those jewels and feathers. Overdressed idiots, all of them eager for the sight of someone in trouble. As long, of course, as that "someone" had nothing to do with them. Hungry, the lot of them, to see pain. And maybe even death.

Not. Mine.

"Rather than have you waste your time in childish games," the emperor continued, "you shall train properly!"

"As my father wills it," Si Cwan said, keeping his voice absolutely without expression.

His father signaled over his shoulder. Imperial guards came forward—no, not just guards. They were dragging a man with them. At first Si Cwan thought that this must be another of the guards, someone who had slipped up somehow and was going to pay for it by being humiliated in a fight with a boy.

A boy? Humiliated? Now I'm starting to think like Father.

But now that he could see the man clearly, Si Cwan knew that this bedraggled, bruised figure could never have been one of the guard. A prisoner taken out of the royal dungeon? His ragged tunic was of plain, rough weave, dingy gray against the reddish brown skin of a commoner. He was built like a warrior, though, muscular and sturdy, with badly healed scars crisscrossing his body.

Some of those scars, Si Cwan noticed, looked pretty fresh. The man hadn't exactly been in gentle hands recently.

"An Enemy of the State," the emperor said coldly.

Well, that explained the recent scars. Enemy of the State. There was a good catchall phrase. In his father's court, Si Cwan knew, that term could mean anything from "here is an out-and-out traitor" to "someone who spoke out too openly against the administration." Si Cwan waited warily, not sure where this was going. His father had already turned him into a torturer. Surely he wasn't now going to be expected to play executioner as well?

Instead, his father added, almost as though bored with the subject: "Fight him."

Looking at the muscular warrior, Si Cwan thought with a youth's certainty, *I can take him.*

But then his father gave an almost absent wave—and to Si Cwan's shock, he saw two of the guards stab their captive. Not fatally, he realized after that first horrified moment, no, that would have been too merciful. They'd wounded the prisoner enough to just weaken him. Give him a handicap.

Curse you, Father, you don't even think I'm good enough to face a warrior who isn't hurt! Where's the honor in that?

A part of Si Cwan's mind noted, *It's worse for the warrior.*

Well, yes. There was certainly a darker fate in store for the man. An Enemy of the State, whatever he'd done (or maybe not done), had definitely been condemned to a one-way trip to the Place of Gentle Correction.

With a stop en route, it seemed, for a little fight.

And oh, look, they'd been . . . kind enough to bring a second man, even more badly damaged, for Zoran to fight.

Suddenly it was all too much to bear. With a roar of pure fury at his father, at himself, at this entire stupid, cruel, pointless situation, Si Cwan flung himself into battle.

The warrior turned grimly to meet him. Wounded or not, the man was still a fine fighter. He caught Si Cwan and, in one smooth turn that made use of Si Cwan's own forward momentum, hurled him aside. Furious at having been caught like that, Si Cwan lunged up, head down, and sent the man crashing back into a wall. That forced a cry of pain from the man, and Si Cwan, to his great astonishment, felt a stab of guilt.

He's a traitor, you idiot, an Enemy of the State!

But the man's sides were slick with blood, and his eyes . . . dammit. His eyes were filled with the same empty questioning that had been in the torture victim's eyes.

Oh, don't do this to me.

But he couldn't help it. Even though he was doing this to show his father he was no weakling, Si Cwan knew that now he was going to be fighting out of pity. This "enemy," whatever his crime, wasn't a monster, just a man. An ordinary nobody who now had no future.

Si Cwan and he exchanged a quick, significant glance. Very subtly, Si Cwan nodded, and saw relief flood the man's face. And that hurt, too.

That's right. You won't face torture. Not if I can save you.

They grappled again, but this time Si Cwan let the man throw him into the watching guards. His face contorted with feigned fury, like someone too angry to think, Si Cwan grabbed the guard's dagger. Glad of his training, he stabbed up and across in a quick, fatal blow.

This time, the man's eyes were . . . grateful.

As the warrior crumpled, dead before he finished falling, Si Cwan, panting and trying not to shake, saw Zoran kill his own opponent—

No, this can't be!

What blazed in Zoran's eyes in that moment of killing wasn't pity or even triumph. It was cruel pleasure.

He's my friend, he wouldn't . . .

"This wastes my time." As though he'd utterly lost interest in the proceedings, the emperor turned to leave, robes swirling dramatically about him. He paused merely to add over his shoulder, "Clean up that garbage," and left. The gaggle of courtiers followed after him in a storm of whisperings.

Si Cwan stood in rigid silence as the guards removed the bodies and servants mopped up all traces of blood. He stood silent as the servants bowed and retreated, leaving the rooftop garden almost alarmingly just as it had been a short while ago. Pristine. Lovely. And over everything that clear blue sky, those bright red wari-birds soaring by and sweet breezes stirring the air, just as though two men had not just suddenly died.

"Zoran . . ."

His friend grinned. "Now that was more like it, eh? I mean, we don't often get a chance to really fight."

"They were wounded, Zoran."

"Well, yes, that was kind of insulting. As if we couldn't handle them otherwise."

"That's not what I mean. They had no chance of surviving, no matter what happened."

"What's your point? They were criminals."

"Yes, but . . ."

Zoran frowned. "Si Cwan? Hello? It wasn't as if they were highborn, after all."

Si Cwan said nothing. He wasn't even sure what he might have wanted to say. Of course the two dead men had been commoners, but . . . well . . . they'd still been living beings. That look the man he'd slain had given him, that undeniable gratitude—thanking him for killing him because the alternative facing him was worse . . .

"Enough fighting for now," Si Cwan finally got out, and left Zoran standing in utter confusion.

That night, Si Cwan lay awake, unable to sleep, his mind racing. He couldn't sleep, because every time he closed his eyes, he found himself replaying the events of the day . . . the man he'd killed and that stare so filled with relief.

A commoner. Remember that. Just a common criminal.

But there had been nothing in that grateful stare to separate commoner from noble.

And then there'd been the man Zoran had killed . . . had killed with such pleasure . . .

Dammit. They were common-born, we're not, and that's the way it is. The way it's always been. Even Kalinda's nursemaid—

The nursemaid whose name he didn't know. The woman took care of Kalinda, his lovely little sister, and he had never even bothered to ask her name.

Yes, but she was a commoner!

If she's good enough to take care of Kalinda, surely that means she has to have some worth.

This chain of thought led inexorably on. Surely that warrior he'd killed had had some worth, too . . . a commoner, but of worth . . . and maybe this meant . . . well, all commoners had some worth, surely. To themselves, any-how. Still, maybe he should . . . no, what could he do?

Look into how the commoners really were treated. See that justice was, well, just.

Si Cwan rolled over onto his side. It was far too much to consider in one night, particularly if he ever did mean to get some sleep.

Tomorrow, though, first thing in the morning, he was damned well going to ask that nursemaid her name!

Si Cwan woke with a start, blinking and yawning. Morning . . . sort of, anyhow. Gray light . . . sun wasn't up yet, was it? Had to be pretty early . . . ugh, yes, far earlier than he usually woke. And he really hadn't gotten enough sleep last night.

But like it or not, he was awake.

All right, you made yourself a promise. Now's a good time to keep it before any-one gets in your way.

Shivering in the dawn chill, Si Cwan hastily dressed and grabbed a bite to eat, waving away puzzled servants, then started down the maze of palace corridors. He'd get this over with before his father could catch him being . . . what? Sentimental? Subversive?

The sudden sound of shouting turned Si Cwan's walk into a dead run. Oh no, no, that uproar was coming from the nursery!

Kalinda!

A kidnapper—an assassin—

But what Si Cwan saw didn't look like either. A sturdy middle-aged courtier had caught a bedraggled, scrawny young girl in a plain gray tunic roughly by the arm, and she was fighting frantically to free herself, kicking and clawing.

"What is going on here?" Si Cwan shouted.

The startled noble whirled, dragging the struggling girl about with him, her bare feet swinging free of the floor. Not surprisingly, the noise had at-tracted the palace guards, too, who were rushing into the nursery, ringing them round. With the guards was—Zoran? What was *he* doing up at this hour? And what was he doing with the guards?

"I repeat," Si Cwan said. "What is going on here?"

The girl said nothing, head down.

"This *scum*," the noble began, giving his prisoner a shake, "this common little scum actually dared try to play with Princess Kalinda!"

"So what? No one got hurt. She's just a kid. Let her go."

"You can't mean to just—"

"I gave you an order!"

"Your pardon, Prince Si Cwan, but you are still a minor. I must take my orders from your royal father."

The girl took advantage of his momentary lack of attention to sink her teeth into the man's arm. He yelped and slapped her so hard she cried out in pain.

That was too much for Si Cwan. That, and the slap to his pride. He swung a fist up, connecting squarely with the man's chin. The noble stumbled back into the ring of guards.

Si Cwan caught the girl before she could try to run. "Don't be stupid," he said under his breath. "You can't get through all those guards."

"Could," she muttered sullenly. "Got in, di'n't I?"

"I usually look at who I'm talking to."

She looked defiantly up at that, a scared kid not wanting to admit she was scared. Her eyes were deeply shadowed and red, as though she'd been crying all night.

Her face . . . was eerily familiar.

Oh.

Oh damn.

The warrior he'd slain yesterday. This had to be his daughter.

I never thought that he might have a kid.

And she was, what, maybe ten at the most. Hardly dangerous. Brave, though, getting this far, or just plain desperate. With no father . . .

Well, her father should have thought about that before he let himself get into trouble.

Maybe so, but that didn't help the kid here and now. She would be in real trouble if this got out of hand. The thought of a kid being condemned to the Place of Gentle Correction—no!

Suddenly inspired, Si Cwan palmed one of his jeweled bracelets. The jewels weren't so big or valuable they'd be notable. They'd be easy to sell. He slyly slid it into the girl's hand and saw her eyes widen ever so slightly.

"Go on, get out of here," Si Cwan snapped, and gave the girl a rough shove. "No!" he snarled at the guards. "Let her go. And you are dismissed!"

They, at least, had the grace to pretend they were obeying his orders, and left. But Si Cwan caught Zoran watching him suspiciously.

And suddenly the cold truth hit, hit with the force of a blow. That moment of oddness when they'd been play-fighting, when Zoran's eyes had gone cold; the way Zoran had tried to pick out Si Cwan's feelings about commoners; yes, and now, turning up here and now when Zoran never got up before the sun and almost never visited the nursery:

Zoran was now spying for the emperor. Spying on his friend.

His former friend.

No matter, Si Cwan tried to convince himself, although a cold weight seemed to have settled in his stomach. *No matter. Someday, I will rule. And then the empire will become a finer, better place for everyone. I swear it.*

He turned to the nursemaid, who had dared steal out again from hiding, Kalinda in her arms, now that it was safe. Si Cwan smiled at her. One had to begin somewhere, after all.

He asked the nursemaid, "And your name is . . . ?"

SELAR
"Q"uandary

Terri Osborne

Prior to joining the crew of the *Excalibur* as chief medical officer, Dr. Selar served a distinguished tenure as assistant chief medical officer on the *U.S.S. Enterprise* for eight years. " 'Q'uandary" takes place during that tenure, primarily (but not entirely) simultaneous with the *Star Trek: The Next Generation* episode "Tapestry."

Terri Osborne

Terri Osborne always knew she wanted to write, and can't remember a time when she wasn't watching and scribbling story ideas about some form of filmed science fiction, including *Star Trek*. Almost thirty years after she wrote her first story, something was finally published: "Three Sides to Every Story" in the 2003 *Star Trek: Deep Space Nine: Prophecy and Change* anthology, which chronicled the lives and friendship of Jake Sisko and Tora Ziyal during the difficult months of the Dominion's occupation of Deep Space 9. Terri is reachable on the Internet at http://terriosborne.com, and is currently hard at work on her first full-length novel. She lives in New York City with Keith R.A. DeCandido and two of the silliest cats ever born, and as close to her beloved New York Yankees as she can possibly get. (Sorry, Bob.)

2364

"Biospectral analysis inconclusive."

Dr. Selar raised one dark eyebrow as the computer informed her of the results. She'd run every analysis she could think of on Admiral Mark Jameson's blood sample. The admiral was aging at an illogical pace, and nothing Dr. Crusher could find made sense. Finally, the task had been turned over to Selar's Vulcan sensibilities.

She thought she'd isolated the compound that was responsible hours ago, but breaking it down even further was proving to be one of the more interesting challenges that the Vulcan had encountered since leaving Starfleet Medical.

A white flash appeared in the corner of the lab, preceding the arrival of a humanoid cowering from something. The being was wearing what looked to be a Starfleet uniform, though a black jumpsuit with the division color across the shoulders over a gray turtleneck was a design of uniform that Selar had never seen before, even at the Academy.

Still, only one creature in the known universe made such an arrival.

"Q," Selar said.

Q pulled its hands away from its face, apparently protecting itself from something. Selar wasn't sure she wanted to know what an omnipotent being would need to shield itself from.

Raising itself back up to its full height, Q looked around sickbay. "I missed again. Your centuries go by so quickly." In a flash, the uniform became a standard-issue, command-track, Starfleet red.

Selar briefly thought the other design looked far more comfortable.

Before Q could say another word, the floor beneath Selar's feet shook.

"Computer," Selar said, grabbing the table for balance, "what is happening?"

"The Enterprise *has collided with the shock wave from a supernova."*

"A supernova? Computer, how long have we been observing this event?"

The ship slowly stopped shaking. *"The* Enterprise *was not observing the phenomenon at the time of explosion."*

"This must have something to do with you," she said, eyeing the strange being that had begun wandering around her sickbay.

"You're Vulcan, aren't you?"

"I fail to see how that is relevant to—"

Q smiled. "We'll meet again, Vulcan."

With a snap of its fingers, Q vanished.

Selar's lips pursed. The *Enterprise* had encountered the Q on only two occasions since departing Farpoint Station, but Selar had never met the being before that moment.

This was why the fact that there was something strangely familiar about the form this Q had taken nagged at her like a strand of hair brushing across the tip of her nose.

"Computer, access the pre-Federation Vulcan database. Is there any mention of someone resembling the entity that was just in sickbay?"

If the reports hadn't mentioned the immortality of the Q, she might not have thought it logical to look so far back in Vulcan history. However, she had what Dr. Crusher might have called a hunch.

"Match found."

She called up the picture. It was an image of one of the first Vulcans to work closely with the Terrans, T'Pol, speaking with two Andorians and a human woman in an old Earth Starfleet uniform during the peace negotiations with the Andorians on Paan Mokar. According to the record, the Andorians pictured were named Tarah and Shran, while the Terran was simply listed as a diplomat assisting Captain Jonathan Archer.

Unnamed or not, Selar would have known those high cheekbones, that long fiery red hair, and that haughty expression anywhere. The "Terran diplomat" was, in reality, a Q.

2367

Selar adjusted a setting on the medical tricorder and ran the scan once again. The bruise on Lieutenant Worf's right anterior cranial ridge was proving to be more severe than she'd initially suspected.

Worf merely growled.

"Do not move, please," Selar said. The results were precisely what she'd thought: The contusion had reached the bone. "Nurse Ogawa, please set the dermal regenerator for a bone contusion."

The tool appeared just under Selar's left arm, but when she reached down to grab it, she noticed something amiss. The fingers that were wrapped around the dermal regenerator did not have Alyssa Ogawa's skin pigmentation.

"Nurse Ogawa?"

"Not quite, dear."

Selar raised an eyebrow, slowly turning away from her patient. At least Q had picked the right uniform this time. "You again."

Q smiled, and Selar briefly thought that any human would probably have found it an unsettling sight.

The Vulcan, however, found it fascinating. Selar had read reports on the various encounters with members of the Q Continuum over the years, and found the paper recently filed by Dr. Julian Bashir of Deep Space 9 of particular interest.

In a microsecond, Selar was transported from ward three and her patient into the middle of a scarred ruin of a landscape. The unmistakable whine of disruptor fire sounded in the distance. Mottled red stone surrounded her, laden with craters she could only presume were from munitions fire. The moonlit night air was thick with smoke and an acrid dust from the cross-fire. Squinting to protect her eyes, she quickly pulled her uniform collar up over her mouth as best she could. It felt as though a mountain had been ground into fine particles and suspended in midair with no hope of dissipation.

Selar considered removing her uniform jacket. Even by Vulcan standards this was a hot planet. She briefly thought that only a reptilian species might have been able to handle the heat on a regular basis. That was when she realized where Q had placed her. "The Vulcan-Romulan War."

"Yes," Q said, leaning against one of the standing black stones as if nothing were amiss. "It's something I thought your less-evolved brain might be able to understand." Walking slowly toward Selar, Q continued, "The Continuum is in the middle of a civil war. We need your help."

Selar raised her left eyebrow. "You require my assistance?"

"That's what I said." Q had barely finished the statement before she began coughing. When it was over, she placed a hand over her mouth in an impractical attempt at a breathing mask.

"Intriguing," Selar said, feeling the grit beginning to work at her own trachea. She could not recall ever tasting anything so metallic in her life. "I thought your species was omnipotent."

Q's hand left her mouth. "We're omnipotent, not omniscient," she said, taking the tone Selar had often heard humans use toward a misbehaving youth. "There are things going on in the Continuum that we've never dealt with before, and we've been around for *billions* of years. We've seen other, lesser beings fight among themselves, but the thought that *we* could stoop to such a level never occurred to us. Our powers aren't working consistently, and that's just the beginning."

Another explosion shook the ground around them, and both Selar and Q reached for the nearest stone outcrop.

"It's getting worse," Q said, her arrogance slipping. "Q are dying."

That piqued Selar's interest. "According to our reports, Q are immortal."

"Apparently not," Q stated snippily. "We're being injured and actually facing death for the first time any of us can remember."

"I understand," Selar said.

"No. No, you don't." Q's lips twisted as she looked around the area. All of the capriciousness that Selar had come to expect from members of the Continuum was gone. She even thought she sensed a flicker of fear. Q stared into the slowly dissipating dust clouds and said, "Nothing is worse than the weapons that an omnipotent race can devise when they want to hurt each other."

The scream of a rocket-propelled disruptor grenade sounded nearby, and it was getting closer. Both women ducked, the grenade narrowly missing them before it impacted with a boulder no more than ten feet from where they stood. Selar managed to shield herself from the flying shrapnel in time, but when the debris stopped raining down, she saw that Q had not been so lucky. The woman was covered in bits of pulverized stone, and being racked by another coughing fit. Selar didn't venture checking on her any more closely until it appeared that no more grenades were heading toward them. By then, Q's coughing had subsided to an occasional hacking.

"Stay down. I need to examine your wounds." Blood trickled down Q's nose from a laceration near the center of her forehead. Upon further examination, it appeared that a thin piece of stone had become embedded just over Q's right eye. Selar tried to think of a possible dressing for the wound from the meager bits of plant life that were tucked here and there across the stone field, but nothing appeared useful. That was when a warm breeze found her arm. She tracked it to a hole in her sleeve. Sticking two fingers inside the wound in the fabric, Selar used them to tear a piece off. It wasn't perfect, but it would do until they found a hospital. Folding the fabric into a compress, she placed it on Q's injury.

"Hold this to your forehead and press as solidly as you can. It will help stop the bleeding. Does this location have medical facilities?"

Q tried to shake her head, but it appeared to make her unsteady. "None that do us any good," she said. "That's why I came to you. We've got all of the power we could ever want, but no idea of how to use it to heal ourselves. Your ship has assisted the Q in the past, so I thought you might be willing to do so again."

Selar managed to stand. She looked around the area for signs of an encampment of any sort in the vicinity. "Why did you not approach Dr. Crusher? She has a background in medical instruction—"

"And is human," Q said, derision in her slowly deteriorating voice. "The others could never accept someone from such an intellectually challenged species as an instructor. A Vulcan is far less deficient. You might even be able to figure out a way to stop this nonsense that we haven't already thought of."

Selar checked to make sure Q was applying appropriate pressure to her forehead before wrapping an arm around her midsection to help her stand. Slowly, they made their way out of the stone field. Explosion after explosion sounded in the distance, growing more frequent by the footstep.

The war was beginning to escalate.

When Q asked for a rest, Selar stopped and assisted her patient to gingerly sit on a small boulder near their path. The air was growing less polluted the farther they walked, a fact that appeared to be helping Q recover herself.

"Why do you believe that I might be of assistance with diplomacy?" Selar asked.

After a few deep breaths, Q said, "I thought you might have picked up something from Picard. He's Q's favorite pet. You might have a better insight into what Q's planning than we do."

Selar thought she heard a touch of bitterness in Q's voice at the mention of another Q. "This other Q you speak of, is it your mate?"

"Supposedly," Q said.

"And your mate is fighting for the opposition in this battle?"

Q was silent for a long moment, long enough for Selar to determine that her hypothesis had a high probability of being correct. She briefly wondered what she would do if she ever found herself on the opposite side of a battle from Voltak, her own mate. As they were both Vulcan, and mated from youth, logic indicated that their approach to the problem would at the very least be similar. Diplomacy would not be necessary between them, as they would logically be on the same side of the conflict.

"I am a physician, not a diplomat. Why do you believe that I would have a solution to a dispute between you and your mate?"

The briefest trace of a smile turned the edge of Q's lip. "Q is leading the revolution, and he's absolutely fascinated by humans. So, I've been studying how humans have approached diplomacy though their history, even talked to a few over the years. There was this one woman, half-Klingon, certainly had a lot of spunk." Q slowly shook her head. "You've been around humans longer than Q. You can give us an idea of how they think, what Q might do with their advice, and then we use it to win. Help us, and when this war is over I can return you to that little ship of yours at the exact moment you left."

Her left eyebrow raised, Selar said, "You have an—unusual—interpretation of diplomacy."

"Yes, well," Q said, her arrogance returning, "we've never really needed it before. I'm sure you Vulcans have never done anything illogical, either."

Selar let the jab slide, but couldn't deny her point. She briefly attempted to envision the Q that enjoyed toying with the *Enterprise* trying to negotiate peace, and failed to get even a mental flicker. For a race that had existed for billions upon billions of years, the Q seemed as ill equipped to generate a diplomatic solution to a conflict as the Vulcans and Romulans had been during the century-long battle between their races. "Perhaps a new perspective will assist you in ending this conflict."

Q appeared lost in thought for a moment. "That's quite logical, since a 'new perspective' started this—wait a minute. I wonder if this has something to do with that Janeway woman. She *did* allow Quinn to commit suicide."

Selar raised an eyebrow. Janeway? Surely she couldn't be talking about Commander Kathryn Janeway of the *Billings?* As far as Selar knew, that ship had no recorded contact with members of the Q Continuum.

"So?" Q asked as she used her free hand to delicately push herself off of the boulder she'd been using as a chair. "How about it? There are other things I need to check on."

Selar slipped an arm back around Q's midsection as they continued to walk onward. "I do admit that the idea of teaching medicine to an omnipotent race is quite intriguing. However, my skills are also required on board the *Enterprise.* How long would you require my services?"

"It's not easy for me to say this, but I don't know," Q replied. "It depends on how long the war takes. Things are different in the Continuum. Time doesn't work the way you're used to it working, to begin with. I suppose we could give you powers equal to our own for—"

The roar of another explosion in the vicinity drowned the remainder of Q's statement out. Selar ducked. The grenade had come down only a dozen meters to their left, but somehow hadn't kicked up enough debris to do them serious damage. Pressing forward, Q stumbled, losing her grip on the makeshift compress when she tried to reach for a stone to regain her balance. Selar reached down and recovered the fabric from the ground, brushing as much of the dirt and dust from it as she could. The compress wasn't as damp with blood as Selar expected. "You are not pressing this to the wound solidly enough. We should find a way to bind it to—"

When Selar looked up, she found Q staring at her, a vague hint of pleading in her eyes. "It's not easy for my people to ask for help, Selar, but we need it."

Selar surveyed the battleground that surrounded them. "I believe you," she said. "And I offer my assistance."

Q heaved a sigh of relief. "Good."

In the blink of an eye, Selar went from the dark menace of the battlefield to a brightly lit chamber. When her eyes adjusted to the change, Selar realized that it was some kind of field infirmary. Three figures draped in white moved between tables, tending to patients with a surprising efficiency, considering they were equipped with the kind of instruments Selar only knew of from history texts. Laser scalpels, old-fashioned hyposprays, even a few pre-Federation medical scanners were neatly arranged on tables through the facility.

Selar slowly began walking between the prone patients, mentally assessing each wound as she went. A broken leg here, a disruptor burn there, it all seemed to be logical battlefield injuries that any capable physician should have been able to handle.

Until one of the injured men began screaming.

Two of the healers rushed to the man, whose cries became interspersed with violent convulsions. They began quickly trying to do their work. When Selar reached the exam table, she noted with some disconcertion that the victim had a severe disruptor wound to the area around his cervical vertebrae and another in his lower anterior spinal region. Whatever Romulan had shot this man had wanted him to suffer before he died.

Selar began to feel something she hadn't known in decades build in her stomach as she watched the two healers work: anxiety. Her discipline had always been more than enough to suppress such rudimentary emotions, so the ease with which they came to her now was surprising. The healers were doing so much that was right, covering his legs with a blanket, giving fluids intravenously, attempting to minimize the damage to the spinal region, but something told her it wasn't going to be enough.

If she only had a surgical support.

She fought the nervousness into its proper place and tried to figure out a treatment using what little she had to work with. Laser scalpels were useless. Medical scanners wouldn't tell her anything she didn't already know.

"Do you have any kelotane?" she asked anyone who would listen. When there was no reply, she began riffling through the medical cabinet that stood against one wall. The only useful substance she could find was a vial of asinolyathin. Admittedly, using such a muscle relaxant was an inelegant solution, but it would at the very least ease the patient's pain while the healers worked.

Once the asinolyathin had been administered, she began to take over care of the patient. She had seen third-degree burns such as this only a few times in her life, but it was enough to know that they were never the same twice. She did everything she could, thought of every possible treatment, but after a few frantic minutes, the antiquated monitors ceased to pick up life signs.

Selar fought to resuscitate the young man, but it was for naught. Finally, she stopped. There was no bringing this patient back. A sharp anger started to fill her, and once again she suppressed it. She took a step away from the exam table.

Across the walkway, the third of the white-robed figures was tending to a seated patient's wounded head. When the healer finally backed away, Selar could see that it was the female Q. Her forehead wound was completely healed, but she was clad in the ancient black leathers and woven silver of a field officer. Q's facial features had also been slightly altered to fit the environment. Instead of curving around her ocular cavity as a human's would, Q's red eyebrows rose as they grew away from the center of her cranial ridge in a typically Vulcan manner.

"What do you think?" she said, turning so that Selar could see her profile. "I'm not sure the eyebrows are quite me." Q tucked a few strands of titian hair behind an ear that now came to a very Vulcan point. "Do the ears work?"

"That man might have been saved," Selar said, ignoring Q's vanity. "Your healers—"

"Need your help," Q finished, hopping off the table. "This is no different from that battlefield, Selar. It's a way for us to show you this so you'll understand it. We're dying. There's no easy way to say it." Q held out her hand, and on her flattened palm appeared a folded item of heavy white linen. "Your robes, Doctor," she said. Q's tone had all of the solemnity of the commandant handing out diplomas at Starfleet Academy—but none of the sincerity.

Selar reached for the proffered garment. "Do you not have more advanced equipment? A medical tricorder, perhaps?"

The words had barely left Selar's mouth before one appeared on top of the folded robes.

"Ah, good. Looks like you're starting to learn how to use your abilities," Q said.

She was? Selar arched one eyebrow. She did feel . . . unusual. Something was tempting her to let go of her mental discipline, to allow her emotions to come to the fore. Was this what true omnipotence felt like?

Fascinating.

But she was Vulcan. She would not lose her so carefully maintained control.

She took the tricorder and the robe. Within seconds she was wearing her new uniform and had her tricorder set, making her comfortably armed for any medical battle that might walk through the door.

"Dr. Selar?"

The source of the voice lowered the hood of her robe, and Selar looked down into gentle dark eyes and a cherubic face that was rimmed in blond hair. Like Q, she also appeared Vulcan, but Selar knew that under the façade was a Q who had been raised among humans. "Amanda Rogers."

"What are you doing in the Continuum?"

Selar briefly entertained the idea of saying that she had come to check up on Amanda, but dismissed it as too undisciplined. "One of your people requested my assistance."

"Yes, dear," Q said, stepping around Amanda to put a hand on Selar's shoulder. "She's going to teach you what you need to know about medicine."

"I thought your primary area of expertise was eco-regeneration?" Selar asked, remembering what she could of the young woman. Dr. Crusher had taken her under her wing when Amanda had first arrived on the *Enterprise*, but Selar had rarely seen the girl thanks to the necessities of the mission to Tagra IV.

Amanda smiled sweetly. "I did some work in neurobiology before Q brought me here."

"A logical choice for a healer. You are one of those that I have come to train."

"The Vulcan capacity for stating the obvious never ceases to amaze me," Q said, smirking. "You'll be teaching all three of them advanced field medicine."

Q called the other healers over. "Dr. Selar, this is Q, and Q."

Selar resisted the sudden urge to shake her head. At least Amanda had kept her name. The dichotomy of reasoning that would lead a race to all name themselves the same thing was vast, indeed.

The first Q lowered its hood, revealing an older female with a kind, maternal face; straight, sandy blond hair down to her chin; and brilliant blue eyes the color of Selar's Starfleet uniform. Holding out her hand in the traditional Vulcan greeting, she said, "Peace and long life." The woman's voice was gentle and melodious, but belied an age far greater than her physical appearance. "Amanda said that lesser species such as yours prefer to give themselves individual names so that others may refer to them without confusion. You may call me Monica."

Ignoring the insult, Selar held her palm out in kind. "Live long and prosper, Monica."

"And you may refer to me as Tenley," the second Q—an older male— said. "We have heard much about you." Tenley's voice was rough, but not overly so, and Selar noted that this Q had done something she had seen in no other: he had appeared with graying black hair. For a race as notoriously vain as the Q, this was unexpected. Still, he appeared no less friendly than Monica.

"You have?" Selar asked. "I was not aware."

"Amanda has told us much about you," Monica said. "She says that you are respected and trusted."

"Yes," Tenley said. "I'm not sure any of our people would have leapt to that Q's aid as quickly as you did. We believe that we can simply visualize whatever we desire, and it will happen. We tend to forget, though, that we have to learn precisely what we desire, first."

"It's like that warp-core explosion that Q set up on the *Enterprise*," Amanda softly interjected. "If I hadn't learned some plasma dynamics, I might not have known how to stop it properly."

Selar gave a short nod. "I will teach you. Should we not begin?"

Her three students exchanged glances.

Amanda finally answered. "Sounds good."

"Wonderful," Q said. "I'll leave you to it. I still need to go find Q. Maybe I'll talk to that Janeway woman while I'm at it. She may have more to do with this than I thought."

In a flash of white light, Q was gone.

Pulling out her tricorder and looking at all of the triage patients, Selar tried to think of the best place to start.

They surrounded the bed of the first patient, a young male whose left femur was distorted by a compound fracture. The fear rolling off of him was almost palpable. "Peace and long life," she said, hoping to settle the boy's mind. "I am Selar."

The Q nodded, his close-cropped hair looking somehow incongruous with the Vulcan features. "Q," he said. "I am Q."

She aimed her tricorder at the injured leg, and got to work.

Selar spent the next few hours—or was it days?—showing her surprisingly eager students how to treat every injury that came through the ward.

As she sat in the drab gray mess hall afterward staring at her *plomeek* soup and spice tea, Selar considered her students' performances. Amanda had proven to be the quickest study, as Selar had expected from everything Beverly Crusher had said. The young Q was picking up ways to handle even the most disabling of trauma, from disruptor burns to grenade-induced amputations and beyond. If she had chosen to remain among humans, Selar couldn't help but wonder how much Amanda's abilities would have benefited the Federation.

Monica and Tenley, however, had required more help than Selar had initially suspected. They were more than adequate healers, but Selar had found it necessary to take over on each of their more seriously injured patients. No matter how often she showed them more subtle techniques, they never seemed to pick them up. Monica had also proven to have an excellent bedside manner, but Tenley made up for that in his lack of communication skills with the patient.

Selar concentrated, and tried to visualize a simple padd. It took a few seconds of focus, but the device slowly coalesced on the table. It looked just like the padds she'd used on the *Enterprise*. Somewhat pleased with herself, Selar slipped the stylus out of its cradle and tapped on the screen.

Nothing happened.

She tapped again—nothing.

How could she have conjured a working medical tricorder, but not a padd? Perhaps this had something to do with Tenley's statement that the Q needed to learn what they desired, first? Selar realized that she had never actually handled a padd beyond making use of it. Dismissing the nonfunctioning padd with a thought, Selar conjured an old-fashioned notepad and pen and began jotting down notes.

"You're that doctor that Q brought in, aren't you?"

Selar looked up from her work to see a middle-aged human male with blond hair that was longer than the modern convention. He was dressed in a simple gray tunic and pants, and his friendly expression reminded Selar of Monica and Tenley if they were a little more patronizing. None of Selar's prior information on the Q suggested they were all so mollifying and cordial around those they deemed lesser beings. Certainly the Q that had tormented the *Enterprise* over the years wasn't such an entity. Selar made a quick note to amend the file when she returned to her universe.

"Yes," Selar replied. "How may I assist you?"

Q appeared surprised by her question. "Oh, I just wanted to see if it was really you. How are you adjusting to life in the Continuum?" He gestured toward her pen and paper. "I see you've brought a few things from your universe here."

"Yes," Selar said. "Not as much as I would like, but—"

"Dr. Selar!"

She turned to find Monica standing in the mess hall doorway, panic in her eyes. "Yes, Monica?"

"You're needed in the infirmary!"

Selar quickly retrieved her notepad and pen, shoving her medical tricorder into one of the pockets of her robes. She sprinted out of the mess hall and across the small compound to the infirmary.

Selar heard the yelling long before she reached the operating chamber. Amanda and Tenley were both working on a patient who had been seriously injured, if the amount of blood staining their robes was any indication.

Selar stopped in her tracks when she realized the blood was red.

First the Q that appeared human; now there was a patient with red blood in the middle of a Vulcan-Romulan conflict. What was happening? Historically, there hadn't been any red-blooded species involved in the civil war, so why were they showing up now?

Another wail of pain pulled her back to the situation at hand. On the exam table was a human male, she couldn't tell precisely how old, missing his leg below the left knee.

"Make sure there is pressure on the wound," Selar said, taking charge of the situation. "Did anyone find the rest of his leg?"

Two soldiers stood off in the corner, both covered in blood. They were staring absently ahead as though they were in their own little worlds.

"Did you find the rest of his leg?" she asked again, a little more sharply than she'd have liked. She quickly centered herself, forcing her emotions back into check.

When control didn't come immediately, Selar reined herself in as best she could. A man's life was in jeopardy. There would be time for proper meditation later.

The two soldiers looked at each other, then down at the darkening morass of blood on their uniforms. They both shook their heads.

Selar inspected what Amanda and Tenley had done so far. The remainder of the leg was properly elevated, and Amanda had her gloved hands pressed firmly to the compress over the wound. Selar conjured a blanket, spreading it over the man's torso as soon as it materialized. Grabbing her tricorder from her pocket, she checked her patient over for any other injuries.

When she was confident that the only injury she was dealing with was the amputation, she went to work, allowing her students only to watch and act as nurses whenever she needed a second set of hands. She didn't need them to hand her instruments, as Selar found it easier to just conjure the tools she needed when they were necessary and place them aside when she was through.

What seemed like an interminable amount of time later, Selar finished sealing the last of the arteries in the severed leg with a laser cauterization unit. It was a crude solution to the problem, but it was the best she could manage at the time.

She thought about trying to conjure a biobed, but it took too much energy for her to bring forth a simple tool like the cauterizer. Selar didn't want to think about what something as complicated as a biobed might do. Having the method to treat the patient was useless if the doctor was dead.

As the young man was taken away to recover, Selar collected the tools that she had conjured onto a medical tray for Monica to remove.

"You're settling in quickly," Amanda said, gathering some of the soiled linens. "I almost wish I'd had it so easy when my powers developed."

Selar considered the idea. Perhaps there was something to Q's belief that Vulcans weren't quite "lesser beings" after all. It was eminently logical, considering the Vulcan mastery of emotion and the intellect. Naturally, the Q would turn to a Vulcan for assistance, just as a Vulcan would quickly adapt to the powers of the Q. "Perhaps," she finally replied. "However, you have also adjusted to your new life well. It has only been a few months."

Amanda gave a soft chuckle. "A few months? Doctor, I've been here for a few years. Time works differently in the Continuum."

"Q mentioned that," Selar said. "That was part of the reason that she gave me abilities equal to your own."

A soft, understanding smile lit Amanda's features. "Otherwise, you'd probably go insane if you were here for very long. I'm told it's happened before whenever one of our kind has brought one of the younger races into the Continuum. It's the multiple dimensions and temporal physics. If you're not born to it . . ." Amanda's voice drifted off. She quickly seemed to shake herself out of whatever train of thought she'd taken. "Have you thought about what you're going to do when the war is over?"

Selar arranged her cleaned instruments meticulously on the stand. "Q has promised me that when you no longer require my assistance, I will be returned to the *Enterprise* at the moment I was removed."

"That's Q," Amanda said amiably. Dropping the linens into a nearby bin, she added, "She likes to keep things interesting."

"That is true. When she first brought me to the Continuum, we ended up on Tyrus III." At Amanda's confused expression, Selar continued, "It was a planet dominated by a Saurian species, until they were the unfortunate beneficiaries of our conflict with the Romulans. The indigenous races of Tyrus III have been extinct since before the Federation was born."

A hand fell on Selar's arm. Turning, she found Monica looking up at her with concern in her blue eyes. "That is what I fear might happen to your universe if our civil war does not end soon. Some aspects of our battle can be felt in your universe, and not even a fully-empowered Q can stop their effects once unleashed."

The memory of Q's first appearance in sickbay flashed in Selar's mind. "When Q first came to me, the *Enterprise* was shaken by a supernova shortly after she appeared."

Monica nodded. "That would be one of our higher-yield explosives."

"And the only way to stop the supernovae is to stop the explosions?"

"Yes."

Selar began considering everything she'd ever done that might prove beneficial to the situation. Certainly, Captain Picard would have been a better choice for a diplomatic resolution to the problem, but—as Q had made abundantly clear—Selar's primary objective had been to help them learn medicine. If she could be half as successful with diplomacy in the Continuum as she had been with medicine, there was hope for them all. Selar almost smiled at the notion that she could return to the *Enterprise* as the entity that single-handedly saved the Q Continuum. There was something almost poetic about it.

"What was the inciting event for the war?" Selar asked.

Amanda leaned against one of the empty exam tables. "The way I heard it, one of us found a way to commit suicide. Quinn got bored and wanted out. After he died, others wanted the freedom to make that same choice, even though it violated some of the ideas we had on space and time—as if physics worked any differently from time here. Some of the others liked things just the way they were, and tried to stop it from changing. Tempers rose, and here we are."

Selar couldn't help but think that her initial idea of a different perspective might have been the exact solution all along.

"Where do you think Q has gone?" Monica asked, glancing at Amanda.

The young girl shrugged. "Knowing Q, she went off trying to find that Q of hers." Amanda smiled. "And knowing *him,* he's off causing trouble someplace."

"You don't think he went to Janeway, do you?" Monica asked. Selar could hear shock in the older Q's voice.

"Maybe," Amanda said with a shrug. Pushing herself away from the exam table, she added, "Come on, let's go get some dinner."

When they reached the open area of the compound, Selar's Vulcan hearing picked up something—or, more appropriately, the absence of something. "The shooting has stopped."

The three women exchanged expectant looks.

Selar scanned the darkness that surrounded the small field hospital, an instinct she hadn't realized she had telling her that there was a problem out there waiting to happen. A flicker of trepidation worked its way up her spine. It was a feeling that she was surprised to discover she liked.

This time, however, she didn't try to suppress the emotion. She allowed it to roll around in her brain for a while, considering all of its nuances and facets. The more she examined it, the more appealing it became.

And the less it threatened to take over her mind, as emotion often did with humans.

For the first time that she could recall, Selar allowed herself to smile.

"Okay, that's a little too weird," Amanda said, the index finger of her left hand extended toward Selar. "They always told me that Vulcans don't smile. What's going on?"

Taking a deep breath, Selar reluctantly forced the lid back down on her emotions. "I believe that using the powers your kind possess I may have discovered a path toward finding balance between emotion and logic. My people are so accustomed to suppressing all emotion and allowing logic to rule that they've denied themselves something as elegantly simple as experiencing fear. We've denied ourselves instinctual emotions that could possibly save our lives. This place—"

Monica gave a soft chuckle. "I believe she is beginning to think like a Q, Amanda."

"Hello, dears. Miss me?"

Selar turned toward the voice, and found Q standing a few steps away. Her hair was pulled up into what appeared to be human pin curls, and she was clad in a full-length mauve floral dress with tapered, wrist-length sleeves and many, many gathers. The enormous hoop skirt looked like an overturned bowl, and the entire dress appeared to be edged in thin white lace. If Selar had her human history correct—something she did not doubt—it looked like something from the era of the United States Civil War. "Where have you been?"

Q turned to her side, revealing the bulge under her dress. "Q and I have been a little busy," she said, backing her jovial tone with a broad smile. Selar couldn't help but note that Q's entire demeanor seemed brighter than it had before.

"Oh my!" Amanda walked over and placed a hand on Q's abdomen. "You're pregnant!"

Q gave her a sideways look. "Been talking to the Vulcan too much, dear?"

"No," Amanda replied, backing it with a short-lived glare. Her smile quickly returned. "I wish we all had names. I've always loved the name Grace. Or maybe Tynan if it's a boy."

"My goodness." Monica dazedly stepped toward Q, shaking her head. "There has not been a baby born in the Continuum in billions of years."

Q patted her stomach. "Well, there will be. . . ." Her voice trailed off as her eyes widened. With a look of abject terror, she looked down at her feet and said in a very small voice, "Soon."

Selar had a bad feeling about the situation. *"No* children have been born in the Continuum? That means nobody here knows—"

"How Q bring children into the world," Monica finished.

All eyes fell on Amanda, but the young girl shook her head. "Don't look at me. My parents had me on Earth."

Selar pulled her emotions back into check. "I'm versed in the reproductive methods of the thirteen species in regular residence on board the *Enterprise,* as well as over one hundred other Federation member species. This cannot possibly be any more difficult than if the child were Andorian."

The cry Q let out at that moment suggested that it might.

"Q," Selar said, "I need you to listen to me. I want you to begin breathing like this. It will assist you in not hyperventilating." She began regulating her breathing in a paced manner. "Do not focus on the pain. Do you understand?"

"*You* try not focusing on the pain, Vulcan!" Q said, her voice a snarl.

"Monica, please assist me in getting Q to the infirmary," Selar said. "Amanda, we're going to need sterile linens. Have one of the technicians tilt a bed so it is at a thirty-degree angle to the floor. We'll use that for Q."

The young girl nodded before sprinting ahead.

Selar and Monica both tried to help Q remain upright as they headed toward their makeshift delivery room, but the hoops in Q's skirt were getting in the way. At that point, Selar decided to try something. She quickly visualized a long, flowing hospital gown like the ones she had sometimes seen used at Starfleet Medical. When the image was fixed in her mind, she attempted to use her new abilities to change Q's attire.

In a flash of white, Selar's attempt worked.

Another cry of pain from Q suggested that the impending mother was too busy to notice.

"Your contractions are getting closer together," Selar said as they reached the infirmary doors. "It's almost time."

Q's voice had a tone that suggested that she not only couldn't tolerate the fact that giving birth was such a painful experience, but also hated that the pain was happening to *her*. "Time for *what?*"

"This child to be born," Monica said, attempting to soothe Q.

"Yes," Selar added, "no matter the species, childbirth is not without discomfort." When Q was settled in on the jury-rigged table, Selar turned to Monica. "See if there is any anesthezine gas in the compound. If not, we'll use the asinolyathin."

Monica immediately went to the medicine cabinets and began searching.

Selar pulled out her medical tricorder and aimed the sensors at her patient. One eyebrow raised when all of the readings came back precisely where she would have expected them to be had Q been human.

That made things much easier.

"What is it?" Q asked between attempts to pace her breathing.

Selar allowed herself to relax, but not too much. "My tricorder is registering a normal *human* delivery."

Q clenched her jaw and groaned.

"Another contraction?"

Q nodded.

The infirmary doors swung open, allowing Amanda to come back with a bundle of linens, and a companion. "Did someone lose a Q?"

"Q! My darling!" the male Q wailed melodramatically as he went to the female Q's side.

Flecks of gray in his black hair made him look older than the pictures in Starfleet's files. Perhaps the war had done more damage to the Continuum than anyone had initially suspected.

The note of mischief that had been in his eyes in every recorded image remained, however. Selar closed her eyes and took several calming breaths. The female Q had proven to be enough of a handful, but Q himself on top of the current situation might be catastrophic.

He delicately wrapped a hand around the female Q's. "Is it time? I can't wait to show this little one his powers."

Selar caught the impishness in the male Q's grin and made a mental note to warn Captain Picard of the impending chaos when she was sent back to her ship. "Yes, Q, it's time," she finally said. "Please allow us to deliver this child in peace."

The male Q gave her a look that questioned her sanity. "What do you think the shooting stopped for? This child will bring peace."

Selar wanted to say that she had a difficult time believing that, but managed to restrain herself. Instead, she loaded a hypospray with asinolyathin and handed it to Amanda. "If he gets out of hand, give him ten cc's of this."

The male Q looked about to feign indignation when the female Q screamed in pain. A scream that was distinctly lower in resonance followed shortly after as the female Q squeezed the male Q's hand. Judging by the level of the scream, Selar wondered if she should not have Amanda check the male Q's hand for broken bones.

Instead, Selar turned back to the medicine chest to load up another hypospray for the female Q. Before she could turn around, she heard a baby crying.

Selar slowly followed the crying back to its mother. The female Q appeared exhausted, but was blearily smiling. Amanda was cleaning off the baby, and wrapped it up in clean linens before handing it to its mother. "Congratulations," the young girl said, "it's a q."

By human standards, the child was adorable. A shock of straw-blond hair stuck up in several directions atop his head, and his cherubic face looked out upon the world with large, dark eyes. Selar felt another smile begin to creep onto her features at the sight.

Grabbing her tricorder, Selar tried to balance her emotional outburst with the mental exercise of examining the newborn. "All readings are normal," she said after a few seconds. "You have a healthy son."

What felt to Selar like a few hours later, she was standing in the middle of the compound with Monica, Tenley, Amanda, and the new Q family. The male Q was beaming with pride over his offspring, and the female Q looked very maternal. The entire Q family had changed into the same Starfleet uniform that Q had worn when she first appeared in sickbay years before.

Selar still thought they looked more comfortable.

"He's so adorable," Amanda said, running a finger over the baby's wisps of hair. "Look at those cheeks! If you ever need a babysitter, Q . . ."

"Thank you," the female Q said.

"Darling," the male Q began, "may I take him for a walk? A little father-son bonding?"

The female Q gently handed q to his father. "Don't be gone for too long. I need to send our dear Dr. Selar back where she belongs, but I want you two here when I get back."

The male Q's expression turned a level of grave that Selar would not have thought him capable of. "Of course, my dear. We won't be gone very long. Perhaps a visit to see Aunt Kathy."

With that, they were gone.

The female Q perched her hands on her hips. "Well, are you ready to go home?"

Selar looked around to the remains of the compound. The lines were a little fuzzy, and her three students had all long since taken on human form instead of Vulcan, but otherwise it looked like the same compound she had been living in all this time.

She had learned so much in this place, more combat medicine than she had seen in six years on board the *Enterprise*. She looked forward to sharing her experiences with Dr. Crusher in Ten-Forward, seeing if there was any way to implement some of the techniques she picked up during her stay. Just the scans of q she obtained during his birth might get her a nomination for the Carrington Award.

Still, as she looked into the faces of Amanda, Monica, and Tenley, a part of Selar did not want to leave.

But she knew that she had to go back. Temporal mechanics had to be taken into consideration. There was no way of knowing what might happen if she tried to stay in the Continuum. "Yes, Q."

Amanda quickly hugged her and said, "Tell Captain Picard that things worked out after all. I'm going to miss you, Selar."

Monica and Tenley both said quick good-byes, then stepped back to allow the female Q room.

Q raised her hand to snap her fingers, but paused. "There's just one thing that needs to be done before you can go home. After all, we can't have an inferior species running around with powers of omnipotence. Q tried that idiotic trick once already. . . ."

"Do not move, please," Selar said, scanning the bruise on Worf's cranial ridge. The results were precisely what she expected.

She thought of a dermal regenerator set for a bone contusion, but nothing happened.

She reinforced the thought, envisioning the device in the most minute detail her brain could manage.

Still nothing.

"Problem, Doctor?" Selar turned to find an inquisitive look on Alyssa Ogawa's features.

Puzzled, Selar looked around sickbay. Something was missing. Why was she unable to conjure a simple tool?

Why did she think she should be able to?

"Where is Q?" Selar asked.

Ogawa shrugged. "Q?"

"Yes. Q handed me the dermal regenerator."

"Why would he do that?"

Selar reached for the dermal regenerator on a nearby supply tray, turning it to the proper setting for a bone contusion before using it on Worf.

"It was not a male Q," Selar said. "It was a female."

"Doctor," Worf interjected, "no one was here beyond the three of us."

Perplexed, Selar stepped back from her patient, handing the regenerator to Ogawa. "Please attend to the lieutenant's injury. I require meditation."

Ogawa nodded her understanding, allowing Selar to escape sickbay. As she walked back to her quarters, she fought with her mind to figure out why she had thought she could bring a piece of equipment into existence simply because she thought it.

Q *had* been there. Selar was sure of it. Why had Nurse Ogawa and Worf not seen her?

Why did she remember talking to a female Q, but not what was said? Why was she so sure that Q had taken something away from her?

Selar quickly found her way to her quarters, ordering the computer to lock the door as soon as it had closed behind her. She found herself growing angrier by the second, and she did not care for the feeling. Further, she did not like the reasons for the anger. How could she trust her memory again? How could she trust *anyone* again?

Calling upon all the Vulcan disciplines she'd learned in a lifetime, she tried to crush the anger, to cast it aside, to be rid of it.

Grabbing a thick white candle from the shelf, she lit it and began a short meditation. The need for candles in Vulcan meditation rituals allowed Selar some leeway in what sensors were enabled in her quarters. Right now, the last thing she needed was the fire-suppression system engaging.

She stared into the flickering flame, slowly beginning the chant that would assist her on the path to mental focus and a return to the Vulcan path of logic.

Eventually, she was successful. Her mind cleared and focused.

But the anger and the resentment over what was taken from her—whatever it was—never quite went away. . . .

BURGOYNE 172
Oil and Water

Robert T. Jeschonek

Burgoyne 172 is a Hermat who is one of only two officers besides Elizabeth Shelby to serve on the *U.S.S. Excalibur* under both Captains Korsmo and Calhoun. Prior to that assignment, however, s/he served on the *U.S.S. Livingston.* "Oil and Water" takes place while s/he was at that posting.

Robert T. Jeschonek

Robert T. Jeschonek wrote "Our Million-Year Mission," winner of the grand prize in *Star Trek: Strange New Worlds VI*. He also contributed the prize-winning "Whatever You Do, Don't Read This Story" to *Strange New Worlds III* and "The Shoulders of Giants" to *Strange New Worlds V*. He is a graduate of the Oregon Professional Fiction Writers Workshop conducted by Dean Wesley Smith and Kristine Kathryn Rusch. Robert studied journalism at the University of Pittsburgh and has worked in radio, television, and public relations. While pursuing a career as a fiction writer, he works as a technical writer in Johnstown, Pennsylvania. His wife, Wendy, makes his fiction writing possible by supplying encouragement, patience, understanding, and editing support. Robert has many projects in the pipeline, including stories and novels exploring the worlds of science fiction, fantasy, mystery, and paranormal romance.

No sooner had Lieutenant Burgoyne 172 tossed aside the body of the Klingon *targ* than s/he heard a crackle of movement from the dense underbrush. Tensing, s/he spun in the direction of the sound . . . just in time to see the tiger leap toward hir in a blur of orange and white fur.

In the split second before the tiger could slam into hir, s/he vaulted to one side, avoiding the creature's flashing claws. As the tiger sailed past and landed in the piled corpses of Burgoyne's previous opponents—the *targ,* a Vulcan *le-matya,* a Rigelian winged raptor-wolf—Burgoyne's lithe body hit the ground in a roll and quickly sprang up onto all fours. It was a pose that s/he normally would never adopt on board ship, but in the privacy of the *Livingston*'s holodeck, in the heat of a down-and-dirty, no-holds-barred battle program, s/he was concerned only with survival, not appearances.

Which was a good thing, because the program was running without safety protocols. It was Burgoyne's treat to hirself after learning that hir nemesis, Chief Engineer Spode Castlebaum, was finally being transferred to another ship. Safety protocols were fine for a little no-risk romp, but there was nothing like genuine danger to make a Hermat feel alive.

The tiger threw itself around and leaped again, striped body soaring over the jungle floor. This time, Burgoyne charged forward on all four limbs, darting under the airborne predator and lashing up a sharp-clawed hand to gash its belly on the way.

The cuts went deep. Blood spattered the ground as the tiger's forelegs touched down, and its hind legs skidded out from under it when they hit. The beast's hindquarters swung down in the dirt, momentum flinging them forward and pitching the creature onto its side.

For an instant, Burgoyne crouched, inhaling the rich scent of tiger's blood on hir talons. S/he flicked hir tongue out for the quickest taste of it, then coiled back and sprang.

The tiger was struggling to get to its feet when Burgoyne pounced, landing with enough force to slam it down again. As the creature roared, the Hermat dug the claws of hir feet into its flanks, then drove the talons of one hand into its throat.

And ripped.

Blood spurted everywhere. Driven wild by the smell of it, Burgoyne drew back hir hand and slashed again, gouging out more flesh. S/he was just about to make the killing strike—and was considering doing it with hir fangs—when three words brought the kill to a screeching halt.

"Computer, freeze program."

Fangs bared, Burgoyne swung hir head around to gape in the direction of the voice. When s/he spotted its source, a familiar wave of irritation surged through hir.

Though the transfer had been finalized, Castlebaum wasn't off the ship yet. Unfortunately, knowing that the arrogant chief engineer would soon be gone did not make having to deal with him now any more pleasant.

And he wasn't alone. Not only had he entered Burgoyne's in-progress holodeck program unannounced, but he had brought someone with him.

Someone Burgoyne didn't know.

Heart still racing, Burgoyne leaned back from the holographic tiger carcass and grinned. "Commander Castlebaum," s/he said, panting from exertion. "Here I thought my next opponent was a Taurian sky-shark!"

"Next best thing," Castlebaum said with a smirk. "But I'd rather not embarrass you in front of our guest, so let's save the sparring for later." Castlebaum was a tall, knobby stick-man in his fifties, all giant nose and giant elbows and giant Adam's apple. Worst of all, in Burgoyne's opinion, was his awful comb-over—gray hair grown long on one side of his head and pulled up and over to cover his bald spot. Many was the time when Burgoyne had wanted to grab that greasy shock of hair (wearing gloves, of course) and hack it off with cable cutters for the good of the entire crew of the *Livingston.*

"I can wait," said Burgoyne. "It will give me something to look forward to." Smoothly, s/he got to hir feet, determined not to show a trace of the awkwardness s/he felt at being seen in full feral mode by a stranger. "So, are you going to introduce us, or shall I do the honors?"

"This is Dr. Dovan," said Castlebaum, looking especially pleased with himself as he nodded at the newcomer. "Dr. Dovan, meet Lieutenant Burgoyne 172."

Dr. Dovan looked human in appearance except for a set of forehead ridges with a rounded knob in the center. The dark-haired newcomer was slim and stood just a little over five feet in height, shorter than Burgoyne and positively dwarfed by the towering Castlebaum. "Burgoyne," Dovan said simply, making a half-bow without smiling.

"Pleased to meet you," said Burgoyne, striding forward with hand extended . . . then realizing the hand was covered in holographic blood and quickly drawing it back. "Computer, end program," s/he said, and the blood vanished, along with the dead animals and jungle surroundings. "Now, let's try that again."

Burgoyne reached out, but Dovan did not complete the handshake. After holding hir hand there for a moment, Burgoyne swung it up and back to smooth hir hair, running it over the blond buzz-cut on top and down the shoulder-length fall in the back.

"The two of you will be working closely together," said Castlebaum, looking and sounding unusually smug. "I'm sure you'll make a great team."

"Teamwork's my middle name," Burgoyne said glibly, flashing hir sharp canine teeth in a friendly smile with just a trace of menace.

"Dr. Dovan's an expert in techno-organics," said Castlebaum, flashing plenty of his own teeth. His grin, in fact, was the biggest Burgoyne had ever seen on that skeletal sourpuss. "Oh," he said. "And I almost forgot to mention one other detail."

As Castlebaum paused, training that cadaverous grin like a searchlight on Burgoyne, the Hermat knew that the other shoe was about to drop. The chief engineer's whole performance since entering the holodeck had been leading up to what he was about to say.

"Dr. Dovan's a J'naii," said Castlebaum. "And Burgoyne's a Hermat," he added for Dovan's benefit.

Burgoyne didn't miss a beat. "And Chief Engineer Castlebaum's a human," s/he said with a wink to the J'naii, "but we don't hold it against him."

Burgoyne laughed lightly and patted Castlebaum on the arm. Though the chief engineer's eyes were still fixed expectantly upon hir, s/he was pleased not to give him the slightest hint that he had gotten a rise out of hir.

Nevertheless, Burgoyne was surprised by the revelation of Dovan's species. S/he had never met a J'naii before, but had certainly heard a lot about them . . . and what s/he had heard was enough to make hir a little uncomfortable.

"This won't be a problem, will it, Burgoyne?" cooed Castlebaum. "Working with someone with no gender?"

"I've been working with you, haven't I?" said Burgoyne. "And by that, I mean working with someone who only has *one* gender, of course."

"Of course," said Castlebaum, smile still fixed firmly in place but eyes twinkling with obvious contempt.

"One or none, it makes no difference to me," said Burgoyne, but as s/he took a closer look at Dovan, s/he felt a mixture of distaste and fascination. As a Hermat, a being who encompassed both male and female characteristics in one body, s/he was disturbed by the notion of a complete absence of gender. The androgynous J'naii seemed unnatural to hir, even less complete than the single-gendered humans . . . and yet, the same differences that struck hir as unnatural also piqued hir curiosity. S/he found hirself more intrigued than repelled.

Generally, Hermats considered J'naii to be unfortunate freaks of nature. Since dual-gendered Burgoyne was used to encountering similar opinions of hirself among the single-gendered majority of Starfleet, s/he really didn't have much trouble setting aside hir own initial squeamishness.

"So, what's the occasion?" said Burgoyne. "I assume we have an assignment involving techno-organics."

Castlebaum lost his smile and dropped into an all-business mode. "A Starfleet prototype ultra-deep-space probe has gone rogue," he said. "It's techno-organic, and it's raising hell on a Federation planet."

"A probe?" said Burgoyne. "How much damage can a probe do?"

"Quite a bit," said Castlebaum, "if it's equipped with biomechanical phasers, shields, a tractor beam, and warp drive. It has the offensive and defensive capabilities of a small starship, not to mention certain techno-organic capabilities. And it's smaller than a shuttlecraft."

Burgoyne raised hir eyebrows. "Fail-safes are offline?"

"We think it's evolving," said Dovan.

"Wow," said Burgoyne, shaking hir head. "Next, you'll be telling me it can reproduce."

"It can," said Dovan. "It has replication capabilities for self-repair and replacement."

"Let me see if I have this straight," said Burgoyne. "This probe is essentially a techno-organic life-form capable of asexual reproduction. Starfleet's assigning a sexually androgynous J'naii and a dual-gendered Hermat to deactivate it."

"Correct," said Castlebaum, and then his wicked grin returned. "And one more detail you'll be interested to know."

"What's that?" said Burgoyne.

"The planet it's threatening," said Castlebaum, "is Damiano."

"Ah, yes," said Burgoyne. "Where the inhabitants can have any of *three* genders." S/he realized that Castlebaum was watching to see if s/he was rattled, as if the thought of dealing with gender assignments other than hir own could possibly unnerve hir. So Burgoyne laughed. "The more, the merrier," s/he said brightly. "How about it, Dr. Dovan?"

"Gender is irrelevant," said the J'naii, staring coldly at the Hermat. "I suggest we focus our attention on disabling the probe."

"I'll leave you to it, then," said Castlebaum, grinning. "We'll reach Damiano in less than twenty-four hours, so time is of the essence."

Burgoyne touched the sleeve of Dovan's khaki coveralls. "Let me just grab a shower, and I'll meet you in engineering," s/he said briskly.

To Burgoyne's surprise, Dovan shrugged hir hand aside and turned to Castlebaum. "I'd like to get to work immediately," said the J'naii. "We've already wasted enough time."

"Right this way," said Castlebaum, gesturing toward the holodeck exit. As the J'naii strode past him, the chief engineer beamed his biggest grin ever at Burgoyne, satisfied that he was making the Hermat's life suitably miserable. "You can catch up with Dr. Dovan when you're done with that shower, Lieutenant Burgoyne."

"That's assuming Dr. Dovan won't have to catch up to *me,*" Burgoyne said cheerfully, trotting out the door past hir boss. "This mission is so right up my alley, I can't wait to get started!"

"That's great to hear," said Castlebaum in a less than convincing tone.

"Oh," said Burgoyne, stopping to turn a look of concern on the chief engineer. "If you feel the need to talk about any gender confusion sort of stuff, I want you to know I'm here for you."

"Thanks," said Castlebaum, nodding with an insincere smile. "You'll be the first one I'll call."

"I think I might want to switch sides," said Burgoyne, leaning over the display table in engineering to stare at the probe's schematics, "because from what I can see, there's no way to beat this thing."

Across from hir, Dovan intently studied readouts on the tabletop. "Suit yourself," the J'naii said stiffly, tapping control surfaces to run a calculation.

Burgoyne supposed s/he ought to jump for joy, because those were the first two words Dovan had said to hir in the half-hour since s/he had finished hir shower and come to engineering. This was especially noteworthy since Burgoyne hirself hadn't stopped talking the whole time.

"I assume you have a plan, though?" said Burgoyne, forging ahead now that the silence had been broken. "I mean, being a techno-organic specialist and all, you must have some tricks up your sleeve."

"There's nothing up my sleeve," Dovan said without looking up from the table.

"That's what all magicians say," said Burgoyne, "just before they make the flock of doves appear from thin air."

Dovan sighed heavily and kept right on working. "Perhaps I should request a different teammate," said the J'naii. "One who doesn't babble quite so much."

"Only problem is, I'm the best nanotechnology specialist on the ship," said Burgoyne. "Plus which, I know you'd miss me if I wasn't around."

Finally, Dovan looked up. "The only way I'd miss you," it said, "is if you suddenly turned into somebody I *liked* and *then* went away."

Burgoyne smiled. "So what kind of person do you like?" s/he said. "Tell me, and I'll see what I can do."

Dovan scowled and looked back down at the display without deigning to answer. Though Burgoyne knew that s/he, too, ought to be concentrating on the job at hand, s/he continued to watch Dovan, annoyed and confused at the J'naii's unconcealed disdain for hir.

S/he wondered how someone s/he had just met could dislike hir so strongly. With the exception of Castlebaum, s/he rarely put people off; as a rule, s/he made excellent first impressions.

The only thing s/he could think of to explain Dovan's repulsion was the gender difference. Perhaps, though Burgoyne had managed to put aside the issue, Dovan was not progressive enough to play nice with a multigendered being.

At least not yet. Burgoyne, being the outrageous and persistent creature that s/he was, was not about to accept Dovan's opinion until it coincided with hir own.

"Okay then," s/he said brightly, tapping hir claws on the display table. "How do you propose we disable this rogue probe? I don't see a weak spot, but then I'm not an expert in techno-organic systems like you are."

Eyes fixed on the schematics, Dovan answered grudgingly. "Parasites."

"Wait," said Burgoyne, leaning over the table toward hir teammate. "Are we still talking about the probe, or are you referring to a personal problem?"

The wisecrack got no visible reaction from the J'naii. "I plan to attack the probe with techno-organic parasites," said Dovan. "I'm growing them from the same biomatrix as the probe, so they should be able to fool its defenses. The probe will think they're part of itself."

"Where are you growing these parasites?" said Burgoyne.

Dovan walked away from the display table. "The cultures are developing in this incubator," said the J'naii, touching a circular silver contraption on a nearby console. The device looked like a poker-chip caddy, but with gleaming silver cylinders mounted in the sockets instead of stacks of chips.

Burgoyne stepped over and leaned down to peer at the incubator. "How exactly will these parasites disable the probe?" s/he said thoughtfully.

"Once attached, they'll bore into the device and hijack its neural pathways," said Dovan. "They'll reprogram it to shut itself down."

Burgoyne nodded. "And you're sure this will work?" s/he said, reaching out to touch one of the cylinders on the incubator.

By way of adjusting a control on the device, Dovan brushed aside Burgoyne's hand. "All it will take is one parasite," said the J'naii. "The only problem we might face is getting past the probe's defenses."

"Hold on now," said Burgoyne, frowning. "I thought you said the parasites would fool its defenses because they're being grown from its own biomatrix."

"Once they're attached, the probe won't repel them," said Dovan. "But they won't be self-propelled. Someone will have to attach them manually . . . and to do that, we'll have to get past the probe's shields and weapons."

"I don't suppose you've come up with a way past those, have you?" said Burgoyne.

"As a matter of fact," said Dovan, making one more adjustment to the incubator and returning to the display table, "I hope to walk right through them."

Burgoyne laughed. "I never knew the J'naii had the power to turn intangible. Or are you indestructible?"

"The probe is programmed for self-preservation. I don't believe it will retaliate against products of the same biomatrix that spawned it. Therefore, I don't expect it to attack me," said Dovan, "because its biomatrix was derived from my own genetic material."

"Aha," said Burgoyne. "You're the probe's daddy . . . or is that mommy?"

"Neither," said Dovan, fingers dancing over the table's controls. "But I did play a role in its creation."

Burgoyne thought for a moment, then walked over to stand beside the J'naii. "Correct me if I'm wrong," s/he said, rubbing hir chin and staring at

Dovan, "but isn't it against techno-organic engineering protocols to derive a biomatrix from humanoid genetic materials?"

"I . . . circumvented protocols," said Dovan, its gaze never wavering from the readouts on the table. "Apparently, this was a mistake."

"Well," said Burgoyne, narrowing hir eyes. "I can see I was wrong about you, Dovan."

"In what way?" the J'naii said coldly. "Not that I care."

"I thought you were the type to play it safe," said Burgoyne. "Not a risk taker. I was wrong."

Dovan said nothing, though its hands slowed their work on the table.

"Interesting," said Burgoyne. "It makes you think, doesn't it?"

"Think what?" said Dovan.

"Maybe you're wrong about me, too," said Burgoyne.

Dovan looked up from the table and directed a frosty glare at the Hermat. "No," said the J'naii. "I'm not."

Without another word, Dovan grabbed a padd from the table and marched out of engineering. Burgoyne watched it go and smiled.

"It won't be long now," s/he said to hirself. "The doctor's really starting to come around."

Later, Dr. Dovan did, in fact, come around. It came around to within a few inches of Burgoyne's face, actually, while hollering full-throttle.

"We must not destroy the probe!" shouted the J'naii, face flushed with anger. "Deactivation will be sufficient!"

Burgoyne drew hir lips back in a grin that revealed hir sharp canine teeth. "I don't know if I'd say you're cute when you're angry," s/he said, "but you're definitely more animated."

Dovan jerked away from the Hermat and turned to Castlebaum, who had joined them for a strategy meeting. "Tell hir!" snapped the J'naii. "Our orders are to *stop* the probe, not *eradicate* it!"

Castlebaum cleared his throat. "Starfleet's orders don't rule out lethal force," he said calmly. "Our primary mission is to protect the people of Damiano. If we have to destroy the probe to do that, so be it."

"We need to *study* it," said Dovan. "Find out what went wrong! If we blow it to pieces, that won't be an option!"

"So if it comes down to sacrificing the probe or the people," said Burgoyne, "you'd rather sacrifice the people?"

Dovan whirled to face hir, seething . . . then seemed to catch itself on the verge of further fireworks. The J'naii's shoulders rose as it took a deep breath and released it, then another. "As I've explained," it said tightly, "the techno-organic parasites will discontinue the malfunctions and disable the probe."

"I hope they do," said Burgoyne, "but I'm not convinced. That's why we need backup plans."

"The parasites will do the job," said Dovan. "The simulations I've run prove it."

"You said it yourself," said Burgoyne. "You think the probe's evolving. What if it's evolved to the point of resisting the parasites?"

Dovan spun around to face Castlebaum again. "It will recognize their biomatrix as its own," said the J'naii. "Having done so, it will avoid damaging them. Self-preservation is one of its most deeply embedded protocols."

"If the probe's evolving," said Burgoyne, "it's no longer the same device you created."

"All the more reason not to *destroy* it," said Dovan, its voice rising again. "It's become something *new!* We need to *learn* from it!"

"Excuse me," said Castlebaum, "but do you know how many people it's killed on Damiano?"

Dovan did not say a word.

"Forty-three. And counting."

Still, Dovan remained silent.

"We have to stop this thing any way we can," said Castlebaum. "We'll try your parasites, but we'll take other measures if they fail."

Burgoyne looked at the chief engineer and couldn't help but feel a twinge of admiration. Most of the time, Castlebaum was so abusive and dictatorial, it was hard to remember how sensible and effective he could be.

"We'll lock the *Livingston*'s phasers on to the probe," said Castlebaum. "As Lieutenant Burgoyne has suggested, we'll program them for rapid frequency modulation. They should break through to the probe, even if it modulates its shield frequency."

"So that's it," said Dovan, throwing up its arms in futility. "You're set on destroying what could very well be the greatest leap forward of all time in techno-organic technology."

"Only if your plan doesn't succeed," said Castlebaum. "And according to you, it will succeed, so this ought to be a moot point."

Dovan sighed and dropped into one of the chairs around the briefing table. "I don't have much choice in the matter, do I?"

"As I said, it ought to be a moot point," said Castlebaum. "Now, how much longer until the parasites are fully operational?"

"Less than two hours," said Dovan. "I just need to fine-tune their programming."

"Burgoyne will assist you," said Castlebaum.

"Actually," said Burgoyne, "I'd like to do more than that."

"Explain," said Castlebaum.

"I'd like to piggyback more parasites on the parasites," said Burgoyne. "Entropic nanobots. We could infuse the parasites with colonies of them."

"To what end?" said Castlebaum.

"The 'bots could be injected into the probe when the parasites make contact," said Burgoyne. "They would literally take it apart from the inside."

"No," said Dovan, glaring at the table. "I refuse. The parasites are meant to deactivate, not destroy."

Burgoyne shrugged. "From what I can see, this probe is next to unstoppable. I vote we strengthen our hand however we can."

"Please," said Dovan. "Give me a chance to retrieve it intact."

Castlebaum looked at Dovan, then Burgoyne. "Infuse two parasites with the 'bots," said the chief engineer. "We'll hold them in reserve in case the others fail."

Dovan blew out its breath in frustration and shook its head.

"Typical," said the J'naii.

"Excuse me?" said Castlebaum.

"I expected better from you, Commander," said Dovan, "though your subordinate's attitude comes as no surprise."

"And here I thought I was full of surprises," said Burgoyne with a smirk.

Dovan rose from its chair and looked disgustedly at the Hermat. "I've dealt with your kind before," said the J'naii. "It's always the same."

"Now, what exactly do you mean by that?" said Burgoyne.

"Morality means nothing to you," said Dovan. "You have no conscience."

Burgoyne smiled dangerously, displaying hir fangs in full view. "Obviously, I do," s/he said quietly. "Otherwise, you would have found yourself the recipient of a rather extreme full-body makeover just now."

"Case in point," said Dovan, and then it left the briefing room.

Castlebaum patted Burgoyne on the shoulder. "I'm glad to see I was right," he said, grinning. "About you two making a great team, that is."

"Oh, I love my teammate," said Burgoyne, fangs still bared. "I look forward to spending more time together in the near future."

"Nothing like quality time to bring two people closer together," said

Castlebaum, glowing with delight at the irritation that Burgoyne was unable to conceal.

"Yes," Burgoyne said stiffly. "Quality time."

Though the team from the *Livingston* materialized inside the office of the governor of Damiano, Burgoyne immediately realized that they had just beamed into a war zone.

Gazing through a picture window at a view of the city around them, s/he saw that the reports of the probe's destructive power had not been exaggerated. Smoking craters yawned in the middle of city blocks, surrounded by the rubble of collapsed buildings and exploded streets. The buildings that remained standing were battered and burned, pocked with impact cavities and bristling with wreckage. In the distance, bright light flashed between structures, signaling a battle in progress. Coinciding with the flashes of light, s/he heard and felt a rumbling like the thunder of an approaching storm.

"Welcome to Iaron, our capital city," said a voice from the side of the office opposite the window. "What's left of it, anyway."

Turning, Burgoyne saw a green-skinned humanoid seated behind a large desk. "Lieutenant Burgoyne, of the starship *Livingston*," said the Hermat, bowing at the waist. "Techno-organic specialist Dr. Dovan," s/he continued, gesturing at the J'naii and then at each of the other away-team members in turn. "Lieutenant Carlsbad, Ensigns Rubio and Snell. We're here about the probe."

The being behind the desk nodded. "I am Planetary Governor Es'sca G'ullho." Like all Damiani, the governor had silver eyes, spiky black hair, and pointed ears. Es'sca also had a pair of silver-gray horns, each several inches long and angled upward at the tips into sharp points.

The horns protruded from either side of Es'sca's head and looked like they could do some damage in a fight; Burgoyne knew that they also served as evidence of the governor's gender. A single forehead horn signified what was known to offworlders as a "he" (though the word "he" was only used for the sake of convenience, and a Damiano "he" did not correspond anatomically to a human male). Three horns signified a "she" (not quite corresponding to a human female), and two horns were the mark of a third gender, referred to as "it."

"This is General Cu'lan T'ullhy," said Es'sca, motioning toward a single-horned Damiano standing with arms folded alongside the desk. "He's the head of our planetary defense forces."

Cu'lan snorted. "This is all Starfleet could send us?" he said sharply. "Five people to stop a menace that has stood against the combined might of our armed forces for days?"

"We have a plan," said Dovan.

"Thank Ho'nig," Cu'lan said sarcastically. "I feel better already."

"We have several plans, actually," said Burgoyne, "plus an entire starship that won't leave orbit until the job is done."

Cu'lan started to say something, but Es'sca cut him off. "You'll have to excuse us," said the governor. "We don't mean to seem ungrateful . . ."

"Yes we do," muttered Cu'lan.

". . . but this is, after all, Starfleet's fault. We want the matter resolved before any more lives are lost."

"Coincidentally," said Burgoyne, "those are our exact orders."

Es'sca cleared its throat and trained an especially meaningful stare on Burgoyne. "I don't suppose I have to remind you that a sizable anti-Federation faction exists on Damiano? And that the longer this situation lasts, the stronger that faction becomes?"

Burgoyne smiled graciously. "No reminder necessary," s/he said.

"Fifty-two Damiani have died," Es'sca said coldly. "That we know of. Much of Iaron is in ruins. This must end immediately."

"I assure you," said Dovan. "Our plan will work."

"We'll see," Cu'lan said with a scowl. "We've been throwing everything we've got at the thing for days, and we haven't even slowed it down."

"There's a reason Starfleet sent us," said Burgoyne.

"Your ship is the only one in the sector?" Cu'lan said scornfully.

"We're the best team for the job," said Burgoyne. "We've never failed. Now let's get to work, shall we?"

Cu'lan snorted and shook his head. "Follow me," he said, marching across the office and out the door.

The team fell in step behind the general, who led them out of the building and onto the street. As Cu'lan moved off for a moment to confer with an aide, Dovan whispered to Burgoyne.

"We've never failed," said the J'naii, "because we've never worked together before."

"Same difference." Burgoyne smirked. "What's the matter, Dovan? Getting nervous about screwing up in front of these inferior trigendered types?"

Dovan glared at the Hermat, then looked away. "Gender has nothing to do with inferiority," said the J'naii.

Burgoyne was not convinced of Dovan's sincerity. The memory of the

J'naii's earlier remarks about hir "kind" and how they lacked "morality" and "conscience" still stung. "Just think," said Burgoyne. "A species with three different genders, and you with none. It really blows your mind, doesn't it?"

"The quality of a person relies on other factors," Dovan said tightly, "which, unfortunately, seem to have been in short supply when your creator fashioned you."

Just then, General Cu'lan returned, ending the conversation . . . but Burgoyne continued to stare at Dovan. For someone who seemed to hate dual-gendered Hermats, the J'naii had voiced some enlightened opinions on gender differences.

Which was why, as the away team boarded a Damiano transport vehicle with Cu'lan, Burgoyne was more preoccupied thinking about Dovan than the mission that lay ahead.

"You're just in time for the fireworks," said General Cu'lan as the team got out of the transport. "We're about to hit that thing hard."

Cu'lan stomped up to a makeshift barricade erected in the street, a wall of thick metal plating with ports through which weapons could be fired. Uniformed Damiani hustled back and forth behind the barricade, setting up gun emplacements and making final adjustments to phaser rifles.

On the other side of the barricade, a wall of armored tanks trained their phaser cannons down the street, humming with power. Airborne fighter pods bobbed in a semicircle overhead, gleaming obsidian bubbles spiked with gun turrets and rocket launchers.

Burgoyne squinted through one of the barricade ports. Light flared from around a corner three blocks away, and a cloud of black smoke rolled out onto the street a second later.

As Burgoyne watched, five uniformed Damiani ran full-tilt around the corner, guns and elbows pumping. "Looks like the battle's already in progress," s/he said as bursts of phaser fire streaked after the fleeing soldiers.

"We're just drawing it in," said Cu'lan from the next port down, peering at the action through a set of binoculars. "Driving it into an ambush."

"Tell your troops to stand down," said Dovan, watching alongside Burgoyne. "We'll take it from here."

Cu'lan lowered his binoculars and glared at the J'naii. "Say again?" said the general.

"The use of firepower will interfere with our plan," Dovan said stiffly. "Now order your forces to stand down."

"And what, exactly, is your plan, Mr. Scientist, sir?" said Cu'lan.

"I will approach the probe and attach these," said Dovan, patting one of the six silver cylinders suspended from the bandolier belts strapped crossways over its chest. "They contain techno-organic parasites that will infiltrate and deactivate the device."

"You'll just waltz right up to it, huh?" said Cu'lan.

"The probe's biomatrix was derived from my genetic material," said Dovan. *"Starfly* will recognize my genetic makeup as its own and won't attack me."

" '*Starfly*'?" said Burgoyne.

Dovan nodded. "The probe's designation. *Starfly One Bioprobe.*"

Burgoyne sighed. "If you were planning to refer to it by its acronym," s/he said, "don't."

Dovan thought for a moment, didn't seem to understand, and shrugged.

Clearing his throat, Cu'lan raised a handheld radio transmitter and spoke into it. "All hands, stand down," he said. "Do not engage."

"Thank you," said Dovan. "This shouldn't take long." Turning, it started to walk off, heading for the end of the barricade.

"Hold on," said Burgoyne, grabbing the J'naii's arm. "You aren't going anywhere."

"What?" Dovan said indignantly. "I have work to do."

"The radio," said Burgoyne, shaking hir head. "It wasn't on."

Cu'lan smirked. "We ask for help, and this is what Starfleet sends," he said derisively. "A J'naii who wants to take this thing on single-handedly. Why in the name of Ho'nig should we take you any more seriously than you take us?"

"You don't understand!" said Dovan. "My plan will work!"

"Let us handle this, Mr. Scientist," Cu'lan said derisively. "You can pick up the pieces when we're done."

Dovan tried to pull away from Burgoyne, but s/he held fast to the J'naii. "General," s/he said. "What makes you think this attack will have any more impact than all the others?"

"We've been hammering it for days," said Cu'lan. "I'm betting we've worn it down."

"And has it shown any sign of being worn down?" said Burgoyne. "Shield fluctuations? Power loss? Anything?"

"Here it comes!" shouted a Damiano soldier along the barricade.

Cu'lan switched on the radio and spoke into it. "All hands, prepare to engage! On my mark!"

Through the barricade port, Burgoyne glimpsed flashes of silver in the black smoke billowing at the far end of the street. Gradually, more of the probe's silver skin became visible, pushing through the cloud . . . until finally, the device emerged fully into daylight, cruising several meters above the pavement.

"Ready!" Cu'lan shouted into the radio.

"Don't do it!" said Dovan, straining against Burgoyne's grip.

Starfly floated toward them, a gleaming sphere studded with weapons mounted on spidery mechanical arms. The sphere was suspended by equatorial spokes in a circular harness with short wings on either side; below the wings, struts descended from the harness to the familiar flattened cylinders of the warp-engine nacelles.

As Burgoyne stared at the deadly construct, s/he was amazed that its designer had managed to pack so much power into such a compact form. Though it was hard to judge exact dimensions from a distance, s/he didn't think *Starfly* was bigger than twelve feet in diameter.

Twelve feet in diameter, and the probe was equipped with shields, phasers, and warp drive. Just thinking about it, Burgoyne felt new respect for the J'naii who had created it . . . not affection, what with Dovan's bigoted behavior toward the Hermat . . . but definitely respect. And a little professional jealousy, to boot.

"All right!" Cu'lan barked into his radio. "Let's show this thing what we're made of!"

Burgoyne turned to hir own security team. They had already drawn their phasers and were standing in positions of watchful readiness. "If the probe breaks through," s/he said, "protect Dovan at all costs."

Turning back to the barricade port, Burgoyne saw that *Starfly* was now less than a block away. The probe glided smoothly forward, weapons arms twitching, surface lights blinking.

"All units, fire!" shouted Cu'lan. *"Fire!"*

Suddenly, the street erupted with the blinding light and piercing whines of concentrated phaser blasts. Every Damiano rifle and fighting machine poured out streams of destructive energy at once, and every single one of them came to bear on the probe.

As focused energy rained upon it from every direction, *Starfly* flared and seemed to disappear in the heart of a brilliant nimbus of light. Still, the tanks and troops and airborne fighter pods continued to hammer away, maintaining a steady flow of deadly force.

Shielding hir eyes with an arm, Burgoyne squinted into the glare, trying to see if the probe had disintegrated under the barrage. All that s/he could make out was the blaze of light, ever expanding and intensifying . . . until it became so unbearably bright that s/he had to shut hir eyes against it.

Less than five minutes later, it was all over.

The street was heaped with wreckage and bodies. Not a single tank or fighter remained intact. Most of the barricade had been atomized.

And *Starfly* just hovered amid the debris without a scratch on it.

Burgoyne and hir team watched it now from behind a pile of rubble where they had taken refuge. If s/he had not seen it with hir own eyes, s/he would not have believed that anything could move so fast and apply so much power with such precision.

"Ho'nig help us," said General Cu'lan, who had also taken shelter behind the rubble. "It's all yours, Starfleet. We've got nothing left."

Burgoyne thought of mentioning how many lives could have been spared if Cu'lan had delayed the attack . . . but s/he knew it wouldn't accomplish anything. "You tried your best, General," s/he said instead. "That was some real heroism we just saw."

"I'm ready," said Dovan, shifting the bandolier straps on which the parasite cylinders were clipped. "Remember, no sudden moves while I'm out there. Don't interfere unless I call for it."

"Got it," said Burgoyne. "Good luck."

Dovan touched each of the silver cylinders on its chest, counting under its breath. "Six," said the J'naii. "Six here, and two in reserve."

"Ten-four," said Burgoyne, tapping the pair of cylinders suspended from the belt at hir waist. One cylinder hung from each hip, like revolvers on a gunslinger.

"Ten and four?" said Dovan, looking puzzled. "But I have six and you have two."

Burgoyne chuckled and shook hir head. "You're right, you're right," s/he said. "Six and two . . . and my two have the nanobot colonies."

"Which we won't need, of course," said Dovan.

"Of course," said Burgoyne.

Dovan took a deep breath, held it for an instant, and released it. "Here we go," said the J'naii, and then it stepped out from behind the rubble in full view of the probe.

Burgoyne clambered far enough up the pile to have an unobstructed view of *Starfly*, then activated hir communicator badge with a touch. "Burgoyne to *Livingston*," s/he said softly. "Prepare for emergency beam-up of Dr. Dovan."

When Burgoyne received no reply, s/he touched the communicator again. "Burgoyne to *Livingston,*" s/he said, a little louder. "Come in, *Livingston.*"

Still nothing. Grabbing the tricorder from hir belt, s/he scanned the area . . . and quickly determined that the probe was broadcasting a jamming field that blocked the communicator's frequencies. For the moment, the away team was on its own, completely cut off from the orbiting starship.

As Burgoyne cursed, movement in the street below caught hir eye. Slowly, arms hanging loosely at its sides, Dovan picked its way through the field of debris, approaching the probe.

Starfly, for its part, remained still, hanging less than a meter above the street, every multijointed weapons arm pointed toward the J'naii. The only visible movement from the probe was the rapid blinking of lights on its silver skin.

Ever so slowly, Dovan proceeded. It was less than twenty meters from the probe now. To Burgoyne's amazement, the J'naii's plan seemed to be working; just minutes after wiping out an entire military strike force, *Starfly* was letting an unarmed scientist approach without a single hostile twitch.

Dovan moved closer. Burgoyne alternated between watching the J'naii's progress and checking the tricorder for spikes in the probe's power levels. An energy surge would tip hir off that *Starfly* was preparing to fire its weapons.

As the J'naii drew to within a few meters of the probe, Burgoyne held hir breath. From that point on, if *Starfly's* power levels spiked, no one could cross the debris field fast enough to haul Dovan out of the way before an attack; even responding to a shouted warning, the J'naii would never be able to run for cover in time to avoid being cut down by phaser fire.

With the *Livingston's* transporters out of play thanks to the communications jamming, Dovan was truly isolated in the danger zone. The fact that it kept walking toward the probe brought Dovan up another notch in Burgoyne's estimation.

The J'naii took a few more steps forward, moving to within arm's reach of *Starfly.* Burgoyne took it as a good sign that the probe's weapons did not reposition themselves to keep Dovan in the crosshairs.

Still moving in slow motion, Dovan pulled one of the parasite cylinders from its bandolier. With great care, the J'naii extended the cylinder toward the probe's spherical body . . . then deposited it on *Starfly's* silver skin. With the same slow, smooth movement, Dovan withdrew its hand and reached for another cylinder on its chest.

Burgoyne nodded, feeling increasingly confident that hir teammate would at least manage to plant all the cylinders. As risky as the plan had seemed to hir, s/he was starting to think that it had a chance of success.

Then s/he glanced at the tricorder readout and immediately changed hir mind.

"Dovan!" s/he shouted as loud as s/he could. "Get out of there *now!*"

According to the tricorder, *Starfly*'s power levels were surging.

Dovan was placing the second parasite on the probe and tried to pull away, but it was too late. Suddenly, silver tendrils sprang from the skin of the sphere and wrapped themselves around the J'naii's arm.

Burgoyne jumped up, ready to dive from the pile of rubble and charge across the debris field . . . then froze as the tricorder chimed for attention. As s/he stared at the tricorder's display, s/he realized that hir teammate was out of reach.

Starfly's shields were up.

As Burgoyne watched helplessly, the probe pulled Dovan into itself. The J'naii was already submerged up to its shoulder in the gleaming sphere and sinking deeper.

And screaming as if subjected to the most excruciating pain imaginable.

"Let's spread out," Lieutenant Carlsbad said urgently. "Fire at its shields from multiple points and rotate frequencies rapidly. Maybe we can punch through."

"Dream on," said General Cu'lan. "Did you see how much firepower we hit it with before, and nothing got through?"

"The general's right," said Burgoyne, scrambling down from hir vantage point atop the rubble. "We need an alternative."

Down the street, Dovan screamed louder than ever . . . loud enough to make the hairs stand up on the back of Burgoyne's neck.

"That thing's eating him alive!" Ensign Snell, an Andorian, was so agitated that the antennae on his forehead fluttered like blades of grass in a stiff breeze.

"Not for long," said Burgoyne, placing the tricorder on a block of rubble and detaching one of the two silver cylinders suspended from hir waist. "It just so happens I have an alternative right here."

"One of the parasites?" said Carlsbad. "But how can we get through the probe's shields to plant it?"

"Not a parasite," said Burgoyne. When s/he gave one end of the cylinder a twist, it slid open, revealing a single red button. "A trigger."

"A trigger for what?" said Carlsbad.

Burgoyne depressed the button with hir thumb. "I just activated the nanobot colonies inside the probe and signaled them to attack its systems."

"Wait a minute," said Carlsbad, frowning. "I thought you said the nanobots were in the cylinders you kept in reserve, not the ones Dovan was carrying."

Burgoyne shrugged. "Seems I made a mistake. Apparently, the 'bot colonies were in Dovan's parasite cylinders after all. The two cylinders Dovan already attached to the probe, to be exact. Lucky for us, huh?"

Carlsbad nodded knowingly. "I'll say. Pretty lucky you happened to have that remote trigger with you, too."

"I'm on a roll, apparently," said Burgoyne. S/he allowed hirself a quick smile, then went grim as another scream burst out of Dovan. "Now let's hope it continues. There's no guarantee the nanobots will work, given the probe's ongoing evolution."

"Then what?" said General Cu'lan. "Yet another alternative?"

"Not a good one," said Burgoyne. "If the *Livingston* doesn't hear from us by a predetermined deadline, she'll hit the probe with an orbit-to-ground phaser barrage. We're betting that will be enough to take out *Starfly.*"

"And Dovan," Carlsbad said gravely.

"When is the deadline?" said Cu'lan.

"Fifteen minutes," said Burgoyne. "So let's hope, for Dovan's sake, that the nanobots have what it takes."

As if Dovan had heard hir, the J'naii let loose with the loudest scream yet.

Burgoyne had never realized that five minutes could seem like such a long time.

For five unending minutes, perched atop the pile of rubble, s/he watched the tricorder readouts for a fluctuation in the probe's defenses . . . and listened as Dovan screamed in agony again and again. Every time s/he checked the tricorder, there was no change in *Starfly*'s energy levels or shield strength; every time s/he looked down the street, Dovan had been sucked farther into the probe.

Before long, over half the J'naii's body had been drawn into the silver sphere, leaving only the head, a third of the torso, an arm, and a leg still free. At *Starfly*'s rate of absorption, Burgoyne was certain that by the time the *Livingston*'s phasers opened up, not a trace of Dovan would remain outside the probe.

Five minutes passed like five hours, punctuated by screams . . . and then, after one minute more, Burgoyne finally noticed a change. It was small and brief, but it might as well have been enormous and long-lasting for the surge of hope it brought hir.

For just a split second, *Starfly*'s power levels dipped. It would have been better if they had stayed down for good, but the fact that they came right back up again did not negate the importance of the fluctuation.

It meant that something was changing inside the probe. It suggested that more changes were on the way.

Burgoyne waited until the next alteration to speak up. "Shield strength is down two point five percent," s/he said, eyes glued to the tricorder. "And back up. The dip was three seconds in duration."

"Call it when our window opens up," said Carlsbad. "We'll focus four phasers on one point for a concentrated burn."

"Five phasers," said General Cu'lan, raising a rifle he'd retrieved from a soldier's corpse.

"There's another dip," said Burgoyne. "Down five percent . . . six . . . ten point three . . . ten point seven. Down twelve percent. And back up."

As Dovan screamed again, Carlsbad scaled the rubble and hunkered down next to Burgoyne. The rest of the group followed with weapons in hand, arranging themselves along the top of the pile.

"Sight in on the side of the sphere opposite Dovan," said Carlsbad. "Target between two and three o'clock, below the phaser cannon armature and above the harness ring."

"Another drop," said Burgoyne. "Twenty percent . . . twenty-five . . . thirty-two . . . thirty-two point three . . . and it's coming back up." Watching the tricorder closely, s/he did hir best to block out Dovan's latest round of screams. "But not all the way back up. Shields are steady at minus ten percent of original strength."

"Seven minutes until the airstrike from the *Livingston*," said Ensign Rubio.

"Down forty percent," said Burgoyne, heart racing. "Forty-three . . . fifty . . . sixty-five . . . and back up. Steady at minus twenty-seven percent."

"We'll go at minus seventy-five percent," said Carlsbad.

For a moment, nothing changed on the tricorder, and Burgoyne started to worry. If *Starfly* had managed to neutralize the nanobots, Dovan was doomed to be vaporized by the *Livingston*'s phasers.

A bead of sweat ran down hir forehead, and s/he wiped it away with the back of hir hand. Dovan wailed with such pitiful desperation that s/he wondered if it was already too late to save the J'naii.

Then, the tricorder reading plunged once more. "Forty percent . . .

sixty . . . seventy . . . seventy-four point five . . . point seven . . . point eight. And *mark!*"

All at once, five phasers opened fire from atop the rubble. The bright beams flared to a stop against the probe's shields, several meters out from *Starfly* itself . . . but continued to pour more energy against the protective screen. The spherical wall of force shimmered like heat ripples in the air, distorting around the impact zone with increasing agitation.

Then, with a burst of flickering sparks, the shields gave way. The phaser beams punched through to the skin of the probe, striking in a single point of blinding light.

Everyone kept pouring it on, frequencies rotating automatically. The skin of the probe dimpled under the bombardment, glowing yellow, then red, then white.

Then returning to silver again.

Burgoyne grimaced. "Time until airstrike?" s/he hollered over the shrill whine of the phasers.

"Five minutes," Ensign Rubio shouted back.

Burgoyne kept the phaser's firing stud depressed for a few more seconds, then released it. "Cease fire!" s/he said, tossing the weapon aside.

The other four beams disengaged. Dovan's screaming, which had been drowned out by the attack, resounded in the street once more, continuous and louder than ever.

"It must have developed some kind of ablative armor," said Burgoyne. "It's dissipating the energy from the phasers."

"Damn," said Carlsbad. "I guess that's it, then. We wait for the airstrike."

"The hell with that," said Burgoyne. "It still has a weak spot."

"Weak spot?" said Cu'lan.

Burgoyne got down on all fours, relaxing into the predatory posture of a Hermat about to draw blood. "There's an opening," s/he said in a low voice. "I'm going in through it."

"What opening?" said Cu'lan.

"Oh my God," said Carlsbad as realization dawned on him.

Burgoyne coiled back, gathering hir strength for the coming struggle. "Dovan," s/he said, and then s/he leaped from the rubble toward *Starfly*.

As Burgoyne charged down the debris-littered street, the probe opened fire. Since *Starfly* was damaged, the shots were erratic, spraying willy-nilly in all directions, but their unpredictability made them nearly as dangerous as if they had been aimed with precision. Several times, beams from *Starfly*'s phasers came close enough to Burgoyne that s/he could feel their searing heat crackling past.

In spite of the random weapons fire and the rugged course, the Hermat never stumbled or slowed. Four limbs pumping, s/he raced over the remains of blown-apart war machines and warriors, scrambled over wreckage and churned-up pavement, dove across craters.

Even as s/he brought hir feral instincts to bear, s/he counted down in the back of hir mind, marking the time until the *Livingston*'s airstrike. Each passing second spurred hir to go faster, accelerating hir heart rate, lengthening hir stride.

Four minutes.

Burgoyne barreled around the smoking hulk of a ruined tank, switching directions just in time to avoid a bolt from the probe's phasers. S/he darted up an incline of upthrust pavement . . . then leaped, arms extended like a tiger's forelegs.

Though Burgoyne had worried that the probe would manage to restore its shields, s/he met no resistance in hir flight. Phaser beams flashed around hir, but none made contact, and s/he landed lightly on the street in front of *Starfly*.

Springing up on two legs, s/he lunged toward Dovan with a snarl. The J'naii was almost completely absorbed now, submerged up to its chin; its free arm and leg were visible only from the elbow and knee down.

Without hesitation, Burgoyne drove hir claws between Dovan's forearm and the skin of the probe . . . realizing that s/he was raking the J'naii's flesh in the process but not caring. If s/he failed to free Dovan, the J'naii would die within minutes anyway.

Three minutes, to be exact.

Grunting, Burgoyne thrust hir claws through the tight seam between forearm and probe, creating a gap by cutting and squeezing Dovan's flesh. S/he forced the claws deeper until s/he felt the tips push past solid mass into open space . . . and then, s/he hooked them into *Starfly*'s skin from the inside and wrenched backward with all hir strength.

The skin resisted, holding fast. Burgoyne braced hir feet against the sphere and heaved backward again.

This time, s/he tore away a jagged silver hunk. As it separated from the probe's surface, bundles of fibers came with it . . . and rubbery pink strands that looked like nerves. Crimson fluid oozed from the broken edges, smelling of brine and metal, covering hir hands. Whatever the exact composition of this techno-organic slurry, it was close enough to blood to send Burgoyne into the killing frenzy s/he needed.

Howling, s/he heaved aside the hunk s/he'd ripped from the probe and gouged out another piece. *Starfly* bucked and quivered, weapons arms twisting and firing randomly.

Now that its integrity was compromised, the probe's skin yielded more easily. Burgoyne was able to hack out bigger chunks with less effort . . . and the more pieces s/he cut away, the more bloodlike slurry flowed out, intensifying hir frenzied strength.

Two minutes.

Burgoyne plunged hir talons into the hole s/he'd opened and slashed away at the tangle of conduits and fleshy tubules connecting Dovan to the probe. Tendrils shot out of the mess of electronics and organics, whipping around hir wrists and neck . . . and s/he ripped them away in a crazed flurry of motion.

Starfly started to spin, but Burgoyne would not be dislodged. Hanging on with hir clawed feet, s/he hacked like a whirlwind at the guts of the probe, shredding Dovan's bonds and anything else within reach.

Finally, *Starfly* shuddered and dropped to the street. A piercing squeal rose from inside the probe, reaching an earsplitting crescendo that made Burgoyne howl in pain . . . and then it quickly subsided. The hum of power that had throbbed all along inside the techno-organic berserker died away to nothing just as fast.

One minute.

Burgoyne hit hir combadge, then kept slashing Dovan free as s/he spoke. "Burgoyne to *Livingston!*" s/he shouted, hoping that *Starfly*'s systems were as dead as they sounded and the jamming field was gone. "Emergency transport! Two to beam up!"

There was no response.

Burgoyne kept slashing. *"Livingston!* Two for emergency beam-out!"

Still nothing.

Hir mental countdown reached thirty seconds.

"Repeat!" shouted Burgoyne. "Two to beam up *now!*"

Fifteen seconds.

When there was still no response, s/he howled and clawed all the harder. If s/he had to die, it was better to go out like this, fighting for survival to the very last instant. At least s/he would die in the full flower of hir true nature, bloody and beautiful in the heat of the kill . . . and even better, laying down hir life for the life of another of equal courage.

Dovan, s/he had no doubt, was hir equal in that regard. Whatever its mistakes in developing *Starfly*, the J'naii had walked out to meet it with little more than bare hands. Dovan had faced its errant creation only moments after witnessing its destructive might in action, and had not flinched.

So there was no shame in this for either of them.

Ten seconds.

Burgoyne hit hir combadge again. "Two for emergency beam-out!" s/he shouted, cutting away the last fibers and tendrils that held Dovan in place.

When no one from the *Livingston* answered, s/he howled one final time, crying out hir rage and pain and joy like a wolf in one of hir holodeck programs.

And then, it was all over. Just as s/he resigned hirself to impending death, Burgoyne disappeared from the face of Damiano in a beam of energy sent down from above.

A transporter beam.

As Burgoyne walked into the *Livingston*'s sickbay, s/he had the distinct impression that Dovan was pretending to be asleep. A whiff of Dovan's scent in the air confirmed it: The scent was deeper, muskier, warmer . . . all results of increased blood flow and a waking, not slumbering, physiology. Though the J'naii lay with eyes closed on the diagnostic bed, Burgoyne had no doubt that the scientist was just as awake as s/he was.

Nonchalantly, s/he strolled over to the bed, hands clasped behind hir back. "I guess I'll have to come back later," s/he said in an exaggerated whisper loud enough for Dovan to hear.

Then, in the process of turning to leave, s/he let hir elbow bump a nearby tray of instruments, sending them clattering to the floor. "Oh, dear," s/he said, whipping around in time to see Dovan's eyes snap open. "Clumsy me! I woke you out of a sound sleep!"

Dovan's eyes were too clear and alert for the J'naii to have been sleeping, but it kept up the pretense. "No problem," Dovan said with what had to be feigned grogginess, letting its eyes flutter shut. "Can't stay awake anyway."

Smirking, Burgoyne plopped hirself down on the side of the bed. "Well," s/he said lightly. "Since you're up for the moment, how about filling me in on how you're doing?"

When Dovan's eyes blinked open again, Burgoyne could see a mingling of irritation and apprehension in them. "Feeling fine," said the J'naii. "Healing fast, but need more rest."

"Excellent," said Burgoyne. "I see your wounds have regenerated."

Dovan sighed impatiently but lifted its arms and turned them over. The shiny patches of newly regenerated skin were the only indicators of where *Starfly*'s connectors had punctured and Burgoyne's talons had slashed.

"Sorry I had to cut you up like that," said Burgoyne, running a fingertip over one of the regenerated patches.

Dovan pulled its arm away and looked at the ceiling. "You did what you had to," the J'naii said tightly. "Now, if you'll excuse me, I really must get some rest."

Burgoyne sat for a moment, then eased hirself off the bed. For once, s/he felt awkward about saying what was on hir mind.

S/he turned to go, then cleared hir throat and turned back to Dovan. "I know you don't think much of me," s/he said slowly, "but I wanted to tell you it was an honor working with you."

Dovan lay silently, staring at the ceiling.

"The design of the probe was incredible," said Burgoyne. "It had a couple of kinks, but it was incredible."

Still, Dovan said nothing.

"And I admire you for confronting it the way you did," said Burgoyne. "That really took guts."

Dovan blew out its breath as if eager for the Hermat to shut up and leave.

"Anyway," Burgoyne said with a shrug. "That's all I wanted to say. See you later, Doc."

With that, s/he moved to the instrument tray, retrieved its spilled contents from the floor, and headed for the door.

Just as the door slid open, Dovan finally spoke up.

"Seventy-seven dead," the J'naii said bitterly.

Burgoyne turned.

"I'm sorry you cut me free," said Dovan, "because I should be dead, too."

The door slid shut again as Burgoyne walked to the foot of Dovan's bed. "It was an accident," said the Hermat. "You didn't intentionally program *Starfly* to cause the deaths of those people."

"My carelessness let it happen," said Dovan. "I took a shortcut and used my own genetic material in the biomatrix."

"And we still don't know if that caused the malfunction," said Burgoyne.

"We'll never know, since the *Livingston*'s phasers vaporized the probe," said Dovan. "And as long as there's a possibility that I caused it, I'll blame myself."

"Give it time," said Burgoyne. "If I had a credit for every scientific pioneer who never made a mistake . . . well, I wouldn't have a credit."

Dovan sighed. "You don't understand. I helped create something that ended up violating everything I believe in. You can't imagine what it's like for a pacifist to be responsible for such destruction."

"Pacifist?" said Burgoyne, frowning. "You're a pacifist?"

"I believe that violence is never acceptable under any circumstances," said Dovan. "It is my most deeply held belief. It is why I found you so repellent."

"I thought you had a problem with my dual genders," said Burgoyne. "You being a J'naii and all."

Dovan shook its head. "When we first met, you had blood on your hands from a violent act. It might have been only a holodeck simulation, but it revealed your true nature. You are a creature of violence."

Burgoyne smiled. "I guess I should be insulted," s/he said, "but I'm relieved."

"I am a pacifist," said Dovan, "and I have caused so much death. To make matters worse, I avoided my own death, the death I deserved, only because you committed more violence. And the worst of it is there's a part of me that's glad to be alive. There's a part of me that's grateful to you for saving my life."

Burgoyne nodded thoughtfully, then walked around the bed and took hold of Dovan's hand. "Well, Doctor," s/he said. "I'd like to tell that part of you that I'm glad you're alive, too. For now, anyway."

Dovan frowned. "What do you mean?"

"You've been through an ordeal," said Burgoyne, squeezing Dovan's hand just a little too hard. "I understand why you feel guilty, especially now that I know you're a pacifist."

Grimacing, Dovan tried to pull its hand away. "You're hurting me."

"This is the kind of experience that could ruin somebody," said Burgoyne, "and I won't let you let that happen to yourself. I think you have some important contributions to make to the universe."

"Thank you," said Dovan. "Now please let go."

"Now that I've taken an interest in your work, I want you to see it through," said Burgoyne. "To that end, if you don't get your act together soon and put that genius mind of yours to work on more techno-organic miracles—*with* undefeatable fail-safes and *without* your genetic material—I *swear* I will hunt you down myself and finish the job that *Starfly* started."

"You're joking," said Dovan, staring up at hir with disbelief . . . and a touch of worry.

"Try me," said Burgoyne, curling back hir lips to reveal hir sharp, gleaming canines. "Just try me."

MARK McHENRY
Singularity

Christina F. York

Despite his rather peculiar nature—which, unbeknownst to all, is due to having a Greek god in his ancestry—Mark McHenry graduated Starfleet Academy along with future *Excalibur* crewmates Soleta and Zak Kebron, and established a reputation as one of the best, if most eccentric, pilots in Starfleet. "Singularity" takes place several years after he graduated from the Academy.

Christina F. York

Christina F. York's fiction first appeared in *Star Trek: Strange New Worlds*. Since then she has sold five novels, collaborated with her husband, J. Steven York, on various works, including *Star Trek S.C.E. #20: Enigma Ship*, and is currently hard at work on a variety of projects. In recognition of her growing bibliography, she has acquired the obligatory writer's cats, who share the Yorks' Oregon home.

Mark McHenry ignored the warning klaxon, and the droning computer voice that kept repeating, *"Shield failure imminent."*

He watched the viewscreen as he steered the runabout, his hands thrust into the holographic control system. The display showed a chaotic tumble of color, light, and darkness. The light appeared in swift, erratic bolts and flashes, then disappeared into a blackness so complete it hurt his eyes.

He could recover. He just had to concentrate, to ignore all the outside distractions and trust himself and his skills as a pilot.

"McHenry!" Colin Murphy's voice was quiet and emotionless over his com link. *"The shields are failing, and structural integrity is critical. Sensors indicate a reading of over two thousand Cochranes—well outside tolerances."*

"Yes," McHenry muttered, his attention never leaving the nav controls. "I just need to—finish—this—maneuver."

With a surge, the ship pulled free of the black hole, and veered away from the gaping nothingness, which quickly dwindled behind him.

Satisfied, McHenry leaned back in his seat, drew a deep breath, then hunched over the control console again. His fingers continued manipulating the controls, moving to some internal rhythm, as he flew the runabout back to the science ship. He had delayed only a fraction of a second. All Murphy and the other engineers would know was that the four-dimensional navigation system worked.

Within seconds, McHenry heard Murphy again. *"Computer, end program."*

The controls shimmered and disappeared. The viewscreens were replaced with bare walls, leaving only the navigator's chair in the middle of the stripped-down holoroom, and McHenry's bare hands hanging in empty air.

McHenry rose from the chair and moved to the hatch. The door slid open, putting him face-to-face with Murphy.

"Good job, McHenry. Debrief in fifteen minutes, fourth-floor conference room."

Murphy turned and left the lab. McHenry allowed himself a moment of satisfaction. He *had* done a good job. But any good pilot could do it. Even so, he felt a small rush of victory. He had done it first.

It was a dream assignment for McHenry. The holographic controls they were developing would make it possible to get closer than ever to black holes. They could learn more, explore more, than ever before. They would be able to navigate on the razor's edge between normal space and the event horizon, at the brink of oblivion.

McHenry was pleased he could be a part of the development. Maybe, if he was incredibly lucky, he could join a mission at the edge of a black hole, once they had worked out all the bugs in the system.

He marveled at his good fortune. He could have been on a ship on the other side of the galaxy, or assigned to some remote starbase, when the project started. He could have been passed over for pilots who were stronger, or more agile. But somehow he had managed to get into the single most exciting project in Starfleet.

He wasn't about to disappoint the engineers. They *would* succeed.

The conference room reflected the personalities of the men and women who used it. Utilitarian, and unadorned, but with the best available technical equipment.

The conference table was worn and small, the bare metal chairs mismatched, as if they had been appropriated from other workspaces when they were needed, and the carpet colorless. In contrast, at each station the table held a state-of-the-art engineering screen linked to all the data available on the 4-D project, and oversized display screens covered the walls.

When McHenry reached the room, about half the stations were already filled. Seetara, Harris, and Crane, the other test pilots, were clustered together at one end. Jill Harris gestured to an empty seat next to her, and McHenry moved to join the group.

At the center of the table, where he could command a view of all the participants, was Colin Murphy. As the chief engineer, he was in charge of the project, and the rest of the staff answered to him.

Though they were all members of Starfleet, McHenry knew that in this room rank counted for nothing. All that mattered was creating a new navigational system, and your status depended on your ability to contribute. Today, McHenry was at the top of the ladder.

McHenry listened as Murphy gave a brief description of today's simulation. Although he assumed a relaxed posture, and seemed to be inattentive, he was sharply focused on Murphy's description of the test.

"Shield integrity showed signs of failure at approximately twenty-seven minutes, flight time. Before failure occurred, the craft escaped the event horizon. The simulation was subsequently terminated at twenty-nine-point-five minutes of flight time." The usually taciturn Murphy could not disguise the note of excitement in his voice. "Ladies and gentlemen, it appears that we have successfully simulated the flyby of an event horizon. Congratulations."

Murphy paused, as if allowing them to savor a moment of success. Then he continued. "Mr. McHenry, your observations, please."

McHenry suppressed a grin as he rose to his feet. He knew what the engineers needed to hear.

"The flight was uneventful through launch and approach." He tapped a command on his padd and a display of his flight path appeared on the screens. "At twenty-five minutes, I experienced increased subspace distortion, at approximately this point." He indicated a spot in his flight path on the display. "Cochrane readings exceeded fifteen hundred at about that same time. A few seconds later, there was a fluctuation in the controls. It was so slight that it may not have registered, but it was there. It lasted only a fraction of a second; then navigational control returned to nominal. The runabout continued on trajectory, taking an elliptical path around the singularity, and drawing closer to the event horizon. At twenty-seven minutes, we reached the closest approach to the event horizon, and began the withdrawal. During the initial withdrawal phase, all controls appeared nominal, and all readings were normal. At about twenty-eight minutes, the warning klaxons sounded a shield-failure warning. However, the ship pulled free of the event horizon and assumed its return course before Mr. Murphy signaled 'end program.' "

"Recommendations, Mr. McHenry?" It was Seetara, the Vulcan propulsion engineer, who asked. It was always Seetara who asked.

"We need to reconfigure the controls here, here, and here." He switched the display to a representation of the controls, and indicated three positions. "The sequence of commands is awkward in the current configuration, and it may have contributed to the sluggishness I detected."

Murphy nodded as his assistant made notes. "Anything more, Mr. McHenry?"

"No, sir. Other than that, she performed flawlessly. As good as any pilot could ask for."

"Thank you." Murphy looked around the table. "Anyone else have questions or comments?"

Murphy paused. No one spoke, though a few shook their heads. Clearly, everyone wanted to get back to work. McHenry could see the design engineer fiddling with his padd, already at work on McHenry's modification.

"Very well. Thank you, Mr. McHenry. Dismissed."

The pilots held back as the engineering staff filed out of the room, until they were alone. Then they all seemed to talk at once.

"What happened, really?"

"How did it feel?"

"Did it work the way we expected?"

Mark finally allowed a grin to spread across his face. "It was incredible! Just what we expected. Wait till you get to try it!"

"I don't know, Mark." Jill's blue eyes were clouded. "It looked like a rougher ride than you're telling us."

"Naw. Piece of cake. You'll see." Mark leveled his gaze at her. "You're one of the best, Harris." He looked around the arc of faces. "You all are. There isn't anything you can't do. I know it."

Seetara inclined his head slightly. "If you say so, Mr. McHenry." His tone indicated he was not convinced.

Frankie Crane let out an impatient whoop. "Forget the doom-and-gloom crowd. You did it, Markie-boy! Let's blow this joint and celebrate!" He threw an arm over Mark's shoulders. "The first round's on me."

Frankie turned to Jill and Seetara, and made a sweeping bow in their direction. "In view of our pal here's accomplishment, I'll even buy you two a drink. But you better hurry up, this is a limited-time offer."

Mark watched Jill's eyes clear, and a smile spread across her face. In the last few weeks, she had clearly developed a deep affection for the baby-faced Crane, and couldn't resist his good-natured enthusiasm.

Even Seetara seemed amused, or as amused as a Vulcan ever got. McHenry could have sworn his eyebrow twitched.

"Sure," McHenry said. "Let's celebrate."

The bar was crowded and noisy, but Crane managed to thread his way through and find an empty table. Harris and Seetara followed him, and McHenry was behind them in tail position.

Crane moved swiftly, and McHenry smiled to himself. Even in a packed waterfront bar, Crane's piloting skills were evident.

They settled in around the table, Jill taking the seat between Crane and

McHenry. She was an attractive woman. With close-cropped red hair and an athletic build, she attracted male attention, but didn't seem to notice.

Seetara sat between Crane and McHenry, his posture relaxing slightly, now that they were out of the lab.

McHenry felt a twinge of nostalgia. This was what it had been like in his Academy days, being part of a team, one of the gang. He wondered where Soleta, Tania, Zak, and Worf were, where their careers had taken them.

But now he was part of a team again. It felt good. They were working together on a huge project, Singularity One, and each of them was eager for the challenge.

Crane had disappeared, but quickly returned, carrying four iced mugs, a head of foam topping each one and running down the sides.

"Stout," Crane said, setting the mugs on the table. "Greatest thing on Earth."

"Hardly an impressive claim," Seetara said, eyeing the mug suspiciously.

McHenry preferred Klingon bloodwine to Earth beer, but he accepted the mug with a smile. This was his celebration, after all. He should try to enjoy it. Even a man descended from gods sometimes just wanted to be one of the guys.

"Good news." Murphy stood behind his usual chair at the center of the conference table. "After Mr. McHenry's successful simulation, and the subsequent flight of Harris, Seetara, and Crane, we finally have authorization to build a prototype."

The room buzzed with excitement, and the four pilots exchanged triumphant glances. Crane grinned widely, and whispered to McHenry, "Thanks for leading the way, buddy."

McHenry shook his head. "Luck of the draw, man. I just happened to get there first."

Murphy shot them a look, and further comment died. They could discuss it later.

Once he had everyone's attention again, Murphy continued. "Construction will begin immediately. We expect to have a functional holographic control unit installed in the runabout *Amazon* in about three weeks. We will begin field trials immediately thereafter."

He keyed his padd, and a star chart appeared on the display screens. "We have selected a location for the trials, and arranged for the use of the science vessel *Glenn.*"

A smile threatened Murphy's usual stoic expression. "You will all receive orders for your temporary transfer to duty aboard the *Glenn,* but that's just a formality. As of now, consider yourselves reassigned, and be prepared to leave at the end of the month. Dismissed."

The meeting broke into knots of engineers, pilots, and technicians, all talking at once. McHenry stood with Harris, Seetara, and Crane. It seemed as though all four were talking at once, but Crane's excited chatter rode over the others.

"Field trials? Field trials! Can you believe it? I mean, of course you can." He looked at McHenry. "You led the way, buddy!"

Mark grinned. "We all did it, Frankie. If we hadn't, they wouldn't be putting the time and talent into building us a prototype."

Walking into the stripped-down common room of the refitted runabout *Amazon* was a déjà vu moment for McHenry. It felt exactly like the simulator in the lab at Starfleet Headquarters, right down to the emergency medikit on the bulkhead.

He sat in the command chair, and imagined the holographic controls in front of him. The chair felt so familiar, he wondered if they had taken it from the lab in San Francisco.

The power coupling was in the same place, under the right armrest, and when he activated it, the controls appeared in front of him, just like in the lab.

Seetara was piloting *Amazon.* On this first round of tests with the new system they wouldn't approach the event horizon. Despite his disappointment at the restrictions, McHenry was happy to be back in a real ship.

Their flight was uneventful. To McHenry, in the windowless holosuite built into the runabout, it could just as well have been back in the lab. Except he could feel the difference in their position in space. Unlike the lab, which was always in the same spatial orientation, the runabout was actually moving, shifting location and direction.

It might look exactly like the lab, but it didn't *feel* that way.

Pilot. 4-D pilot. Observer. McHenry, Harris, Seetara, and Crane cycled through all three positions, in every combination. They polished the skills they had developed in the lab, and grew familiar with the nuances of the new installation. They still could not fly near the event horizon, but each round of tests brought them closer.

McHenry was next in the rotation, when Murphy called them into a briefing. "We have just received clearance for a flyby," he said without preamble. "Mr. McHenry, you're up. Are you ready?"

McHenry felt a surge of excitement. Ready? They were all ready. "Yessir!"

Murphy nodded. "We will begin tomorrow. Each flight will get progressively closer to the event horizon. Regular flight rotation will be followed. Any questions?"

They shook their heads, and were dismissed.

As they headed down the corridor, Crane turned to McHenry. "I do have a question for you, buddy."

"What?"

"Just how in the hell are we supposed to sleep tonight?"

Mark grinned at him. Crane would pilot the runabout in tomorrow's flight, and McHenry understood how he felt. "I don't know, Frankie. You think Zefram Cochrane had this problem before his first flight?"

Crane laughed. "I think every pilot who ever broke a barrier must have had the same problem. Did you ever hear the stories about Yeager, the first guy to break the sound barrier?"

McHenry nodded. He devoured historical minutiae, and Chuck Yeager was one of the greatest pilots of twentieth-century Earth. He had read everything he could find about the man.

But that didn't stop Crane from launching into a long and involved tale of the first Mach 1 flight.

McHenry had to admit it: Crane was a good storyteller. He could only imagine what Crane's version of tomorrow's flight would be like, but it would probably make a great story.

McHenry watched the holographic viewscreen intently. Every few seconds the display would fluctuate, the colors a shade less intense, the focus softening almost imperceptibly. It passed in the blink of an eye, an instant of change that disappeared before it could be analyzed.

But Mark knew each time it happened. He could feel the difference between their actual location and what the displays were showing him. It just felt *wrong*.

At the helm, Crane seemed to share the same sense of wrongness. McHenry could hear it in the tone of his voice, and feel his hesitations.

They drew in nearer to the event horizon, crossing the invisible line in space, which they had not crossed before. There was no dramatic change, no sudden shift, but McHenry could feel a subtle shift in the speed and direction of the runabout. It was fully in his control now, the 4-D controls offering a dizzying number of choices and combinations.

McHenry reacted with confidence and precision. This was what they had trained for, the job they were here to do.

The flight ended almost as soon as it began. At least, that was how it felt to McHenry. All the months of work, of training and drill and practice, came down to a few seconds of flight time. As he surrendered control to Crane, he wondered how long Zefram Cochrane's first flight had been.

Buoyed by the success of his first flight, McHenry was eager to see what an approach looked like from the outside.

Crane was the 4-D pilot, Harris at the helm. McHenry and Seetara watched from the bridge as *Amazon*'s image grew smaller on the viewscreen.

"Magnify."

The tactical officer responded to Murphy's command. The view focused in on the runabout as it neared the event horizon. Without the 4-D displays, the colors and lights seemed dim and monochromatic. They reminded McHenry of the thunderstorms back on Earth: powerful and dramatic, but nothing like the brilliant chaos he had seen from the holodeck.

Amazon approached the event horizon, then assumed a course that followed the rim of the singularity. The open com channel between *Glenn* and *Amazon* relayed every sound from the runabout.

Crane had assumed control, and his muttered monologue provided a running commentary on his every move. He ran through the navigational routines, his fingers following his mumbled instructions. His words tumbled out faster and faster as he tried to keep pace with his flying fingers.

The sequence reached the most dangerous point, disengaging, and Crane's voice rose. He was breathing fast, and talking faster, as he completed the maneuver and returned control to Harris.

Crane's exaggerated sigh of relief drew a chuckle from the assembled crew. They had all felt the tension, and success now allowed them to relax. For a minute.

"*Ouch!*" Crane yelled, startling the assembled bridge crew.

The doctor instantly tapped his communicator. "Mr. Crane? What seems to be the problem?"

"*My fingers. Cramped,*" Crane answered through what sounded like gritted teeth.

McHenry winced in sympathy. The command sequences were long and complicated, and had to be executed swiftly.

"Mr. Crane?" Murphy said.

"Yes, sir."

"Can you still operate the controls?"

"Negative."

The single word stopped them all. It wasn't a failure; Crane had already completed his part of the flight. But McHenry could see concerned glances passing among the members of the design team.

Crane and Harris returned to *Glenn* without further complications, but there was an air of uneasiness in the conference room as the team assembled. The pilots were subdued, taking their places without their usual discussion and horseplay.

Murphy ran through the debriefing, covering the operation of the runabout and the data collected by the monitoring systems. Finally, he turned to Crane.

"Mr. Crane, can you tell us what happened after Harris resumed control of the flight?"

Crane gingerly rubbed his hands together for a moment before he answered. Although the cramp had passed, the movement still looked painful.

"After I completed the transfer to Harris," he began, "I shut off the holo controls, using the prescribed shutdown procedure. Everything worked the way it should, except for my hands." Crane looked down at the offending digits, as if they could offer an explanation. "They just cramped up. Clenched, and I couldn't relax them for a couple minutes."

Dr. Trent took over from Murphy. He asked questions, and nodded as Crane answered. Satisfied, he turned to Murphy.

"I think this is simply a muscle-fatigue problem. We're asking these pilots to perform at their maximum physical output. Is there some way the sequences can be streamlined?"

Murphy was a good engineer, but he had the best on his design team, and he passed the question along to them. A few were nodding, and two were already bent over a padd, sketching changes.

"Looks like it," Murphy said. "Let's see what the team comes up with."

Murphy looked back at Crane. "How are the hands now?"

Dr. Trent answered. "He's fine. As I said, it appears to be a muscle-fatigue response."

Murphy nodded. His attention was already on the engineers. His dismissal was almost an afterthought as he moved to join the impromptu brainstorming session at the end of the table.

*　*　*

McHenry eagerly assumed his position in the command chair. The mission would launch in ten minutes, but he was ready now.

This rotation should have been Seetara's, but the doctor had grounded the Vulcan. Some foolishness about exposure to a virus. Instead, Seetara had come to the hangar bay to watch McHenry take the runabout out.

"Sorry for taking your mission," McHenry said. Even though he was anxious to fly the new configuration, he didn't like to see his friend disappointed.

"There is nothing to be sorry for," Seetara replied evenly. "It is not my mission for you to take. It is the mission of the next pilot in the rotation. Since I am unable to fly, you are the next pilot. It is your mission."

Harris and Crane arrived. Harris took her place at the helm, and Crane joined Seetara. Soon, Murphy hailed the hangar, and told them to prepare for launch.

Crane and Seetara left the bay, and Harris took them out. McHenry activated the holographic controls. Over the com link, he heard Murphy give the order, and heard Harris reply, *"Here we go."*

He watched the displays as they sped toward the spot of darkest space, which held the black hole. Light shimmered on the edge, and disappeared into the darkness within. Colors danced at the rim. Streaks of red swirling into blue, then a flash of green, combinations and shades that Mark had no words for. Each millisecond brought another permutation.

McHenry logged every change. He could feel the dip and sway of the ship as the subspace distortion increased. He knew, without sensors or readouts or displays, their precise location in space, and the limits of their navigational instruments. It was as if he were a part of the ship.

"Transferring control," Harris said over the com channel.

McHenry knew Murphy, on board *Glenn,* was monitoring them. For his benefit, he replied, "Roger that."

Control of the ship was now in his hands. He entered the command sequence for the flight without hesitation. They had all drilled, were all trained to back up the other pilots. So far, it was a routine test.

As they approached the event horizon, McHenry veered off, skimming the ship along the edge of safety. The simulated viewscreen showed the black emptiness moving along their starboard side, sliding past them.

The ship's speed grew erratic, as they approached the space-time distortions of the event horizon. McHenry held *Amazon* to the prescribed trajectory, letting the sensor array read the fluctuations.

McHenry sensed a sideways slip in the ship's course. It felt as though it had moved, though no more than a fraction of a millimeter, in the time *between* milliseconds.

He calculated the consequences. They were in an unstable time-space. Slippage could occur in time that did not exist for the rest of the galaxy. Unchecked, it would drag *Amazon* in, and there would be no escape.

Fingers flying, McHenry made a minute course correction, pulling *Amazon* back into the proper space-time. It was all over in the blink of an eye. *Amazon* was safely back on course.

When neither Murphy nor Harris commented on the correction, he hesitated. Had it actually happened? Or had it only happened in the exact time-space where *he* was, and not for anyone else?

After a few seconds, the sensor array indicated that they had finished collecting the data the engineers needed. McHenry brought *Amazon* about, pulling free of the event horizon, and putting the ship on course for their return flight.

"Returning control," he said.

"*Roger,*" Harris replied. She resumed control of the ship, and McHenry leaned back in his chair. His eyes closed, and he looked like he was asleep. But his thoughts were racing, already planning the next mission, when he would have the helm.

Next time, Crane would have the controls. McHenry would just be along for the ride.

The event horizon shimmered on the forward viewscreen. It was closer than McHenry had ever been, closer than he ever wanted to be.

Amazon bucked, speeding up and slowing down as the temporal shifts battered it. He could hear Crane's harsh breathing over the open com channel.

McHenry knew the concentration required to hold the ship on course. He had done it on the last flight. Surely Crane could do the same. Just a few more seconds, and they would be clear.

The ship rolled, and McHenry clutched the arms of his chair to avoid being thrown to the deck. Crane was breathing faster now, panting with the exertion.

McHenry hesitated. Crane could do this. McHenry just had to have faith.

He sensed the minute Crane lost control. Before the sensors could detect it, before the warning klaxons sounded, McHenry knew.

"Computer, end program. Authorization McHenry-Alpha-Zero-Three." Without waiting for orders, McHenry assumed control of the ship.

Amazon's standard controls lacked the fourth-dimensional modeling of the holograph, but McHenry might be the best astronavigator in Starfleet.

And if he wasn't, he and Crane were both dead.

His fingers flew across the controls. The ship veered, and in his imagination he heard welds creaking with the strain. McHenry wished he had the added capabilities of the 4-D system, but he couldn't reach it. He had to rely on the standard controls.

The ship bucked again, but McHenry anticipated the movement, and continued his frenetic pace. They were slowly coming back on course.

Gravitational shear pulled at the off-course ship. The starboard side of the ship was somehow traveling *faster* than the port side. The Cochrane readings were spiking well above safety limits. The ship might literally tear itself apart.

McHenry shut out the warning klaxons. He ignored the readings and the displays. He knew where to go and how to get there. He just had to *do* it.

Amazon made another slip, this one in the right direction. She shuddered and slipped again. In a few moments, McHenry knew he had the ship back on course.

"You all right?" he asked Crane.

There was no answer. McHenry continued to manipulate the controls, his concern for his copilot growing with every second of silence.

The turbulence had been momentary, but both intense and unexpected; at least, it was to anyone who wasn't Mark McHenry.

The event horizon receded. *Amazon* broke free of its influence, regaining her normal stability. McHenry instantly set the autopilot and leaped from his seat.

He stepped through the hatch to the holodeck, and into a nightmare.

Crane's chair was still anchored in the middle of the empty room, but Frankie wasn't in it. The holographic controls were still functioning, but there was no one to operate them.

Instead, Crane was crumpled against the far wall of the cabin, where he had been thrown by the turbulence. Blood stained his shirt, and poured from beneath his scalp. One leg was bent at an unnatural angle.

But the noise was the worst. He wasn't exactly breathing, but instead snorting and gasping as though unable to draw air into his lungs.

From an emergency med pack mounted on the bulkhead, McHenry pulled a medical tricorder. "Computer, monitor readings," he commanded as he ran the tricorder over Crane's body. "Recommend treatment."

McHenry knew the runabout was relaying the tricorder readings to sickbay aboard *Glenn*. It had been only a couple of minutes since the last time he had heard from Crane. But how long could he survive without oxygen? How long before McHenry had to act?

His combadge chirped, and then he heard Dr. Trent speaking from *Glenn*. *"Recommend you place Lieutenant Crane flat. Do not move his left leg any more than necessary."*

McHenry began shifting Crane's body, laying him flat on the floor, as the doctor continued. *"It appears his airway is obstructed by his posture. Can you send another scan?"*

"Affirmative," McHenry said through gritted teeth. Crane was heavier than he looked, and McHenry had never been much for weight-lifting.

Still, he managed to lay Crane out. As he ran the tricorder over him once more, Crane gasped again, and shuddered as he drew in a huge lungful of air.

"He's breathing again!"

"No need to shout, Lieutenant. We have his telemetry. We know he's breathing."

Mark wasn't sure, but he thought he heard a note of amusement in the doctor's voice. There sure as hell wasn't anything at all amusing about this situation.

"Then you know he's still unconscious, and he's still bleeding," he said, trying to keep his anger from showing in his voice. "Shouldn't we do something about that?"

"The head wound is superficial. Put a pressure pack on it. You'll find one in the medikit," the doctor replied. *"And he'll come around soon enough. Just get him back here so we can patch him up."*

Murphy broke in. *"We'll beam him to sickbay as soon as you're in range, McHenry. We'll debrief after Crane's through with the doc. We want to know exactly what happened out there. The sensors went nuts here, we lost telemetry for a few seconds, then we had you in control and moving away from the event horizon at top speed. We're anxious to hear what you and Crane can tell us."*

"Returning to *Glenn*. *Amazon* out."

McHenry tapped his combadge to end communication. He put a pressure pack on Crane's head, and tried to make him a bit more comfortable. It was hard to tell if it did any good, since Crane was still unconscious.

McHenry was hurtling through space with an injured crewmate, an experimental ship that no one else could control, and a growing feeling of guilt.

In his ignorance, he had assumed anyone could do what he had done.

He had refused to admit his unique abilities, to acknowledge that he was different from the other pilots in the program.

But he was. He could do things Crane and Seetara and Harris and Murphy couldn't do. He could fly to the thin edge of the event horizon and back again, knowing the exact limits of his control. But no one else could.

He looked down at Crane. He was still deathly pale, but he was breathing steadily. The blood no longer flowed down his face, though his uniform shirt was soaked with it. He looked like he was sleeping, but each time he moved, however slightly, his face was creased with pain.

This was the cost of McHenry's ignorance, and someone else was forced to pay it.

They were nearing transporter range. McHenry returned to the pilot's seat and resumed control of the runabout.

Within seconds he was hailed by Murphy. "We're ready to transport Crane to sickbay."

McHenry felt the acceleration as Crane's weight was removed from the ship; then the ship adjusted and resumed its proper speed. He would reach *Glenn* in two and a half minutes. And what would he do when he got there?

McHenry cycled the door of the runabout open. He sprinted down the corridor in the direction of sickbay.

Halfway there, Murphy intercepted him, grabbing his arm. "What happened out there?"

McHenry shook off his grip and kept moving. Murphy fell in beside him, not letting him get away. "What happened?"

"How's Crane?" McHenry countered.

"He'll be fine. The doc's already working on him." Murphy was panting as they ran. His sedentary engineering duties didn't keep him in shape for running.

"Good. Then I can see him for myself."

They ran through the door of the sickbay, and then McHenry stopped, looking for his injured crewmate. He spotted Crane and hurried to his side.

Crane was still unconscious, but his face was no longer marked with pain. He looked relaxed, as though he were simply resting.

McHenry caught the doctor's arm. "How is he?"

"Better than I expected, frankly." The doctor pulled free of McHenry's grasp and continued his work. "And he'll continue to improve, if you'll let me do my work."

"Sorry." McHenry stepped back, letting his hand drop. What was he doing here? He didn't know, but he knew he had to stay. "Can I wait here?"

"As long as you don't interfere, I don't care where you wait. But if you get in my way again, I'll call security."

McHenry retreated a couple steps, giving the doctor plenty of room. "Yes, sir," he said quietly.

Murphy was still at his side, but he was also quiet. The fact that Crane hadn't regained consciousness seemed to have dampened his demands for information.

The room was silent for long minutes, as the doctor circled the bed. He scanned Crane, administered hyposprays, and treated him with instruments McHenry didn't have names for.

Finally, after what seemed like hours, Crane opened his eyes. There was an instant of panic on his face, then swift comprehension of where he was. And then, as clearly as if he had spoken aloud, the relief of finding himself alive and more or less in one piece.

But that moment of panic on Crane's trusting baby face would stay burned in Mark McHenry's memory. He was sure he would carry that image with him, in everything he did, for the rest of his life.

"Good to see you, buddy," McHenry said.

Crane gave him a shaky thumbs-up. "Good to see you, too. Didn't figure I'd be seeing anybody again."

"Hey, I couldn't let anything happen to the second-best navigator in Starfleet, could I?" McHenry nearly choked on the truth of the old joke. It was one he swore he would never use again. "Not to mention what Harris will do to me for letting you get hurt."

"No way you could have stopped it."

McHenry could feel Murphy hanging on their conversation, listening and weighing each word. He chose his words carefully.

"No," he lied. "I don't think there was."

He felt Murphy stiffen. "Let's not be too hasty," he said.

"We're not being hasty, Murphy." McHenry turned to face Murphy. If he was going to kill the man's dream, he should at least have the guts to face him. "The ship was beyond our control. Period. I don't know how we got out of there, and I doubt we could do it again."

Murphy looked stricken.

"There are things we can't see," McHenry continued. "Time and space are distorted in ways we can't understand, can't simulate, and can't compensate for."

McHenry wished he could tell him the whole truth, but even the truth would do him no good. Because the truth was that McHenry *could* understand. He had a unique gift, a gift that could compensate for the distortions. A gift he could not share with another being. And without that gift, the 4-D project could not succeed.

"We can't do it, Murphy. I wish I could give you a better answer, but look for yourself." He gestured at Crane, still lying on the exam bed. "This is the answer. We can't do it."

"Maybe there's another way—"

"There isn't." McHenry's voice was unnaturally harsh. "Not with what you've got. You could go back to square one, Murphy, and start over. But you can't do it with what you've got."

"Then we'll go back to square one. We'll try a new approach, new designs. Go in a new direction. We have a good team here."

McHenry felt the words as though they were physical blows. He could never be a part of the team. Not now. Not when he knew the danger his abilities posed to the others.

"Yes," he said. He clenched his hands into fists, hidden behind his back, channeling his tension and frustration into the rigid muscles. He kept his face calm and his voice steady. "You have a good team. But I can't be a part of it any longer. This has always been a voluntary assignment, and I am requesting immediate reassignment."

Murphy swallowed the news as though it were a particularly bitter pill. But he took it. Closing his eyes, he stood immobile for a few seconds, then shook his head.

"That's it, then. I'll recommend the program be restructured. You," he nodded at McHenry, "and any others that request it, will be reassigned."

Murphy left, his rigid posture silent testimony to his steely control.

McHenry watched him go, feeling like a traitor. But it was the only thing he could do.

He turned back to Crane. "You sure you're okay?"

"Yeah. I owe you a beer, though. Thanks." Crane started to say something more, but something in McHenry's face stopped him. He shifted uncomfortably in the bed, and glanced around the room as if looking for some way to change the subject.

Crane turned back, and his face lit with a tentative smile, but he wasn't looking at McHenry. He was looking past him. McHenry looked behind him, and saw Jill Harris coming through the sickbay doors.

"Yeah," McHenry said. "I think you are."

McHenry slipped out of sickbay as Jill came to Crane's bedside. He glanced back in time to see her take his hand in hers, and saw Crane's smile grow. The baby-faced pilot was going to be fine.

Murphy had told them to expect reassignment, but McHenry couldn't wait for orders. He now knew he could never be just one of the gang, and that truth was going to take some time to accept.

He had some leave coming. It was time to go.

AREX
The Road to Edos

Kevin Dilmore

Arex served a distinguished tenure on the *U.S.S. Enterprise* under Captain James T. Kirk in the latter days of that ship's historic five-year mission. After being accidentally sent forward eight decades in time, he was assigned to the *U.S.S. Trident* as chief of security under Captain Shelby. When he first arrived in the twenty-fourth century, however, he had to assimilate into the future. "The Road to Edos" takes place during that transition period in Arex's life.

Kevin Dilmore

After fifteen years as a newspaper reporter and editor, Kevin Dilmore turned his full attention to his freelance writing career earlier this year. Since 1997, he has been a contributing writer to *Star Trek Communicator*, writing news stories and personality profiles for the bimonthly publication of the Official *Star Trek* Fan Club. With Dayton Ward, he has written a story for next year's *Star Trek: Tales of the Dominion War*, six installments of the continuing eBook series *Star Trek: S.C.E.*, and a forthcoming two-book *Star Trek: The Next Generation* tale, with more to come. Look for Kevin's interviews with some of *Star Trek*'s most popular authors in volumes of the *Star Trek* Signature Editions this fall from Pocket Books. A graduate of the University of Kansas, Kevin lives in Prairie Village, Kansas, with his wife Michelle and their three daughters.

Still fumbling with his data padd, Agent Stewart Peart rushed down the hallways of Starbase 211 as if he were racing time itself. Hardly looking up from his handheld display, he sidestepped the contents of a toolkit splayed across the floor near a pair of busy technicians, then nearly jogged into the path of a workman's antigrav cart before spinning himself out of the way. All the while, his eyes never stopped scanning the data before him.

Although rushed, Peart found himself smiling at his own enthusiasm, a feeling that caught him somewhat by surprise. Despite the hasty, on-the-run scan of the padd's mission dossier—*his* mission—the young man surged with confidence. His mind raced with ideas, wanting to leave nothing to chance once his superiors put him in charge.

He slowed to a walk while hastily keying several commands into his padd. Stilling his hand until the padd softly beeped in confirmation, he then looked up and strode between a pair of sliding doors bearing its designation with little fanfare.

STARFLEET COMMAND—DEPARTMENT OF TEMPORAL INVESTIGATIONS.

His stride was abruptly broken by a reception desk that blocked his access into the array of suites beyond. As he panted to catch his breath, he awaited some acknowledgment from an older, neatly coiffured woman at the desk, who stayed intent on a flat viewscreen on the desktop's surface. He cleared his throat somewhat lightly, and the woman almost imperceptibly raised herself to look Peart in the eyes. Her lips barely parted as she spoke.

"Yes?"

"Yes, good afternoon," Peart said in a crisp voice too loud for an office. Catching himself, he lowered his volume. "Good afternoon. Um, Temporal Displacement Division?"

"Two doors down on the left," the receptionist replied, now staring Peart down as he shifted his weight from one foot to the other.

"Yes, thank you," Peart said, pausing again as he noted that the woman was making no moves to facilitate his entry. "Um . . . Special Agent Dulmer?"

"Two doors down on the left."

"Yes . . . he, um, called me to a meeting?"

The woman drew a heavy breath and let it escape slowly. "Son, I need your identification."

"Right! Of course," Peart said as he set his padd on the desk and fished into his shoulder bag to produce a slim metal card. He thumbed a sliding switch on the card's face, revealing a data wafer encoded with his likeness, Starfleet serial number, and security clearances. As the woman studied the card, letting her eyes flit from it to Peart's face, he could not help but note how free from motion she remained in her chair. He wondered whether her limbs would creak if she tried to reach for something, let alone walk.

The receptionist nodded but slightly. "Hmm . . . first assignment?"

His eyes widened as a noise escaped his startled lips. He leaned closer to the woman and spoke in a low voice. "Does it show?"

Without a spoken response, the woman invisibly triggered a mechanism causing what had appeared to be an extension to her desk to slide into the adjoining wall. "Second door—"

"To the left, right," Peart finished for her as he snatched up his padd and stepped through the newly opened access. "I mean, 'correct' right. It's on the left, I mean."

The woman silently pivoted in her chair, never allowing her gaze to leave Peart's face.

"Um, right," he offered as he broke off to head down the hallway. In a few jogged steps, he reached the door and pressed his finger to a translucent plate next to its frame triggering a chime to announce his arrival. The door silently slid away and Peart stepped into the room, his blood pounding in his ears more from excitement than from exertion.

"Ah, Agent Peart, I appreciate your haste," said a blond, tousled-haired man as he rose from a chair behind the office's lone desk. While never having met the man in person, Peart immediately recognized Temporal Investigations Special Agent Dulmer from his required scourings of department communiqués and classified files. It did not take long for him to pick up on the fact that Dulmer's name figured time and again among those agents taking part in temporal cases of the highest profile.

Any feelings of familiarity faded, however, as he turned to the individual seated across the desk from Dulmer. Peart was certain that he never had encountered anyone quite like this in his life.

"Peart, I'd like you to meet Lieutenant Arex Na Eth," Dulmer said, smiling. "Arex was among a shuttlecraft party carried to 2376 just yesterday courtesy of a wormhole in the Argolis Cluster."

Peart took a hesitant step toward the lieutenant, who was unlike any being that Peart had met in person. Not that Peart was unnerved merely by the appearance of the displaced Starfleet officer, who rose on three spindly legs from his seat. He did not flinch when his proffered hand was taken in greeting by a three-fingered, red leathery mitt on an arm connected to the center of Arex's chest. Arex seemed to raise a question in Peart's mind, more of a nagging feeling for the young agent.

Shake it off, Stew. Be on top of your game, here.

"It's a pleasure to meet you, sir," said Peart, hoping a confident tone of voice would put him more at ease. "And, welcome."

Arex's bony, bald head more teetered than shook on his slim neck as he seemed to force his angular face into an uncomfortable approximation of a humanoid smile. "Thank you, Mr. Peart. It's good to know that Starfleet continues to thrive after these . . . what . . . seventy-one years, is it?"

Peart knit his brow at the sound of Arex's gravelly voice. The unspecified question continued to nag at him, but he shrugged it off as his appreciation for Arex's situation began to sink in.

Seventy-one years. A generation at least—probably more. What would I do if I were in his place? My family and friends . . . all gone. My whole experience changed. Where would I even begin to rebuild my life, my place in this new world?

"From the logs of your shuttlecraft, Mr. Arex, that's what it appears," said Dulmer, retaking his seat as Peart and Arex did the same. "It's a brave sacrifice you have made for the Federation, Lieutenant, one that could be surpassed only by giving up your life. Starfleet wants to honor that sacrifice, and I have been authorized to put this department and its personnel at your disposal."

Arex nodded once again. "I appreciate that offer, Mr. Dulmer, which is why I have approached you with my request."

Peart straightened himself in his seat, sensing that Dulmer was ready to address him and dole out his first assignment as a Temporal Investigations agent. He sat ready to puzzle out the nature of the wormhole and its impact on the timestream. He was prepared to correct this temporal anomaly using any means necessary and reset the course of history. He was ready to wrestle time and space to put all as it should be.

"Agent Peart," Dulmer said, "your job is to accompany Mr. Arex, with all haste, to the home of his parents."

He felt his shoulders slump. "Um, that's it? That's all I am supposed to do?" Peart felt a chill in his veins as Dulmer's eyes widened to glare back at him. He blurted out before silence could continue to fill the office. "Oh! Right! Absolutely I can play the valet—I mean, um, attaché to Mr. Arex."

Dulmer's voice took a more threatening edge. "I want to impress upon you, Agent Peart, that escorting the temporally displaced is not a duty we take lightly in the department, particularly in this case. Mr. Arex needs your help in getting home within the next twenty-four hours."

Peart turned to Arex, who was staring downward at his three clasped hands. "It is a solemn time for my family as tradition dictates we gather at our ancestral home. My arrival has coincided with a grave event. The Day of Death is upon my father."

"Your father is still alive?" Peart regretted his words of surprise as soon as they shot from his mouth.

Arex looked up at Peart with yellow eyes and attempted his twisted form of a polite smile. "You seem surprised to learn this? It is no secret that my people are long-lived by your standards."

"Right, but of course they are. Please excuse my rudeness." Peart laughed, hoping his words would cover what he was sure came across to the others as self-doubt as he put his finger on the nagging question.

His people . . . his people . . . dammit, Stew, think . . .

"While they are not members of the Federation, we owe a lot to Mr. Arex's kin and culture," Dulmer said. "Their contributions to science, architecture, mathematics, and the arts would be hard to calculate. And Starfleet has gained much from the service of officers with the physiological advantages of Mr. Arex and other—"

Aha!

"Yes!" Peart's outburst startled them all as his mind seemed to engage anew. "Yes, right. Contributions all discussed in detail in xenosociology classes at the Academy. How could I forget, I mean, um, lose sight of that?"

Peart tried a polite laugh as a cover for his refreshed memory as he turned his attention to his trusty data padd. He worked feverishly, his fingers speeding through commands as silence returned to the room. In less than a minute, he looked up at Dulmer with a renewed sense of pride. "Sir, I've accessed Starfleet vessel assignments and course filings from the starbase computer, and we're in great luck. The *U.S.S. Musgrave,* a ship assigned to the Starfleet Corps of Engineers, is headed on assignment to Starbase 129. With some discussion with its captain, I am sure we can arrange a high-warp trip there and catch passage on the *U.S.S. Prokofiev,* which in ten hours is headed from there to Gamma Trianguli—but not before a stop at Mr. Arex's homeworld. I daresay that it's a trip we can make well within your deadline."

"Nice work," Dulmer said, nodding agreeably as the edge faded from his voice. "Mr. Arex, I will turn you over to Agent Peart, who can brief you on any aspect of life today as you travel."

"But we need to leave right away, as the *Musgrave* ships out in fifteen minutes," Peart said, adopting his best ambassadorial tone. "Mr. Arex, I tend to travel light, so I am ready to go. May I assist you with your belongings?"

Arex shrugged. "I have no belongings. I was told that the contents of my living quarters were shipped to my family fifty years ago."

Peart winced inside as Dulmer spoke, trying to sound apologetic. "It's Starfleet policy to declare a missing officer as 'presumed dead or displaced' after twenty years."

"Please, Mr. Dulmer, I do understand," Arex said.

Dulmer rose from his seat. "You two need to get moving. Mr. Arex, I am sure that anything you might need for the trip can be replicated for you onboard ship. And I'll get to work on reactivating your personnel file, security clearances, and duty status so by the time your visit home is over, you'll be free to move about the quadrant just as you used to do."

Arex sprang to his three feet and extended his center hand to Dulmer. "I cannot express my appreciation enough. This is a grievous time for me and my family, so you are doing us all a great service."

"It's the least we can do in return for your sacrifice of seventy-one years. Travel safely and I am sorry for your loss," the supervising agent said as the travelers set off. "Oh, Agent Peart, can I have one more moment?"

As Arex left the room, Peart drew a breath to speak. He wanted to leave with one last bit of confidence. "Sir, I'll take care of everything."

"See that you do, Peart. So far, you're off on the right foot," Dulmer said as he leaned forward on his desk. "This is your shakedown cruise. Pull it off, and trust me, it will be a tight pull, then we'll see what we can do about beefing up your case rotation."

"Yes, sir!"

"But blow this case, Peart, and you'll be done in this department. Plenty of people want to be where you are, and we don't have time for second chances," he said in a stern tone. "Am I clear?"

Peart felt his stomach flutter. For years, he had worked toward a posting in DTI. His boyhood dreams had been filled with the possibilities such a posting offered, such as traveling through time, observing history firsthand or glimpsing the future, and possibly meeting some of the legendary figures of Starfleet and Federation lore. And it all seemed to be riding on his making two flight connections with an amiable alien denizen of the past.

How hard can this be?

"You are clear, sir. I'll check in when the assignment is complete," Peart said. Striding to the door, he let loose his urge to lighten his supervisor's concerns. Turning, he said, "And next time, maybe we'll run into Captain James Kirk or something."

Dulmer froze. "Don't talk to me about James Kirk, Agent Peart. Just don't."

Peart broke into a jog down the hall, catching up with Arex at the reception desk. The gray-haired woman continued to sit all but motionless as he passed her. "Let's be on our way, shall we?"

As the two left, Arex said, "She does not move all that much, does she?"

Peart laughed. "Maybe she's drying out."

"I thought the same thing," Arex said. "It made me a little wistful for home."

The young agent puzzled that comment out briefly before tapping his combadge. "DTI Agent Stewart Peart to *U.S.S. Musgrave.* Two to beam aboard, please."

Within seconds, a hum filled Peart's ears as the room faded amid a cascade of shimmering light. He always sensed a slight light-headedness at the peak of transportations, although he assumed it owed more to his imagination than to his physical discorporate state. Once his mind—his whole being—was translated into energy particles, the concept of his continuing to have a train of thought or physical sensations was one he internally disputed. Clarity quickly returned, however, as his new surroundings shone through the fading light and he found himself in a palpably different location.

"Permission to come aboard?" Peart asked, and smiled, but only because he had few opportunities to do so. The transporter chief of the *Musgrave* confirmed and reported to the bridge as he gestured for Arex to lead the way off of the pad. They were met by a Gnalish officer, who showed the pair to separate quarters, something that Peart admitted he appreciated.

"Mr. Arex, I'll be by in a few minutes if that's okay with you," he called down the corridor as they separated. It looked as though Arex nodded silently, but Peart could not be sure. He found himself a bit mesmerized by watching the stride of his companion. Arex's three legs moved in series, not so much as a person on crutches might walk but more as a pinwheel's blades might spin. Maybe the rushed departure wore the alien down more than Peart himself realized.

Okay, Peart thought, *step one accomplished.* From here should be smooth sailing.

A sonic shower and a *raktajino* later, Peart was ready to check on his charge, the subject of his first department mission. And he came armed with treats. His walk down the corridor to Arex's guest cabin aboard the *Musgrave* drew a few stares from passing crewmen, especially given what Peart carried: a large, sealed jar, through which could be viewed about a dozen palm-sized fluttering insects. The colorful, mothlike creatures flicked their wings on the sides of the jar, making an ululating noise he truly hoped Arex would find appetizing.

The door chimed to signal his arrival as he stopped before it; then it quietly slid open. Peart saw Arex placing several items into a hard-shelled travel case that was standard Starfleet issue for personnel traveling on civilian business. Setting the jar down on a nearby desktop, he said, "It looks as though you were able to get what you needed."

"Yes," Arex said, wrapping a small circular tin container in an earthen-toned gauze. "The ship's replicator had no problem creating this *meechacha* ointment, for instance, so that I may present it to my father on his transition as is our custom."

"And this flute?" asked Peart as he held up a slim, wooden instrument to admire for a moment before passing it to Arex. He noticed that, while replicated, its appearance would make it difficult to distinguish from one handcrafted and used for decades.

"Ah, my *sessica*. As we travel, I must observe the Contemplation. I need time to myself to reflect in honor of my father's sacrifices for our family. That reflection is begun by my rendition of the Song of Heritage," Arex said. "But what I find more interesting than my meager possessions is this jar of insects you have brought."

Peart beamed with pride. "Well, in our meeting, I added one instruction for our travel manifest. I had the *Musgrave* take on some of your native foods. I crosschecked the xenobiology files and starbase food stores during our meeting and made a few quick selections. I hope they are to your liking. These are, um, desert silk flies, I think."

Arex approached the jar and studied its contents. "Well, they may be. But as much as I appreciate the gesture, I won't be eating them."

"Really?" Peart felt a bit let down. "You're not hungry?"

The alien's reddish face puckered into a smile. "I do not eat living insects."

"You don't? Um, do you eat anything alive?"

"Well," Arex said, "not while it remains alive, no."

Peart was stumped. This was the first time he could remember that his skills at information access through his trusted padd had failed him. And of all times now, on his first mission. He resolved not to let this show in his demeanor toward Arex. "I do apologize then," he said. "I'm sure you will find something more to your liking then when you arrive on Edos."

Arex stiffened. His head slowly bowed as he drew a breath. "Agent Peart, now may be a good time to tell you that I am not Edoan. I am a native of Triex."

"What?" Peart thought his knees would buckle but caught himself on the edge of the desk. That was it. That's what his nagging mind was attempting to spur while talking with Special Agent Dulmer.

You should have paid attention *in that damned Academy class, idiot!*

"Um," Peart began as he regained some control of his thoughts. "Pardon me, did you say, um, Triex?"

"Yes."

"Um," Peart mumbled as he tried to recover somewhat gracefully, "common mistake?"

"Not really, I must admit," Arex said. "Edoans are a much more, well, animated race."

"No kidding?"

"I fear that my native world is far from Edos," Arex said calmly. "This may require a change in our travel arrangements."

"Ah, a *change?*" Peart shouted as he rummaged through his shoulder bag and grabbed his padd. Practically pounding his fingers on its surface, Peart started to panic once his requested data started to flow. "We're going in the opposite direction!"

"As I said—"

"I know! I know!" Peart looked up at Arex quickly then back down to the padd as he paged through data. "We can't go all the way to Starbase 129. It would cost us twelve hours at least. We have to get off of this ship. I'm going to speak with Captain Dayrit."

"I hate to be any trouble."

Arex's face looked almost sympathetic to Peart as he met the alien's gaze. His mistake certainly cost them time, he knew, but it might well have cost Arex his one chance to see his dying father after more than seventy years. "No, sir," he said. "This is on my shoulders. I brought this on us. I can fix it."

Peart raced out of the room and into the first turbolift he could find, directing it to the bridge of the *Musgrave*. When the doors opened, he practically burst onto the bridge, which was sparsely staffed and bathed in low illumination. His voice cracked the air like a red-alert klaxon.

"Captain! This is an emergency! We're going the wrong way!"

The woman sitting in the bridge's center seat snapped to face Peart as if he had lassoed her. Her tone was just as terse as his, from being startled if nothing else. "The captain is asleep, sir. And how do you figure that we're going the wrong way?"

"Oh! Oh, sorry," Peart said, lowering his volume and attempting to adopt his professional tone despite his heart's pounding in his throat. "Um, I meant that *we're* going the wrong way, it appears. My companion and I need to leave the ship immediately."

"Okay," said the duty commander, "I'm game. How do you suggest we do this? Shall I slow to warp three and open a hatch for you?"

Peart paused a moment. "Well, um, I'm still sussing that out a bit. I don't suppose we could borrow, say, a shuttlecraft?"

The woman rose from the command chair and walked over to the railing of the command well where Peart now leaned. "I'm aware we are to be at your disposal, Mister . . ."

"Peart, Stewart Peart," he said, and smiled a bit too slyly. "Some people call me Stew."

The woman laughed and extended a hand. "Renee Varella," she said as they shook.

"The pleasure's all—"

She dropped Peart's hand and held her palm to face him. "I don't need the charm lesson, Mr. Peart, and we have only two shuttlecraft on a *Sabre*-class ship. But I'm open to your taking one if you let me know where to pick it up."

He sighed in some relief. "Well, um, I suppose our going to the nearest starbase is in order."

"Agreed," Varella said as she turned away. "Helm? Tell me the starbase closest to our current position."

Peart craned around to see the answer come from an Andorian male—or was it a female?—at the navigation station. Peart cursed his xenobiological deficits for the second time in these few minutes. He resolved then and there to look into a crash course on the subject as soon as he was able.

"It looks like," the navigator said, "Starbase 37."

"Thirty-seven?" Peart's disgust at the revelation tainted his voice. "No, not 37."

"Could have been worse," Varella said with a smirk. "It could have been Starbase 36."

Peart allowed a breathy laugh when the navigator spoke again. "Commander, just so you know, a straight-line course from here to the starbase is going to run right through the Mewesian asteroid belt."

"Oh, of course it will," said Peart, rolling his eyes. "Why wouldn't it?"

Varella let a serious tone into her voice. "That's not a big deal for a starship's shielding, but it could pose some problems for a shuttle. Take care in plotting that course."

"Thanks, I do appreciate that, Commander, but time is not quite on my side," the agent said. "How quickly might the shuttle be prepared for travel?"

"Mr. Peart, this is an S.C.E. ship," Varella said and smiled. "We're always prepared for anything."

"Right," Peart said, and smiled as he stepped toward the turbolift.

Now if only I were.

Listening to the Pan-like, lilting tones of Arex's *sessica* helped put Peart more at ease as the two made a beeline through space to Starbase 37 as fast as the shuttle could carry them. Reclining a bit in his pilot's seat, he let his mind drift as the music, which Arex said chronicled the history of his Triexian forebears, created images of a people practically unknown to him before now.

At least it did for the first hour of their trip.

As Arex played into its second hour, Peart respectfully maintained silence for Arex, but began busying himself with almost anything he could find to do within the cramped confines of the shuttle. He calibrated sensors, he monitored the flow of energy to the craft's nacelles, and he ran diagnostics on any shipboard system he could isolate and test. He even considered engineering some problems that he could turn right around and fix, but he considered that to be pushing his luck—particularly on this trip.

In the third hour, he tried to sleep. He fitfully attempted to get himself comfortable in the pilot's seat, but decided he might as well have tried to do so on top of some cargo containers. He faded in and out of a slumber that would have been equally restful for him were he sleeping next to a snoring Tellarite.

Fading, and then awakening with a start, Peart checked the shipboard chronometer. It marked their fourth hour in space.

And Arex played on.

Partly on purpose, Peart looked toward Arex and coughed loudly as he stretched and brought his seat into an upright position. The alien's yellow eyes snapped open and music stopped issuing from the *sessica* as if Arex had thrown a switch. "Oh! Are you ill?"

"No, no, Mr. Arex," Peart said, now a bit embarrassed that he had done it. "I'm fine. I'm just not used to sitting like this for so long. I daresay that our trip won't be so cramped once we get to Starbase 37."

Arex paused, then moved to place his *sessica* back into his travel case. "Maybe you would enjoy a break from my playing."

"Oh, not at all," Peart lied. "But I must admit that I didn't expect the performance to be so, um, rich in detail."

"You mean 'long,' Mr. Peart," Arex said, and smiled. "I am sure it seemed a bit droning for you. But this is an important part of my observing my heritage as I prepare for my father's Day of Death. Each motif of the Song of Heritage tells a tale important to my family surviving and thriving over many centuries on Triex. It is a song to be performed in its entirety only on events as nodal to my family as this."

Peart felt sympathy for Arex's coming loss gnaw at his growing embarrassment. "I do not want to interrupt your ceremony. Please continue."

"Not for now," Arex said. "I was nearing its conclusion, anyway. I was about to recount my grandfather's clash with a tusked *gradak* that cost him an arm and a leg."

Peart coughed again, this time to stifle an involuntary giggle.

"Are you sure you are well?"

Peart scrambled for words. "I must admit, Mr. Arex, that I am finding my interest in your people growing. I would like to hear more."

"Maybe you would like to hear more about a great many races of the Federation, young man?"

He felt the bottom of his stomach drop out as Arex's voice took a serious turn for the first time on their trip. "Um, pardon me?"

"I have to wonder whether Triexians are not the only race for which you have a lack of information."

"Well, um," Peart stammered, feeling as if his hand had been caught in a cookie jar. "Does it show?"

Arex tried his twisted smile again, and Peart relaxed a bit. "And you think some of you do not look the same to me? I just wanted an honest response. It is a way for us to learn each other's capabilities. We are in this mission together, you know."

Peart knit his brow. He had not really considered this trip *their* mission, only his. But certainly, it was fair to consider that Arex had just as much personal investment in their success as he did. Sure, the success of the trip could be a career-breaker for him, but Arex had his own obligations to a family he revered—and had not seen in more than seventy years. It was time to lay his cards on the table, as Peart recalled his uncle Neil used to say.

Yes, we are *in this together.*

"Right. Well, I was raised on Earth, in England, actually, if it matters," Peart said. "I've always been much more interested in history than I have been in space and life in the 'great beyond,' as my father is fond of calling it. My studies led to Starfleet and my aptitude scores guided me to Temporal Investigations, which I must admit fascinates the hell out of me. I am pretty good at getting information on the fly and I scored well on mechanics and all, but, um, I fear I did pretty lousy on all the alien things."

Arex nodded. "The alien things being?"

"Oh, all of it. I barely passed xenosociology," Peart practically gushed, feeling a sense of liberation in his honesty. "I can recognize most races on sight, but I have no facility with languages or physical attributes or cultural commonalities. For practical purposes, assume I can't tell a, um, Caitian from ah . . . ah . . . a Calamarain."

"You could if you had served with one, Mr. Peart," said Arex with what Peart saw as almost a wistful look in his eye. "Well, this is good to know. Anything else?"

"Well, I have some experience in—" Peart's words were cut off by a rapidly repeating audible signal from the shuttle's control console. "It's a proximity alert. We must be nearing that asteroid belt they warned us of."

"I see," Arex said, with that smile of his not leaving his face. "Now, Mr. Peart, it's your turn to learn about some of *my* skill sets. Slow us to impulse and raise the shields."

"Are you sure you want to go through this belt, Arex?" Peart surprised himself by his lack of formality in speaking while he tapped the commands into the console before him.

"I have confidence we can navigate this belt without much difficulty," Arex said. "My most intensive Starfleet training was in navigation, and I doubt the equipment has changed so much that I can no longer use it. And in turn, to be honest as you have been with me, I admit that our travel time is a growing concern for me. We are unsure of our passage beyond the star-base, and by traversing the belt, we will make time work in our favor."

Peart wanted to speak more from concern than from curiosity, so he chose to risk appearing blunt to Arex. "Did your family say he was failing fast?"

Arex moved forward in his seat. "I have not spoken to my family. I am going by the content of an electronic written communication I received from them not three days ago."

Peart nodded. "Yes, but, um, you arrived only yesterday."

"This is true. The timing was quite fortunate for me."

"And this letter was sent three days ago? That's . . . not possible."

Arex laughed lightly; at least, Peart imagined the clucking noise that came from his mouth to be a laugh. "Why, of course it is."

"And you haven't spoken to them?"

"No. They are sure to have begun observing the Contemplation. They will not respond to any communications from me."

Peart was becoming more frustrated with what seemed to be nonsense answers from Arex. "But they sent the letter to you!"

"Yes, they did."

"But they don't know you're here in 2376!"

"Mr. Peart," Arex said in a steady voice, "I am quite sure they don't know I left 2305."

"Um, come again?"

Arex laughed lightly once again. "I have a family that is long-lived and large in number compared with those in human custom and familiarity. We have much family activity to follow among my parents and twenty-five siblings—"

"Twenty-five?" Peart practically shouted.

"With eleven brothers and thirteen sisters, I make twenty-five, yes. So with that, and our concepts of passing time being so different from yours, it did not surprise me that members of my family continued their regular contacts."

"But they never got a letter back in seventy-one years!"

"Well, I never was a good one to stay in touch, myself," Arex admitted.

Peart paused a moment to sort out the past moments of conversation while feeling his frustration rise into his voice. "So you flew a shuttlecraft into a black hole—"

"I was not piloting, and technically, it was a wormhole."

"Wormhole, right," Peart said, not missing a beat. "You come seventy-one years forward in time, get picked up by Starfleet, you go someplace to check your electronic communication log and sort through seventy-one years' worth of messages only to find out that your father is dying . . . today!"

Arex said, "It was kind of Starfleet to keep my log active as long as it continued to receive messages. And I was declared missing, not dead, so there was no reason for my family to think the worst."

"It's been seventy-one *years!*"

"Can we focus on the matter at hand, please, Stewart?"

Peart stopped short at hearing his given name, noticing that Arex was leaning forward and peering into a small data viewer. While his crash course in Triexian logic continued to baffle him, Peart chose to set Arex's family matters aside for later discussion. "Right," he said, and followed with a heavy exhale. "What can I do to help?"

"Focus the scanners and gather the most detailed reading you can of the belt ahead," Arex said. "I want as much as you can get about each asteroid: individual mass, trajectory, spin, and speed, all within a one-kilometer swath on either side of the shuttle. Then I want you to feed the data into the navigation computer banks in a constant stream. I want the most current scans fed in directly. Can you do that?"

Peart set to work, his hands working the console with the same speed and dexterity that he displayed when using his personal padd. After a few moments, he spoke. "You should be getting some data now."

Arex growled as he continued to peer into the viewer. "If only this thing were bigger . . ."

"That I can fix," Peart said, his hands again flashing across the console. With a final entry, the image on the shuttle's main viewer was replaced by a tactical rendering of the asteroid belt. Yellow crosshairs centered on each tumbling chunk, some of which were larger than the shuttle itself.

"Excellent work, Stewart," Arex said, turning to look at Peart. His expression must have registered a bit of surprise, prompting Arex to speak again. "We can set formalities aside for the mission's duration, don't you think?"

"Absolutely, um, Arex."

"Wonderful," Arex said as it was his turn to start working the shuttle's console. His three arms whirled, keying in commands at a speed that Peart had not seen bested. "Yes, this is not altogether different from what I am used to working. Now, I appreciate that you trust me, but even the best navigator and pilot team is not as fast as a computer. So, we're going to be along for the ride here, for the most part. Your job is to keep those sensors tuned and let me know if something unexpected happens. I will monitor the flow of the navigational information and the computer will be in charge of acceleration and actually flying us through this mess. Sound acceptable to you?"

"Um, that presumes I have a choice, Arex."

"You always have a choice, Stewart," he said. "We always could turn around and head in some other direction."

He needed little time to mull that option. "Let's go."

Arex nodded and pressed a finger to a glowing red light on the console's top.

And there they sat.

"Um, what's wrong?"

Arex tapped a few more commands. "It appears that the computer is weighing probabilities regarding asteroid collisions and optimal times to enter the belt. When it's ready, we will go."

"So it could be a few minutes," Peart said.

"It could at that."

Peart drew a breath and exhaled, drumming his fingertips on the armrests of his seat. "So . . . you have thirteen sisters?"

Arex turned and smiled at Peart. "They all are bonded for life."

"That's not what I mea—aaaah!"

The shuttle surged ahead as the young agent gripped his seat's armrests. They appeared to bear directly on a large asteroid when the craft plummeted downward, making Peart feel as though he were in a runaway turbolift. He felt a jolt to his right and almost got knocked from his chair.

"We've been hit!"

Arex's voice was loud yet calm as his arms flashed across the console. "It was not an impact. The shuttle's thrusters are going to make a lot of sudden, pinpoint corrections and we are go—"

The Triexian's body hurled toward the console as the shuttle lurched nose-up. He would have slammed face-first into the controls were it not for his center arm, which grabbed the edge of the console and propped him up. "Take off my boot, Stewart! My center boot!"

Peart hesitated for an instant, and then left his chair to hug the pod's floor. He grabbed Arex's center leg and tugged at his boot, which after two hard pulls came free. Arex shook his foot as if to unfurl his toes, then raised it. "Is that all?"

"Lock my chair from swiveling!" Arex called as the shuttle heaved to the right, rolling Peart against his own chair. He flipped himself and reached for the opposite seat's anchoring post, grabbing a metal lever and twisting it down to lock the chair into position.

Peart scuttled to his belly, then pushed himself upright and fell into his chair. He watched Arex as his three hands fed navigational data into the autopilot while his legs formed a stabilizing tripod with his center foot firmly in the chair behind him. Peart grabbed another breath and turned his attention to the sensor logs. All appeared well until a loud klaxon blared in the cabin. "Impact! We're going to get—"

The two flew from their perches and struck the cabin's ceiling, recoiling from an asteroid strike from above. Peart tried to shake off what felt like a small concussion. "Arex! Are you all right?"

"Fine," he shouted. "Give me a reading on the shields!"

The agent looked at a readout on his console. "I don't believe it! We're already down to forty-two percent!"

"I believe it," he said. "That asteroid was twice our size and probably should have broken us in half. I'm sorry, Stewart, but it was my fault we hit it."

Peart almost was shaken as much by Arex's decision to be contrite at a time like this than he was by the impact. "Just get us through this and I'll not say a word about it."

The shuttle continued to bob and weave while Peart watched the scanners. "It looks like the belt is thinning out!"

"Yes . . . yes," Arex said, his hands flashing as his head nodded on its skinny neck from the console up to the screen and back again. "Maybe another twenty seconds."

The shuttle dipped forward and banked to the left as Peart felt a lurch for which the inertial dampers could not compensate. The impact sent the shuttle into what felt like a flat spin as the lighting flickered. He leapt forward to study the console. "We took another hit. The shields are gone!"

"We have lost thruster control on the port side as well," Arex said. "At least we cannot argue with the timing of that last strike. It appears we are out of the belt."

He looked to the screen, which showed a black field save for a grouping of yellow crosshairs that swept through their view at a precise interval as they spun away from the conglomeration of damaging space boulders. Peart keyed in a series of commands that restored the shuttle's viewer to its normal view. It would have appeared normal, Peart thought, were the shuttle moving in a normal fashion. Its flat spin, however, made the star field appear constantly to be rushing to their right.

"Well, Arex," said Peart. "Are we in agreement to send out a distress call?"

Rather than meet his gaze, Arex bowed his head a bit. "I was not as successful as I hoped, Stewart. I am sorry I have failed us."

"What, are you kidding? We're still breathing, right?" Peart reached down and plucked Arex's loose boot from the floor, then passed it to the sheepish-looking Triexian. "I'll get you home as soon as I can. I promise."

Arex accepted the boot and began to put it on. "I will hope our luck improves on Starbase 37."

Peart let loose an exasperated laugh. "I'd not set those hopes too high."

"Why do you have such reservations about the place?" Arex asked. "The last time I was there, it appeared to be a top-notch facility."

"Oh yeah? Tell me, Arex, when was the last time you visited Starbase 37?"

"It must have been last . . . oh, my . . . seventy-two, maybe seventy-three years ago."

"Precisely my point," said Peart as he moved to access the shuttle's subspace communications system. "Times have changed for Starbase 37, but there's something in me that is guessing you still will recognize the carpeting."

An unceremonious towing by a passing ore freighter, a mind-numbing debriefing by an overly officious commander, and a checkup in an automated sickbay later, Peart now found himself standing before the door of the noisiest gathering place on Starbase 37. Arex paused them both at the threshold while he tapped his memory.

"The Admiral's Lounge! That's what this establishment used to be called," Arex said with a bit of pride at his memory. "Not that I frequented the place."

"You won't be wanting to frequent it any more now, although I admit that Galactic Barry's is a bit catchier a name for a pub," Peart said. "Our goal is to hire a charter pilot. We have the resources of the department to pay someone to take us straight to Edos."

Arex shot him a harsh glance.

"Triex! Right, right, Triex," Peart said. "Maybe I shouldn't be the one doing the talking."

"You will be fine," Arex said. "I will wait by the door and keep my eye on things from here."

The two shared one more glance as the door before them slid open.

Waves of sound and scent engulfed the pair as they walked into Galactic

Barry's. Peart could not recognize the style of music coming from a sole performer in the one lit corner of the bar, but it looked as though patrons were meeting the clanking sounds he produced with approval. He did recognize various smells, much to his disgust, including bursts of Klingon food, Merakan incense, disinfectant, and the body odors of dozens of unwashed races mingling together to assail his nasal passages.

He began to step toward the central bar, but not before feeling a tug on his sleeve. He turned to see Arex holding him with his right hand and gesturing him back to a corner booth with his other two hands.

"What?" Peart stage-whispered over the cacophony.

"Just a few things, quickly," said Arex. "Do you see those two males laughing loudly a few tables away?"

Peart squinted into the dim light and tried to single out the table Arex indicated. "You mean the Nausicaans?"

"Yes, Stewart," Arex sighed. "So you know about Nausicaans, then."

"Oh," Peart said, rolling his eyes. "Give me some credit, please."

"Fine, fine. Just do not approach the Nausicaans," he said, scanning the bar once again. "The big one near the musician is a Brikar. You would do well to stay away from her, too. In fact, Stewart, maybe you should just limit your contacts to humans."

Peart scowled at Arex as he returned his twisted smile. The sight made him laugh despite himself. "Five minutes, and we'll be out of here."

"I do trust you, Stewart, especially now that I have gotten a good look at the place," Arex said.

"That made a difference?"

"It did, because you were right about one thing," he said as he nodded toward the floor. Peart looked down to see Arex scraping a boot toe against the soiled flooring. "I do recognize the carpeting."

Peart laughed again, thankful that Arex's even temperament was helping a bad situation seem a bit brighter. "I'm getting a drink. Want anything?"

Arex mulled a moment. "Q'babi juice sounds good today."

"So much for my reputation in this place." Peart made his way to the bar and placed his order for an Andorian ale and Arex's Q'babi juice. Before he could be served, he noticed an odd-looking humanoid sidle up to his right. Definitely an older male, the haggard-looking spacer seemed friendly . . . too friendly to the overly wary Peart.

Great, what race is this guy?

"Welcome," said the bald spacer, who followed his greeting with a split-toothed grin. "You are known as Starfleet? An investigator, not true?"

Peart felt his adrenaline surge a bit as he remembered he still was wearing his combadge and departmental pin. If this gap-toothed spacer already had identified him by his attire, who could guess how many people had made him when he walked in the door. His unease with the spacer began to grow.

"I'm just enjoying a drink, sir," Peart said, trying not to look him in the eye.

"Oh, forgive!" Peart was unsettled by his volume and theatrics as he gesticulated somewhat exaggeratingly. "Simple trader am I, and new to this place. You seek services of I, to the bar come."

"Certainly, sir, to the bar come," Peart said as his drinks arrived. He placed his thumb to a data padd offered by the barkeep, then grabbed the glasses and moved away from the spacer. He scanned the place and found Arex, but a flash of glitter caught his eye. Turning, he saw a pair of human-looking women . . . beautiful women . . . at a nearby table and he could not help but follow his gaze to their sides.

"Well, hello, ladies," Peart said as the taller of the two swept back her tightly braided black hair with a bobbing move of her supple neck. "Um, either of you wouldn't happen to be, um, charter pilots, perhaps?"

The tall woman flashed a smile, exposing a set of metallic, razor-honed teeth, giving her an inhuman and definitely unnatural look. "Back off, Starfleet," she grumbled in a voice two octaves lower that Peart thought befitted her womanly figure. "Get your own ship."

Wordlessly, Peart took two quick steps back and spun on his heels to walk—and stepped full force into a wall, spilling his drinks against it.

"This is a new blouse," said the wall.

Shocked, Peart slowly looked his way up the wall and into the eyes of the Brikar, who apparently had moved away from the musician. His first instinct was to start wiping the remaining liquid from the front of the now-soiled blouse, but his arm was seized in the Brikar's grip before he could swab a drop. Returning his gaze, Peart tried a smile.

The Brikar was not amused.

"If I was in your shoes, I would be—"

"Um, leaving," finished Peart. "What a good idea." He felt himself being helped along to the main door by the massive being, his feet barely brushing the floor. Arex spotted him and moved quickly to trigger the door's automatic opener, and with a kick of his feet tripped the mechanism. As they neared it, Peart decided to set aside any pride in favor of a little pleading.

"Don't toss me, please," he said. "It was an accident!" He winced and squeezed his eyes shut as he felt his body being swept upward and out into the brightness of the hallway . . . where he was gingerly deposited on his feet.

"I do not just toss people," the Brikar said. "I am a lady, after all."

Peart slowly opened his eyes, to see the female in standard lighting. She stood two heads taller than him, easily, with a face that looked to him as more stone than skin. Her eyes peered from a mantle of a brow as her slit-like nostrils flared a bit and her gash of a mouth made for a solemn expression.

"Of course you are," Peart said, and forced out a laugh. His arm had been released, and he snatched it close to rub at where the Brikar had grabbed it.

"Not like your toothy friend in there. I've seen her bite chunks from someone's hand or neck just for fun," the being said as she extended a three-fingered hand. "I'm Mirg, and you said you were looking for a charter pilot."

"Yes, *yes!*" Peart returned the greeting and watched his hand get swallowed in Mirg's massive mitt. "I need to get Mr. Arex to his homeworld as soon as possible. How fast can your ship travel?"

"I can get warp five if I push it. I don't like to push it," Mirg said as she turned to greet Arex. "Triexian, right?"

Arex smiled and looked more at Peart than at the pilot. "A distinction not easily made by some. Thank you for offering your assistance."

"I did not say it was going to be cheap," Mirg said.

Peart, who had scooped his data padd from his shoulder bag and was rapidly entering commands, spoke without looking up. "At warp four point five, we can make Triex in twelve hours. If we arrive in less time, Starfleet will add twenty percent to your standard rate. Is that acceptable?"

"Did I say warp five was pushing it?" Mirg asked as she led them away from Galactic Barry's. "A push is probably closer to warp six. . . ."

For the first time since they left Starbase 37, Peart decided to interrupt Arex's hours of meditation. For a thankful change of pace, Peart thought, it was with good news. He activated the chime at the door of the Brikar cargo ship's lone guest cabin, and it slid open to reveal Arex seated on the floor of the room with his legs folded under him. His yellow eyes were closed and his breathing was deep and regular. His *sessica* lay at his side.

"Um, Arex," Peart said softly. "Arex?"

The still figure slowly opened his eyes. "Have we arrived?"

"Yes, and ahead of schedule," Peart said. "Mirg is starting her landing procedures. Do we need to contact anyone for you?"

"That is not necessary," Arex said as he rose. "My family is likely to be prep—"

A rumble that began rocking the ship cut Arex's thoughts midstream. Peart braced himself against a bulkhead as the creaking and quaking of the ship continued to increase. "Turbulence?"

Arex shook his head. "Not exactly, but I fear we may have another problem."

"What?" Peart asked as Arex moved past him and toward the cargo ship's bridge. "What? *What?*"

He caught up with Arex and they entered together as the shaking continued to increase. Mirg struggled in her pilot's seat, her hands gripping a joystick control. "The atmosphere is ionized," she said. "We're going to shake ourselves apart."

Arex perched close to Mirg, looking over her control panels. "Can we remodulate the shields?"

"I tried that, but this ship just isn't equipped for this," she said, fighting the controls. "Is the whole planet like this?"

"I am afraid so," said Arex. "Severe ion storms are a natural phenomenon on Triex. It can pose a problem in some cases."

Mirg looked up at Arex. "I'm sorry, but I have to pull out. Even if I got us down okay, I can't guarantee I'd ever take off again."

Arex nodded as Peart felt panic rising in his blood yet again. "What do you mean we're pulling out?"

"Mirg's ship cannot land in our atmosphere," said Arex. "We may be stranded."

"Stranded?" Peart asked. "So just beam us down."

The ship's attitude noticeably stabilized, prompting Mirg to loosen her grip on the joystick. "Transporters won't work in this. Too risky."

Arex agreed, saying, "Even with pattern enhancers on the ground, chances of a successful transport on Triex are slim. Our people use transporters only in the direst of emergencies."

"Okay, then, how are we getting down there?" Peart's question hung in the silence of the room. "Anyone?"

"You could wait for another approaching ship and hitch a ride down with it?" Mirg offered.

"Who knows how long that might take," Peart said dismissively. After a moment of thought, he asked, "Does this thing have a lifepod?"

"Sure, but it . . . Wait a minute," Mirg said. "What, you want to ride that thing down to Triex?"

"Any other ideas?" Peart turned to Arex, who seemed to favorably mull the option. Peart smiled a bit at himself. "Then let's get on board. A standard pod should be heavily shielded enough to withstand reentry through nearly any atmosphere."

"I only have one, and it's a one-seater," Mirg said.

"Sure, but a Brikar one-seater should be roomy enough for two of anyone else," Peart said. "Let's get going."

"And I'm not going down after it, so I'll have to add it to your fare," she said. "Those things aren't cheap."

Peart smirked and said, "Hey, this one's on Starfleet."

He felt sure of himself and his idea right up until the moment Mirg loosened the pressure hatch and he actually got a look inside the pod. With one body couch, a sparse control panel, and no viewports, the lifeboat looked to Peart more like a coffin. He turned to Arex, who tossed his cylindrical travel case inside.

"I guess that settles it," Peart said as he crawled into the pod. "Mirg, you have the coordinates of our destination. Give us your best shot."

Arex moved his spindly form inside the pod as Peart did his best to hug the wall. The Triexian did not seem to take up much room, Peart decided, but the situation rapidly redefined his idea of personal space.

"Best of luck," Mirg called inside before sealing the hatch.

Lighting within the pod dimmed a bit as Peart attempted to shift to a more comfortable position. He felt completely cocooned and might have been able to relax were it not for the bony pressure in his abdomen.

"Um, Arex, I think your knee is in my side."

"Oh, pardon me," he said, making an adjustment in his position.

"Nope, your other knee."

"All right," he said, patiently shifting again.

"Um, try your *other* other knee."

A shift, and with it, Peart felt some relief. "Thanks, that's got iiiiiiiiiiiiiit!"

His head struck the pressurized hatch of the cramped pod as it shot away from the freighter. Peart felt as though the tiny craft were skipping along a watery surface while in a shallow spin, mental images that only intensified a wave of nausea.

"Uhhh . . . um, Arex, I'm going to be ill," Peart sputtered, trying to brace himself against the curves of the lifepod's hull. "No . . . check that . . . I'm going to passss . . ."

*   *   *

A slamming thud jarred Peart's head against something hard, snapping him back to consciousness. Before he could shake it off, two more thuds bounced him into a wall, then into Arex, who moaned a bit in response.

"Where are we?"

The Triexian's voice quavered. "I know the drag chute deployed. I am guessing we are on the surface of Triex." A pause, and then he spoke again. "The readings show a Class-M atmosphere. We must be down. Shall I blow the hatch?"

"Please, Arex," Peart strained to speak. "I think I'm sitting on my head here."

A rush of sound and orange light filled the lifepod's compartment, and Peart extended an arm into the brightness. Feeling around for a purchase, he gripped something and was able to steady himself to his feet and peer out.

Wow . . . If this is Triex, I might not have left.

The lifepod had settled in a green field teeming with waist-high grasses. It was bounded by what looked to be a lush forest, and Peart spied snow-capped mountains on the horizon. He hopped out of the lifepod and was joined a moment later by Arex.

"This is a beautiful place you have here, Arex," Peart said, genuinely impressed. "It's tough to get to, but worth it."

"This is an exceptionally lovely region of my world, so do not be unduly awed," he said, "but thank you. I must admit that the view is very welcoming to me. I just hope it means what I believe it does."

"And that is?"

"That we are not far from my ancestral home," Arex said.

A whipping, whooshing sound started to fill the air, and Peart turned to the source of the noise. What appeared to be an open-cockpit hovercraft sped toward them, piloted by a pair of Triexians.

"Welcoming committee?" Peart asked.

"Law enforcers, I imagine," Arex said. "We have nothing to fear."

The hovercraft came to rest within steps of the downed pod, and Arex greeted its occupants with a series of gravelly chitters and clicks. What Peart took for a conversation ensued for a few moments, and then Arex motioned him into the hovercraft.

"They said they received a message from a Brikarian freighter and locked on to our position as soon as we were launched," Arex explained as Peart settled into his seat. "Amazingly, we landed not fifteen kilometers from our intended destination."

Peart felt a cool breeze tousle his hair as they sped away from their drop zone and across the field. "So you're almost home?"

"Almost," Arex said as his expression began to fade into a neutral, solemn state. "I must meditate. Please excuse me."

The agent settled in for the ride as Arex withdrew into his own thoughts. Peart noticed that he had lost track of time in a personal sense, but a quick check of his data padd confirmed what he suspected. Since he got the assignment, fewer than twenty hours had elapsed on their journey to Triex. Arex should be arriving in plenty of time for his family obligations, under Special Agent Dulmer's estimations. Peart rested his eyes, letting himself slip into a meditative state of his own, to a point. He dozed a bit, letting the rocking of the hovercraft lull him during these last few min—

SKRRREEEEEEEEE!

The shrill screaming from the front seat jolted Peart awake just enough for him to see the produce cart they were about to broadside.

"Arex!" He shook the meditating form beside him to alertness just as the hovercraft smashed into the cart, sending the quartet of passengers sailing out of the open cockpit and into the air. He saw the pilot and his fellow officer plunge headlong into the contents of the cart just before his own world went soft and wet.

He sputtered out a mouthful of pulpy fruit with a sloppy sound, wiping wetness from his eyes in time to see Arex rush into a nearby cottage. Peart breathed a sigh of relief that Arex was uninjured by the mishap, then dredged himself from the sickly sweet mess and shook some of the glop from his arms and legs.

Peart bounded through the door of the cottage, panting and still dripping with reddish pulp. He squished his way into the room, listening for some sign of the home's occupants, and then his ears picked up the faint sounds of sobs echoing down a hallway. Leaving soggy prints in his wake, he slowly moved down the hall, which turned into a large bedroom. Peering into the room, he stopped and held his breath.

Several dozen Triexians had packed themselves into the room, all surrounding what Peart assumed was Arex's father's deathbed. As he crept forward, the crowd parted slightly, affording him a better view. His eyes widened as he recognized Arex from the back, kneeling at the side of the bed. After a few moments, Arex rose and turned toward the crowd, silently making his way from the prone figure upon the bed.

As he approached, Peart saw Arex's wet, swollen eyes set within a dour expression, which softened a bit when Arex noticed that Peart had arrived.

"Thank you, my friend, but I was too late," Arex said softly. "My father has passed."

"No," he whispered as tears welled up in his eyes. Peart pushed ahead to get his own look at the frail form of the Triexian, ashen and almost translucent against the pillow-strewn bed. His heart sank deeper into his chest as his breath came in gulps. The stilled patriarch of this solemn Triexian family died without knowing the extent of the personal sacrifice his son, a Starfleet officer, had made for the Federation. His long life ended before he realized how hard Arex had struggled just to be at his side one last time.

Peart turned away, letting tears run down his cheeks unimpeded. He wept for his new friend's loss and for his failure in getting them to Triex on time. He hesitated to approach Arex again; almost fearing that he might hear Arex's heart—

CRACK!

The agent heard a gasp fill the room as he stopped in his steps. A second brittle pop fractured the room's silence, followed by some steady crackling sounds. He felt compelled to turn his gaze back to the supine Triexian . . .

And Peart saw the ashen form split down the middle.

A voice shouted, *"Iglappa!* It begins!" Peart felt his jaw go slack as the ashen form of the Triexian elder started falling away from the bed in flaky pieces. A soft chant of *"Iglappa! Iglappa!"* swirled in the room as a trio of pinkish, slimy hands worked from the center of the husk to clear it away.

Arex stood by Peart, grabbing him on the shoulders. The shocked agent turned openmouthed to Arex, stunned into silence. "Um . . ."

"The Day of Rebirth is upon us, Stewart! My father returns to us!" Arex jogged up to kneel once again at the bedside as the elder raised his damp, pinkish head from its resting place.

"What is this?" the newly molted being asked. "Arex? So, you bothered to join us at last? I thought for sure you would miss my third Rebirth in a row."

Arex nodded as the crowd erupted into laughter. "I regret my lateness, Father. I have been away for some time."

The elder smiled, and smiling seemed to be much easier for him than for Arex, Peart noted as he caught his breath for the first time in what seemed minutes. As Arex passed him the opened container of *meechacha* ointment, he dipped into it with one hand and began spreading it onto his puckered, moist form. "My life begins anew, my loved ones! Let the feasting begin!"

A cheer filled the room as joyful Triexians filed past an incredulous Peart and into the hall. He stood motionless until Arex walked past, then snatched out to him as if his arm were a striking serpent. He walked with the startled Arex into a quieter corner of the room.

"What is this, a joke? He just *molted!*" Peart wanted to loosen a mixture of rage and frustration that had quickly boiled to the surface.

"I beg your pardon, Stewart," Arex said calmly. "This is a celebration of my family, the most important one in twenty-five years."

"He does this *every* twenty-five years?" Peart felt blood churning in his ears. "I risked life and limb time and again to get you back here to see your dying father, and now he's not dead after all? He's just . . . just . . . *pruney?*"

Arex laughed. "Stewart, calm yourself, please."

"This happens to you Triexians all the time?"

"Well, we don't talk about it much," he said. "It is hardly a topic of discussion in xenobiology classes, I can assure you."

Peart felt his rage start to subside. "So . . . so, I didn't blow this mission?"

"Not at all. You did nothing wrong. We have arrived just in time. In fact, you were present for a Triexian rite that few offworlders get to see," Arex said, putting a hand on Peart's wet and sticky shoulder. "You certainly are welcome to join my family at the Feast of Rebirth . . . minus the ripened waterfruits, obviously. But first, we must report our success to Special Agent Dulmer."

Peart felt the tension ease from his shoulders as they left the elder Triexian and some attendants to his preparations. "So I will get a passing review?"

"Absolutely," said Arex as they approached a large dining room. "I daresay that my father may even bestow upon you an honorary birth ranking as his twenty-sixth child. Assuming you pass the feats of physical prowess."

"Um," Peart said, "and just what does that involve?"

"We arm-wrestle," said Arex, and smiled, until he must have noticed Peart's unhidden expression. "Stewart, *that* was a joke."

D'NDAI OF CALHOUN
A Lady of Xenex

Peg Robinson

Under the leadership of M'k'n'zy of Calhoun and his brother D'ndai, Xenex was able to throw off the yoke of Danteri oppression and become a free world. After this historic occasion, but before M'k'n'zy would leave Xenex and join Starfleet under the new name of Mackenzie Calhoun, M'k'n'zy was obligated to help a widow from his clan named Catrine sire a child since D'ndai, the older brother, was away on business. "A Lady of Xenex" takes place shortly after M'k'n'zy performed this service to Catrine, following D'ndai's return to Xenex.

Peg Robinson

Peg Robinson lives in Lompoc, California, with her husband, her daughter, and four very bossy cats. She's sold stories to *Star Trek: Strange New Worlds* Volumes I and II, *Marion Zimmer Bradley's Fantasy Magazine,* and several magazines that died before she could actually see her stories in print; she's also won an honorable mention from L. Ron Hubbard's Writers of the Future Contest. She lives quietly, and likes it like that. She also cooks one heck of a fine saag panir, among other things, and her figure shows it.

It wasn't the worst of times, but it wasn't the best, either. It was the dawn of a new era on Xenex, and if you'd asked D'ndai of Calhoun, freshly returned from his first trip off his home planet, it looked like the era was starting badly.

Old Man V'rdan, G'lyndr of Clan G'lyndr, was a cocky bastard. He leaned with his butt propped on the fountain in the courtyard of Calhoun's administrative building and bellowed his greeting up to D'ndai, standing on the entry landing above.

"Praise to the Calhoun, and the house of the Calhoun, and the hair of the Calhoun's head, may it never grow less!"

As a child D'ndai had dreaded him. He still did at twenty-four: V'rdan made famine, war, and plague look safe.

D'ndai forced himself to welcome his guest.

"Praise to the G'lyndr, and all his men, and his flocks and herds and his *lirga* lying fat in their styes."

He wondered why V'rdan and his retinue had popped up barely two days after his return from Danter. It reeked of secret agendas. During the rebellion Calhoun and G'lyndr had been allied against the Danteri, but they had once been famous feuding partners.

V'rdan squinted up at D'ndai and gnawed the fringe of his mustache, ignoring the Calhoun retainers that ringed his party, hands hovering by their weapons.

"So your trip to the Federation and Danter hasn't made a mincing little phaser-fighter out of you. "

"They only had me for six months," D'ndai responded, dryly. "I'm still a proper Xenexian dry-gully back-stabber."

V'rdan brayed with laughter. His men joined in.

"Next he'll invite us to drink and poison the flask," a G'lyndr war boy said. D'ndai recognized him: G'nard, heir to Clan G'lyndr.

G'nard and D'ndai had never liked each other.

"You mean like Argil of G'lyndr did to Sa'am of Calhoun? I won't copy G'lyndr. If I kill you I'll come up with something original or I'll stick to tradition and cut your throats."

Everyone knew it was a joke. If it hadn't been, the G'lyndr party would already be dead, or at least too busy fighting to waste breath laughing. D'ndai laughed harder than anyone. Then he leaned forward on the rail of the balcony.

"So, G'lyndr," he said, with a touch of grit in his voice, "what brings you to Calhoun?"

V'rdan pushed his son forward like a prize *venn*-ram being considered for breeding.

"I have come for a *Calhoun* bride for my heir. I seek Catrine, widow of the hero An'dr, for my dearest son: a treasure for a treasure!" His eyes glittered with mischief and challenge. "So, Calhoun: What do you think of that?"

Matchmaking was a key source of feuds on Xenex. Therefore D'ndai struggled to maintain a bland façade. It wasn't easy. He'd come home early for a reason, and that reason was named Catrine.

V'rdan's grin grew even bigger. "G'nard will be chief when I'm gone, Calhoun. Get him and you get an alliance with G'lyndr. Turn him down and . . . let's just say Clan G'lyndr would be insulted."

"You and An'dr always said she was a beautiful woman," G'nard said, smirking. "It seems a shame to leave a beautiful woman unwed." The glitter of malice in his eye left no doubt he'd been looking forward to D'ndai's dismay.

The thought of Catrine with that puffed-up braggart was not a happy one.

Neither was the thought of catapulting Clan Calhoun into a feud.

"The tribal elders must confer," D'ndai said, firmly. "Catrine is a Calhoun widow. Calhoun must insure her future." He was relieved to see Elder Sh'nab jittering nervously by the archway that let out onto the street. "Sh'nab, arrange refreshments for our guests. Then meet me in the sand garden." He didn't wait for Sh'nab to agree, just nodded to V'rdan, and entered the building. Once out of G'lyndr's hearing he began to swear.

He was still swearing when Sh'nab joined him. D'ndai scowled up at his advisor. "What is going on that you haven't told me about?"

Sh'nab tugged one side of his mustache, and shifted uneasily. "Quite a bit. You've only been back for two days, after all. The first day you had warp lag and mostly slept. That night the clan gave you a party, and you mostly drank. The second day you mostly threw up. Not a good time to give a briefing."

D'ndai said a very rude word. "What does V'rdan think he's doing black-mailing Clan Calhoun? And what makes him think I won't have him and his filthy heir killed in some alley before I ever let G'nard make a match with any Calhoun woman?"

"That wouldn't be wise," Sh'nab said. "Clan G'lyndr has allied with the Thallonians." The way Sh'nab said it, it sounded a lot like "You've got three weeks to live" or "There are tribbles in your silo."

"So? *We've* been dealing with them for over ten years. V'rdan of G'lyndr's not stupid. Of *course* he's dealing with the Thallonians."

"G'lyndr has an exclusive deal."

"Impossible. The Thallonians wouldn't limit themselves that way."

Sh'nab gave him a very old look. "Of course they would—if they thought they'd profit by it. G'lyndr's trying to push us out. Thallon is bet-ting they'll succeed." The elder shook his head. "They want to be the sole power on Xenex. Danter and the Federation could threaten that. You dealt with Danter and the Federation. Case closed."

"Bastards. Do they think the Federation gave me anything beyond a free trip around the sector and an earful of sanctimonious advice? As for Danter—they can crawl through the tangle-lands and Xenex still won't deal with them. Truce is as good as they'll get." He scowled, then shook his head. "So Thallon is too stupid to realize that. We still have to block their plans."

Sh'nab gave a tight little shrug. "No matter what, G'lyndr wins. If we turn them down we insult them publicly and start a feud. If we accept then the other clans know we backed down to them, and they gain a share of our political clout. But the marriage is the better choice—we can't afford a feud so soon after the rebellion. Give the woman to G'nard. It's a good marriage for her and a cheap marriage for us." His eyes flicked away from D'ndai and back, as though he were weighing his thoughts and words very carefully. "It could solve . . . a number of potential problems. Catrine can't exert much pull on us; she's only a Calhoun widow, not a Calhoun daugh-ter. They could have asked for one of your child-debt girls. Imagine having to deal with G'nard as your son-in-law."

D'ndai took a deep breath. "What if I married her myself? Calhoun owes her child-debt, and An'dr was my friend. There's obligation both ways. That should override any insult G'lyndr tried to claim, shouldn't it?"

Sh'nab had turned a peculiar shade of pink. "You? Marry Catrine?"

"Yes, me."

"You." This time it wasn't a question, it was a pronouncement of doom.

"I'm not exactly *lirga* dung," he snapped. "I'm the Calhoun. I'm young, I'm healthy, I'm fertile—with plenty of debt children to prove it. And just *once* I'd like to sleep with a widow because I wanted to, not because tradition demanded it."

Sh'nab shivered. "*You* want to sleep with Catrine? An'dr's-widow-Catrine? That Catrine?"

D'ndai hated it when he blushed. It made him feel even younger than he was. "Um. Yes. I mean, I'd hoped . . ." He started pulling leaves from the honey-berry vine that ran up a tree next to his seat. "I always thought An'dr was a lucky man. But you don't drool over your best friend's wife. Then he died." He shrugged, and tossed the leaves on the ground. "The traditional year seemed like long enough to mourn. I planned on asking her when I got back. That's why I pushed to come home early."

"Not early enough." Sh'nab sat heavily on the far end of D'ndai's bench. He knitted his hands together and scowled at the locked fingers. "You should have come home three weeks early instead of just two. She's already petitioned Clan Calhoun for a debt baby."

The words hit hard, deep inside where the bleeding wouldn't show.

D'ndai rested his head on his hands, fingers threaded through his hair. "M'k'n'zy, of course. He was the only other Calhoun of rank. Is it too much to hope my dear baby brother treated her like a woman of value? Gods know, I've seen him lead girls into the shadows one evening, then treat them like beggars by next morning's light."

He could hear Sh'nab shift uneasily. "Er . . . They were only together one night. But Catrine has made no complaint." Sh'nab sounded like a man trying to swallow a live sand mouse. D'ndai knew he was holding something back. He was fairly sure whatever it was, he didn't want to know.

"No. She wouldn't." He stood, then, feeling wrung out but very clear-headed. "I'll go speak with her. If she wants M'k'n'zy she'll have him, if I have to hold a phaser to his back through the whole ceremony. If she wants me—I'm here. If she wants G'nard . . ."

"She can have him, too?"

"Not a chance," D'ndai said, firmly. "If she wants G'nard I'll just have to have him killed. That gloating excuse for a war boy won't have Catrine so long as there's a Calhoun alive to prevent it."

"Um—she's just a woman. Do you really want to start a feud over a woman?"

D'ndai grinned a sharkish grin. "Why not? G'lyndr and Calhoun have been swapping women for centuries; bride raids, seductions, husband-slaying, treaty trades. We've been feuding over the results for all that time. Why stop now?"

D'ndai took the time to bathe and dress in his best before he set out. It was a familiar route, but one he hadn't walked often since An'dr's death.

"Hey, Calhoun—going courting?" a woman shouted as he passed. She was a classic Calhoun matron: gap-toothed, tough as sandal straps, and able to gut a Danteri soldier or a fowl for the stew pot with equal competence. She looked him over appreciatively. "Looking tasty, chief. Very tasty."

"As are you, O star of my skies," he called back, politely if untruthfully.

"Tell my husband that," she responded, a bit bitterly. "He needs to be reminded."

"He is a fool, then," he laughed, and passed on his way.

D'ndai had longed for Calhoun while he'd been gone: he'd felt dwarfed by the wealth and the overwhelming development of the Federation and Danter. Now that he was home all he could see was that his people were poor, the buildings shoddy, the streets packed earth, the land outside town arid and bleak.

The women who'd called out to him, and all Calhoun's people, were D'ndai's patrimony. Every choice he made would affect them—including who he married. During the rebellion he'd been able to ignore that. Who knew if he, or anyone, would survive another day? Now he had to live for that woman as much as he lived for himself. The thought was not cheering.

A feud could destroy Calhoun. Maybe Sh'nab was right—maybe it was best to give Catrine to G'nard. As Calhoun he could command her, no matter what she wanted.

D'ndai stalked along, kicking a rock ahead of him, looking for some way to satisfy his duty without sacrificing his own desires—or Catrine's.

"I hear you're having trouble with Clan G'lyndr," a Danteri-accented voice said at D'ndai's elbow.

D'ndai had spent too long fighting Danteri: He had the man pinned to a wall with a knife at his throat before he recalled Xenex's victory, or the treaty he'd just signed.

"What do you want with me, Danteri? Make it quick—I'm a busy man, with important things to do."

"More important than your planet's future?" the man asked. He raised a finger and pushed D'ndai's wrist until the knife no longer touched his skin. "I just want to talk, Calhoun. I'm Warain—Warain of the DEA."

"Danteri External Affairs." The name felt nasty in his mouth—like rancid grease mixed with rotten egg. Dedicated to off-Danter concerns, the DEA on Xenex had functioned as the intelligence branch of the military. "A Danteri spy."

"Only a diplomat. Spies get a bigger budget and much more exciting weapons. Diplomats get more women, though—we get more practice being charming." When D'ndai failed to laugh, Warain sighed deeply. "I'm sorry I surprised you. I hoped we could speak before the Boy General convinced you I was—what did he call me? Oh, yes: the bastard spawn of a Danteri deserter and a *lirga* sow. I could be a good ally against G'lyndr and Thallon."

"I don't ally with Danteri," D'ndai growled. He stepped back and sheathed his knife.

The man stayed where he was, leaning on the whitewashed wall of the building—a wall covered with graffiti and stained with urine, with unpatched cracks so deep D'ndai could have hidden an entire arsenal in their shadows. He was a small man, and slender, dressed in the loose cream tunic and trousers affected by Danteri civilians. His hair was clubbed back into a latinum clasp, a latinum stud set with a glowing green stone graced one ear, and his shoes were so supple they made D'ndai think of women's wedding slippers. Yet Warain of the DEA was not someone he wanted to underestimate.

He could hate a man so soft and deadly. He could also envy him. What was it like, to be so elegant, so powerful, to play such dangerous games?

"But you do ally with Danteri," Warain said, gently. "You signed the treaty: Danter and Xenex are now equals, determined to promote peace, trade, and the well-being of our peoples." His light voice expressed an infinity of irony laced with amusement.

"We've promised to stop killing your soldiers if you stop sending them."

"That too."

"That's enough. Xenex doesn't need more from Danter."

Warain looked incredulously up and down the street. "Pardon, but you need a universe of things from *somewhere*. Sanitation systems, weather control, water generators for irrigation works. Libraries, schools. Power grids. Hospitals. Tractors. You might as well get those things from Danter." He smiled a thin, wicked smile. "Sharp dealing is the best revenge, Xenexian. Just think how you can make us bleed."

D'ndai shook his head. "I may be M'k'n'zy's older, dumber brother, but I'm not that dumb. We've seen your idea of trade: Danter takes, Xenex suffers. I don't think that's changed." He walked away without waiting for a response.

Warain's words followed him. "The Federation is too distant to be a good trade partner. Thallon will happily throw Calhoun to G'lyndr, if it buys them monopoly. You need us, and Danter needs you. After three hundred years our economy's tied to yours."

"Start learning to untie knots, Danteri."

"You're bound to us, too."

"Not for long."

"You won't find a better market for your *harish* or your *lodoen* crop. Danter's economy's in a tailspin since you cut off our supply. You have leverage, if you've got the guts to use it."

D'ndai didn't answer. He *couldn't* deal with Danter. He'd had three great goals ever since his father had been killed: Take care of M'k'n'zy; watch over the clan; and fight Danter.

Now the Danteri were defeated, M'k'n'zy was leaving—and what the clan needed most was a healthy, thriving Xenex.

His world spun around him like sand around the eye of a dust devil.

He had to deal with all of it. But he had to deal with Catrine first and worst.

He'd known the house for most of his life. As a boy he and his older friend An'dr had chased poultry around the dusty yard while his father and the other men sat in the shade of the scant-leaved *arona* tree drinking home-brew. When he was older he'd picked up assignments there: He ran messages for the rebellion. He delivered weapons. He reported conversations heard in the market. But it was only after his father's death that he'd learned how much of the rebellion had been run out of the little four-room house.

He raised his hand and knocked.

There was no answer.

He considered leaving. Instead he walked to the side of the house and opened the gate leading to the yard behind.

Catrine was lying on a reed chaise under the old *arona* tree, eyes closed, hair knotted carelessly up off her neck. Her dress was simple and light, suited to the hot summers of Calhoun. Her fingers were fanned protectively over her belly. Her skin, hair, white dress, all seemed to glow in the shade of the tree.

She opened her eyes.

The silence stood between them. At last she said, softly, "You came back early."

"Not early enough." He shifted, miserably. "You went to M'k'n'zy for your debt child."

She heard the question he didn't ask. She rose and walked slowly toward him, looked calmly into his eyes, her head high.

"M'k'n'zy wasn't An'dr's near-brother. I never held him while he cried for his father—or let him hold me while we both cried for my husband. There's already too much between us, D'ndai. Your brother never even noticed me. He was too taken up with his own vision." She smiled, then, regretful. "He is beautiful, brilliant, he is a son of Calhoun and owed me what I wanted—and he was not you. I could ask of him what I couldn't ask of you."

She was almost six years older than he was. When he'd been younger it had seemed like an impossible difference. She had been the adult wife of his adult friend.

"An'dr was lucky," he said.

"*I* was lucky. I still am." She looked toward her house. "I think I'll move away from Calhoun. There will be fewer memories."

"Do you love M'k'n'zy?"

She laughed then, in frustrated amusement. "I can't have him. His future's too tempting for him to stay here, married to an aging widow, raising a child in another man's name. He'll never threaten An'dr's memory. He'll never occupy my life."

"But do you love him?"

She sighed, and D'ndai's heart broke. "I love him like I love the camp songs of the rebellion: as something scarred, and lovely, and sad."

"But you will never marry him."

"No."

"V'rdan of G'lyndr wants you for his son, G'nard."

"If I'd wanted to marry again I could have done so." He could hear a sharp twist of pride in her words. "I am not so old, or poor, or of such ill reputation that I could not have my pick. I choose to stay as I am." Her hand strayed again to caress her belly. "I will have a child to carry An'dr's name. I need no more."

"G'nard is heir to G'lyndr."

"You are the Calhoun of Calhoun. M'k'n'zy is the Boy General. I want none of you."

"They'll make the clan pay for the insult."

She touched him, then, her hand tracing the line of his cheek. "You're the Calhoun. You'll find an answer."

"It would be easier if you'd marry me—or M'k'n'zy," he added, bitterly. "Marrying one of us would allow G'lyndr to save face."

"No."

"I could command you."

"Could you?" Her eyes laughed.

He sighed. "No."

"Then go," she said. "I am only your first dream, not your last."

"M'k'n'zy can marry her," D'ndai said to Sh'nab. The two men were sitting in the cabin D'ndai had lived in since his father's death, getting drunk. It seemed like the right thing to do. "For once he can do what *I* tell *him,* and marry Catrine."

"Sometimes I wish I belonged to any clan but Calhoun," Sh'nab said, mournfully. He topped off their drinks and leaned into the leather back of his chair. "Calhouns are so stubborn. She won't marry him. *He* won't marry her. He's got Starfleet on his mind, and . . ." He gritted his teeth, then said, cautiously, "He's not ready to marry, Calhoun. Please, believe me—the boy's nowhere near ready to marry."

D'ndai's temper shattered. He rose, braced his hands on the table, and leaned so close to Sh'nab that the elder was forced farther back in his chair. "I don't give a damn if he's ready!" He straightened, ignoring the way the room spun. "I'm tired of running the world to suit the Boy General. Whatever M'k'n'zy wants, M'k'n'zy gets. Arms out of nowhere, soldiers from thin air, money for bribes. He has visions—I turn them into reality. He gets the glory—fame, honor, Federation officers begging him to go be a genius for them instead of Xenex. Any woman he wants. I get nothing but responsibility. This time *he* can be the responsible one. Better him than G'nard."

"She won't marry G'nard, either," Sh'nab moaned. He shot back his drink, and quickly poured himself more. "Calhoun, forget Catrine. She's making you crazy."

D'ndai just reared his head back and hollered—a shout he'd perfected over years of bluffing men older and larger and more experienced than he was.

"M'k'n'zy! Where is my baby brother?! Somebody fetch the Boy General, or I'll have you all shaved bald and sent to the Pit to chase visions." He could

hear the scurry of feet in the chief's compound as oath-men scrambled. He nodded and fell into his chair. "Can't forget her. I love her."

Sh'nab laid his head on his arms and moaned. "I could have been a stable boy. I could have tended *lirga*. Instead I'm liege man to the damned Calhoun of Calhoun." His fingers hooked into his thinning hair. "I thought I did the right thing. I thought, *D'ndai is gone, and he's tired of bedding widows, and the woman asked for M'k'n'zy. Why not let the boy do An'dr's widow a good turn?* But it's never easy when you're dealing with the most sand-squall-perverse family on Xenex. First M'k'n'zy is . . . *whatever*. And now you've gone crazy. I think that today I will die. It will save me a lot of trouble in the years to come."

D'ndai stared at the door, waiting for M'k'n'zy like a predator waiting for a desert lizard to come out of hiding.

It wasn't long before the boy arrived.

D'ndai loved M'k'n'zy. He admired him. He'd given a substantial portion of his life to raising his brother, protecting him, supporting his insane—and insanely successful—campaign against the Danteri.

Looking at the young man, though, it occurred to him that he didn't like M'k'n'zy very much. It's hard to like someone who's smart, handsome, outrageously successful, popular, romantic, idealistic—and completely clueless where lesser mortals are concerned.

"You got her pregnant," he said. It was hard to get the words out.

M'k'n'zy jumped, and looked reproachfully at Sh'nab—or at the balding top of the man's head, for that was all that showed. "What did you *tell* him?"

"Nothing. I told him *nothing*," Sh'nab snarled.

M'k'n'zy didn't look reassured. "Nothing?"

"Nothing you'd care about."

"Oh." M'k'n'zy looked at his brother. "You *are* talking about Catrine?" he asked. There was something wary in his eyes, a hesitation in his voice.

If D'ndai had been less obsessed, he might have wondered at M'k'n'zy's panic—or at Sh'nab's evasive response. All he cared about, though, was that M'k'n'zy seemed more like a child caught stealing sweets than a grown man soon to be a father.

Catrine deserved better.

"Is there anyone else you're likely to have gotten pregnant?" he growled. "You'd better tell me if there is. Clan Calhoun's responsible for Calhoun begottens."

"You should know," the boy said, jutting his chin. "You've bragged enough about yours."

"I live up to my obligations," D'ndai replied, trying to look dignified. "I've got *dozens* of debt-begots, and who knows how many pleasure babes as well," he went on, using a line he'd used to impress the men in the rebel camps. A boy clan chief with little to boast of but debt babies to war widows had to take his bravado where he could find it. "I'm a *man*. Men don't go waltzing off to the Federation and leave their women and their babies to look after themselves."

M'k'n'zy didn't look impressed. He just looked scared. In all the years of fighting, the only time D'ndai could remember his brother looking scared was just after their father had died.

"You don't expect me to stay here on Xenex?"

"You don't have to make it sound like Danteri torture," D'ndai said, reproachfully. "You'd have a woman—the finest woman on the whole planet. A home. Status. Power. A chance to build our future, the same way you built our freedom. Think about it, M'k'n'zy. Stay."

He hadn't realized how much he wanted his brother beside him till the words were out. M'k'n'zy was his only living family, his tactical wizard. For most of their lives he'd been D'ndai's most pressing obligation and his most valued asset. Facing the future without him was scary as hell.

He wanted M'k'n'zy to stay.

"I can't." The words squirted out of M'k'n'zy like seeds from a *rogan* fruit. The boy's voice cracked pitifully on the final word.

Sober and sane D'ndai might have understood that his brother had reached the end of one dream, and didn't know where to look on Xenex for another.

D'ndai was far from sober, and almost as far from sane. All he heard was the rejection.

"I see."

"D'ndai, I have a *destiny.*"

"How nice for you."

"My future's out there, not here."

"Of course not. Places like Xenex are for *ordinary* people, like me."

"You understand!" He grinned his cocky, trusting grin—the grin he flashed every time he came up with a new plan and handed D'ndai the mess that went with it. "I knew you would. You're a great brother, D'ndai!"

Fratricide was too good for M'k'n'zy. It was, however, the best D'ndai could arrange. He wondered whether to cave his brother's head in with the jug or just break his neck.

Sh'nab raised his head, recognized "critical mass," and grabbed D'ndai's arm. He looked at M'k'n'zy. "Don't say another word. Just go, boy, before it's too late."

The hell of it was, M'k'n'zy did just that, bouncing out of the room as if he'd never known a single care. He didn't even look back.

"I think I'll have him tortured before he's executed," D'ndai said. "Slowly. It should hurt lots."

Sh'nab stood, then caught himself as he wobbled. "Too much home-brew," he said, then looked cannily at his leader. "We've both had too much."

"I've just started." D'ndai reached for the earthenware jug. Catching Sh'nab's frown, he added, *"M'k'n'zy* gets visions in the Pit. Me? I never got to Search for the Allways. Da was killed right about the time I started thinking about it, and after that . . . Well, the Calhoun of Calhoun can't risk himself, can he? So," he continued, pulling the jug close, "I'll just have to find my visions here, won't I?"

Sh'nab pinned his arm to the table before he could pour himself another glass. The old man had lived life the hard way, and had the wiry toughness to prove it. "You still can't risk yourself. Whether she marries or not, Catrine will need you—you're her clan chief and always will be. Clan Calhoun needs you. Xenex needs you. You're the Calhoun of Calhoun, and *this* is your destiny. You can't hide from it in a jug."

"I think I hate him, you know," D'ndai said, sadly. "Damned brat. I wish I could trade destinies. He got the easy one."

Sh'nab patted him clumsily on the shoulder, and took the glass from his fingers. "If you can't hate your brother, who can you hate?"

D'ndai made sure to tell Sh'nab all the ways the next week stank.

"It stinks worse than a ten-day-dirty *lirga* sty, old man. It stinks like a dead Danteri soldier left to rot in the swamps down near Vedrine. It stinks like a latrine after a battalion with the flux has . . ."

"Shut up, D'ndai."

D'ndai grinned, glad to know he'd finally gotten past the elder's cast-iron good nature. "But it does stink."

"So does a Danteri's crotch cloth, but it's not something I need to hear about. Look," he said, waving a Federation-style padd in the air, "just look at this. Please? V'rdan and G'nard have given a statement to the Argive newsies suggesting we're provoking an intertribal feud. They spent an extra ten minutes promoting the 'New Economic Vision.'"

"The new what?"

"Apparently it's something G'nard has 'seen' while sitting in a smoke pit meditating on his left big-toe nail. 'A vision of a New Xenex, a Xenex free of want and need and poverty and pain.'"

"Sounds nice." D'ndai leaned his chin on the heel of his hand. "So how do we get this nice new Xenex?"

"Establish Clan G'lyndr as first among equals and make V'rdan executive of the Council of Clans—what else?"

"Of course. I should have guessed. It's obvious once you think of it." D'ndai pushed his own mempad across the desk. "Thallon's terminating all prior trade agreements with Calhoun, and threatening sanctions unless 'certain provisions are met.' Any guesses what they have in mind?"

"All hail Clan G'lyndr," Sh'nab intoned. "V'rdan's not playing *dath*-toss for kisses. He's determined to push us out and take over the planet."

"He sent me a private message, yesterday," D'ndai said. "Auto-erase, and no way to prove it. If I don't give him Catrine he'll force a feud."

"Then give him Catrine," Sh'nab said. "I know, I know, she doesn't want to marry—and you don't want her to marry G'nard. But what's one woman compared to the good of the clan?"

"What's the point of the clan, if it's not to look out for the good of the women?"

"Tell that to the world," Sh'nab said. "To me just say, 'I love her.' That's what it's really about. It's why G'lyndr picked her, too, though damned if I understand how he knew." He began to gather up the papers and pad. "G'lyndr were always bastards to feud with. They do love to twist the knife."

The next afternoon a herdgirl rushed into the courtyard, shrieking. She'd found a wild *harg* gutted on the high plateau where the *venn* grazed.

The *harg* was Calhoun's banner-beast. The knife left in the *harg*'s eye was etched with G'lyndr's flying nighthawk.

"They'll steal some of the herdgirls next," Sh'nab said. "After that? Bride raids, duels, ambushes, cattle runs. Give them the woman, D'ndai."

He couldn't.

M'k'n'zy left, beaming up with nothing more than the clothes on his back, a battle pack he'd had for years, and a happy grin. He didn't mention Catrine at all.

The clans began to mutter when a herd of *venn* was rustled during the night. They muttered louder when a fifteen-year-old girl went missing—even when she turned up safely married to a nomad boy her family detested.

Feud was in the air. Everyone was afraid.

D'ndai still couldn't make himself give in.

He couldn't hold firm, though, either. Not when the good of the clan was at risk.

He took to walking the town, hoping for an excuse to either kill a G'lyndr or be killed.

It would serve M'k'n'zy right if he died, he thought. Then the boy would learn the real cost of power: unending obligation. A mean, angry grin grew on his face as he imagined his brother called back from his precious Academy to face what D'ndai faced daily. Each beggar child, each scarred old veteran hobbling one-legged across the square in Calhoun was D'ndai's responsibility.

Let M'k'n'zy try plotting his way out of that.

D'ndai was sitting in the sun in the public square of Calhoun, eyes closed, trying to find a way out of the mess, when he heard a reedy voice he'd heard before.

"I hear you've got trouble."

"I was born to trouble," D'ndai said. He opened his eyes and looked reproachfully at the dapper DEA agent. "Why are you pestering me, Danteri? Don't you have better things to do?"

"Not really." Warain settled on the low plinth the bench sat on, reached deep within his silk tunic, and pulled out a beautifully etched duraglass case. He flipped it open and offered it to D'ndai. "Have a *mek* tab? They're from Serrias. Good, if you like them strong and spicy."

D'ndai ignored the offer. "We have nothing to say to each other."

"You may be sworn to silence. I'm not." Warain popped a tab in his mouth and rolled it around, savoring the burn and the faint narcotic rush. "I have some information you might be interested in. That's one nice thing about being DEA: gossip, rumor, speculation, sheer fantasy, you can hear it all if you show some interest. This particular rumor concerns Clan G'lyndr and a certain widow."

"Leave the gossip to the market peddlers. They give it away with every basket of greens."

"All a matter of fair trade," Warain said. "Give a little, get a little, and thus we all prosper. I'm willing to give a lot to get a lot."

"Stale goods. News of G'lyndr and—certain widows—is old news."

"Perhaps. Perhaps not."

"I don't deal with Danteri. I definitely don't deal with DEA."

"My goods have a short shelf life."

D'ndai pushed off from the bench. "Too bad for you, then. I need no DEA rumors, fresh or otherwise." He ambled away, determined to show no sign of interest or anger.

"She'll be lost if you delay," Warain said, so softly D'ndai almost didn't hear him. "G'lyndr's going for the kill."

D'ndai wanted to keep moving. The best he could manage was to stand, frozen. "Lost how?"

Warain hummed softly to himself. "Fresh goods, fresh and sweet. Who will buy? I'm sorry, Calhoun. I don't relish forcing your hand. But for Danter's sake I can't—no, I *won't* give goods away free. Not even when a woman's future is at stake."

"What's your price?"

"You know the price."

D'ndai turned and squatted on his haunches, looking fiercely at the DEA agent. "Xenex *hates* Danter. If I made a deal with you I'd be destroying my own clan as well as betraying my planet. When word got out G'lyndr would make an example of me Xenex would never forget."

"It wouldn't be betrayal if it helped Xenex. As for V'rdan . . . he can't destroy you if he can't make a show of it. All you need is plausible deniability or a good enough excuse." He came and crouched by D'ndai, offering the tab case again. "Come, now. No one will doubt Calhoun's loyalty to Xenex."

D'ndai snatched the case from Warain's hand and took a tab. The *mek* burned like fire and set his blood racing. "It would have to be a damned good excuse, Danteri."

"It would be nice to be called by name," Warain said. "I haven't been called anything but 'Danteri' for the past three months. If you deal in good faith, you'll have all the excuse you need for the short term. Greed and pragmatism will provide for the long term."

"I'll deal in good faith." It was a lie—but he suspected Warain knew that.

Warain gave a soft snort. "Sold, to the man in the Calhoun regalia!" He paused, and looked at D'ndai a bit wistfully. "Very well. You've sold your soul. You deserve something back for it. There's to be a bride raid tonight. Thallon is transporting G'nard and his war boys. They'll beam them out once they've accomplished a traditional snatch with the whole street watching."

"So we move Catrine."

"They'll only try again. You need to beat them like your brother beat us: so completely there's nothing left for them to do but back down."

"Of course. How?"

Warain chuckled. "Oh, I have a few ideas."

Warain wasn't as clever as M'k'n'zy, but the man had his own brilliance. D'ndai quickly found himself working with the man much as he'd worked with his brother: filling in, shoring up, adding definition to a sketchy concept. It felt good—better than anything had felt since the war had been won. D'ndai felt alive and on top of things.

He and his men were beamed down to Catrine's house late at night, long after everyone on the peaceful little street was asleep. They huddled together on the landing, peering at the black-market Federation tricorder, watching the life readings of Xenexians at rest.

D'ndai had taken part in ambushes before. He knew the creeping tension, the flick of eyes, the near-silent shift of feet as men tried to ease muscles kept still too long.

He'd wanted to tell Catrine. He'd wanted to beam her away so she'd be safe during the fighting. Warain had insisted that they needed her reaction—her shock, her rejection of G'nard, her fear. This was a battle of rumor and spin, not just of knives and phasers. What the witnesses saw on the street would matter.

Catrine's honest reaction frightened D'ndai worse than the thought of dying in the scrimmage.

She'd never forgive him.

Sh'nab, hunched low by the stairs, pointed at the patterns on the tricorder screen. "They're coming," he hissed. The old man had demanded a part in the battle, saying he'd been in at the start of this mess and he intended to be in at the end. Not that D'ndai had minded. Sh'nab was old, but he was a canny fighter, and loyal.

They could hear G'nard's party approaching. They weren't trying to be silent: They wanted as many witnesses as they could get. They came howling down the street, setting off firecrackers and shouting G'lyndr battle cries.

"Wait," D'ndai whispered. "No moves till they've broken in."

A murmur came from the bedroom: Catrine, disturbed by the noise below.

G'nard was shouting something about a man's needs and his love for a woman. The words were overblown and sappy, like something from a traveling opera.

In the bedroom feet hit the floor. Catrine was awake, now, and swearing. D'ndai heard her window open.

"Keep quiet down there or I'll empty the piss-pot on your heads!" she shouted. "Some of us need our rest."

"Forget rest, O beauteous dawn! You shall light my way to bed this night, or I am not G'nard of G'lyndr."

Of course G'nard had to make sure everyone knew who he was. That was the whole idea, wasn't it?

Catrine was silent a moment. D'ndai shivered, thinking of her fear. Then her voice rang out, clear and cutting. "G'nard the Small? I've heard about you."

"Good things, I hope?"

"Tiny things," she snapped, "and very unsatisfying. Now go away. I'm not interested in G'lyndr drunks."

D'ndai's men were choking back laughter. G'nard's men and the neighbors weren't so constrained: They roared as Catrine slammed the window closed.

G'nard must not have liked having his carefully planned little romance turned into a farce. He swore, then ordered his men on. One-two-three thuds later the door onto the street burst in. G'lyndr men tumbled into the entry.

"Now." D'ndai stepped out onto the stairway, dagger drawn. His men pushed in behind, slithering into the hall, taking down G'lyndr liege men before they knew they had any opposition.

Above, Catrine's door swung so hard it slammed into the wall. She shrieked: not a frightened shriek, but a banshee skreel of rage.

D'ndai, below, slammed the butt of his dagger into a G'lyndr chin. It was stupid, but he hoped Catrine would see him and know he was fighting for her.

"Men," he heard her growl. "Stupid, stupid *men*. Aaargh!" Her voice Dopplered down the stairs. He heard something hard hit something fleshy with a meaty thud. Someone swore sharply. Given the edgy contralto note it was either Catrine or a very unhappy man suffering a very personal injury.

D'ndai felt the fight move like a tidal surge out the door and onto the street. Men were panicking—not just G'nard's men, but D'ndai's also.

Behind them, wielding a very large iron lantern stand, came Catrine. Her form wasn't all it could be—though there wasn't much precedence for lantern-stand work in Xenexian military traditions. Her spirit more than made up for it. She was every frothing cannibal war goddess ever imagined.

G'nard was an experienced fighter. D'ndai saw him shift, heard him calling his men together.

D'ndai dodged a fist, sidestepped a dagger thrust, and faded back to stand beside Catrine, blocking a strike from—no, not a G'lyndr, but a neighbor who'd apparently decided it was a open-entry fracas with all targets fair play.

"We're here to help," he shouted to her.

"In a *lirga*'s eye," she snarled. But she didn't hit him.

Some sappy part of his brain stored the rest of the fight away in the most sentimental shadows of his mind: the one time he and Catrine were a couple.

The entire neighborhood had joined. G'nard realized he wasn't going to win this round. He batted frantically at a combadge pinned to his tunic.

"Beam us out! Now!"

No shimmer arrived to whisk the G'lyndr men away.

The group tried to bolt but the crowd was too dense, the fighting too enthusiastic. Soon the raiding party was surrounded. They huddled by a streetlamp in the guttering light of the oil lantern. Few had any weapons left. None had much dignity.

Catrine, still clutching her lanternstand, paced forward. "You dared. You *dared.*" She began to raise the stand.

D'ndai blocked her arm. "We won. Let them live with the shame." He directed his next words to G'nard, making sure he was loud enough to be heard by all present—and maybe even by people several streets away. "Calhoun protects its own. It always will. But if you give me Clan G'lyndr's oath of truce I'll give you safe passage out of Calhoun."

G'nard stared past D'ndai to Catrine, with a look too intense for D'ndai's comfort. "You're everything An'dr and D'ndai claimed," he said, softly. "G'lyndr needs a lady like you."

Catrine growled, low in her throat. "G'lyndr needs its ba—" She stopped herself, abruptly. "Just go."

"I'll return," G'nard said, sounding too sincere. He shook his head. "What a fighter! I can make you the mother of warriors!"

"Spare me the honor," she hissed, and turned to D'ndai. "I want this finished, Calhoun. No more. Not you, not your brother, not the next fool who wants to play politics over my desires. You're chief: Find a way to end it. Or I swear I will leave Xenex forever, if I have to sleep with every crewman on a Danteri junk freighter to pay my way."

D'ndai had never considered himself the genius in the family—at least he hadn't since M'k'n'zy had started spouting visions and plotting sneak attacks on Danteri encampments.

Desperation and inspiration are nonidentical. There is a statistical correlation, however.

"Land marriage," he said, softly.

"What?" Catrine looked more peeved than enlightened.

"Land marriage," he repeated. He raised his voice, looking around the faces in the faint light of moon, stars, and oil lantern. "It's an old tradition, from back in the days before the Danteri conquered us. When a widow wanted to protect her estate, or her honor, or her children by her first husband, she'd marry her own land. From then on she'd be the Lady of Long Acres, or whatever her lands were called."

G'nard made a disgusted noise. "Oh, I can just see it: This woman wasted on a grubby little house in a grubby little town, tied here forever. It might please you, but it won't please anyone else."

D'ndai felt a glow like the one he'd always thought M'k'n'zy must feel at the height of a successful battle. "No. Catrine, you're going to marry Xenex. You'll be free to go anywhere in the world, and the marriage is binding. A bride raid isn't enough to override a valid marriage."

G'nard just snorted. "But no child rights. No sane woman wants to give up her child rights forever."

Catrine looked first at G'nard—a cool, calculating look with no sentiment in it at all. Then she looked at D'ndai, and her expression softened. There was something there: not love, or passion—that was too much to hope for—but affection and respect.

She laid her hand on D'ndai's arm. "But G'lyndr, Calhoun has already paid my child-debt."

There was no question that G'nard assumed that D'ndai had given Catrine her hoped-for child. There was also no question that Catrine had intended to give that impression.

D'ndai covered her hand with his, squeezing it in thanks. "All it takes is a public oath," he said. He looked out at the faces around him. "We have plenty of witnesses. Shall we proceed, then?"

"Oh, yes," Catrine said, with a low, gloating purr. "Absolutely."

D'ndai had to improvise. He'd heard of land marriages, but he'd never bothered to study them in any detail. He was pleased, though: He managed to leave one small loophole in his phrasing that would allow Catrine to annul the bond if she chose.

Catrine took her oath in a firm, loud voice.

Then it was done. D'ndai stepped away from her, presenting her to the throng. "Behold: a Lady of Xenex! May she live long and happy in her land's embrace!"

There was a good deal of cheering and back-slapping. Neighbors skittered into their houses and brought out an impromptu wedding feast.

As G'nard and his men slipped sullenly away, a figure stepped from the shadows at the end of the street and nodded pleasantly.

Warain. Of course the man had to show himself—he needed G'lyndr and the clan's Thallonian allies to see *his* victory, too.

D'ndai found Catrine happily wolfing down sweet cakes and sour tea on a neighbor's stoop. He stole her glass and gulped down half the tea. Then he nerved himself, taking her hand. "You can still change your mind."

She slipped her hand back. "No. I'm sorry, D'ndai. This is a *good* answer."

"You're not old. You could live years—a long time to stay celibate."

She chuckled. "You mean Xenex is going to be a jealous husband?"

"Um . . ."

"No, my dear. I'm not planning on taking lovers. Even if I were . . . D'ndai, let me go. From now on I'm a Lady of Xenex, and happy that way." She stole back her glass and finished the last of the tea in one gulp, as though she too needed the emotional cover the action provided.

It was over, then.

He slapped his men on the shoulders. He smiled at Catrine's neighbors. He accepted compliments on his fighting style.

As he passed out of the street, Warain joined him.

"A good answer. I *am* impressed."

"Genius runs in the family," D'ndai said dryly. But something inside him warmed to the compliment. He did feel smarter, more as though he was in the same league as his little brother. He slipped on a M'k'n'zyesque rogue's grin, trying it on for size. "My brother had to learn it all somewhere."

Warain laughed. "Of course, my friend. I should have realized."

D'ndai felt obliged to return the compliment. "That jamming field you used to block the Thallonian transporter—it worked perfectly. Poor old G'nard was pounding his chest and shouting for a rescue, and nothing happened. I thought he'd have a heart attack he was so frustrated."

"Ah, but that Lady of Xenex notion: simply brilliant!" Warain moved silently through the rising fog, a sleek feline padding beside a stockier canine. "I think I'm going to enjoy working with you, Calhoun."

D'ndai felt a flicker of guilt, knowing he planned to abandon the DEA agent as soon as possible. Yet there was no point abandoning the alliance too soon. D'ndai could see many ways it could prove to Clan Calhoun's benefit.

"Likewise," he said, feeling amiable and empty and drained of passion. "You wouldn't happen to have any of those *mek* tabs with you? They were very fine."

The etched case passed between the two men. They commented on the fine blend of the *mek*. They plotted plots, and planned plans. And so they sauntered into the dawn of a new Xenex day.

U.S.S. EXCALIBUR
Making a Difference

Mary Scott-Wiecek

The *Excalibur* has a long and varied history. After serving as part of Captain Picard's blockade between the Klingon and Romulan Empires during the Klingon Civil War of 2368, the ship was given to Captain Morgan Korsmo and Commander Elizabeth Shelby as commanding and first officers, respectively. The ship continued to serve with distinction up until the second Borg incursion into the Federation. "Making a Difference" takes place during that incursion, simultaneous with the movie *Star Trek: First Contact*.

Mary Scott-Wiecek

Mary Scott-Wiecek is a stay-at-home Mom/aspiring writer who lives in Ohio with her husband, three children, and various pets. Her other *Star Trek* short stories have appeared in three of the *Strange New Worlds* anthologies (Volumes III and VI, grand-prize winner in Volume V). Other interests include art and Tai Chi. She would like to thank Penny "The Mouthpiece" Proctor, Kev "The Rev" Killiany, and the rest of the *SNW* "gang" for their support and camaraderie. Youse guys are da best!

Insufferable arrogance. That's what it had been, he decided, as he watched the Borg cube on its inexorable course for Earth. Insufferable arrogance—to believe that he, Captain Morgan Korsmo, could have made an iota of difference at Wolf 359. Just as it was insufferable arrogance to believe that he could make one now, as part of Admiral Hayes's hastily assembled defense force.

No—had he been at Wolf 359, his ship would have ended up just like all the others, a smoking, drifting shell, full of dead officers and crew. He didn't want to believe that was what was going to happen this time. In the six years since that first, devastating standoff, the Federation had learned a great deal about the Borg, and had come a long way toward developing effective defensive strategies against them. He himself had survived two Borg encounters in that time, although he knew that had been more a matter of luck than anything else. The battles had been brutal and deadly; he'd lost a lot of good people, and the *Chekov*, his previous ship, had been damaged beyond repair. He had survived, though, along with most of his crew. The Borg weren't invincible.

But this cube seemed different, somehow. It was barreling along with a passionless, purposeful determination that filled him with foreboding. Here in Sector 001, the Borg ship's destination, the blue orb that was his home—and the Federation's center of operations—looked vulnerable and even fragile. He felt despair, and a near-violent surge of protectiveness. They *would* stop that cube. They had to.

Admiral Hayes's task force was assembled and preparing to attack. Twenty-three starships, all together, geared up for battle. Oddly enough, the *Enterprise*-E was not among them. This didn't seem like the sort of mission Picard would want to miss, with his illustrious and seemingly charmed career. It still vexed Korsmo—just a little—that no matter what he accomplished, Jean-Luc Picard always seemed to be two steps ahead of him, from their days at the Academy to the present. Still, it would be good to see him now. The newly refurbished *Enterprise* was Starfleet's most advanced ship. Perhaps it just hadn't arrived yet.

The battle strategy for the fleet was almost comical in its simplicity. Their job was to make the cube stop and turn around. To somehow, in some way, draw the damned thing away from Earth. If they could get it on the defensive, perhaps they could find a way to destroy it.

As simple as the strategy was, its execution was another matter entirely. In front of him, he could hear his operations officer, Ensign Kothari, speaking to First Officer Shelby in urgent, clipped tones, as they monitored the designated frequency for tactical coordination. The battle plan was a triumph in strategic planning, with specified, shifting targets for all of the ships of the task force, and random shield and weapon resonance modulations across the board. It very likely wouldn't be enough, but they had to try. What other option was there? He studied the information Shelby was sending to his station with grim approval.

It was time.

"All hands to battle stations!" he called out, over the shipwide com. They were already at red alert, and now everyone finished with their last-minute preparations and focused on the challenge ahead.

Admiral Hayes's voice sounded over the ship-to-ship channel. *"All ships, prepare to engage the Borg. Team Alpha—fire!"*

The first wave of starships surged forward, phasers and photon torpedoes blazing. The cube was illuminated by dozens of explosions. Its shields absorbed the energy at first, but as the barrage continued, a few breaches appeared. The task force immediately took advantage of them. Remarkably, after the first run, the cube sustained at least some damage to its weapons arrays, Team Alpha's primary targets. Hayes called for Team Beta, and the second line moved in. The Borg cube was responding now, in full force. Torpedoes burst forth from the monstrous ship. One of them immediately found a mark, and a *Norway*-class starship vaporized in a cloud of sparks and glowing debris. Korsmo wasn't even sure which ship it was, and he didn't have time to think about it now.

"We're up next," he said. "Helm, move us into position—bearing three-fifty mark twenty."

"Aye, Captain." Lieutenant T'Shanik, his Vulcan conn officer, a remarkably efficient young woman just a few years out of the Academy, was already maneuvering into position.

"Team Gamma—fire!"

"Engage!" Korsmo called out, and they were off. T'Shanik piloted the ship in a graceful arc around to the port side of the cube. "Target phasers, and fire!" he said. "Fire torpedoes!"

T'Shanik was already pulling the ship up and away as the last torpedo found its mark. They rocked, briefly, as a Borg phaser beam grazed their shields. Korsmo looked toward Shelby expectantly as she monitored the data coming in.

"At least one of them got through," she said, grinning. "We've taken out our secondary target—a power relay."

Scattered cheering erupted on the bridge, but everyone knew the battle was just beginning. As T'Shanik moved the *Excalibur* into position for its second run, Korsmo allowed himself the luxury of watching the viewscreen.

Resistance apparently wasn't as futile as it used to be. The surface of the cube was riddled with torpedo craters and phaser scars. Inside the cube, he could see the green glow of a half-dozen plasma fires. He knew Borg drones were already being dispatched to deploy forcefields and repair the damage, but it was a satisfying sight for the moment. The cube had stopped, too, and wasn't that half the goal already?

His flash of optimism faded quickly, as slowly, unbelievably, the Borg ship lumbered into motion, resuming its course for Earth. The mood on the bridge darkened, and the disappointment and dread of his crew was palpable. It almost seemed that the entire task force was nothing more than an inconvenience to the cube. Nothing was going to distract it from its goal this time.

Korsmo wondered what the cube would do when it reached Earth. Would it carve out chunks of the planet to study the technology, as the Borg had done in so many other systems in the past? The resulting loss of mass would alter the planet's orbit and turn it into a lifeless chunk of ice. Those unlucky enough to survive the initial attack would slowly starve, or freeze to death.

But no, the Borg had other plans for Earth. If it were possible for a collective of soulless automatons to hold a grudge, the Borg surely held one against humanity. They meant to assimilate both the planet and its population. Korsmo tried to picture how it might look—flat gray and mechanical, with relays spidering over the surface like Borg facial implants. He thought about his sister and her family in Prague, and what would become of them. Her youngest was only three.

"*All ships—pursuit course. Fire at will!*" Admiral Hayes shouted over the com.

The Borg chose this moment to broadcast their standard greeting. *"We are the Borg. Lower your shields and surrender your ships. We will add your biological and technological distinctiveness to our own. Your culture will adapt to service us. Resistance is futile."*

Like hell it was. Korsmo stood up, furious and with renewed determination. "Reconfigure phasers," he barked. "Shelby, how are the shields?"

"Still at ninety-five percent," she replied, "but we should shift the nutonals, just in case. We were lucky in our first run, but the Borg could still have adapted."

"Do it," he confirmed. "Lock phasers, ready torpedoes, and engage!"

This time, their weapons did some real damage to the cube's hull. One torpedo created a soul-satisfying display of pyrotechnics and left behind a crater filled with debris.

But then their luck ran out. The Borg were firing their torpedoes randomly and constantly, and one of them struck the ship head-on. *Excalibur* was jolted violently by the impact, and people were thrown off their feet. Korsmo managed to grab hold of the arm of his chair and crawl back to his seat.

"Report!" he bellowed. The bridge crew was still struggling to get back to their stations.

"Our shields are down!" Shelby said. "Damn!"

"Evasive maneuvers," he called out to T'Shanik, but before she could respond, he felt a familiar percussive thud and jolt that settled right into the pit of his stomach. He'd felt it before, and he knew what it meant.

"Tractor beam!" Lieutenant Martins cried, from tactical, confirming his worst fears. "They've caught us in a tractor beam."

"All engines—full reverse," he and Shelby said, simultaneously. They exchanged a glance, but he didn't mind her duplicating obvious orders in a battle situation, and she knew that. They'd both been down this road before. When the Borg tractored a vessel, they intended to hold it in place for their cutting beam.

"Fire all phasers. Target the source of the tractor beam," he ordered. He stepped up next to Shelby, behind the helm. "I thought I told you to take that 'Borg cutting beam—slice here' sign off the hull after the last time," he said to her, sotto voce.

She snorted. "I'm sure it's nothing personal, sir," she said. "We just happen to be closer to the cutting beam than their nearest phaser banks."

"Great," he said. "I'd hate to inconvenience them."

"Our engines are unable to pull away, sir," T'Shanik told him.

"Modulate the resonance settings . . ." he started to say, but it was too late. The unforgettable green cutting beam shot out of the cube, and pierced *Excalibur* a fraction of an instant later.

Because of the tractor, there was little jarring on impact. But although he couldn't actually hear the sounds of screeching metal, he knew what was happening to his ship. It was an instinct that most starship captains developed over time. He'd have sworn he could feel the cut, right down to his bone.

Alarms began to sound at almost all of the bridge stations. "Hull breach!" Martins shouted from tactical. "Sections twenty-five through twenty-nine, decks nineteen and twenty. Engineering."

"Keep firing phasers," he shouted over the cacophony of klaxons and multiple damage reports. "Modulate the resonance settings. Get a damage-control team down there—emergency forcefields!"

On the main viewscreen, he saw another ship come streaking in, phasers flashing. The *Endeavor* had noticed their predicament. With both ships firing simultaneously, the tractor beam went down, but he knew it would only be temporary. The Borg were nothing if not persistent.

"Hard about," he yelled in T'Shanik's general direction. "Bearing two-twenty mark seveteen. Full impulse." He slapped his combadge. "Engineering—report!"

The response was slow in coming, and when it did, he could hear a lot of shouting and pounding in the background. *"Burgoyne here."* It was the assistant chief engineer. *"Warp engines are offline. Impulse engines are down to fifty percent. Main power is fluctuating, but we're on it. And, sir, Commander Argyle is dead."*

For Korsmo, the sounds of the battle converged into a dull roar, and the moment seemed to stretch out in all directions. Argyle had been a fine officer, and a good friend. This was the second time he'd lost a chief engineer to the Borg. For just an instant, his mind flashed back to his last encounter, nearly four years ago. That time, it had been a small Borg scout ship, a fraction of the size of this one. But size didn't matter much when a Borg cutting beam was involved. . . .

"Warp and impulse engines are offline. Main power is offline. We've lost both shields and weapons," Shelby told him. Her face was covered with blood from a gash on her cheek. "Damage reports coming in from all over the ship. Twenty-two dead. So far. And three . . . missing."

They both looked at the viewscreen, where the Borg ship was moving away, with a large chunk of engineering in its tractor beam. The fate of the three crewmen inside was unknown.

"Sir, we're being hailed," his tactical officer, Lieutenant Lowe, reported.

"If it's the Borg, ignore them," Korsmo snapped. *He was sure no one was in the mood for the "resistance is futile" speech.*

"It's not the Borg. It's . . . it's coming from engineering, sir," Lowe said, and his voice wavered as he realized the significance of the source. *"Deck eighteen, section twenty-nine. Audio only."*

Shelby gasped, and they both looked in horror at the pillaged portion of their ship still being carried by the retreating cube. *"Dear God,"* she whispered, *"someone's still alive over there."*

"Can we lock on with the emergency transporters?" he asked Shelby, quietly.

She glanced quickly down at the helm console. *"No, we're out of range,"* she said, her voice filled with frustration and regret.

"Call down to what's left of engineering," he told her. *"Find out if there's anything . . . anything we can do at all."*

She nodded as he turned to Lowe and gestured for him to open the channel.

"Korsmo, here," he said. *"To whom am I speaking?"*

"Lieutenant Marika, here, Captain," *a woman's voice responded.* "Crewmen Ramirez and Howard are with me. The Borg have erected some kind of forcefield around this section. I guess they must want. . ." *She stopped briefly to regain her composure, before finishing, courageously.* "They must want us alive."

Marika Wilkarah, a Bajoran engineer. He knew of her. She and her husband were both officers onboard. *"Marika, we're doing everything we can to retrieve you,"* he told her, not bothering to add that there wasn't a hell of a lot they could do. Even if, by some miracle, they could get within transporter range, the chances of them being able to lock on through the tractor and a forcefield were not good.

"Captain," Lowe interrupted. *"The Borg are creating a transwarp conduit."*

And they were running out of time. He turned to Shelby, and she shook her head, confirming what he already knew. They had no options at all.

"We appreciate your efforts, sir," *Marika said.* "Can you tell me what my husband's status is? I wasn't able to raise his station."

He didn't even need to look at Shelby. Out of the corner of his eye, he saw her hurry over to ops.

"We're trying to find out for you," he told Marika, wishing with all of his heart that he had something else to offer her.

"The conduit is open," Lowe reported. *"The Borg cube is accelerating toward it."*

"Captain," *Marika said, her voice shaking,* "it's been an honor serving with . . ."

The line went to static as a bright white flare filled the viewscreen. The warp con-

duit had closed behind the cube, and the slice of his ship that it still held in its trac-
tor beam, like a damned trophy. He sat down heavily in his command chair.

Biting her lip and fighting back tears, Shelby stepped up to his side. "Marika
Errid has been taken to sickbay. He's injured and unconscious, but expected to sur-
vive," she told him, softly.

Unable to suppress the surge of fury that rose up inside him, he slammed the arm
of the chair with his fist hard enough to make Shelby jump, and undoubtedly break
some of his bones. He didn't care. Yes, he'd managed to save his ship, and he knew
that was a significant victory. It didn't feel that way now, though. So many dead. So
many injured. His ship, perhaps, damaged beyond repair. And a woman, calling out
to him on her way to a fate even worse than death, and he'd been utterly powerless
to help her. He hadn't been able to do even the simplest thing for her—like tell her
whether her husband was dead or alive. How could anyone, ever, hope to make any
difference at all when faced with such a cold, intractable, malevolent enemy as the
Borg?

A now sickeningly familiar jolt pulled Korsmo back to the present, and
he realized that things had just gone from bad to worse. "The tractor beam
has locked on to us again," Martins called out from tactical.

He felt the same helpless rage now as he had then. Nothing he had done
had helped. He couldn't stop the cube, or do anything at all to save Earth.
And now he was going to lose his ship and crew as well. He remembered
the lists from Wolf 359, thirty-nine ships and thousands upon thousands of
faceless names. He bristled at the thought of *Excalibur* and her crew being
just another collection of names on just another damned list, if anyone was
even around to compile one this time.

Well, they weren't going down without a fight. "Target the tractor
again," he ordered. "Fire phasers!"

The Borg cutting beam beat them to the punch. The impact was closer
to the bridge this time—across the saucer support strut, he estimated, from
the perspective on the screen—and the force of it sent him sprawling over
the ops console with Kothari. A split second later, the beam cut through a
critical system, and the console exploded.

He was thrown away from ops in a shower of sparks and debris. For a
moment, he was both blind and deaf, and acrid smoke seared his throat. He
felt himself sliding into unconsciousness, and fought it. As his head began
to clear, he discovered that he was lying on the floor of the bridge next to
the now lifeless body of Kothari. He noted, grimly, that there was no need
to look for a pulse. She'd borne the brunt of the explosion; the hole in her
midsection testified to that. There was no time to grieve.

Looking down, he saw that he was bleeding, too, although not excessively. He felt an odd heaviness in his chest, and sensed that something was terribly wrong, but he'd have to worry about it later.

"Report!" he shouted, hoarsely.

"Hull breach—deck thirteen," Shelby said, hurrying to his side. "Emergency forcefields are in place. Captain, you're injured. I need to get you to sickbay." She reached up to tap her combadge.

"No time!" he snapped, in a voice that would brook no argument. "Take over at ops."

She hesitated for only a moment before complying, as he lurched unsteadily up to tactical. Martins had been thrown over the railing. He stopped briefly to feel for a pulse, but found none. Another bridge casualty. He looked around, but mercifully everyone else was up and about.

Only when the tractor beam caught them again did he realize they'd been briefly free of it. It was unusual for the Borg to have lost their hold, even for a moment, but he supposed the collective had a lot on its mind. Perhaps they could take advantage of that.

He hit his combadge. "Korsmo to engineering. Burgoyne, are you still with me?"

"Yes, sir," the unflappable Hermat responded. There was a lot of bustle in the background—a good sign. *"We still haven't been able to stabilize main power, but impulse is up to sixty percent."*

"Good," he said. "We're going to need that. What's the status on weapons?"

"The forward torpedo launch tubes were damaged by the cutting beams, but we still have dorsal phasers at about eighty percent," s/he said.

"Good," he said, again. He couldn't understand why his chest felt so heavy, and why he was suddenly so cold. There was some pain, but mostly he was just having a hard time getting enough air. He had to concentrate to draw in enough breath to speak. "I need more phaser power," he said. "Make it top priority. Take it from wherever we can spare it. Coordinate with Shelby. We need to evacuate some decks—you can shunt some power from life-support."

"Acknowledged," Burgoyne said, closing the channel.

"Target the tractor . . ." he began, until he remembered that he was manning tactical and therefore giving orders to himself. He shook his head, closed his eyes, and took a slow, deliberate breath. He had to stay focused, now. His hands were clammy, and he wiped them hurriedly on his tunic. When he managed to take in enough air, he targeted the Borg tractor himself and began firing.

"T'Shanik," he called over to the helm. "If we get free of the tractor, we're going to need to get out of range in a hurry. Go to the port side of the cube. There's more going on over there—we won't be as tempting a target. Bearing and mark, your discretion. Stand by."

"Yes, sir," she acknowledged, glancing quickly his way. It was unusual for him to give orders in advance, but he was afraid he might lose consciousness and he wanted to make his intentions clear.

The phasers were, as yet, ineffective, but he could see the power indicator steadily rising. Whatever Burgoyne was doing was working. Argyle had told him repeatedly what an innovative engineer s/he was. S/he was certainly coming through for them now.

He randomized the phaser resonance settings to a different set of fluctuating patterns, then fired. For an instant, he felt a slight change in his ship—a subtle interruption in the vibrations of the deck plating. Although it wasn't obvious that their resistance was having an effect, he was sure it was. The phasers were up to ninety-five percent, and he fired again.

"Come on, you bastards, let go!" he muttered.

The cutting beam lashed out once more. It made contact, but shut off again quickly. The lights went down, and the bridge glowed red as the emergency lighting kicked in.

"We're losing main power," Shelby said. "We've lost life-support on two more decks. I'm evacuating them. And sir, the flagship has been destroyed."

He couldn't even acknowledge her, or spare a thought for Hayes and the men and women who'd served on that ship. He needed every bit of his will and energy to remain upright, and to keep his hands from shaking. He'd begun to shiver almost uncontrollably.

"Captain," she said, "the phaser banks are nearly drained, and there's been no change in the tractor readings."

That might well be, but he knew—he *knew*—this was working. He could feel it. Doggedly, he reset the phasers again, and fired.

The tractor beam flickered, then shut down. This was it, their only chance.

"*Now,* conn!" he rasped. T'Shanik responded immediately, sweeping off to the left. The tractor beam reached for them again, but she evaded it. The cutting beam shot out, and grazed the port nacelle, but *Excalibur* swung around the edge of the cube, out of range.

Another small explosion rocked the bridge—systems were overloading all over the badly damaged ship. But Korsmo knew the worst was behind them.

"Main power is offline," Shelby reported. "Impulse engines are down."

That wasn't the problem it would have been thirty seconds ago. Their momentum was carrying them out and away from the battle zone. On the screen, he could see the *Defiant,* absorbing brutal torpedo blows. Korsmo wished they could help, but at least the smaller ship seemed to be holding its own.

He tried to brace himself against the tactical console, but sheer force of will was no longer enough to keep him upright. He felt himself slide slowly down to the floor. It was increasingly painful and difficult to draw in breath now, and he knew he'd sustained serious internal injuries, which he'd probably exacerbated by moving around so much. He wasn't going to make it this time. He'd tempted fate once too often. *Excalibur* was out of danger, though, and that was the main thing.

"There's another ship coming in," Shelby said, excitedly, from ops. "It's the *Enterprise!*"

Korsmo looked at the viewscreen through half-closed eyes just in time to see the sleek *Sovereign*-class ship shoot by, phasers firing. If he could have found the energy or the breath, he'd have laughed out loud. Starfleet's golden boy—*or golden old bald guy,* he thought, wryly—racing to the rescue again. He'd once told Shelby that the one constant in the universe was that Jean-Luc Picard would always be around to save the day. It was nice to know it still held true, even now. He was at peace with his old friend and rival at last, and genuinely pleased to see him. The Borg might not know it yet, but the momentum of the battle had just turned Starfleet's way.

Picard's voice came over the tactical channel. *"This is Picard of the* Enterprise. *I'm taking command of the fleet. Target all of your weapons onto the following coordinates."*

Korsmo was now shaking violently, and his voice came out as a thin, quavering rasp. "Can we assist?" he asked Shelby.

"Not a chance, sir," she said, turning around. When she saw him, a look of genuine alarm flashed across her face, and she was up and running toward him, calling out orders on her way. "Lock down all nonessential systems, and try to keep us out of the fleet's way with the thrusters."

She reached his side, and slapped her combadge. "Medical emergency," she said. "Transport the captain directly to sickbay."

"Transporters are down, and so are the turbolifts," sickbay responded. *"We've sent a medical team up to the bridge, but they have to use the Jefferies tubes."*

Shelby swore softly.

"Too late," he told her, in a whisper. "It's all right," he managed to get out, hoping to comfort her. The viewscreen lit up as dozens of starships fired at the coordinates Picard had specified. The cube's hull began to break apart, showing pockets of glowing green within. Then it exploded, in a gratifying burst of light and gray metal. He had to close his eyes against the brightness. He could hear the bridge crew cheering.

He could rest now. The cube was gone, his friends and loved ones on Earth were all safe, and his ship was out of danger. He mourned the people he'd lost—Kothari, Martins, Argyle, and undoubtedly many others. But when he thought about the survivors, he felt a deep satisfaction. T'Shanik was the best natural pilot he'd ever seen, and Burgoyne in engineering had a brilliant career ahead of hir. And, of course, there was Shelby. In the years that he'd known her, she'd grown in experience and wisdom. She was going to make Starfleet a hell of a captain. These were good people, and he was proud to have had a hand in making them who they were, and preserving their lives this day. Sometimes, he now understood, you just had to make a difference wherever you could. And it might well be that, in some small way, he had helped to distract the Borg long enough for someone to find a way to destroy them. Perhaps a little bit of insufferable arrogance on the part of many small Starfleet captains was necessary when facing the mighty Borg.

He opened his eyes slowly, and Shelby was kneeling down beside him, looking uncharacteristically emotional. Were those tears in her eye? His vision was going gray around the edges. He could see that she was holding his hand, but he couldn't feel her touch.

One more duty to perform. "Commander," he said, his voice no more than a wheeze, "you have the conn." There. He'd left his ship in the hands of the most capable first officer in the fleet. Everything was all right, now. With effort, he drew in one more uneven breath. "See to the safety . . ." he began, but then everything went black and silent.

He didn't see Commander Shelby blink hard, then reach down gently to close her captain's eyes. He didn't hear her voice break a little as she completed his final order.

". . . of all hands. Yes, sir."

KAT MUELLER
Performance Appraisal

Allyn Gibson

Before joining Captain Shelby on the *U.S.S. Trident* as her first officer, Commander Katerina Mueller was the "nightside" commander on the *Excalibur*, a post she also held on the *U.S.S. Grissom*, under the command of Captain Kenyon. "Performance Appraisal" takes place during Mueller's tenure on the *Grissom*, before Commander Mackenzie Calhoun was assigned as that vessel's first officer.

Allyn Gibson

Allyn Gibson lives in Raleigh, North Carolina, where he works as a store manager for one of the leading video game retailers, ironic given that he rarely plays video games. The publication of "Performance Appraisal" and the upcoming *Star Trek: S.C.E.* eBook *Ring Around the Sky* fulfills one of his long-standing ambitions: to be a published author by the age of thirty. When not working, writing, or trying to coax sociability out of his anti-social cat, Allyn can usually be found watching *Doctor Who* videos. You can find out more than you ever wanted to know about Allyn at http://www.allyngibson.net/.

"Lieutenant Mueller, please report to the bridge." Hearing the voice of Cray, the *Grissom*'s Andorian chief of security, calling her name startled Katerina Mueller, and she dropped her hydrospanner.

Rachel McLauren gave Mueller a wide smile as Mueller picked the hydrospanner up off the engineering deck. "You've gone and done it now, kiddo." Mueller looked McLauren squarely in the eyes from her squatting position. McLauren stood not more than a meter tall and was powerfully built, the native of a high-gravity Earth colony. It wasn't only her height that distinguished her, though; she kept her head shaved, leaving only her bushy red eyebrows as a sign of her natural coloring.

A look of concern crossed Mueller's face, flashing white the scar that ran across her left cheek. "I haven't done anything, Rachel."

"I'm just teasing, Kat. The captain probably just wants to talk about the sensor probe we modified."

Mueller had spent little time on the bridge, occasionally operating the engineering console during gamma or delta shift over her ten months aboard the *Grissom*. So when the turbolift doors parted to reveal the bridge, she saw the less familiar alpha-shift crew. Romeo Takahashi at ops and Mick Gold at conn she knew only by name; she had worked with First Officer Christine Parsons, Lieutenant Cray at tactical, and Lieutenant Chu'lak at sciences on the Sarn mission.

"Lieutenant Mueller reporting to the bridge, as ordered."

Commander Parsons rose from the center seat. "Lieutenant, the captain wishes to meet you in his ready room."

Mueller nodded silently and tapped on the ready-room door chime.

Captain Kenyon's deep voice answered, *"Come,"* and the doors swished open.

Mueller entered the room and stood ramrod straight. "You wished to see me, Captain." Only then did she notice Commander Todd Kogutt, the

Grissom's chief engineer, standing off to the side. Sitting atop Kenyon's desk was the sensor probe Mueller and McLauren had modified the day before.

"I did, Lieutenant. At ease. You may have a seat. You, too, Commander," Kenyon added with a look at Kogutt.

As Mueller took the proffered seat, Captain Norman Kenyon took a glance at a padd on his desk. Mueller knew Kenyon more through reputation than personal experience. He was a heavyset man in his mid-fifties with thinning gray hair. A career Starfleet officer, Kenyon had lost his previous ship, the *Harriman,* by intervening in a confrontation between a Klingon cargo transport and a Romulan warbird near Nimbus III a year and a half before. Among the casualties was Kenyon's wife, Marsha, also his science officer, and while Starfleet had wanted to ground Kenyon to give him time to recuperate from the twin losses, he instead asked for another command, the *Grissom,* which Starfleet granted after a brief review.

"You are assistant chief engineer, is that correct, Lieutenant?"

Mueller nodded. "Yes, sir."

"One of three, Captain," added Kogutt.

"Thank you for the precision, Commander." Kenyon looked directly at Mueller. "I read Mr. Kogutt's report on the sensor array delivery system you've developed and inspected the probe myself. I must say, Lieutenant, I'm impressed."

Mueller felt her spirits buoyed. "Thank you, sir. It was a team effort."

"Oh?" said Kenyon.

"The initial idea was mine, sir, and with Lieutenant McLauren's assistance, I modified a class-one sensor probe to test its feasibility."

"McLauren?" prompted Kenyon.

Kogutt replied. "Rachel McLauren, assistant chief engineer."

"One of three, correct?" said Kenyon as he gave a sly smile.

Kogutt returned the smile. "Yes, sir."

Kenyon cleared his throat. "In all seriousness, Lieutenant, the sensor arrays Starfleet deployed a century ago along the Neutral Zone no longer have the sensitivity to be a useful early-warning system, and your solution for deploying new sensors without attracting Romulan attention holds promise." He indicated Kogutt with a tilt of his head. "I asked Commander Kogutt to show me your probe. Starfleet Command, as you might imagine, has concerns with the recent Romulan reemergence onto the galactic stage, particularly after last month's attempted defection by Admiral Jarok to the *Enterprise.* If we have a stealthy method of deploying sensor probes along the Neutral Zone we're going to take it. Tell me, Lieutenant, how exactly will the sensor deployment work?"

Mueller took a breath and launched into the explanation, wondering only briefly why Kogutt hadn't provided those specifics. "The *Grissom* will launch the probe toward a cometary nucleus on a ballistic trajectory. When it lands on the surface, heating units inside the casing will switch on, melting the frozen surface gases and allow the probe to sink into the nucleus. Once it has achieved a preset depth, the heating units will shut off, the comet's surface will refreeze, and the sensor probe will be in place."

"Why a ballistic trajectory?"

"A ballistic trajectory expends no motive energy, hence nothing to be observed by Romulan sensors. The probe would appear for all intents and purposes to be space detritus. By melting a probe into the comet's nucleus, the probe's deployment would have all the signs of being a routine outgassing, whereas if the probe drilled into the nucleus, its power supply could be detected by Romulan sensors."

"How did you come up with this idea, Lieutenant?"

"Basic chemistry and physics, sir. Starfleet engineers tend to overthink simple problems and come up with complex solutions. But putting a sensor array inside a cometary core doesn't require a complex solution, not when a nucleus is essentially ice."

Kenyon nodded. "And ice melts."

"Correct, sir," Mueller answered. "Comets are more than just water ice—there's also hydrogen ice, helium ice, ammonia ice, and these have melting points far below that of water. An object at room temperature would melt the cometary ice on impact and vaporize the volatiles to their gaseous state, all without the energy that drilling into the nucleus would entail."

"Have you tested the system yet?"

Mueller shook her head. "Not yet, sir. My team has run several simulations and built the one prototype, but we've had no real-world test as yet."

Kenyon smiled. "Lieutenant, you'll have your real-world test."

"How soon?"

Kenyon drummed his fingers on his desk. "The *Grissom* is currently en route to a rogue cometary field near the Neutral Zone. How long will it take to equip six or eight probes with the necessary hardware?"

"No time at all, sir. Perhaps two hours per probe."

Kenyon nodded. "Very well. Our ETA is tomorrow's alpha shift. Have your team equip eight probes with the internal heating units." He paused. "Good work, Lieutenant."

Mueller smiled. "Thank you, sir."

Kogutt stood. "If that will be all, sir?"

"Yes, Todd, thank you." He handed Kogutt the probe and dismissed him with a wave of his hand. "Lieutenant, if I could have a few moments of your time?"

"Of course, sir," Mueller said, an edge of confusion creeping into her voice.

Once Kogutt departed, Kenyon folded his hands on the ready-room desk. "As you may be aware, I will in all likelihood have a command vacancy shortly."

"Commander Parsons is taking command of the *Tolstoi*." Seeing no confirmation in Kenyon's face, she quickly added, "Or so I've heard."

"The lower decks are remarkably well informed. Christine's promotion hasn't yet been finalized."

"One hears things."

"Obviously," said Kenyon sardonically.

"The position of first officer is vacant, then."

"Assuming all goes to plan, I've made a tentative offer of the first-officer position to Paullina Simons." Commander Simons served as the *Grissom*'s executive officer, the commander of the nightside watch. While her duties as executive officer differed in no respect from those of the first officer, the move from XO to first officer was considered a promotion and a stepping-stone to eventual command.

"The nightside commander position is available, then," Mueller said in a flat tone that indicated a statement, not a question.

"Again, assuming all goes to plan, correct. I intend to fill it from within the *Grissom* community." Kenyon paused. "Commander Kogutt thinks highly of you, and I trust his judgment. I like the elegance of your solution to placing the sensor probes. It shows thinking outside the conventional box, a prerequisite of command. And I understand you have command training."

Mueller frowned. "My command training is limited, sir, just a year in the command program at the Academy."

"You received high marks. Admiral Stell noted that you had a fine tactical mind."

"I wasn't aware that the admiral thought highly of me, sir," Mueller said. Admiral Stell taught Historical Perspectives on Military Tactics. "His class was one I had difficulty with."

"It might surprise you that he noted in your file that your analysis of the

Battle of Ghioghe demonstrated convincingly to his mind that it was Kirk's recklessness that led to the loss of the *Lydia Sutherland,* and had he shown more patience the battle might have been avoided altogether." Kenyon leaned back in his chair. "I've known Stell since I attended the Academy. Let me assure you, Lieutenant, he doesn't often offer praise. Yet, you left the command training program after taking the *Kobayashi Maru* examination."

"My performance in the simulation was not . . ." She paused, searching for the right word, then decided to start the thought fresh. "I felt that Starfleet would be better served in command by someone capable of achieving more than I did in the simulation and that I had more to offer the engineering services." She sighed deeply. "I lost my command to the Romulan warbirds without destroying a single one. I should have managed at least one kill, and the *Kobayashi Maru* was still lost."

Kenyon smiled. "Even though everyone loses the ship?"

"Not everyone. James Kirk survived the simulation and rescued the ship."

"It's not widely known, but Kirk also reprogrammed the simulation and played by a different set of rules. I wouldn't count Kirk as a standard to hold oneself against in the *Kobayashi Maru.*"

"It's said another cadet—I think his name was Quintin Stone—survived the simulation a decade ago." She looked intently at Kenyon. "It can be done."

Kenyon's smile upturned slightly on the left side of his mouth, his head nodded slowly, and his eyes narrowed. "You set high standards for yourself, Lieutenant."

Mueller's facial scar turned white. "If I don't, sir, no one else will." She fixed Kenyon with a concerted look. "Might I ask who else are you considering for the XO position?"

"Cray."

Mueller frowned.

Kenyon shook his head. "I know you and Cray haven't had the best of relationships—"

"The Sarn mission," she said.

"I wouldn't let that concern you, Lieutenant. I've begun the selection process, not ended it."

"May I ask what is your timetable for filling the position?"

Kenyon rose, and Mueller did likewise. "Commander Parsons will be aboard as first officer at least until we reach Starbase 65. Assuming her own promotion goes through as anticipated, I expect to have a decision made by that point."

Mueller nodded. "Thank you, Captain, for the opportunity."

Kenyon held out his hand. Mueller took it. "Thank you, Lieutenant, for your interest."

Mueller turned, and as she reached the ready-room doors Kenyon said, "One last thing, Lieutenant."

"Yes, sir?" she said.

"I'd like you on the bridge tomorrow when we deploy the first sensor probe. It's your project. You deserve to be there."

Mueller nodded. "I appreciate that, sir."

As she stepped back onto the bridge, Cray gave her a withering glance. She had never been close to Cray, less friends than acquaintances, and he hadn't spoken to her at all since the Sarn incident. She knew that Cray had blamed her for the explosion of the colony's fusion-reaction core in his postmission report. In contrast, both Commander Parsons and Lieutenant Chu'lak reported that, even had the *Grissom* crew arrived to stabilize the ruptured core hours earlier, the damage had already been done and it was only a matter of time before it went critical. Shaking her head, Mueller stepped into the turbolift and tried to put the thoughts of that mission behind her.

"How did it go, Kat?" said Rachel McLauren as Mueller stepped into engineering.

Mueller smiled. "The captain wants to consider me for the XO position."

"Oh, Kat, that's wonderful!" She threw her arms around Mueller.

"Unfortunately, the captain is also considering Cray."

McLauren backed away. "Oh," she said. "That can't be good."

Mueller sighed. "I don't have anything against Cray. I barely *know* Cray. But he hasn't spoken to me since Sarn—"

"That was six months ago. No one blames you for that. It wasn't *anyone's* fault."

Mueller frowned, biting the inside of her cheek. "He's the chief of security. He serves on the bridge during alpha shift, alongside the captain day in and day out. The captain knows Cray's work and his reputation. He only knows what Kogutt tells him about mine."

"I wouldn't get worked up over it." McLauren frowned. "I have to get back to calibrating the antimatter containment fields. Meet me in the lounge after shift? I'll buy you a drink."

Mueller nodded wearily. "Thanks, Rachel."

"You worry too much, kiddo. You'll give yourself wrinkles to match that scar of yours," McLauren said, cutting her right hand across her cheek. "Promise me you won't dwell too much on Cray and Sarn."

"I promise," Mueller said as McLauren disappeared into the bowels of engineering, but for the rest of her shift she couldn't help but think of taking orders from Cray.

Against the icy blackness of space and the distant suns of the Romulan Star Empire the cometary nucleus appeared as nothing more than an indistinct smudge on the *Grissom*'s main viewscreen. So distant was this comet from the closest star that even at maximum magnification no surface details could be discerned, so little was the light of reflected starglow.

Kenyon rose from his command chair and gave two quick tugs to his uniform top. "What do you make of the comet, Lieutenant Chu'lak?" he asked.

The Vulcan science officer turned from his console and looked to the drifting comet. "A typical nucleus, Captain. Thirty-five kilometers long, eighteen kilometers wide, ten deep. Composed of various ices—water, ammonia, methane, other organic compounds—and a nickel-iron core within. Surface temperature stands at eight degrees Kelvin."

"An iceberg of the spaceways," said Kenyon.

"Essentially, sir, yes."

Commander Christine Parsons leaned from her chair toward Kenyon. "You're thinking this would be a good test bed for Lieutenant Mueller's deployment system?"

By way of an answer, Kenyon turned to Mueller at the engineering station. "What do you think, Lieutenant?"

"It's a perfect candidate, sir."

Kenyon gave a quick nod and resumed his seat. "Mr. Gold," he said, addressing the conn officer, "bring us to a position two kilometers above the nucleus's equator."

"On our way, sir," replied Gold as his hands danced across the helm console.

The captain tapped the companel on his chair's armrest. "Kenyon to engineering."

"Kogutt here, Captain."

"Commander, have one of Lieutenant Mueller's probes sent to the launching bay."

"Aye, sir. We'll have one there in five minutes."

"Thanks. Kenyon out."

"Captain," said Cray, his right antenna twitching, "given our proximity to the Neutral Zone, I recommend yellow alert."

Parsons nodded. "I concur, Captain. We're ten AUs from the Zone. If the Romulans don't know we're here, then they're not paying attention to their own doorstep, and that would be out of character."

"Very well, Number One." Kenyon turned to Cray. "Go to yellow alert, Mr. Cray."

Cray inclined his head in a curt nod. "All decks confirm, Captain."

Kenyon smiled. "On top of things as always, Cray. Carry on."

"Thank you, sir," said Cray.

"Tactical plot on viewscreen," ordered Kenyon.

"Aye, aye, sir," replied Hash at ops. Given the lack of natural light, the only way to track the sensor probe would be a tactical plot.

Kenyon touched the companel. "Torpedo bay, are you ready?"

"At your command, sir."

"Stand by." Kenyon closed the channel, and turned his command chair to face the rear of the bridge. "Lieutenant Mueller, it's your project. The word is yours."

A look of genuine surprise crossed her face, and she found herself at a temporary loss for words. "Thank you, sir," she finally said. She stood, straightened her uniform top, and looked at the main viewscreen. "Mr. Cray, launch sensor probe."

"Aye, Lieutenant," Cray replied, touching his tactical console.

A sensor-enhanced image of the comet dominated the viewscreen; moments after Mueller gave the order, a moving dot representing the sensor probe appeared.

"Ten seconds to impact, Captain."

"Thank you, Mr. Takahashi." Kenyon took a step forward toward the viewscreen.

"Captain!" cried Hash. "I've lost contact with the probe."

Every face turned toward Kenyon at the center of the bridge. The viewscreen showed the comet, and the notation representing the probe had vanished.

"Mueller, report," said Kenyon. "Was the probe destroyed on impact?"

Mueller looked from screen to screen on her engineering console. "Captain, as best I can tell, the probe didn't land."

"Hash?" said Kenyon.

"Confirmed, Captain. The probe was four seconds from comet's surface."

"Three point eight-seven," said Mueller. "To be precise."

Commander Parsons came around the bridge railing and looked over Cray's tactical displays. "Captain, we are reading probe debris approximately ten kilometers above the comet's surface." Parsons looked at Kenyon. "It appears the probe struck something."

"But what, Commander?" said Kenyon.

"Captain," said Cray, "Romulan ship decloaking directly beneath us." Onscreen, a Romulan *D'Deridex*-class vessel shimmered into existence between the *Grissom* and the nucleus.

"Well," said Hash, "that answers that."

"Cray, raise shields. Red al—" Kenyon's order trailed away as the bridge lighting dimmed from the natural lights and took on a reddish tinge.

"Red alert, aye."

"You jumped the gun, Cray," said Parsons.

Cray's right antenna twitched. "Time was of the essence, Commander."

"Belay that, Number One." Kenyon turned toward the tactical console. "What's their status?"

Cray consulted his readouts. "Phaser banks charged and locked. Torpedo tubes loaded. They have not raised shields." Cray looked meaningfully at Kenyon. "If they mean us harm, they can."

"Our status?" asked Parsons.

"All departments report red alert. Weapons systems standing by and awaiting the captain's orders," said Cray.

Kenyon resumed his command seat. "Thank you, Lieutenant."

"Captain," said Chu'lak, "I read the Romulan vessel as the *Hiyll'aeh.*"

"Captain, we're being hailed," said Hash.

Kenyon took a deep breath and sighed. "The moment of truth. On screen, Lieutenant."

The image of the *D'Deridex*-class ship changed to an image of the Romulan bridge.

Kenyon rose from his command seat and strode to the center of the bridge. "Tomalak."

The Romulan inclined his head and smiled thinly. *"Captain Kenyon, it has been far too long."*

"Not long enough," Kenyon said, his voice barely a whisper.

Tomalak nodded his head sympathetically. *"The regrettable incident near Nimbus III, I believe."*

"Regrettable?" said Kenyon, his voice rising, his face reddening. *"Regrettable?* I lost my ship, Tomalak." Kenyon paused. "And my wife."

"As I said, Captain, a most regrettable incident." Tomalak bit his lower lip, and took measure of Kenyon. *"I hope this is not another 'regrettable incident.' What explanation have you for your attack on my vessel?"*

"Attack? What are you talking about? Your ship crossed the Neutral Zone in defiance of the Treaty of Algeron."

"The weapon you launched struck my vessel. Even now we are assessing the damage."

"We fired no weapon, only a sensor probe. Our mission, whether you chose to believe it or not, is to survey primordial bodies in deep space. That our survey happens to be near the Neutral Zone is merely a matter of coincidence."

"A likely story, Captain." Tomalak looked off to the right of the viewscreen. *"I shall have my navigator double-check our position, and should I find we are on the Federation side of the Zone, we will gladly concede our error and return to our own side."*

"Thank you, Tomalak. I appreciate your candor."

Tomalak waved his hand dismissively through the air. *"Think nothing of it, Captain. Neither of us seeks an interstellar incident, not over an insignificant comet survey."* A centurion stepped into the com image and handed Tomalak a padd. He studied the padd for a moment, looked again to the right, back to the padd, then up toward the viewscreen. *"A minor navigational error, Captain, surely."*

Kenyon smiled wearily. "As I thought, Commander. Return across the Neutral Zone, and I won't make note of this incident in my log."

"Return?" said Tomalak. *"It is not I that has committed a navigational error. It is you."*

Kenyon snapped his fingers twice. "Com channel muted, Captain," reported Hash. Onscreen, Tomalak mouthed silent words.

"Hash, confirm our position. Which side of the Zone are we on?"

The ops officer's fingers flew across the console. He turned toward Kenyon. "I'll want Lieutenant Chu'lak to double-check, sir, but we're close. Damn close."

"Which side, Ensign?" said Kenyon with some malice.

Hash shook his head. "We can't get a clean pulsar read."

"Chu'lak?" said Kenyon.

"We are within a thousand kilometers, Captain. Which side we are on I cannot determine."

Kenyon squeezed his nose and breathed deeply. "Damn." He crossed his arms. "Reopen the channel."

"Aye, sir. Reopening channel."

"Well, Captain Kenyon?"

Kenyon shrugged. "We're double-checking now, but if we crossed the Zone, it was only by accident and not by malice."

"You violate our sovereign space and attack my ship, and say you have committed an accident?"

"Tomalak, as a show of good faith, we will withdraw to a distance of one light-year." He turned to Gold. "Take us out, one-half impulse power."

"On our way, sir," Gold replied.

"Close channel, Hash."

"Aye, sir."

The image of Tomalak's bridge vanished, replaced by a sensor image of the comet beyond the *Hiyll'aeh*.

"Think he'll let us go, Captain?" asked Parsons.

"We can only hope, Number One."

The *Grissom* rocked and red alert klaxons sounded.

"Captain," shouted Cray, "ventral shields are down twenty-three percent! The *Hiyll'aeh* has fired upon us!"

"There goes our show of good faith," said Parsons.

Kenyon steeled himself in his command chair. "Helm, increase speed!" shouted Kenyon over the din.

"Aye, sir. Three-quarters impulse," said Gold.

The ship rocked again. "Aft shields down thirty-four percent," said Cray.

"Captain," said Parsons, "we're no match for them."

Kenyon rubbed his chin. "I know, Number One."

"Captain," said Cray, "phasers and photon torpedoes ready to fire at your command."

Kenyon stood up, braced himself by planting both hands on the back of his command chair, and glared at Cray. "Dammit, Cray, I won't instigate a war with the Romulans."

Cray glared back. "With all due respect, Captain, the Romulans *have* instigated the conflict. Our duty is to finish it."

Hash turned from ops. "Captain, the *Hiyll'aeh* is gaining on us."

"Go to warp, Captain?" asked Gold.

The ship rocked, and Kenyon steadied himself. "Not yet. Tomalak would just overtake us and destroy us in warp."

"We can't outrun them forever, Captain."

"I know, Number One. Tomalak might break off the attack once we're out of the Zone, but he's too tenacious an adversary for that."

"Captain," said Mueller, stepping forward, "I have an idea."

"All right, Lieutenant. Make it quick."

Mueller cleared her throat. "Turn the ship around, head back toward the cometary nucleus, and plunge the *Grissom* into the comet. We'll melt through, the Romulans will think we destroyed ourselves, and then we can effect an escape from the other side of the nucleus."

Parsons shook her head, causing her bangs to fall over her eyes. "It won't work, Captain. The *Grissom* will break apart on impact."

"If it works for a sensor probe, it will work for a starship," Mueller said. *"Especially* a starship, since the hull is heated from the inside already."

Parsons said, "Captain, the temperature differential from the comet's surface to the ship's outer hull will be so extreme that the engine housings will crack open, destroying the *Grissom* and the Romulans."

"Captain," said Mueller, "this *will* work. A starship can travel faster than light. A starship can do this."

Kenyon looked from Parsons to Mueller and back.

He made his decision.

"Mueller," said Kenyon, "the conn is yours."

"Commander, the *Grissom* is altering course!"

"What?" cried Tomalak.

"The ship is turning." T'sae, the *Hiyll'aeh*'s navigator, looked back to his console for confirmation. "They are heading back toward the Zone."

Tomalak rose from his chair and crossed the bridge to the navigational console. "The Zone? Why?"

T'sae looked up at Tomalak standing over his shoulder. "Unknown, Commander."

He studied the *Grissom* on the viewscreen, fleeing into the black depths of Romulan space. "Helm, bring us about. Increase speed."

"As ordered, Commander," replied T'sae.

Elhumne, the ship's weapons officer, called out, "Commander, torpedoes are standing ready."

Tomalak turned to Elhumne, then at the *Grissom* on the viewscreen. What was Kenyon doing?

"Centurion," ordered Tomalak, "fire."

The *Grissom* rocked as another Romulan torpedo slammed into the aft shields, throwing Kenyon and Parsons from their seats.

"Bridge," came Kogutt's voice over the intercom, *"engines are overheating!"*

Kenyon toggled the intercom as he pulled himself back into his seat. "Todd, I hear you. We'll do what we can." He turned to Cray. "Shield status?"

Cray looked up from his tactical console. "Aft shields down to thirty-four percent. Another photon-torpedo hit may cripple them."

"Chu'lak," called Mueller from her seat to Kenyon's left, "distance to comet's surface?"

"Two-hundred fifty kilometers and closing rapidly."

"Gold," she said, "be ready to execute the maneuver."

Gold nodded his head sharply. "Aye, sir."

"Chu'lak, distance?"

"One-hundred fifty kilometers."

"Tactical," said Mueller, "drop shields."

"I must object, Captain," said Cray.

"Objection logged, Cray. *Drop the shields!*"

Cray shook his head. "Shields down."

"Commander," said T'sae, "the *Grissom* has lowered their shields!"

"What?" shouted Tomalak. He turned to the weapons officer. "Fire another torpedo!"

"Torpedo launched, Commander!"

"Helm," ordered Mueller, "all stop and reverse."

Gold shook his head and stabbed at the contact on his console. "Brace yourselves."

The *Grissom* lurched as the impulse engines disengaged and began providing reverse thrust. On the bridge, inertial damping fields kicked in slightly after the engines reversed, throwing Hash and Chu'lak from their consoles and across the deck and jarring others despite their bracing themselves for what they knew would come.

Onscreen, a bright explosion illuminated the comet's surface. "Torpedo missed us, Captain," said Cray.

"Too close," said Parsons.

"Gold," said Mueller, "go to thrusters." She looked to Kenyon on her right, and he nodded once. "Take us in."

"Commander, this cannot be!" shouted T'sae.

Tomalak rushed to his console. "Explain."

"The *Grissom*. She is crashing into the nucleus!" T'Sae looked up at Tomalak. "They are destroying themselves."

"Magnify!" snapped Tomalak, turning to the spectacle of the *Grissom* on the viewscreen.

Driven forward by the inertial momentum of a two-million-ton starship slowing from one-eighth light speed to barely a kilometer per second, the leading edge of the *Grissom*'s saucer made contact with the comet's nucleus.

A comet ordinarily spent its existence in the frozen wastes of deep space, far from heat and light. Only when pulled through the shifting of gravity into the heart of a solar system and past the unholy fusion engine that was the system's star did a comet resemble anything more than a lumpy bit of icy coal, outgassing ices suddenly made vapor and producing a tail that stretched for millions of miles.

This bleak cometary landscape felt heat for the first time in its existence. Gases that had been frozen for ten billion years, gases that had never felt a temperature warmer than ten degrees Kelvin, vaporized instantly when exposed to the naked skin of the starship radiating heat from within, heat that kept the starship's crew alive.

A gassy fail rose from the impact site of the *Grissom* and grew in length and intensity as the ship dropped further into the nucleus, vaporizing even more of the frozen gases.

The *Grissom* plunged forward.

"What's happening?" asked Tomalak.

"Sir," said T'sae, "the *Grissom* has vanished."

"Vanished?" Tomalak repeated. The viewscreen showed a hazy bluish glow surrounding the pitch-dark nucleus as the released cometary gases reflected the light of the *Grissom*'s warp nacelles.

"I cannot be certain, Commander. Sensors are confused by the nucleus's outgassing, but it appears the ship broke apart upon impact." T'sae looked meaningfully at the viewscreen. "The *Grissom* does not appear to be intact."

"Take us in closer. I want to be certain."

"As you wish, Commander," replied T'sae.

"Sir," said the science officer, "I am reading a buildup of gases within the nucleus." He turned away from his console and looked at Tomalak. "I recommend we maintain a distance of at least fifteen hundred meters, lest an explosion within the nucleus present a danger to the *Hiyll'aeh*."

"T'sae?" said Tomalak, seeking confirmation.

T'sae shook his head. "Vah'thoal overstates the danger, Commander."

Tomalak looked from one to the other. "T'sae, pursue the *Grissom*, as far as we must go."

The nucleus grew in size on the viewscreen, and the blue glow had vanished, leaving the nucleus shrouded in darkness.

The *Hiyll'aeh* rocked slightly, buffeted by ejecta from the comet's outgassing. "Report!" shouted Tomalak.

Vah'thoal said, "Chunks of rock thrown from the nucleus, sir. Again, I caution us against proceeding closer until the outgassing ceases."

Tomalak rose from his command chair, his face turning a deeper shade of green in fury. "I will *not* allow the *Grissom* to escape me, Vah'thoal! They invaded our space and attacked my ship! Either we destroy them, or they destroy themselves, but they will *not* leave Romulan space!"

The bridge lights flashed dim, then came back full. The deck shook, and Tomalak stumbled.

"T'sae, report!" said Tomalak as he fell back into his seat.

T'sae turned in his command chair to face Tomalak. "Sir, we have—"

The *Hiyll'aeh* shuddered, and the bridge plunged into darkness. Emergency lights came on, bathing the bridge in an eerie green glow, and fans switched on to circulate the still air.

"It is as I said, Commander," said Vah'thoal. "We have lost main power. The engines were overwhelmed by the comet's tail. The nucleus's outgassing has disabled the ship."

Tomalak rose, crossed the darkened bridge to Vah'thoal's console, and slapped him across the face. Vah'thoal fell to the deck, rubbed his hand across the base of his nose, and felt blood.

Tomalak then kicked Vah'thoal in the abdomen. "Get this vermin off my bridge." He turned to T'sae. "How long until main power has been restored?"

T'sae shrugged, a very un-Romulan gesture. "It could be the matter of a few hours. It may be days."

Tomalak stared at the dark viewscreen. Kenyon had bested him yet again.

The *Grissom* emerged from the opposite side of the cometary nucleus, a stream of gases trailing her warp nacelles and water boiling away from the engine housings. She flew free again, banked sharply to the right, and came around the nucleus, heading toward Federation space.

"Captain," said Chu'lak, "we are clear of the cometary nucleus."

"Excellent," Kenyon said.

Mueller turned to Kenyon and gave him a slight smile. "Sir, I relinquish the conn to you."

Kenyon stood and patted her on the shoulder. "Thank you, Lieutenant. Good work." He paused. "Don't crash my ship again."

Mueller smiled wider and returned to the engineering station.

"Cray," said Kenyon, "status of the *Hiyll'aeh?*"

Cray displayed the tactical plot on the main viewscreen. "Disabled, sir, apparently by the comet's outgassing as we passed through the nucleus. Their main engines are offline, weapons and shields are down."

"Should we offer assistance, Captain?" asked Parsons.

Kenyon shook his head. "I would, Number One, but Tomalak is nothing if not resourceful. He'll be back in business soon enough, and I for one would prefer not to be in the vicinity when he is." He looked at the disabled *Hiyll'aeh* on the viewscreen. "He won't press the incident, with his government or with ours, because nearly losing his ship makes him look bad. If we helped him, that would only be more agony for him."

Parsons smiled. "You should have been a diplomat, Captain."

Kenyon smiled broadly. "I'll leave that to my brother." He turned to the engineering console. "Mueller, damage report."

She looked back to Kenyon. "Minor damage, sir. Engineering reports several bulkheads collapsed. Sickbay reports minor casualties and teams are responding."

Kenyon stood and clapped his hands together. "Mr. Gold, take us out. Mr. Cray, go to yellow alert and keep an eye on the *Hiyll'aeh.*" He tapped the intercom. "Engineering, this is the captain. Can we go to warp?"

"Bridge, this is McLauren." She coughed raggedly; Mueller deduced that there was some kind of chemical leak down there. *"It's a bit rough down here right now, but we'll have the mains back online in about thirty seconds. Just don't put us through any more risky maneuvers like that."*

"No more today," Kenyon said with a smile. "Give my compliments to Commander Kogutt on a job well done."

There was a pause on the other end. *"Sir, Commander Kogutt is dead. We had a bulkhead collapse, and he took the brunt of the explosion."* She paused again. *"I'm very sorry, sir."*

Kenyon looked at Mueller. "Lieutenant—" he began. There was no need for him to finish this order. She knew what he was going to say. The expression of pain and sorrow that crossed his face told her in a way that words could not. He had lost so much to the Romulans—his ship, his wife, and now his best friend. What more could a man lose?

Mueller nodded. "On my way, sir." She stepped into the aft turbolift and leaned against the wall. "Engineering," she said, wishing she had been there all along. If she hadn't been on the bridge, none of this day's events would have happened.

Mueller lay on her bunk, staring at her cabin's ceiling. She had dimmed the lights after pulling a double shift in engineering repairing the damage sustained by the *Grissom* in the cometary encounter. Physical damage to the ship appeared to be minor, mostly hull plates that cracked when directly subjected to temperatures barely above absolute zero in the comet's nucleus. McLauren had headed up an EVA team that inspected the warp nacelles and the nacelle struts for signs of damage, but surprisingly nothing more than a hairline fracture in the port strut could be found.

How long it would take the crew to recover, though, was an open question. Casualties were light—twelve killed in the Romulan attack, and another four dead in engineering when a bulkhead exploded, including Commander Kogutt.

Mueller sighed and closed her eyes. Kogutt had been a good friend and a good mentor. He had a great love of beagles, she recalled; his family had raised them for generations.

The chime to Mueller's cabin sounded. "Come," she said, and the door swished open.

Against the light of the corridor she could only make out a vague silhouette that took a tentative step into the cabin.

"I'm not interrupting anything, am I, Lieutenant?"

Startled by the voice, Mueller sat up. "No, Captain, not at all. Please come in."

He nodded his head. "Thank you." He took another step into the dim cabin and the door slid closed behind him.

"Computer, lights one-half." She rose from the bunk and rubbed her eyes.

"I can come back later, Lieutenant."

"No, it's all right, sir. I'm tired, but can't sleep."

"Understandable. Commander Parsons tells me engineering took a beating during the encounter."

She pulled a chair out from the desk and gestured toward Kenyon. "Please, sir, have a seat."

He took the proffered chair. Mueller sat back down on the edge of her bunk.

"Several bulkheads ruptured in engineering. Commander Kogutt and three others were killed." She paused. "I'm very sorry about your loss. I know you and Commander Kogutt were close."

He nodded slowly. "Thank you. I served with Todd for almost fifteen years, since we were both lieutenants aboard the *Lankhmar*. He was my chief engineer on the *Harriman* and the *Grissom*. He had a very practical mind for an engineer, one that I learned to rely upon." He sat silently for a moment. "I was proud to call him my friend. Probably my best friend in the service, other than my wife."

"I'm so sorry, sir," Mueller said, barely audible.

They sat in silence for several moments.

"I'm going to need a new chief engineer," Kenyon said at last.

"Yes, sir," said Mueller.

"What's your opinion of Rachel McLauren?"

Mueller blinked quickly and her head jerked back slightly in surprise. "Rachel? She's very capable, very knowledgeable. She knows the ship well, and there's not a person in engineering that she doesn't get along with." She took a deep breath and let it out slowly. "She'll make a fine chief engineer."

"Disappointed, Lieutenant?"

Mueller bit the inside of her lip, narrowed her gaze, and looked hard at Kenyon. "Frankly, sir, yes. I feel I'm more qualified for the position than Rachel."

"I agree, Lieutenant. Completely."

"Then why—?"

"Because I would rather have you as my XO. Your natural talents would be wasted on the engineering deck."

"But, sir, I endangered the ship. If maneuvering the ship into the comet hadn't worked—"

"You're second-guessing your actions on the bridge."

Mueller nodded.

Kenyon shook his head. "Don't. You went outside the traditional command box and gave me a better option than either Christine or Cray could give." He took a deep breath. "Christine didn't have an option, because there were no good options and she recognized that. Cray's option was to go down fighting because that's his way, but it's not the right way when dealing with Romulans."

"But you couldn't have known my plan would work."

"Poppycock. You wouldn't have suggested the course of action if it wouldn't. A commander knows what a ship can do. An engineer knows how to do it. You can do both." He paused. "The position is yours, Katerina, if you want it." He rose and held out his hand.

"Thank you, Captain. I *do* want it." She took his hand.

Kenyon smiled. "Congratulations, Lieutenant *Commander.*"

"Thank you, sir."

Kenyon shook his head. "No, thank *you*. If it hadn't been for your quick thinking, we might not be having this conversation at all."

"One question, sir."

Kenyon nodded. "Of course."

"What about Cray?"

"What about him?"

"Why did you select me over him?"

"A good question. Cray has his talents, but thinking outside the box is not one of them. He is a very focused individual, and that suits him at tactical and in security. But in command?" He nodded his head pensively. "He isn't ready yet. Assuming he will ever be."

As Kenyon turned to leave, Mueller said, "I won't disappoint you, sir."

Kenyon's smile turned into a wide grin. "You haven't yet." The door to her cabin swished open, and Kenyon stepped into the corridor.

She sat back down on her bunk, her head swimming in giddiness. She had to tell someone. Who?

She tapped the companel on her nightstand. "Mueller to McLauren."

A groggy voice responded. *"Go ahead, Kat."*

"Did I wake you, Rachel?"

She heard a stifled yawn on the other end. " *'Course not. What's up, kiddo?"*

Mueller finally allowed herself a smile as the realization of her promotion sank home. "You won't believe what just happened. . . ."

Even after a week, Katerina Mueller couldn't help but finger the third hollow rank pip on her collar. In time, she knew, the thrill would wear off, but for now the pip was new, and running her thumb and forefinger across it gave her an emotional high, and she smiled wistfully.

"Ah, Lieutenant Commander," she heard.

Mueller looked up from her half-eaten lunch. Cray stood before her, a food tray in his hands.

"Cray," she said with the sudden realization this was their first conversation in months. "What can I do for you?"

His eyes narrowed and both antennae bent in toward her.

"I'll be watching you, Lieutenant Commander. When you stumble, I will be there."

She pushed the tray away from her and folded her arms in front of her on the mess hall table. "Watching me?"

"The promotion to XO was mine. It should have been mine."

"Captain Kenyon disagreed."

"Sarn—" Cray began.

"—is in the past, *Lieutenant*. Captain Kenyon made his decision based on the *present.*" She opened her hands magnanimously. "You'll have other opportunities."

Cray's scowl became a sneer. "I will prove to the captain that he should have chosen me, and when you make a mistake I will see to it that you suffer for it."

Mueller rose, planted her hands firmly on the table, and looked at Cray with such fury that the facial scar stood starkly white against her reddened face. "Are you *threatening* me, Lieutenant?"

Cray backed away and smiled. "Not at all, Commander. I never threaten. I only promise." He turned and walked toward an empty table at the far end of the mess hall. Mueller watched him go.

She returned to her seat and rubbed her chin slowly. Cray would bear watching. Andorians never made promises lightly, nor promises they didn't intend to keep.

XANT
Redemption

Glenn Hauman & Lisa Sullivan

One of the biggest thorns in Captain Calhoun's side in Sector 221G has been the "Redeemers," a group of religious zealots who worship a god called Xant. "Redemption" provides us with a bit of insight into the figure behind the *Excalibur*'s foes.

Glenn Hauman & Lisa Sullivan

Glenn Hauman has been called a "young Turk of publishing" by the *New York Observer* and a "Silicon Alley Veteran" by *Crain's New York Business*, and his new business, LotAuctions.com, is making great headway in the online auction space, though he suspects "Weird Al" Yankovic won't be doing a song for him anytime soon. He has been a featured speaker on the future of publishing at numerous industry trade shows. His *Star Trek: S.C.E.* eBook *Oaths* was recently reprinted in the omnibus edition *No Surrender*, and he's working on more eBooks; he's also been an editorial consultant on many *Star Trek* CD-ROMs. He is, among other things, the webmaster for PeterDavid.net.

Lisa Sullivan received her MA in Early Church History from the University of Georgia, and has completed several years of doctoral studies in the same subject at Union Theological Seminary in New York City. She has previously written for the academic journals *Semeia* and *Studia Patristica*, and has presented papers at conferences in her field both nationally and internationally. She has no idea how she ended up writing for *Star Trek*, but figures if it's good enough for Dr. Marc Okrand, it's good enough for her.

Before his ascension, the great god Xant was walking through the woods and he came to a stream. Gazing across the stream, he saw a nibor, an aquatic animal, and a pygram, a stinging insect, arguing.

The nibor wanted to cross the stream to get some berries on Xant's side, but feared Xant looming over him from across the water. The pygram had no way to cross the stream by himself, but was capable of slaying Xant with his fatal sting. Of course, he was also capable of killing a nibor as well, and pygrams often did so to fill their stomachs. Nibors often ate pygrams when they could, as they considered them menaces, and rightly so.

The pygram spoke to the nibor. "Friend! If we tie our fates together, then none can stop us. Carry me across to the other side, and I will protect you from the huge creature over yonder! I shall frighten him away with my deadly poison!"

"How do I know that if I try to help you, you won't try to kill me as well?" asked the nibor hesitantly, staying a safe distance away.

"Because," the pygram replied, "on the other side of the river, the huge creature is the greater threat, and while I slay him, you can gather your berries and then escape. If I try to kill you while we are in the river, then I would die too, for you know I cannot swim!"

Now, this seemed to make sense to the nibor. But he asked, "What about when I get close to the bank? You could still try to kill me and get to the shore, before I kill and eat you!"

"This is true," agreed the pygram, "but then I wouldn't be able to get back to this side of the river!"

"All right then . . . how do I know you won't just wait till we get back and *then* kill me?" said the nibor.

"I could ask the same thing of you! How do I know you won't just wait till we get to the other side and I scare him off, and then you will devour me?" said the pygram.

"Ahh . . ." crooned the nibor, "because you see, once you've taken me to the other side of this river, I will be so grateful for your help that it would hardly be fair to reward you with death, now would it?"

"And I would not kill you either. But I do not trust you, nibor!"

"Nor I you, pygram!"

The two beasts continued to yell at each other, becoming louder and shriller, until it seemed that each had forgotten why he had started to argue, only knowing that he had to win the argument. Xant looked at the two of them from across the stream, laughed, and seated himself atop a large boulder.

"A very difficult dilemma, is it not? And you . . . what would you do?" Then Xant turned to look down at . . . me.

"This is a dream," I said.

"Perhaps," said Xant. His voice was clear and calm, with the muted sounds of the birds and small animals around him and leaves of thick brush swaying in the breeze. "Or perhaps it is the long-awaited vision of me that you have prayed for all your life."

"A vision of Xant?" I asked. "I've neither waited nor prayed for such a thing. I must accept Xant if it will save my world from the accursed Redeemers, but I do not *believe* in him. He is not my god."

"Yet here we both are, together," said Xant. "You must believe in my existence to some extent, or I would not—indeed, could not—be here. Incidentally, have you ever received any visions from Kolk'r, the god of your ancestors?"

This had not occurred to me. "N-n-no—I have not," I stammered. "But why would the great god Xant appear to me, a nonbeliever? There are many who are more faithful, more deserving of visions, than I."

The figure on the boulder looked at me intently. A cold chill passed through me, and my mind began to race.

What if this really is Xant? I thought. He did bear more than a passing resemblance to the iconic figure that was displayed so prominently around the town. *Am I insulting a god? Better to be safe than sorry, even if it is only a dream. . . .*

I fell to my knees in front of him. "I . . . am not worthy of this great hon—"

"Hah! What honor?"

"This vision of you—"

"Perhaps this is not a vision after all, but merely the delusion of madness, of one who dares to rise too far above his station in life." And Xant suddenly began to look strange and sinister as he loomed above me.

"Or perhaps this is indeed a simple dream—like the dream in which you stand naked before your teacher and you feel like a dunce. Well? Are you a dunce?"

"I—I—"

"Hmmm. You certainly *sound* like one."

"—I am no dunce!"

"That remains to be seen. However, it would only be polite to take you at your word. This is your dream, after all. Perhaps."

His words confused me. "Is this—is this some sort of a test, my lord?"

"Hmm. A test. I suppose it could be, couldn't it?" Xant smiled, although I could not tell if it was the smile of an indulgent teacher or of a being laughing at a cosmic joke that only he had the awareness to perceive.

Xant slid off the boulder, landing lightly on the ground in front of me. "Walk with me," he said. I started to walk behind him, but he stopped before we had taken three steps. "No, no, no. Do not follow me. Walk with me, Eben." He smiled. "Of course I know your name. You are Eben Saxosus. Child of Kayi and Teir, brother of Falo. I know many things about you. And that is why I want you to know many things about me."

I took two steps forward to be alongside him, and continued for another two steps beyond. Xant, however, stayed standing where he had been, a slight smile on his lips as he watched me. Slightly aggravated—but trying to keep the hint of it out of my voice—I turned to face him and said, "I can go no further if you do not lead me, Lord Xant."

"You speak more truly than you realize. Shall we?" And we walked off downstream.

We continued along for a while, with Xant looking calm, but somewhat more unsettled than I would ever have suspected a deity could be. "My lord—"

"Please. Just call me Xant. For us to truly hear each other, we must be able to speak as brothers."

"Xant, is . . . is this really you?"

"You still do not believe?"

"Well, it's just that—I never quite thought of you as real."

"But everyone on your planet believes in me."

My mind cried out that this was obviously not the truth, but I bit my tongue. "We believe that you existed in a historical sense, of course . . ."

"Ah, you doubt my divinity."

"I would not dare to do such a thing, Xant . . . but . . . if you *are* a god, why do you walk and talk like a mortal now?"

"I was once like you," Xant said.

"Yes, I know that you were mortal for a time, before you reached your state of divinity."

"No. Wrong."

"You mean you were always divine, even when you walked among mortals?"

Xant sighed. "Wrong. Wrong. Wrong. You listen, but you do not hear."

Confusion must have been evident on my face. "I *am* divine now, Eben. Could one who was not divine do this?" Xant raised his hand upward and swept it across his field of vision. A glorious rainbow appeared, shooting overhead and across the sky. He turned to look at me expectantly. "Well?"

I must still have appeared unconvinced, for Xant grew impatient.

"What tricks must I perform to make you believe?" He gestured again, and the rainbow turned into a giant arc of flame.

I looked back at him. "I am sorry, but I still do not know if I am dreaming, Xant, and all things can happen in dreams. I suppose I could be wrong . . . but then, here, everything could be wrong."

Then he did smile, as if I had passed his test. "Skepticism is a healthy trait. You mistrust your own perceptions?"

"Yes, I suppose I do."

"Then shouldn't you mistrust your mistrust?"

I started to answer, but found I had no suitable reply. Instead, I grew quiet as I looked ahead, toward a village we were approaching and that Xant apparently meant for us to enter. Our path took us to a marketplace. It was not one I was familiar with, and it was populated with the people of Xant's race. They did not, I was relieved to see, dress in the ceremonial garb of Redeemers.

As Xant and I walked silently into the crowded market square, the crowds parted to let us through, almost unconsciously. I looked at them and then looked again, intrigued.

The crowds did not part so much as they seemed to be repelled from our path. It was much the same effect as when one brought like poles of a magnet together, and yet it all flowed naturally, and the crowds themselves seemed unaware of our passing. I wondered why I was not pushed away in the same manner.

"You are not repelled because I choose to have you by my side," Xant said. "Yes, I know your thoughts. Omniscience is one of my many traits, though I tend to allow people their privacy for the most part." He smiled. "You have an active imagination, Eben."

I was startled. Why hadn't I thought of it? Of course a god would be able to read my thoughts. I ran quickly back over my last twenty minutes of silent musings, hoping desperately that I had not been thinking anything that was too offensive.

"Don't worry," said the god. "Your skepticism, your independent thought—these are the things I value most in you. Do you think I'm not tired of the constant kneeling, prostration, and shouts of 'Yes, Lord'?"

"Well, I . . ."

"I have retained the love of challenging discourse and need for mental stimulation that I had before my ascension, and it is not often now that I get to enjoy it. In fact," Xant continued, "being omniscient has taken away most of the opportunity, but I always learn something interesting when I am with a mortal. It is part of the reason I have sought you out. I speak to those who know to hear not with the ears of the body but with the ears of the mind. Many have sought after the truth and have not been able to find it, but when the mind has been opened to me all things are knowable."

This time, I was the one who smiled first. "You have much greater depth than your High Priests allow us to know. I still do not consider you my god, Xant, but you do fascinate me."

The god smiled back at me. "Thank you, Eben." He leaned in conspiratorially. "Truthfully, I admit that I do enjoy the 'Yes, Lord'-ing just a bit."

We had reached the center of the marketplace, where we stopped.

"Yes, I enjoy learning things from mortals," Xant said. "But now it is time for you to learn from me. Pay close attention." He turned to face the crowd. "Out of all these people—where am I to be found?"

I scanned the faces of the crowd—here and there some looked similar to Xant, but none looked very close. "I don't see you."

"Then listen for me."

I heard nothing but the distant sound of hoofbeats, getting closer.

"Yes," Xant said reluctantly. "That's it."

I didn't know what he meant, and I turned in the direction of the sound. And I saw a band of marauders on horseback, coming through the town at full gallop. The people in the market scattered in fear before them.

The marauders drove forward with unsheathed weapons, slicing at the crowd without regard to whom they might hit. Old or young, male or female, it made no difference to them—they were in the way, and so they were cut down. I saw an old man lose a hand above the wrist, I saw a girl of no more than twelve summers fall to a blade, and I saw an infant's blanket trampled. I could not tell if the baby was still wrapped in it.

Chaos was all around me, and it seemed all that I could do was keep my balance—yet I was spared. No steel touched me, no hand attacked me; the only thing that assaulted me was a cacophony of terror and smells of blood and death.

In the frenzy, I lost sight of Xant. We had become separated in the melee, and I feared for my life away from his protection. I cried out, "Xant! Where are you? Where have you gone?"

"Over here," I heard his voice call. I was able to hear, because the screams and other noises had begun to abate.

I looked desperately around me. The battle—if a massacre on the order of what I had just witnessed could be graced with that name—was, for the most part, over. The invaders were milling about in the market square, slapping each other on the back and laughing as they cleaned their blades. I still did not see Xant.

"Over here, Eben," I heard him call again, and realized that he was speaking to me alone, directly to my ears.

Where are you? I thought intently, as if my words would make him speak more clearly. *Show me!*

"I am right in front of you," the voice said sadly.

I turned and saw naught but the butchers who had slain the crowd. Then one rode forward, dressed in the finest armor. He surveyed the carnage his men had wrought, and began to laugh.

"Xant . . . this is you? This barbarian?"

"No," said another of the horde who had ridden up behind his leader and stopped, looking straight at me. *"This* is me. The barbarian's right-hand man."

It had been a bloodbath.

There had been no mercy. The village had been scoured.

Xant was the last to leave the field of battle. He had surveyed the carnage—no, he had supervised it. He had presided over the destruction of the village. After all the soldiers went away, I looked on as the god stood quietly in the ruined market square, watching the shadows cast by the fire of burning buildings, listening to sounds only he could hear.

Later, Xant and I walked down the path and away from the village. He appeared to be wrapped up in his own thoughts, and I . . . I was still stag-

gered by what I had seen, and trying to come to grips with the fact that
Xant had been an active participant in such a heinous act. *Is this the kind of
behavior that qualifies one for godhood?* I thought bleakly, aware but no longer
caring that he could hear my unspoken words.

Xant led me through the forest, toward a clearing up ahead. He finally
broke his silence. "I know you have questions, Eben. You should not hesitate to ask them."

From all the thoughts turning through my mind, all I could manage to
summon up was "What . . . what happened to the people of the town?"

"The usual. The surviving men were slaughtered anyway. The women
were taken to be concubines in harems or as cheap labor for wealthy
households. And the children were led into slavery, the raw fuel and materials from which the war machine's next generation would be built."

"That—that is truly horrible, Xant."

"It was the way of things. It was what was done."

"But it has just been done, just now! Can't these people still be saved
from that horrible fate? Can't you help them?" I cried.

"Both they and their persecutors are long gone, Eben," the god quietly
replied. "I am the only one left. I show you what and when I need to show
you in order to make my point clear. Now follow and watch again."

By this time we had entered the clearing, and I could see now that it
was the place where the marauders had made camp before their attack on
the village. Those who had returned first were already reveling in their victory, enjoying the spoils of their plunder, and they paid us no mind. We approached the most ornate of the tents, located near the center of the camp,
and Xant pulled the flap back. Inside, I saw the one who had led the attack
against the village, eating a sumptuous meal with his bare hands.

"My lord Shadis," Xant said to the barbarian. I stared at his addressing
someone else as "lord."

"Ah, Xant. Come in. I was beginning to think you couldn't find your
way back from the town."

Xant entered, and I quickly followed. I whispered to Xant, "Shadis?
Who is he?"

"An absolute brute," Xant said, making no effort whatsoever to be
quiet as he answered. Indeed, Shadis seemed wholly unaware of Xant's
comments to me. He continued to rip the roasted meat from the bones
that lay on his plate. "A savage who cut a swath across a continent, all for
his own power and glory. And he may have the worst table manners in
the galaxy."

Shadis belched loudly, as if to underscore the point. "How went the cleanup?" he said, his mouth half full of food.

"As expected, my lord," Xant replied, turning to his leader, his conversation with me ended. "There are no farmers left that would dream of opposing you now."

"You sound almost disappointed, Xant."

"I do not see the wisdom of scouring the land simply to stamp out minor discontent. You command the mightiest hammer, yet you use it to squash the smallest of enemies."

"You would rather I wait until the enemies become larger, and could pose an actual threat?" I could not tell if Shadis actually spat at Xant, or if it was simply the force of his speaking combined with the fullness of his mouth.

"I do not see how ones such as they could ever threaten your rule."

"Of course they couldn't! I crush them before they can!"

"And with this, you hope to hold on to your empire forever? You already rule as far as you can possibly see. Why do you want more?"

"If it is good to rule over the few, how much better it is to rule over everyone? It is my destiny to be exalted above every congregation and every people, prominent in every respect, with all people as vessels for my divine vision, having become master over every power that could thwart me."

"Even the power of nature itself?"

"I would smite the stars themselves if they dared oppose me!"

Xant merely looked at him, his face blank. Whether he was showing deference to his commander or the caution one shows when faced with a stinging pygram, I could not tell.

"Listen to my advice, Xant," Shadis bellowed. "Do not show your back to enemies and flee, but rather, pursue them as a strong one. Be not an animal, with men pursuing you; but rather, be a man, with you pursuing the evil wild beasts, lest somehow they become victorious over you and trample upon you as on a dead man, and you perish due to their wickedness." His voice grew louder, deeper. "Wretched one, what will you do if you fall into their hands? Protect yourself, lest you be delivered into the hands of your enemies. Entrust yourself to *this* pair of hands and no one will be victorious over you. The soldiers say, 'May Shadis dwell in your camp, may he protect your gates, and may his mind protect your walls.' Do likewise, Xant. Let my will become a torch in your mind, burning the wood which is the whole of weaknehhkk!" And Shadis began to choke on his food. He gestured wildly for Xant to help him.

Xant went to stand behind Shadis's chair. Reaching down to the table, he picked up a cloth napkin, still unused. Then, with the speed of a striking serpent, Xant grabbed Shadis by the neck with one arm, jammed the cloth into the man's mouth and covered it up with his hand.

Shadis struggled for what seemed to be a very long time while Xant held on to him, his dark visage betraying no emotion. The captain tried to reach for his attacker, but failed. Finally, after a hard shudder, Shadis collapsed in Xant's grip and the god gently, almost tenderly, brought him to rest on the floor. He removed the napkin from the dying man's mouth as Shadis looked up at him, unbelieving. "Why, Xant?" he gurgled. I could not believe that he still had strength enough to speak. "Why have you done this thing to me? Why have you betrayed me?"

"Because you are a fool, Shadis."

Shadis struggled for his last breaths. "Why . . . am I a . . . fool?"

"Because," said Xant, "you insist on taking everything personally." He knelt, and kissed the captain's brow. "I'm sorry, my lord." And I heard the last breath escape from the body of the man Xant had sworn to follow.

"Do you see, Eben?" Xant did not look at me.

I stood mute. What I saw was one of Shadis's hands, still clenched around a bone from his last meal.

Xant finally turned and met my eyes, half accusing, half pleading. "Do you understand why I have done this thing?"

"Why you have killed—killed this—" I waved halfheartedly at the body of the one he had slain.

He advanced on me. "Do you ever wonder why a man would want to take on such a burden as godhood?" He strode over to the captain's desk, taking a swallow of the wine that stood in a flask there before continuing. "He takes it on because it must be borne by *someone*, and because the one who bears it now is a bloody butcher who sours and savages everything around him. It is a duty, do you understand that? I hated what Shadis stood for, even as I was sworn to uphold his command. He was my ruler, and I knew that in a universe such as this, someone must always bear the burden of leadership. I decided that there was no one who could do it better than I. Certainly I could be no worse than he was. It is a painful, horrible burden indeed, and it has tested me and tainted me. But I had to take it on if there was to be the hope of a better world.

"So I have done things that disgust me," Xant continued, "and I have done things that demean me, but I have done many right things as well. I have worked to build a world that would no longer need me. I have used my position of power to preach, to proselytize, to prevent pain. It is better to preach faith and justice from a throne than from an armchair, is it not, Eben? I have become unto a god so that I might try and rid people of their need for gods."

I sat down wearily upon a stool, staring at the man Xant had slain, unable to take it all in. "This is not how I was told it had happened."

"I know. You probably got the story of how, in the time of our world's greatest struggle over a millennia ago, I appeared with a glowing angel over each shoulder, full of wisdom and foreknowledge, a beacon of light against the darkness."

" 'Xant is light, we are darkness,' " I intoned.

"Eben, it never happened. Not that way. Oh, there are a few grains of truth buried here and there in what they call 'the true word of Xant,' but they are hidden deeply, and can be identified only with great diligence."

"But—what *did* happen then?"

Xant grimaced. "Every god has his disciples . . . but it always seems to be the traitor who writes the biography." He pulled back the tent flap, and, instead of the camp from which we had come, I saw a laboratory beyond the opening.

We entered the lab, and as we passed through I looked back toward the tent we had just left. It was gone. By this point, I was not surprised at all.

One of Xant's people was inside the lab. He was dressed in a white coat and was scurrying briskly back and forth among his beakers and books, his flasks and flames. He was oblivious of us.

"It was a mere twenty years after I had gone beyond. My deeds had already achieved fame during my lifetime, but they now became burnished with the fire of legend. Eventually, as I grew more remote from the understanding of my people, I also became set in their minds in a certain way. They grew placid and conservative. Mortals like their gods to be predictable, after all—surprises don't go over very well on this sort of scale. In any event, the ultimate result was that they ended up relying on me more, rather than less.

"Now some of my followers came to think that my movement as a whole had lost its way since I had gone beyond, and resolved to set everyone else straight or die trying. The hardest of the hard core burned with the fire of true believers, ideological shock troops in a world that was no longer receptive to shocking. These hard-core believers soon began to alienate the people around them who were quite content to live in peace and prosperity. They spoke out and criticized their comfortable lifestyles. They banded together to have themselves elected and appointed to positions within the government, and from there they began a systematic campaign of harassment against those who did not remember the same Xant that they did.

"Worst of all, a number of them came to believe that a great god such as Xant desired—nay, demanded—great sacrifices. This one—" He indicated the man hurrying about in his white coat. "—was one of the worst."

I stared at the little man. Old and slightly withered in appearance, he nevertheless moved briskly about his business as if possessed by some great purpose known only to himself. The man finally stopped in front of a machine that emitted an indigo light. He rolled up his sleeve and placed his arm under the light, which soon began to iridesce. As he stood there, I approached him and looked him straight in his eyes. He took no notice of me at all, of course, thanks to whatever camouflage it was with which Xant had surrounded us both—but still I felt that this man would not have seen me even had I not been shielded from his view.

"Who is he?" I asked.

"His name was Dr. Revoo. He was a physician, a man of science who healed the bodies of those who came to him seeking help, and yet he was also a man of great moral rigidity, just as dedicated to saving the souls of those around him. He believed that his inability to save all of the lives that were entrusted to him was a sign that those patients had been judged by me and found lacking. He was also . . ."

Here Xant paused for a moment, obviously searching for the right words. He sighed.

"Revoo was also one of the most fervent believers in what had become the false image of me. He ultimately became convinced that it was he himself, not his patients, who had somehow strayed from the path of righteousness." The god's voice grew softer. "His devotion to me knew no bounds. Sadly, neither did the lengths to which he would go to carry out what he thought was the will of the one he served. Revoo believed that he had been tested and found lacking. But if he, Xant's most ardent disciple, did not measure up—then, well, what about the rest of the world?

"He decided that only the greatest sacrifice would be sufficient to expiate the grievous sins of his fellow mortals. And he loved me so much, in his own narrow way, that he was willing to sacrifice his own life to do what needed to be done."

Dr. Revoo finished with the analysis of his arm, nodded, and shut off the machine. He gathered a few notebooks into a carrying bag and left his lab, Xant and I following behind him.

The lab was a solitary building, standing high on a hill. A hundred meters below, people were harvesting fruits from a field. Revoo gazed down on them for a short time, then pulled a book from the bag—I could see it was a book of the teachings of Xant. He fell to his knees and began to read aloud from the sacred text:

"We give thanks to you! Every soul and heart is lifted up to you, Xant, who has been honored and praised with the name God. You have given us minds, that we may understand you; speech, that we may expound you; knowledge, that we may know you. We rejoice, having been illuminated by your knowledge. We rejoice because you, who once walked among us, revealed yourself to us. We rejoice because you share your divinity with us through your knowledge."

"Poor soul," I said.

"His thanks and rejoicing would consume a world," said Xant.

I said nothing, but continued to listen as Revoo droned on. This particular litany, I knew, had eighteen verses, and it was coming to an end.

"We do not fear anyone except Xant alone, the Exalted One. We accept his light for our eyes, and cast the darkness from ourselves. We live in Xant, and we will acquire treasures Beyond, in the land where Xant now dwells. Wisdom summons us, saying, 'Come to Xant, O foolish ones, that you may receive the gift of understanding, which is good and excellent. I bequeath to you a high-priestly garment woven from every kind of wisdom.' We know that the eternal realm of Xant has no shadow outside of it, for Xant's limitless light shines everywhere within it. But its exterior lies in shadow, in darkness. We give thanks to you, Great Xant, for the reflected light you allow to be cast upon us!"

He reached into his bag and pulled out a scalpel. He began to speak, "Oh, Xant, sanctify this blade, for as you used a blade to redeem the heathens and unbelievers, I, too will use a blade to redeem myself and our people. We rejoice in you, O Xant."

"No—*no!*" I shouted even before I fully realized what it was that he was doing. As I ran toward him—it felt as if I were moving in slow motion—I saw him take the blade and draw it across his own throat. The blood was flowing down his clothing before I could even reach him, and I watched him crumple before me.

"I was too late for him," I cried to Xant.

"You have always been too late for him," said the god. "And sadly, you were also too late for them."

He bade me look at Revoo's body again. It had already begun to decay, and the grass over which the blood had spilled had begun to wilt. Down below I heard one of the workers in the fields begin to cough. Then another. And another. And still another.

Xant spoke again. "It was Revoo who created what is known as the Redeemer virus."

I looked down at the farmers. "You mean that all those people . . . ?"

"Yes. They'll all be dead within hours. There was no saving them." Already I could see that one frail youngster had fallen to her knees, her body racked with horrible coughing. "The only ones who survived belonged to an obscure religious sect that had hermetically sealed itself off from the outside world. Revoo belonged to this same sect, and he knew that its members would have taken the precautions necessary to isolate themselves from the virus during its active period, praying for salvation all the time."

Suddenly we were in the fields. I walked closer to the young one who had fallen. She had already stopped breathing. Xant continued to speak, heedless of the agony all around him. "When Revoo's sect emerged from its self-imposed cloister, they beheld the purged world they now had all to themselves, conveniently free of all secular unbelievers. They eventually discovered the body of the dear old doctor, who had left detailed notes and instructions describing what he had done. And they felt it was an honor and a duty to take his knowledge, replicate it, and apply it to themselves."

The enormity of what Xant was saying struck me like a slap in the face, and I turned on him, grabbing his tunic and pulling him roughly toward me. "You! Why did you let this happen to these people? *How* could you let this happen?"

"What made you think I didn't want it to happen?"

"But why would you have wanted random deaths and murders to have been committed, or this young girl"—and I gestured at the body which lay at our feet—"to have suffered in your name?" I began to shake him. "Why didn't you stop it?"

"How could I have?"

"How could you?" My hands were at his throat. "You are a god! You said you were divine! You are! You must be! You—" I stopped. If this was a true god of power, how could I hold him in my hands like this? My hands slackened. "If you are not a god, then what are you?"

Xant looked unruffled at this affront to his—personage? divinity? "I? I was alive once, a very long time ago; now I am little more than dust and ideas." He smiled at me sadly. "Perhaps that is all one really needs to become a god, Eben. Maybe we should make *you* into a god."

"I do not want to be a god! I want to stay as I am!"

"Are you sure? You were so adamant, so certain that I could have— *should* have—prevented all of the pain and suffering we have witnessed in our journey together; doesn't that mean that you believe you would have made better decisions?"

Please, no. I began to panic. "But for me to become a god, wouldn't I have to—die?"

"Yes," said Xant. "You would." And suddenly my body became weak, and I felt the terrible cough come upon me, and my flesh began to burn with fever. I fell hard upon the ground at the god's feet.

"I do not want to die, Xant!"

"Everything does. Even gods. You will too, sooner or later. Why not get it over with now, and let your death lead to something great?"

"Because . . ." My body was racked with spasms and chills and coughs, but I went on. "Because there is still much I must do in life! I do not want to die!"

"No? All right then—I suppose we'll make do with turning you into a prophet or some such thing . . . of course, we'll have to make sure that you're up to the job."

A test! So all of this *had* been a test of some sort. . . . I would have been more overjoyed at knowing I'd been right, had I not already been feeling a strong urge to vomit up my last meal. A mocking tone entered Xant's voice, as he continued.

"Yes, yes, call it a test if you like. And now you must try and give me the answers. Tell me, O exalted Eben, what was the great enemy that Revoo was fighting, really? And what is the great enemy that the Redeemers fight to this very day?"

My head swam with all that I had seen, but the darkness of illness had begun to overpower me. Even Xant, whom I knew to be standing right in front of me, was fading into a haze. His voice grew harsher, sharper; the sound turned like a knife in my misery.

"Tell me, boy! Why do these people who stride forth in my name do the things that they do?"

I choked on my swollen tongue, but managed to reply. "Because they are afraid?"

"Ahh. And what are they afraid of?"

"They are afraid of . . . you."

"Closer, Eben, you've almost go it. . . ."

"They—they are afraid of ideas! They fear any idea that might change their understanding of you!" New strength flowed back into my limbs as I spoke.

"Go on!"

As my vision began to clear, my voice grew firmer. "The Redeemers fear that they are not worthy of your ideals. In order to prove to you how worthy they truly are, they have taken it upon themselves to systematically impose your . . . their . . . will on entire worlds, whether or not the inhabitants even possess the ability to understand what it is that the Redeemers want."

I swallowed hard, and continued. "Even when they meet with little opposition, even in the face of their overwhelming victory, the Redeemers are unable to tolerate the idea that not everyone believes as they do. They insure that the terms of any debate are as one-sided as possible, and they are appalled when they encounter dissent. They have the power to sentence a planet to death, yet they feel they must shut out questions, silence any and all opposing voices. They fear that these things pose a very real danger to persons less able then they to withstand such blasphemy."

Xant nodded. "And what else do they fear, Eben? What is the one fear they dare not face?"

The thoughts were coming faster now, as my body rejuvenated.

"They fear that they might be wrong! The Redeemers cannot bear to think that they might be misguided in their actions. If they ever did come to think so, the guilt stemming from what they have done would be too much for them to bear."

And finally, I understood.

"They do not see because they choose not to see. They have surrounded themselves with the darkness of blind faith, and because they live in the dark, they fear the light—the light of truth! They say it themselves! 'We are darkness, Xant is light!' "

"Then what is it that they really want, Eben?"

"They want . . . they want . . ." I hesitated, because it just didn't seem possible, and yet it had to be true. "They want redemption, too."

"Yes."

"And here we are again."

The darkness parted in front of me, and I saw that we had been returned to the stream where we'd first met. The nibor and the pygram were still there, still arguing about how they would get across the body of water, neither one trusting each other any more than they had when we'd left them.

"I have shown you many things this day, Eben. And now, I want you to show me—have you learned anything?"

I looked across at the nibor and the pygram, quarreling as ever. And then I looked at Xant.

Without a word, I reached down and picked up a long stick. Then I turned and waded into the stream, using the stick to keep my balance in the water. I heard Xant speaking softly behind me, but I could not understand what he was saying. When I reached the other side, I grasped the stick with both hands and raised it above my head. And, with a silent prayer, I smashed the stick down hard on the head of the pygram.

The pygram was wounded and stunned but it shook off its injury and leaped, hissing, to attack me, stingers exposed and glistening with its fatal poison. I swung my staff at the pygram and hit it into the water with a resounding crack, and it was swiftly carried away by the current.

I turned then to the nibor, which looked up at me with fear in his eyes, unsure whether or not to flee. I spoke gently to him, saying, "Do not be afraid, little one. I bear joyful tidings."

"Are you going to slay me as well?" asked the nibor.

"No. I mean you no harm."

"Then have you come here to bring me the word of Xant?" the nibor said.

I hesitated. From the other side of the stream I saw Xant watching me.

"No," I said at last. "I am not here to bring you the word of Xant— that is something you must find for yourself. I am here to protect you, and to shepherd you and all others who are weak from those who are treacherous, coercive, and tyrannical. I speak truly when I tell you that the righteous are plagued on all sides by the inequities of the selfish, nibor. In the name of charity and goodwill, I am my brothers' keeper. And I will strike out at those who would attempt to poison and destroy those that I protect."

"Blessed are those who protect the weak from the coercive, and the traitorous, and the tyrants," said Xant. He gestured. "Come back to me, Eben."

I turned back to the nibor. "Would you like to come across with me?"

"Thank you, good sir." I held out my hand, and the nibor hopped into my open palm. I placed him onto my shoulder, then strode to the shore and set foot upon the stream—and discovered that my foot would not enter. I walked across the water's surface to the far side, and the nibor, with a final word of thanks, leaped from my shoulder and scurried off into the marsh.

Xant gripped me by the shoulders and smiled, as if truly seeing me for the first time. "Well done. If you must persist in thinking of our time together as a test, it would appear that you have passed. Not only have you unlearned the lessons taught by the actions of the Redeemers, but your actions have shown that you have taken a new lesson to heart: You now understand that you cannot change the essential nature of a weed, Eben; you can only learn to identify one as it comes up in your garden, and tear it out as it grows, lest it multiply and spread."

"Thank you, my friend."

"No, thank you, Eben. You are the first person in far too long to speak to me as a friend, rather than call up to me as one above all. And that is a precious gift indeed." Xant sighed. "You have faced many trials, and you may be sure that there are more still to come. Your path is murky, but rest assured that your cause is a good one for you have been called to help people help themselves. You will build, but not control. Strive, and not yield. And when you do these things, you will be victorious over all your enemies. They will not be able to wage war against you, nor will they be able to resist you, nor will they be able to get in your way. But listen: If any do, they are to be despised as deniers of truth. They will speak to you, Eben, cajoling you and enticing you, not because they are afraid of you, but because they are afraid of those who dwell within you, namely, the guardians of the divinity and the teaching."

"I understand, Xant. I will not be swayed."

"Then it is time for your greatest trial, Eben. It is the last trial you must face before you achieve true illumination."

"What is that, Xant?"

"Awakening." Xant placed his hand to my brow, and the world began to spin and grow light. It was as if a door had begun to open in my mind, and I was being forced through it by a power that screamed, *At last you see! At last you understand!* And as I felt my spirit fold in on itself to enter the brilliance on the other side of the doorway, I could hear Xant laughing, saying, "They always start off so strong and pure . . ."

I opened my eyes.

My mouth was dry as ash. I was in my own town, lying against a building. Bodies lay everywhere about me on the street. They were all dead, and rapidly turning to dust.

I had seen this before. This was the work of Revoo's plague.

My limbs proved weak and shaky as I struggled to get up. It was as if I hadn't used them for days. I braced myself against the wall, and finally managed to stand upright. My body felt great pangs of hunger, but I had things I knew I must see before I attended to the needs of my flesh.

I walked to the center of town, to Xant's Great Temple. The pews inside were filled with dead people who had obviously used their last breaths to pray to the god to forestall this judgment upon them, to save them from their suffering.

It would seem that I wasn't the only one who thought Xant was supposed to prevent things like this from happening, I thought, slightly hysterically.

I wandered into the High Priest's private quarters, already knowing in my heart what I would find there, yet still needing to see it with my own eyes.

The High Priest lay in the washtub at an unnatural angle. He had fallen and broken his neck, and he had died. And because of his untimely death, the Redeemer virus had been unleashed on an unsuspecting world.

My world.

There had been no blasphemy or heresy uttered, no assault on the body of the High Priest, no rhyme nor reason for his death. Millions of people and countless other living things had died because this Redeemer had been unable to keep his balance on a wet surface. Everyone on my planet was dead.

Everyone but me.

I picked up the staff of the High Priest and walked back out into the main sanctuary. I climbed the stairs to the main pulpit and spoke. "Xant, if it is within your power, guide these people to a place of peace. They have—they were innocent of wrongdoing. They did not deserve this punishment because of one who lacked grace. Grant them some measure of justice, and help them find peace."

There was no answer. But that was all right.

With that out of the way, my thoughts turned to more immediate concerns. First, of course, I must eat. I could not stay on this planet for long—there would be no meat or dairy soon enough. I would have to figure out how to operate a spacecraft and leave, before any Redeemers came to witness the poisoned fruits of their labors.

And then—then I would have to see to redeeming the Redeemers. I would search to the ends of the galaxy to find them and free them from their own blindness, and free the people they dominated from their terror and tyranny.

I will do this in memory of Xant. . . .

"So I thought I would tell you of it, and say: Buy it in the presence of those sitting here, and in the presence of the elders of my people. If you will redeem it, redeem it; but if you will not, tell me, so that I may know; for there is no one prior to you to redeem it, and I come after you." So he said, "I will redeem it."

—Ruth 4:4

SOLETA
Out of the Frying Pan

Susan Shwartz

After taking a leave of absence from Starfleet, Soleta travelled the galaxy on a personal mission of scientific inquiry. One such trip, a decade prior to her assignment to the *Excalibur,* took her to the Thallonian Empire's homeworld, where she had to be rescued from a Thallonian prison by Ambassador Spock, who was on Thallon for his own reasons—with the surprising aid of Si Cwan. "Out of the Frying Pan" takes place immediately following Spock and Soleta's departure from the dungeons of Thallon.

Susan Shwartz

Susan Shwartz's most recent books are *Second Chances*, a retelling of *Lord Jim*; a collection of short fiction called *Suppose They Gave a Peace and Other Stories*; the novels *Shards of Empire* and *Cross and Crescent*, set in the Byzantine Empire; the *Star Trek* novels (written with Josepha Sherman) *Vulcan's Forge* and *Vulcan's Heart*; the novel *The Grail of Hearts*, a revisionist retelling of Wagner's *Parsifal*; and over seventy pieces of short fiction. Her next novels will be *Hostile Takeovers* (which draws on over twenty years of writing science fiction and almost twenty years of working in various Wall Street firms, combining enemy aliens, mergers and acquisitions, insider trading, and the asteroid belt) and the *Star Trek* trilogy *Vulcan's Soul* (also with Sherman). She has been nominated for the Hugo twice, the Nebula five times, and the Edgar and World Fantasy Award once, and has won the HOMer, an award for science fiction given by CompuServe. Some time back, you may have seen her on TV selling Borg dolls for IBM, a gig for which she actually got paid. She lives in Forest Hills, New York.

To turn around as if one expected to be pursued was to invite pursuit, Soleta scolded herself. She had all she could do to keep pace with Ambassador Spock's long, determined strides as he headed toward his rendezvous with the freighter captain who represented their escape offworld. By the time Spock finally paused, Thal, the capital city of the Thallonian Empire, was only a distant haze of buildings, smoke, and low-hanging clouds in which the last brilliance of sunset was fading. From deep within his robes, he pulled out a battered scanner on which a blinking light flashed.

Soleta edged closer, raising an eyebrow to request permission to lean over Spock's shoulder and study the tiny scanner.

"Akachin left orbit when we came within sensor range. I estimate landing within three-point-two minutes," said Spock. "Given your experience with this planet's geological anomalies, I suggest we be ready to take off as quickly as possible."

Which was a very diplomatic way, Soleta thought, of saying that if a sinkhole hadn't swallowed her ship, she wouldn't have needed Spock to rescue her, she wouldn't have to depend on him for a way offworld, and he could have continued to go about whatever important business he had set in hand on Thallon.

Wind whipped her improvised hood away from her hair, which was clasped once again with the IDIC symbol that Lord Si Cwan had returned to her along with her life. There had been no logic in the prince's capricious act, which had released her and Spock, but she was thankful for it.

"If your freighter captain's shuttle raises a backwash, I suggest we move out of range," she said.

Spock nodded. "Captain Akachin will not be rash enough to operate with running lights," he said. "Incidentally, it would be best not to ask him why a navigator from Qualor is running freight."

"Got it," Soleta said, then regretted her informality of expression for the additional one-point-three minutes it took the tiny, dilapidated shuttle to land.

As its hatch opened, she and Spock ran forward. With every step, she wondered if some seismic tremor or other was going to crack open the ground underfoot and swallow them, too.

Spock hurled himself through the hatch with the energy of a much younger Vulcan. "The land is unstable," he warned the ship captain, whose face was marked not just by the drooping folds of pallid skin characteristic of natives of Qualor II, but by an expression of chronic worry and discontent. "An expeditious takeoff would be advisable."

Although the ground had begun to tremble ominously, the shuttle achieved a swift and surprisingly smooth liftoff. Once in the air, the captain set it into a steep climb, banking sharply away from the city to avoid onlookers as well as patrols.

"I'll have you know this shuttle is not as shabby as it looks," said the being Spock now introduced to her as Captain Revex Akachin. He resembled, Soleta decided, nothing so much as a nervous Terran shar-pei who had spent a rainy night outdoors. "I'm the Portmaster's cousin. I could afford a fancier-looking craft any time I wanted, but I just think it's smart not to draw attention to myself."

"Prudent," said Spock. "Logical, even."

Akachin preened visibly, his facial folds flushing, then went back to his litany of complaints. "You didn't tell me about a second passenger. Not to mention a female," he told Spock. "It's a good thing I maintain my shuttles carefully, or . . ."

"The Qualor shuttlepod 41Y," Spock cut in smoothly, "has fuel and life-support to sustain four people for approximately eight-point-three-five days, as we both know. I will, of course, adjust your compensation."

Revex Akachin huffed, then sniffed something that sounded like "I wouldn't have expected anything else."

The shuttle gained altitude. Despite a huffed-out breath from Akachin that warned Soleta not to come too close, she bent forward to study its instruments, hoping not to see the blips that might mean patrol craft coming to investigate an unauthorized takeoff from Thallon's surface.

"Just don't think," the Qualor freighter captain said, "that because I've fallen on hard times, I don't take care of my ship. Or my passengers. Qualor II is known for its fine ship-handling and maintenance. If I say my ship will get the job done, it will get the job done. The ambassador knows that. I just hope, however, you're not a fine lady who expects a luxury liner. You'd better not be."

Soleta arched an eyebrow at Spock in recognition of her lack of choices. As long as the ship was a ship, not a dungeon, and held air and—luxury of luxuries—a sonic shower, she would believe any stories Revex told her. Or appear to believe them.

"There," said the captain. *"Qualor's Pride."*

He didn't sound very proud. And, as the shuttle made its docking approach, the ship didn't look like it had much to be proud of. But Revex and Spock were watching her, so she fell back on what a Starfleet Academy classmate from Iowa used to call the Midwestern Mantra. "I'm sure," Soleta said soothingly, "that it will be very nice."

Spock nodded approval. She would have expected he'd know that mantra too. After all, Captain Kirk had also come from the Midwest.

Akachin's hands never stopped what Soleta realized were astonishingly competent maneuvers at the controls. He brought them into the cramped docking bay quickly and smoothly enough to earn her respect. As the doors closed behind them, the *Pride* left orbit.

Standing orders, no doubt, or part of that astonishing fugue he'd played on controls during the trip from the surface. Three-point-four minutes later, Revex turned his passengers over to a crewman.

"I'll need to be on the bridge till we leave Thallon's system," Akachin said. "It's not as if the *Pride* is a Romulan or Klingon ship with one of those fancy cloaks. When we came in, we had to dodge system patrols three times. They'd have treated us like common smugglers!"

"Imagine that," Soleta said. The captain took her irony for sympathy. Spock gave her a Look.

The crewman—a Bolian with a swagbelly that made him look like a hairless blue bear—escorted Spock and Soleta to their quarters. The two adjoining cabins with their jury-rigged refresher were cramped and bare, but they were at least clean.

"Replicator's on the blink," said the crewman. "You can try it, though, and if you fix it, we'll all be in your debt. That crate holds rat bars . . . field rations. Cap'n says to tell you none of them contain animal protein."

"Thank you," said Spock. "We appreciate the consideration."

Turning to go, the crewman said, "We're kind of cramped here, and we run a tight operation. Better you stay in your quarters as much as possible. Ship's gym, though . . . feel free within reason . . . ship's map is outside, by the lifts. But otherwise, better stay here."

"Thank you," said Spock again to the man's wide back as the hatch slid shut behind him.

"What a garbage scow!" Soleta exclaimed, starting to look a gift ship in the mouth.

Spock pointed at the bulkheads, which had been enameled white and trimmed with green stripes running parallel to the deck. Ultimately, the attempt to camouflage the fact that their quarters had started out life as holds for perishable or valuable cargo might be kindly meant, but it was futile.

It was only logical to suspect that sensors had been activated. Sensors set to spy on them. What humans called "bugs." She nodded understanding.

"I believe the term 'garbage scow' is one that Terrans call 'fighting words.' It is also inaccurate, Soleta. *Qualor's Pride* is most laudably clean."

She nodded, turning to prod a bunk that was pretty much a pad of drab recycled fibers over a battered metal shelf. "Looks almost Klingon," she commented wryly.

"Klingons would not provide mattresses," Spock replied. "At least, however, no one will expect us to eat *gagh*. Or to watch them doing so." He was opening crates and hatches. "Here," he said, and tossed a ship's coverall, worn but serviceable, at her.

No wardroom. No officers' mess. Not even a tour of the ship and bridge access, as was customary for Starfleet officers and high-ranking diplomats.

Be logical, Soleta. Captain Revex Akachin doesn't know you're Starfleet. For that matter, you're not sure you're still Starfleet either.

"No *gagh* on the menu is indeed an advantage," she conceded. *Is he trying to find out if I still observe Vulcan dietary laws?*

Stop that, she told herself. It was going to be a long, long trip if she subjected every remark Spock made to analysis and used it to reproach herself. "Well, what do you suggest we do first?"

"Wash," said Spock. "Seeing as you were imprisoned longer than I, I suggest you go first."

"I'll hurry," she said.

"Acceptable," Spock said. "The olfactory memory of dungeons is most disagreeable, and"—he raised a hand to one hollowed cheek—"this artificial pigmentation is beginning to itch. While you wash, I shall endeavor to disable the sensors that have no doubt been set to observe us."

She'd stepped into more powerful sonic showers, but the improvised hookup finally got her clean enough that she could pull on the coverall and stuff her old clothing (and Si Cwan's cloak, whose lavish fabric had acquired a ripe odor of dungeon) into the recycler with an illogical sense of relief.

Even more illogical was a sensation that Soleta identified as chagrin. She had told Spock she was half Romulan. *"I'm not sure why I'm telling you. Perhaps because you are the last individual with whom I shall hold a relatively normal conversation. I have very little to hide."* Even now, she remembered how she had shrugged, a most un-Vulcan gesture indeed.

Now, however, with her continued survival guaranteed, at least for the present, her statement was no longer true. Moreover, she had plenty to hide, especially from a Vulcan ambassador, the close personal friend of admirals and captains, a living legend in the Federation.

Plenty to hide from yourself, too, she suspected that Spock would point out.

He'll probably be too pleased at the chance to get clean to analyze you, she assured herself and emerged from the fresher.

"Your turn!" she called as she went into her cabin. She heard the sound of panels being returned to positions and boxes being opened before the fresher's hatch closed and the whine of the sonic shower started up again.

No point in wasting time, she told herself, and began to rummage through the storage compartment at her bunk's foot. She might be no kind of Vulcan, least of all an eidetic scholar like those from Gol, but she had vivid recollections of what she'd observed on Thallon as well as from her dig, and it was logical to record them before the memories faded. She found a padd that, although battered, appeared operational and set to work.

The Spock who tapped at her compartment, requesting entry, was clean and considerably paler now that he was no longer an imitation Thallonian. He glanced at the bulkheads.

"Be my guest," she told him. As he hunted for and disabled surveillance devices whose blinking green and amber lights quickly faded, Soleta made note after note.

"You are reproducing your field notes?" Spock asked. He disabled the last of the telltales and straightened, dusting his hands in an illogical "well, that's that" gesture. "That would indeed be productive. But let me suggest what might be a more profitable subject of study for us both."

Soleta set down the padd. When a senior officer—and even though Spock had resigned his commission, he was still an elder—made that sort of suggestion, what could she do but say, "Yes, sir," and wait for her assignment?

Spock walked over to a bulkhead and pressed a button. A section of bulkhead lowered, becoming a foldout desk that contained a computer. "My cabin has a similar unit. I suggest we use them to investigate this ship."

"The ship's awfully old," said Soleta. "It probably still has duotronic circuits."

"Very possibly," Spock agreed. "Because the *Pride* is approximately sixty-point-five years old, its systems are likely to be not just unfamiliar, but more complicated than the technology which you studied at the Academy. I suggest that becoming familiar with them might prove to our advantage. In particular," he added, "its command, communications, control, and intelligence systems. Not to mention weapons and navigation."

Soleta looked up at him.

"Furthermore," he added serenely, "since it appears that we are to be isolated, we have no need to ask anyone's approval. As Captain Kirk always said, it is always much easier to get forgiveness than permission."

Something had to be going on, Soleta suspected. And she was sure Spock thought so too. But just in case their quarters contained bugs that Spock hadn't found, neither mentioned these suspicions to the other. They simply acted on them as if they were a team that had operated together for years.

"Sir, this navigation system isn't just primitive," she said. "These circuits are ancient."

"Much can be achieved with old technology," Spock assured her. His eyes took on the distant, remembering look she remembered from the dungeon. "Even technology as primitive as stone knives and bearskins."

"These characters, for instance," Soleta said. "They turn up initializing every system, but they're no cipher I know."

Spock glanced over casually, as if he expected a careless student mistake. After all, he had been one of Starfleet's outstanding computer scientists. His gesture stung Soleta. No, she might not be a computer specialist, but rigorous work on small and large systems had been part of her general scientific training.

If you think it's so easy, you *try it!* she challenged him in her thoughts. The tricky bits of code caught Spock's attention and held it. He tapped out a phrase or two, erased them, then tried again. Finally, his back straightened, and, if he hadn't been Vulcan, he'd have chuckled.

"These are prefix codes," he said. "Very old prefix codes."

Soleta realized that the ambassador spoke the truth. Starfleet encrypted its ships' codes, and had been doing so for over eighty years. It did not surprise Soleta that Captain Akachin used an older version of the encrypted security, as that would be more cost-effective.

"If we can secure the prefix codes," Spock said, "we have a ninety-six-point-nine-eight percent chance of controlling this ship from our quarters."

With difficulty, Soleta suppressed a grin. In all the stories about Spock, no one had ever said he thought small.

Three days out from Thallon, Soleta ran one hand across her dark hair, bound up again with the IDIC pin that Princess Kalinda had stolen, but been ashamed to keep. Two days ago, Captain Akachin had called a red alert owing to some ships that looked as if they were either smugglers or trying to hunt down smugglers. She and Spock had been confined to quarters.

Although the lockdown had speedily been lifted, she and Spock had used their next "free period" to seek out ship's lockers for breath masks and to hunt, with little success, for weapons. She suspected her desire for a weapon other than her hands and her mind must be the Romulan in her coming out. Someone must have discovered the attempt, because they had been asked to confine themselves to their quarters once again. Now Soleta missed even the limited physical activity of the ship's cramped gym. Even more unsettling was what might be going on throughout the ship. She had mastered enough of the ship's navigation systems to know that the *Pride* had changed course several times. Now they were headed not toward the central worlds of the Federation, but even farther out.

"There!" said Spock. "I believe I have achieved a fine enough calibration on ship's sensors that they can detect tachyon particles."

This accomplishment seemed to please him, because he abandoned his work on the sensor array and proceeded to involve himself with communications while Soleta, as she had been ordered—or courteously requested, which amounted to the same thing—continued working on the navigation and weapons systems.

The buzzer requesting admission to their quarters made Soleta start. Spock, more cautiously, swept diagrams and stray components away into the storage compartment at the foot of his bunk. Soleta ghosted behind the hatch.

"Come," Spock called, and the hatch slid open. "Captain Akachin."

Even the shadows beneath the folds of the skin on the Qualorian's face were pale and unhealthy looking, and he sported a distinct black eye.

"What has happened?" Soleta demanded, coming up behind him.

The freighter's captain jumped. He was frightened to the point of panic.

"You Vulcans aren't the only ones to be able to know when there's a problem," Revex Akachin said. "Once we got by the system patrols, it took me this long to figure it out and pry the truth out of my crew. My own crew, I ask you. Is that fair? Is that loyal?"

"What happened?" Spock asked, with considerably more composure than Soleta thought necessary. Her IDIC ornament, applied to the man's fingernails—if he had fingernails—might get the truth from him, she thought, then dismissed the idea as far too Romulan.

"Ambassador, I don't know if you're aware of how merchant ships are commonly owned outside strict Federation control," Akachin said. "Because of the capital expenditure involved, they tend to be joint owned, a covenant among the captain and his crew, who buy shares, each according to his means. From this disposition, the ship's complement derives proportionate shares of the ship's profits."

"And I assume that if funding is tight, you may turn to an outside lender to raise capital," Spock said. "Is that correct?"

Revex Akachin looked away. "I had been so proud that we'd avoided bringing in outsiders. My ship. My crew. No debts—that is, we had none to speak of. But apparently, before we reentered Thallonian space to pick *you* up—" His emphasis on the *you* seemed to imply that Spock was to blame for the current state of affairs. "—some of my crew had a little too much to drink portside. They started gambling and . . ."

"Don't tell me," said Soleta. "They wagered their ship-shares."

"And then some."

Soleta sat on her bunk. She could see where this was going. Why couldn't the fussy little man simply tell them what was worst-case, instead of fussing and babbling as he led them step by step through his history of petty calamities?

"They couldn't pay their gambling debts. Ordinarily, I'd say 'That's hard luck, boys' and pick them up after they'd finished serving their sentences, but I ran into two problems. First, my men somehow managed to lose to a kind of aliens they didn't know. They didn't want to press charges, which was good. But they did want, very much, to take control of a small, neat freighter like the *Pride*. And—here's where the trouble started—they were aware that debts against ship-shares can be used as a lien on the ship."

Soleta glanced over at Spock.

"So in other words, these aliens . . ."

Revex Akachin buried his head in his wrinkled hands. "Have essentially taken ownership of the *Pride*. They've let us continue running her, but, the point is, we're at their orders. And Rakhal, who's spent half the trip in sickbay anyhow, with a reaction to something called Huyperian beetle snuff, don't ask me to describe his symptoms, Ambassador, they're terrible, just terrible . . ."

"Rakhal did what?" Spock asked. Although he did not raise his voice or stir from his position by the workstation, Akachin cringed.

"Rakhal told them we were open to charter as well as free-trade. And that, this trip, we had a very important passenger indeed."

"You can make warp seven at least," Soleta said. "Why not run? Turn yourselves in to the nearest authorities and ask for protection. You'd probably get off with a fine, maybe some counseling, but you'd be able to keep your ship . . ."

Assuming he wasn't already in trouble with the law.

"You don't understand," Captain Akachin wailed.

Now, thought Soleta, she did. Only too well. She suppressed a most un-Vulcan sigh.

"I've seen our . . . our creditors' ship. It doesn't look like much, but it's got weapons that could crack *Pride* like a Denorian groundnut. I tried to explain to the ship's captain that my deal with you was a preexisting contract. After all, their own law states, 'a deal is a deal.' Their captain wouldn't even appear onscreen, but he did point out that clause two of that law is 'until a better one comes along.' And besides, they don't consider contracts between aliens binding."

"So," said Spock, "what is it that they want? I can hardly be expected to have funds sufficient to pay back your loans. Nor do I think your creditors would accept repayment if a freighter is what they want."

Soleta suppressed a cynical smile. Spock's family was one of the noblest—and richest—on Vulcan. If Spock wished to buy a freighter, he probably could. But the adage that Vulcans did not lie had always been a convenient myth, and Spock was half human at any rate.

Something on Akachin's belt, almost hidden by his belly's overhang, went "beep." "I had a proximity alarm set!" he cried. "They're here!" He looked wildly about the cabin as if Spock and Soleta could do anything to help him. "I've got to get to the bridge."

Soleta didn't even wait for Spock's gesture. They followed him out of their quarters and up to the *Pride*'s cramped bridge, a space of battered, polished metal and weathered blacks and grays. Each station looked different from all the rest, as if they'd all been cannibalized from a variety of ships, but each was well maintained and appeared to be running smoothly.

"Captain's just come in," said the Bolian, extending his hands toward a blank screen in a gesture meant to be placating.

"You're late!" the words crackled out.

"We had three run-ins with local authorities," Akachin started to explain. "I told you. What's the point in owning a controlling interest in a free-trader if it's been impounded?"

"Rule Number 62. The riskier the road, the greater the profit."

"That's what I'm telling you. There's no profit if we're blown out of space."

"So, because you've got a problem, we should suffer? Do you think latinum grows on trees? Unacceptable, Revex, you idiot. But, you're here now. And these fools say you've got the merchandise."

"I'm a freighter pilot, not a slaver!" Revex wailed. "It's not a crime to carry passengers!"

"We've already established what you are. What we're talking now is price. And the price is your life and the lives of your wretched crew. Who, incidentally, should never gamble. Why, my youngest son would have seen through some of the tricks I used! Did you bring your passenger on board?"

"I've got . . . "

Spock pushed past the Qualorian before he could say, "I've got *two.*"

"The Federation does not pay ransom," said Spock. "I urge you to abandon this plan before charges can be filed."

He spoke as composedly as if he spoke in negotiations or from the bridge of a starship with plenty of firepower. Soleta suppressed the urge to protest, which would give away her existence, which was clearly something he did not wish to do.

"Oh, the Federation is hardly the be-all and end-all, Mr. Ambassador. The field of bidders for the rights to obtain you is quite wide."

"I wonder who those bidders would be," Spock mused. "For example, I face two sets of capital charges on Romulus—for espionage in 2268 and again in 2344. The logical assumption is that a spy can be executed only once, but Romulans can be very creative."

Which just might be one more reason why Romulans preferred to suicide rather than be taken prisoner. Soleta looked down. It wasn't just that he was criticizing half her heredity, but Spock had already cheated death once, and she was still Vulcan enough to be concerned that talking about someone else's resurrection could be construed as a violation of Vulcan's strict customs about personal privacy.

Besides, the Romulans were hardly the only species who might want Spock—and Soleta, once they learned of her existence—dead. Even if the crew simply turned around and returned them to Thallon, what assurance did they have that Si Cwan would feel like being generous a second time? Or that he'd even know they'd been sent back? She thought the only thing Chancellor Yoz would willingly tell Si Cwan was to drop dead.

"So," asked Spock, "when does the bidding start?"

"*Rule Number 79: Beware of the Vulcan greed for knowledge,*" the alien voice crackled disagreeably. "*And if 'never argue with a Vulcan' isn't a Rule of Acquisition, it should be. Take him away. Put him someplace safe. Someplace I don't have to listen to him.*"

In despair, Revex Akachin gestured. Four crew members rose to escort Spock and Soleta back to their quarters, apparently turned brig for the duration. They did not dare to touch them, but swept along behind them like the most deplorable shore patrol Soleta had ever seen.

"I still can't decrypt these prefix codes," Soleta complained approximately seventy-two-point-five hours later. All of the likely algorithms, and some of the severely exotic ones, including a few she'd invented on the spot, had failed. Akachin's encryption might have been old, but it was effective.

Spock muttered under his breath.

"I ask forgiveness," Soleta said, surprising herself with the formal courtesy.

"I said 'damn,'" Spock said. "I too ask forgiveness for my language; I learned the habit from my wife. Who is, incidentally, half Romulan. The first half-Romulan, in fact, to attend Starfleet Academy."

Soleta lifted her hands from the keyboard and flexed aching fingers. *There is no pain,* she told herself. Right. Whatever adept said that mantra worked had clearly not spent seventy-two hours attempting to crack these damnable archaic prefix codes.

"Captain Saavik," Soleta said. "That's right! I'd forgotten she was half Romulan."

"Soon to be admiral, if I know anything about it," Spock said. "So you can see that being half Romulan does not preclude an eminently successful Starfleet career."

"But Captain Saavik never lied about her background." *And it didn't hurt that she'd had one of Vulcan's first families backing her.*

"Nor did you," said Spock. "However, unless we master this ship's systems, I would estimate that we have a ninety-two-point-six-seven percent chance of not needing to continue this discussion. If the algorithms we have employed have not decrypted the prefix code, then it is logical to assume that it is concealed by a simple cipher. Here is my hypothesis: The key to that cipher is most likely in Captain Revex Akachin's head."

Soleta felt her lips curving up into an unpardonable and completely feral smile.

Spock shook his head imperceptibly, one side of his mouth quirking up as if he saw something familiar.

"So, what we have to do is get the captain down here," Soleta said. "Starting a fire or a riot would not be helpful. He would probably only send the crew, or he'd try to knock us out with anaesthezine gas because they don't know we have masks."

Spock opened a storage locker and produced one of the spy-eyes. "I think we need more information," he said. "It may be possible for me to reconfigure this so it can listen as well as transmit. After all," he said with a ghost of what looked like humor, "the bridge meant to spy on us; it seems logical to spy on them."

He bent to the task.

"I'm ready to test our bug," Spock told Soleta. "You might want to stand away from the bulkhead. I am not quite certain about the volume lev . . ."

"YOU BANKRUPT, NO-LOBED IDIOT!" came a shriek from the bulkhead before Spock could turn the volume down. *"It's simple enough. You played. You lost. You owe. What's more, my ship's got better guns and more of them than your pathetic excuse for a freighter. If you do not drop your defense and permit yourself to be boarded . . . we can always say your warp core overloaded so we can at least collect insurance."*

"The situation does not sound promising," said Soleta.

"No?" asked Spock. "I've dealt with Captain Akachin, on and off, for five-point-eight years. He's a good enough navigator, but his stress management leaves a great deal to be desired. I expect that he will come here, to wring his hands and explain and apologize before turning us over to his creditors in . . . ten . . . nine . . . eight . . . Do you hear footsteps, Soleta?"

Buzzz.

"Come!" said Spock. Treating Akachin to a raised eyebrow, he asked, "I wonder that you would bother to ask for admittance, seeing as this is your ship—barring those shares squandered by your crew—and you are about to hand us over to their creditors."

"I'm sorry, Spock," said the captain. "But I don't know what else to do. That ship's got enough firepower to blow us halfway to the Delta Quadrant."

"So you expect us to yield to the logic of necessity," Spock said. "And in case we proved recalcitrant, you brought along your phaser." He gestured at the weapon, which Revex had tried to conceal by wearing a drab maroon jacket over his coverall.

The shipmaster sagged. "What do you want of me, Spock? I've done everything I could. Now, you're a Vulcan. Smart. And a diplomat, too. Can you think of any way to get us out of this?"

"I can," said Soleta. "Let us help you. We are experienced, trained ship-handlers with combat training. Release the ship's prefix codes. Give us a fighting chance."

"I can't do that," protested Akachin, his eyes wide. "You'd have full access to every system on board."

"That was the general idea," Soleta admitted.

"You've never flown in combat," Spock's voice overrode her. "We have. It is logical, therefore, to turn control of the ship over to those who have the best chance of defending it, and themselves. "

The Qualorian was shaking his head, backing toward the door as Spock gestured, almost imperceptibly, to Soleta. She pounced on him, feeling his yelp of protest, his easily quashed resistance as release after all this time of imprisonment. Efficiently, she disarmed him and placed the phaser by her computer.

"You think the crew would care if I took him out, Ambassador?" she asked. "I think the exec would take over, and he'd still turn us over to who-ever's out there."

"Clearly," said Spock, "diplomacy has failed. See what you can do with Revex. But remember, we need him." He stood back, as if leaving the nervous, now-whimpering ship captain to his fate.

"I see, Ambassador," Soleta said. "I do see."

She let herself grin. It came as an even better tension release than beating Akachin's head against a bulkhead until the knowledge she wanted popped out of it.

She gave him a shake that made him yelp and made the folds on his face wobble up and down.

"I'll only say this once," she told him. "Ambassador Spock's probably told you about his belief that Vulcans and Romulans can be reunited. Now, I'm one of his students. Does that give you any hints to what I'm about to say? I am not at all averse to prying the information I need out of someone in any way I can. In fact, I think it is only logical. So, are you going to give me the cipher for the prefix codes, *or am I going to rip it out of you?* And don't you even think of fainting! I'll wake you and ask the questions all over again."

Spock held out a cautionary hand as Revex Akachin gave him a despairing "see what you got me into" look. "I'll enter the codes," he said. "Let me sit down."

"How do I know you won't blow up the ship?" Soleta demanded. She moved the phaser out of reach and managed not to snort in disdain. The setting was barely strong enough to stun.

"Because I'm not Romulan and I'm not crazy. I only want to live!" her prisoner wailed. "Look, if you don't trust me near the computer, let me write the codes down, then. If I speak them someone might hear. I posted guards outside the door."

"Our escort to the enemy ship, no doubt," Spock said.

Soleta gave Revex one more shake for good measure. "Your ship's in danger. You're in enemy hands. And you're worried about your crew overhearing a cipher you can change any time you want? I find your priorities illogical in the extreme."

"Don't break the captain, please, Soleta," Spock requested as mildly as he might have asked for more *plomeek* soup at dinner. "We may still need him."

Akachin grew so pale that Soleta eased her grip on the front of his coverall to allow him to breathe.

"I won't break him," she promised. "But I won't release him until he writes down his precise codes. Here!"

She thrust stylus and padd into his hands and waited until they stopped shaking.

"Got them," said Spock. "I'll program them now. You take navigation. I'll take communications and tactical."

Spock's fingers danced on the console, activating weapons, modifying communications protocols, sending a message Soleta couldn't read from this angle. "By the way," Spock said, "I commend you on your acting abilities."

"What made you certain I was acting?" Soleta asked. "And sir, that was not a rhetorical question." Before Spock could answer, however, she cried, "They're trying to override my course changes, no . . . got it! I have helm control."

"Warp factor three," said the older Vulcan.

"Seal that hatch if you know what's good for you!" Soleta snarled at the ship's captain. "And if anyone tries to get us out, you order them to stop."

"Yes, Commander!" he cried.

"And don't call me 'Commander.' "

Soleta met Spock's eyes over the computer and thought they glinted with humor.

She put the freighter into a sharp dive, building up to warp seven and shrieks of "You'll blow the stability fields, you'll overload the warp core; she can't go faster than warp seven-point-one!" from Akachin.

"Alien ship is gaining on us and will overtake in two-point-eight-one minutes," Spock said. "It has brought weapons systems online. I am preparing to fire warning shots."

He fired, and the ship jolted as energy left its weapons, but not nearly strongly enough to indicate any significant firepower.

"They're still gaining." Soleta, her fingers dancing over the keyboard, watched Spock prepare to fire yet again. "If I fire all this ship's weapons at once, perhaps I can strike one of the other ship's weapons ports and damage it."

And perhaps humans will build a ski resort on Mount Seleya, she thought.

The ship jolted again.

"Structural-integrity field down to ninety percent," Soleta reported.

Screams erupted outside their quarters, screams in at least five languages, as the guards protested. Someone pounded on the hatch. Soleta glared, and Revex yelled back.

"Direct hit on aft weapons array," Spock said. "How long can your ship maintain this speed?" he asked Revex Akachin.

Again Soleta glared meaningfully at the man, who twisted to put as much distance between himself and the "Romulan" as he could. "An hour. Maybe two."

"Imprecise," said Spock. "Maximum speed, please."

Soleta pushed *Qualor's Pride*'s faltering engines as hard as she could. They fled before the larger, stronger vessel, a stubby, ugly, copper-colored thing with bigger weapons and a determination that was the match of theirs.

Spock, monitoring communications, and firing to cover their retreat, called out. "Do you see that asteroid? Set a course for it!"

"We haven't got any weapons to seed it with, Ambassador!" she said.

"But we may be able to hide in one of its craters. At least long enough for them to become discouraged and leave. I estimate a thirteen-point-nine-eight-percent chance."

Soleta didn't find those odds particularly promising. Nevertheless, the ambassador's experience was greater than hers, and he'd given her a direct order. Dropping out of warp so quickly their pursuer overshot them, she headed for the asteroid and maneuvered the ship into one of its craters.

"They're trying to break down the door!" screamed Revex. Soleta had been concentrating so hard that she hadn't heard the banging, thumping, and phaser blasts before. She considered giving Akachin back his phaser for no longer than it took to mutter "preposterous" under her breath.

"Sorry," she muttered to herself, and triggered the command that released anaesthezine gas throughout the rest of the ship. She heard coughs, muffled yells, and then bodies hitting the deck. "You did say there was something to be said for brute force," she reminded Spock.

He raised an eyebrow at her.

"The gas is nontoxic," she said. "It won't harm them."

"And if it did? Don't the needs of the many outweigh the needs of the few?"

Soleta closed her eyes in frustration. They were fighting a battle, and Spock chose this time to chase the oldest ethical dilemma in Surak's book?

Is there a better time? she suspected he would ask.

"I would say," she began deliberately, "that it would depend upon their motivations. And the overall circumstances."

"And not on whether you happened to belong to the few or to the many?"

"Spock," she dropped the title, "are you testing to see just how Romulan I am?"

"The Romulans I have known best had a well-developed sense of honor that had very little to do with self-preservation. Sometimes greatly to their detriment. I suggest that you, too, should consider the subject from all points of view."

"I've got something else to think about, Spock."

"Indeed? What?"

"That ship's spotted us inside this crater. I estimate it will be in weapons range in fifteen-point-nine-three seconds. Better brace yourself."

"Locking on target," said Spock. "Firing."

The ship didn't as much jolt as convulse from the hit it took. "Shields reduced to fifteen percent. Hull breach on decks three to five."

"Weapons systems down to sixty percent efficiency. Firing." Apparently, Spock was resolving his own needs-of-the-many crisis in favor of self-preservation too. "I suggest we retreat."

She turned the ship and called for speed fast enough to cause warning lights to break out all over the screen.

The other ship pursued, firing as it advanced. "They're targeting the warp nacelles—ugh!" She reeled away from controls, then regained her balance. "We've taken another hit." The ship shuddered again. "Shields are down. And warp engines are offline. Shall I proceed on impulse?"

"Stand by," said Spock.

If I were really Romulan, she thought, *I would have blown this ship up before I let whoever those people are board and take me prisoner.*

"Now what?" Soleta asked.

"Now, we wait. Please scan for tachyon emissions."

"Aye, sir," she said, good little Starfleet lieutenant at the last. "Nothing yet . . . wait! Tachyon levels rising . . ."

Spock opened a channel to the enemy ship. "I am giving you one last chance. We are awaiting reinforcements. It would be prudent for you to leave the vicinity of my ship at once."

Raucous laughter resounded over the hailing frequency.

"Tachyon level rising . . ."

She really wasn't that stupid, she thought. She only had to be hit over the head three times before she realized. Spock hadn't expected to be able to escape; he had hoped that her best efforts would buy sufficient time . . .

. . . for reinforcements. Cloaked reinforcements.

"Captain!" The title burst out of her. "Ship decloaking at five thousand kilometers. Weapons systems online. It's a Klingon bird-of-prey. Message coming in now. Shall I open a channel?"

"Thank you, Lieutenant. Please welcome our Klingon friends. And tell them they may fire when ready."

Soleta raised both her eyebrows at Spock. The solution was logical, of course. Spock had been in contact with the Klingons since the destruction of Praxis and the Khitomer Accords. Although it was crass and illogical (given human, Vulcan, Romulan, or Klingon nature) to expect payment for duty done, the Klingons did owe Spock big time, and he was skilled enough to summon them to pay off an installment on their debt.

"This is your last chance," Spock told the other ship. "Surrender or die."

They howled mirth and defiance at him. If they jeered that way at the Klingons' challenge . . .

"Klingons are firing, sir," Soleta informed Spock.

"I grieve for thee," Spock whispered to the *Pride*'s creditors as the Klingons blew their ship out of space. The freighter rocked and bucked from the shock waves, but its shields held.

Over the com, Soleta could hear the victorious howls of the Klingons.

Captain Akachin gave a small moan. He actually seemed relieved to faint, joining his crew in blissful slumber.

★   ★   ★

It would take, Soleta thought, the heat death of the universe to throw Ambassador Spock's appearance into disorder. Granted, he wore a ship's coverall rather than the elaborate gemmed robes and tabard of a Vulcan official. But his hair, dusted only lightly by the silver of time, was impeccable; his shoulders were straight; and his face was composed, as opposed to Soleta herself. She knew perfectly well that her own hair was tumbling down about her shoulders, and her hands ached from the tension of orchestrating a ship takeover from the computers in their quarters.

Glancing away from Spock, she tugged her hair back into order, then bent to see to Captain Akachin.

"Spock of Vulcan! Thank you for the battle. It is always an honor to assist you. Lower shields and prepared to be boarded . . . if you please."

"Now that," remarked Soleta, "is a considerable concession."

"A triumph of diplomacy over brute force," Spock agreed.

He bent to check on Revex. "Captain Akachin appears to be coming around. It might be advisable to vent the gas that subdued the *Pride*'s crew. It would hardly do to render our benefactors unconscious."

"Spock here," he told the Klingon ship. "A moment, please. We have been assisting this ship's captain in defending his ship not just against the invader you destroyed but against a mutiny. We have gassed the crew and need to restore them to consciousness."

"Hah!" the ship's captain laughed. *"I am Klovagh, son of Klaa, master of the K'raiykh. We saw your battle, with those pathetic weapons I would not give a child. My father, who served with you and General Korrd, always said his service with you was too brief. He praised your skills as a gunner. I can see he said too little."*

"He honors me," Spock said, inclining his head at the computer screen. "I remember his valor."

Sensors showed the gas levels throughout the ship dissipating.

"The air is now acceptable," Spock said. "If you would be pleased to come on board?"

"We'll bring guards to assist your brave captain."

Revex Akachin stirred at the term "captain," saw a Klingon's face on the screen, and fainted again.

"On your feet, mister," said Soleta, and suited actions to words by means of one hand at the throat of his coverall, hauling him up. "They think you're a hero, so don't tell them any different."

Releasing the doors, she went out into the corridor to see to the recovering crew.

She informed various moaning, burping, or otherwise under-the-weather crew, "We've got Klingons preparing to board. Yes, Klingons. Do you think they're going to bring you medical officers? They're likelier to bring guards: Ambassador Spock told the Klingon commander, who turns out to be the son of an old comrade, that we were helping Captain Akachin resist a mutiny."

Perhaps that was not the most effective way of convincing them to stand on their own two feet. At least, those of them who had only two.

Spock and Soleta went to the *Pride*'s bridge, where the Klingons materialized in the red blaze of a transporter effect. Green cassocks covered what she was certain was the officers' finest parade armor, donned in honor of Ambassador Spock. Large red gems adorned the spiked collar and leash of the Klingon commander's *targ*. Its head came up higher than its master's waist, and he was at least half a meter taller than Spock.

The Bolian cast an appealing glance at Soleta. "Stand straight," she murmured under her breath. "Klingons can smell fear. And if they can't, that *targ* can."

Spock cast her a faintly reproachful glance.

"It is a logical assumption," she told him. "The *targ* is a predator; predators have keen senses of smell. Therefore . . ."

"Lieutenant, you are old enough to know the meaning of the term 'rationalization.' " In other words, he knew she was enjoying herself in a most un-Vulcan manner, and he was calling her on it.

Must be the Romulan coming out in me, Soleta thought. *Just wonderful.* But she'd been locked up with a living legend in this miserable ship for days; she'd helped fight a ship's action that logic, assuming they'd bothered to listen to it, said they should not have started, much less won, and she was, pure and simply, frustrated with the whole situation, which was the sort of thing she'd once heard her Midwestern classmate describe as "out of the frying pan into the fire."

Interesting place, Iowa must be. If she survived this trip, maybe she'd put it on her itinerary of places to go so she didn't have to go back to Starfleet. Or home to Vulcan.

But which fire did the humans who'd coined that phrase mean? Soleta could think of several. She suppressed a sigh that she was sure would permanently have lowered her in the ambassador's estimation, assuming she could fall any further, and braced herself to welcome their Klingon rescuers appropriately.

Whack!

Captain Klovagh's slap on Revex Akachin's back sent the little man halfway across the bridge. He caught himself against a guardrail, and Soleta wondered if any of the disks in his spine had been ruptured. "Captain defends his ship with the help of two Vulcans, even when one of them is Spock himself . . . little man, you've got more *butlh* than I'd have thought."

Soleta glanced down at her own fingernails, under which there was, naturally enough, no dirt at all. Poor grooming as a synonym for male, or ortho-male, pride? Highly idiomatic, she decided, and potentially improper. She filed the reference in her capacious memory, which, right now, felt as if she needed to download at least half of it to storage and then lose the storage unit.

At a gesture of Klovagh's elaborately gloved hand—and a flash of the metal studs that turned glove into deadly weapon—guards dispersed throughout the ship.

With the business of mopping up after a victory now taken care of, Klovagh and his personal guards turned toward Spock. As one, they saluted, a noisy matter of chests being thumped and *bat'leth*s brandished. Even the *targ* seemed to raise its tail in salute. At least that's what Soleta, standing a respectful two paces behind and to the side of the ambassador, hoped was all that the *targ* was doing. She managed to keep her nostrils from flaring at the creature; the Klingons might misunderstand even so trivial an involuntary physical reaction.

Klovagh strode forward, clearly intending to clasp arms with Spock, if not to embrace him, but something in the Vulcan's demeanor kept him quite literally at arm's length.

"Captain," Spock said. "May I present . . ."

"A female," said Captain Klovagh. "A Vulcan female." He grinned, exposing crooked, yellowed teeth that looked very strong. "But Ambassador, though I do not mean to intrude"—which had to be a first, Soleta thought, while keeping her face expressionless—"on Qo'noS, we had not heard that you took a new mate."

"This is Starfleet Lieutenant Soleta, indeed of Vulcan," Spock said with immense dignity. "She is my student."

Klovagh bellowed laughter, then advanced on Soleta, who drew herself up in a salute to keep him at bay. "Your student, you say! And what do you *study,* Lieutenant?" he demanded.

Under such close observation, Soleta knew she was on her own. She couldn't even flash Spock an "I'll get you for this!" glance—which would have been extremely disrespectful, at any rate.

"Ship's design, sir," she said. "And psychology. Applied alien psychology."

Klovagh roared again. The *targ* barked, turning the noise into a duet painful to sensitive Vulcan ears.

"I am glad to hear this, Ambassador. Your mate has deserved well of us, and we would not wish to have her angry at us."

"I agree, Captain. It would be profoundly illogical for me to take a new consort. Not to mention life-threatening."

As Klovagh roared, thinking Spock had made a most un-Vulcan joke, Soleta glanced down and away. She had never seen such a master of lying with the truth, even with truths that must not be spoken of before outsiders.

Someone touched her sleeve. Quickly, she turned, suppressing a combat-honed reflex to send Revex Akachin back along the trajectory he'd gone when Klovagh slapped his back. "Lieutenant? *You're* a Starfleet lieutenant?"

She tilted her head at him. "That is indeed my title. I am, however, on extended leave of absence."

"But I thought . . . you made me think you were a . . ."

Her impersonation of a Romulan on a really bad day wasn't a subject she wished to discuss at any time, let alone in front of the Klingons. "I told you nothing of my origins. You made inaccurate assumptions. You would be wise to attend the ambassador and the Klingon captain. I believe they are discussing your best interests."

"Well, Captain," asked Klovagh as the Qualorian turned toward him with the expression of a man facing slow, painful execution, "what shall be done with your crew? Not just disloyal but incompetent! One man—and two Vulcans—against an entire ship, and you held out. Our bards would sing of it, if only you were Klingon. As it is," the Klingon captain said, becoming all business for one brief moment, "we will probably tell this story in bars, which is honor enough for one not born a conqueror. Tell me about your crew. Shall we shoot them naked out your ship's airlocks? Feed them to my *targ*? He was last fed two days ago and should be hungry soon."

"You might render your *targ* ill," said Spock. "That would be regrettable. Not to mention a waste of a fine *targ.*"

"So it would," Klovagh said. He tossed his head, sending his great braided mane flying. "Your ship is disabled. Here is what you will do: We shall take your ship in tow to our nearest base and repair it. There will be no charge; it is an honor to help so noble a fighter, as well as Spock, friend of our Empire. You will remain on board your ship with guards, although you will dine with us tonight. Fresh *rokeg* pie! And we shall make the bloodwine flow and your blood burn!"

This time Spock looked down and to the side too. And was that a faint flush of green Soleta saw starting on the tips of his ears?

"Ambassador, I ask for the privilege of having you and your . . . student as my guests. She will learn much among my crew."

Soleta inclined her head two degrees further than Spock and held her bow four seconds longer as he accepted for both of them.

"So that is settled!" Klovagh slapped his gloved hands together. "I have ordered my private shuttle to take you to my ship so you may be received in all honor," he told Spock. "If you would be pleased to go to the docking bay? Captain, you and I will escort the ambassador." He grabbed Captain Akachin and propelled him to the head of what became a very rough-and-ready procession. The *targ* sniffed at his buttocks, and Akachiu jumped forward, suppressing another moan.

Soleta took the opportunity to lean closer to Spock (but respectfully so, now that Klovagh's inappropriate suspicions were allayed for the time being). "Sir, I neglected to consider all possibilities in context. I didn't know . . ."

"A master of human philosophy once said that admitting ignorance was the beginning of wisdom. In that statement, T'Plana-hath, Matron of Vulcan philosophy, concurred. You might wish to consider this. When I began my career, the Klingon Empire was the enemy of the Federation. Now we are allies, and Klingons have just saved our lives. It may be that the Romulans will follow that same path."

"Do you truly think so?" Soleta asked.

"There are always possibilities, Lieutenant. As I told you back on Thallon, life is anticipation. Life is constant surprise."

She paused for a moment, trying to work it out.

"And I suspect," said Spock, "that we should find out what surprises await us on the Klingon ship."

Soleta followed Spock out of the "frying pan" of the *Qualor's Pride* into what she fervently hoped would not be yet another fire. But even if they ran into more trouble, she suspected that she and Spock could come up with a few surprises of their own.

BURGOYNE 172
Through the Looking Glass

Susan Wright

After hir term on the *Livingston*, Burgoyne became assistant chief engineer of the *U.S.S. Excalibur* under Captain Morgan Korsmo. "Through the Looking Glass" takes place in that time period, about two years prior to hir promotion to chief engineer when Captain Calhoun took command of the ship.

Susan Wright

The first novel of Susan Wright's science fiction trilogy, *Slave Trade*, was published in April 2003. She has written nine *Star Trek* novels, among them *Dark Passions*, *Gateways: One Small Step*, and *The Badlands*. She also writes nonfiction books on art and popular culture, including *Destination Mars*, *UFO Headquarters*, and *New York in Photographs*. For more information, go to www.susanwright.info.

Burgoyne stripped off hir clothes and dropped them on the fancy tiled floor. Hir suite was in the best R-and-R resort on Argelius II. The Hermat leaped toward hir private pool, going down on all fours to pick up speed as hir arms and legs bent at joints normally hidden by hir uniform. The oblong of clear green water yawned under hir as s/he neatly dived in without a splash.

Burgoyne resurfaced as Keeten Planx, a joined Trill whom Burgoyne had met during shore leave, slowly applauded hir feat. "I didn't know you were so talented, Burgy! That's some fast moving."

Burgoyne floated on hir back, kicking with hir legs. "There's plenty of room in here. But I have a standing rule . . . no clothes allowed."

For a moment, Burgoyne thought the burly Trill would refuse with his customary grin. "Why not?" he agreed. "But I'm warning you, my entrance won't be as spectacular as yours."

To Burgoyne's delight, Keeten Planx slipped off his vest and kilt, revealing a male physique worthy of applause himself. Keeten flexed his chest and arms, tightening his spectacular abs for Burgoyne's benefit, before strolling forward with true athletic grace. His dark spots ran from his forehead all the way down to his toes. He dived into the pool and swam underwater toward Burgoyne with strong, sure strokes.

Burgoyne had been eyeing Keeten Planx ever since the Trill had arrived at the resort a few days ago. This was hir last evening before returning to *Excalibur*, so Burgoyne intended to make the most of it. Captain Korsmo had been generous to grant hir two weeks of shore leave, and hir request had been duly approved by *Excalibur*'s first officer, Commander Shelby.

Keeten emerged from the water, letting it pour off his head and shoulders. Burgoyne was drawn to him. Desire had lurked in every word and look they exchanged. S/he leaned forward, hir lips brushing against his cheek and mouth. His arms slid around hir back, holding hir close. Just as s/he suspected, Keeten didn't need conversational foreplay like most other people. It would be like jumping into a raging fire—

"Burgoyne? I saw your lights on," a high, singsong voice called out. Sharanna, a diminutive woman with creamy gray skin and straight black hair, appeared on the open patio of Burgoyne's suite. "I thought I'd stop by before the party—" She stopped in confusion at the sight of Burgoyne embracing Keeten Planx in the water. "Oh! You're not alone. . . . You're not dressed!"

Burgoyne's fingers tightened on Keeten. S/he hoped that Sharanna would be polite enough to leave. But Sharanna had been in this very pool with Burgoyne yesterday, as well as the night before.

Her eyes blinked rapidly as her smile faded in realization. "Oh . . . *Burgoyne!*"

A world of pain and resentment was conveyed in hir name. "Sharanna, I thought we were going to meet at the party later." Burgoyne gestured to the Trill. "You know Keeten Planx."

"We've met," Sharanna said faintly.

At her tone, Keeten glanced at Burgoyne. They both knew that shore-leave romances were fleeting at best. But Sharanna was a higher-education student attending the tech school on Argelius II, so she wasn't an ordinary resort pickup. Burgoyne had found her in one of the native dance clubs. S/he always did like to sample the local cuisine.

"Sharanna," Burgoyne said reasonably. "Are you all right?" S/he almost got out of the water, but was afraid that would embarrass the rustic woman even more.

Keeten had no such qualms. He pushed himself up to sit on the edge of the pool. He seemed to care as little as Burgoyne about nudity. That was one thing s/he loved about joined Trill. They were mentally and emotionally free of the confines of gender, much like Hermats.

Keeten asked politely, "Why don't you join us for a swim?"

"Me?" Sharanna stared from him to Burgoyne. "With you? I don't think so!"

With that, Sharanna turned and fled.

"Sharanna!" Burgoyne jumped out of the pool and jogged after her. But she didn't pause, slamming the door closed between them.

Burgoyne felt sorry about hurting her feelings, but surely Sharanna hadn't expected more than a fling with a visiting Starfleet officer? Yet her reaction indicated she had become emotionally attached. Burgoyne dejectedly trailed water back to the pool.

"Now you're not moving so fast," Keeten commented.

For a moment, Burgoyne thought s/he had messed up hir chances with the Trill, too. "I'm sorry. I think she misunderstood my intentions."

"Too bad." A gleam rose in Keeten's eye. "Something similar happened to one of my previous hosts, but that time the guy joined in. I have to say, it's a highlight of my sexual memories."

"Well, you do get two in one with me," Burgoyne reminded him, slipping back into the pool.

"Maybe you should lock the door this time," Keeten suggested. "Who knows how many other jealous lovers you've managed to pick up during your shore leave?"

Burgoyne almost made a smart retort, but after Sharanna's reaction, it was no joke. S/he climbed out of the pool and went to lock the door.

Burgoyne almost got away clean from Argelius II. Keeten had been so much fun that s/he missed the late-night party in town. In the morning s/he commed Sharanna, but there was no answer. Burgoyne quickly recorded an apology, thinking it was better that way.

Then Burgoyne checked out of the fancy resort with a lighter heart. As bad as s/he felt about the misunderstanding, s/he really didn't want to go through a rehash of hir short yet intense affair with Sharanna.

In the transporter room of the resort, hir foot was lifted to step onto the disk when Sharanna appeared in the archway. "Burgoyne 172," she formally stated.

Almost, Burgoyne said to hirself. S/he forced herself to turn and smile warmly at Sharanna. It wasn't her fault that Burgoyne disliked needy, clingy lovers. "Sharanna! I tried calling you earlier. I didn't mean to hurt you."

"I know." Sharanna stood away stiffly, her expressive mouth twitching as she tried to remain impassive.

"I'm a traveling Hermat," Burgoyne reminded her. "I'm not like the rest of my people. I thought you understood."

"I do."

Burgoyne was afraid Sharanna was about to burst out in some kind of tirade. She had been so self-sufficient a few days ago, but now she looked emotionally unstable enough to make a scene in a public transporter room. Burgoyne hated that.

S/he glanced back at hir small traveling case sitting on the disk. *"Excalibur* is prepared to transport. But if you want to talk, I can tell them I've been delayed. We can go somewhere."

"No. I only wanted to give you this." Sharanna handed hir a cylindrical pendant that hung from a silver chain.

"Sharanna!" Now Burgoyne felt even more awkward with nothing to give her but apologies. "You don't have to do that."

"Take it." Her hand jerked the chain, making the filigreed cylinder bounce.

"Thank you." Burgoyne held up the pendant. The cylinder was as long as hir finger with silver caps and tiny bars forming a cage. Inside was a bristling crystal. The sharply fractured prisms of the crystal caught the light, casting bright rainbow chips into hir eyes. "It's beautiful! Is it a necklace?"

"It's from Rabolum, my home." Sharanna had talked often about her frontier homeworld. Her government had sent her along with a group of young technicians to Argelius II to get much-needed training so they could improve the industrial base of their planet. "I'm part of the *sacritorum* caste, so I have access to these sorts of pendants."

"Sharanna, I can't take this if it's some kind of national treasure!" Burgoyne tried to press the pendant back into her hands.

"It's private, but they're not all that rare on my planet." For the first time, she faintly smiled. "I knew you'd like it, Burgoyne. Sometime when you're alone, look into the crystal and think about me."

"Sharanna," Burgoyne said helplessly. S/he wanted to plead that s/he never meant to deceive her into sharing lust. But Sharanna already knew that.

"The transporter chief is waiting for you," Sharanna reminded hir.

Burgoyne stepped forward to hug her, but Sharanna turned away. Burgoyne got a shoulder in hir chest and a faceful of fine black hair.

So s/he marched back to the transporter disk. Holding the gift, Burgoyne forced hirself to smile at Sharanna. Then s/he glanced at the transporter chief. Hir eagerness to get away must have been clear, because he hardly waited for hir nod before beginning the dematerialization.

The transporter room faded into a sparkle of energized particles, and reformed as *Excalibur*'s main transporter room. Burgoyne enjoyed letting go during transport, relishing that glorious slide into nothingness. It felt thoroughly invigorating when s/he rematerialized.

Along with the chief on duty at the terminal, Commander Shelby was waiting in the transporter room. "Welcome back, Lieutenant," Shelby said briskly. "I hope your leave was pleasant?"

"Er—yeah, it was great." Burgoyne swept up hir traveling case, slinging Sharanna's present over the handle. "You'll never guess who I met, Commander. You should like this, since you served on board the *Enterprise.*"

"Never play guessing games with a tactician," Shelby reminded hir. "Who was it? Commander Data? Captain Picard?"

"No, a little older than that." Burgoyne grinned. "It was Chief Engineer Scott! I ran into him in a dive of a bar, drinking something he called 'scotch.' We talked warp engines for hours. That guy sure knows his stuff."

"You mean *Montgomery* Scott? Of Kirk's *Enterprise?*" Shelby raised her brows.

"I know that's a bit before your time, Commander. But it seems like everyone who's served on board *Enterprise* has a certain nostalgia for the old *Constitution*-class."

Shelby smiled, always the professional commanding officer, yet clearly trying to be friendly. That's why Burgoyne encouraged her. Some of the crew were put off by Shelby's forceful presence. But Burgoyne always like to give hir fellow crew members the benefit of the doubt. S/he had unearthed some real gems that way during hir Starfleet career.

"Once you've settled in," Shelby requested, "I'd like your assistance in creating a weekly maintenance schedule for the key engineering systems. Chief Engineer Argyle suggested you, Lieutenant."

"Sounds like a plan, Commander," Burgoyne agreed. It was a quick change from Argelius II, but s/he was ready to get back to work. "Just let me drop off my gear on the way."

Shelby nodded to the dangling cylinder. "That's pretty. Is it a souvenir?"

"Something like that."

Shelby looked at hir more closely. "Are you well, Lieutenant? We could wait until later to begin."

"No, I'm all right. It's just sometimes you get more than you expected from shore leave."

Burgoyne fell right back into the rhythms of being assistant chief engineer of the *Excalibur* and was so busy reconfiguring the constrictor coils on the warp core that s/he didn't have time to think about hir vacation on Argelius II. S/he also had to catch up with hir friends on board. That cute lieutenant in hydroponics was still interested in having fun during off-duty hours. Whenever anyone asked about hir shore leave, Burgoyne told them about Chief Engineer Scott. S/he didn't mention how hir sexual escapades had unfortunately gotten crossed.

But one evening, after a hearty dinner and faced with nothing special to do, s/he noticed Sharanna's gift draped over the table sculpture where s/he had tossed it that first day. S/he picked it up by the chain. Even though the

lights were dimmed, bright rainbow sparks flickered from the faceted crystal. The detailing on the cylindrical setting was also quite fine. Burgoyne
felt another pang at the thought of Sharanna giving up something precious. The pendant was so brilliant that it had to be special.

Burgoyne turned it, watching the tiny lights flash, wishing that Sharanna
could have enjoyed herself without getting overly attached. Burgoyne
hadn't seen it coming. Usually s/he had a good nose for anything that
smacked of possessiveness or commitment. S/he had talked about hir rov-
ing ways and travels in Starfleet until it had to be clear. Sharanna was fine
until she had stumbled on hir in the pool with Keeten. . . .

Then Burgoyne was standing in a strange house with windows on three
sides. She had never seen the place before, but it felt right somehow. The
interior held some low, beige furniture and glass tables with nothing to detract from the dramatic view. Purple, jagged mountains rose on every distant horizon, with varying tones indicating their relative closeness.
Nothing could be seen in between except for the undulating ground
frosted with lacy plants. The land was exposed, its dusty red and gray rocks
poking through the crust. But it felt *right*. . . .

"I'm home," s/he said experimentally. It was nothing like Hermat, but it
felt like home.

There was another scent layered above the dry, tangy breeze. Burgoyne's
nostrils flared as s/he turned. A female humanoid, that was certain. But
s/he couldn't pin down the undefined textures.

Burgoyne followed hir nose into the adjoining room. There stood a female. Burgoyne couldn't quite see her face but her voice sounded professional like Shelby's. She spoke as if everything were perfectly evident. Yet
as hard as Burgoyne tried, s/he couldn't understand what the woman was
saying.

The emotions Burgoyne felt were the most important thing. S/he was
tied to this woman. S/he could only go closer, s/he couldn't pull away. This
woman was hir partner, and they lived in this house together in domestic
bliss—

Burgoyne wrenched hirself away, every fiber of hir being resisting the lure
of those feelings. That wasn't hir! S/he would rather die than wither away
in boredom with one woman for the rest of hir life.

Panting, s/he sat on the sofa in hir own quarters on board *Excalibur*.
S/he tossed the pendant away in disgust, not wanting it anywhere near hir.

As Burgoyne gradually calmed down, s/he realized that Sharanna had laid a trap for hir. That little scene of coupled happiness was Sharanna's dream, not hirs. Burgoyne wanted nothing more than variety and change—she was a rolling meteorite in space. That piece of hallucinogenic crystal had it all wrong.

But after a while, Burgoyne was able to laugh about it. At least s/he didn't feel bad about Sharanna anymore. Obviously a girl who could pull a prank like that could take care of herself.

Yet the engineer in Burgoyne was curious enough to overcome everything else. How could the crystal invoke a hallucination without some sort of energy exchange?

Burgoyne set up hir tricorder to record everything that happened. Taking a deep breath, s/he stared into the crystal again, counting off the seconds. S/he also braced hirself to feel that awful, stifling sensation of dependency on someone else.

S/he thought it wasn't working at first; then s/he found hirself back in that desolate house with hir shadowy partner. S/he was aware of what was happening, and this time s/he fought the fuzziness, trying to discover the identity of the woman. S/he expected it to be Sharanna. But the scene played out exactly as before, as if the tracks of hir vision had been permanently laid down the first time.

When Burgoyne snapped out of it, everything was the same, except this time the tricorder was running. S/he eagerly checked the readings, but there were only nineteen seconds, exactly what s/he had counted, between the time s/he started looking into the crystal and when s/he shook hir head, reaching for the tricorder. But the vision felt as though it had lasted two minutes from beginning to end. Apparently it was all in hir mind.

Burgoyne tossed the pendant into a drawer and tried to forget about it. S/he was a big Hermat and could handle it.

S/he forced the image of that shadowy mate from hir mind and read the latest technical manual on Ambassador-class shield generators from cover to cover. Yawning, s/he eventually went to bed. But s/he couldn't sleep. It wasn't because of that unnerving feeling that s/he could actually be in a partnership. S/he decided it was anger at Sharanna for forcing hir to feel that way nonconsensually.

Burgoyne had unfortunately run into some humanoids who culturally didn't approve of free love. They restricted sex into certain strict categories that were considered to be "acceptable." But Burgoyne had never lived hir life according to what other people thought. That was one reason s/he had

352 Susan Wright

left Hermat, because hir homeworld was claustrophobically closed. S/he had broken free so s/he could be completely true to hirself.

Sharanna wasn't going to have the last word.

Burgoyne got up and put on an off-duty sarong and tank top. Holding the pendant gingerly by the chain, s/he went down to engineering. Everything looked the same, but there was no one around. That's what s/he liked about gamma shift. A person could concentrate without distractions.

S/he went into the diagnostic and repair room on the upper deck of engineering. The level-one diagnostic unit was empty. Often it was occupied by faulty phasers or components that were rigged for operation while an intensive scan was performed. Burgoyne knew this machine inside and out. If anything could figure out how Sharanna's crystal worked, a level-one diagnostic would do the job.

The pendant fit into the small slotted clamp. Burgoyne positioned it inside the imaging chamber and closed the hatch. When s/he could no longer see the crystal, s/he relaxed. S/he would likely have to trigger it again under the diagnostic for a complete reading, but s/he wasn't looking forward to it. That deadly dull feeling made hir spine crawl.

First s/he physically verified the operational test sequences. A diagram of the pendant appeared on the screen of the terminal. There were two major components—the cage and the crystal. The cylindrical cage was unremarkable; a mix of silver, tin, and various other minerals.

The crystal, on the other hand, was unusual. Instead of a lattice of atoms, it was actually a crystallized energy field. That's why hir tricorder had detected nothing. But if it was a stasis field, there could be something inside. Burgoyne had never seen a stasis field so tiny, or one that didn't require a continuous energy source to be maintained. Internal quantum mechanics could account for the generation of the energy field, but no system could be completely closed.

It took some time, and Burgoyne had to open the viewport on the diagnostic unit and look at the pendant one last time, to get the key. S/he shuddered as s/he came out of the vision of the desert home with hir partner. S/he was almost gagging at the cloying, stupefying sensation of being stuck with one person.

But s/he finally unraveled the mystery. The tiny stasis field wasn't uniformly maintained. Every twenty-six-point-eight-seven seconds there was a pulse that allowed a few subatomic quanta to be released. These particles resembled chronitons, but with significant variations, including a shortened life span. The diagnostic unit designated them as chronometric particles.

Chronometric particles were temporally charged. The diagnostic indicated that the particles decayed within thirty centimeters. When Burgoyne queried the diagnostic unit about how chronometrics would affect humanoid brains, the answer was: *"Symptoms include sensory distortions, time displacement, and hallucinations."*

It only took a simple computer query to get citations for chronometric particles. One Starfleet deep-space-exploration ship, the *Equulus,* had harvested chronometric particles from a temporal vortex nearly seventy years ago. The vortex was four light-years from an inhabited system, outside of Federation space at that time. Rabolum was the name of the fourth planet from the sun—Sharanna's homeworld.

So that explained it. The pulsed stasis field allowed enough particles to escape to induce a short-term vision. Sharanna's *sacritorum* caste probably used pendants like this to control people on Rabolum, giving them visions that conformed to their cultural values. Burgoyne shuddered at the idea. At least s/he was well away from Sharanna.

Burgoyne felt much better knowing the vision was the ordinary result of a known physical property. S/he liked understanding how things worked.

The stasis was the most interesting part. If s/he could duplicate the stasis field, that could have real practical uses. Using a tachyon-particle stream, Burgoyne tried to get a reading on the stasis field itself. But it was impenetrable. There was a spike in the readings only when the pulse occurred. But the diagnostic unit could barely detect the chronometric particles. There wasn't enough time to get a fix on the internal dynamics of the field itself.

Burgoyne initialized an antiproton beam and focused it on the crystallized stasis field. If the computer timed it perfectly, the beam could lodge open the pulse, allowing the diagnostic unit to get a thorough scan of the interior. Since the chronometric particles had affected hir only at close proximity, it should be safe.

"Here goes," Burgoyne muttered as s/he triggered the antiproton beam.

Burgoyne realized s/he was running in long strides, down on hir hands and bare feet, stretching to cover the grass-covered hills and meadows. It felt good to let loose without having to worry about mowing down people or avoiding things in the way. S/he was on Hermat, where life was free-range all the way.

Another Hermat appeared beside hir, catching up. Burgoyne was spurred ahead, trying to beat the other Hermat, who laughed as s/he gamely kept pace. This other Hermat was hir lover, even though Burgoyne didn't know hir name. That wasn't unusual on hir homeworld. Hir lover was sleek and powerful, with a sense of humor to match Burgoyne's because s/he apparently delighted in the chase.

There was a settlement on the banks of a river ahead, a place where they could get food and a soft place to sleep for the night. The distant sounds of singing and drum-beating indicated it was a party night, which would make things even more exciting.

But hir lover caught hir there on the hills and brought Burgoyne rolling down into the grass. Burgoyne grabbed hold, carrying hir lover along with hir. They slowed to a halt, already kissing in passion. Burgoyne didn't mind sleeping outside under the stars. S/he had hir tricorder in hir hip belt with the latest technical specs on reactant injector valves that would give hir interesting reading tomorrow. Meanwhile, s/he had a lovely new Hermat to play with.

It was all so familiar and sweet, much like Burgoyne's adolescence, that s/he didn't realize what was happening until it faded away. . . .

Burgoyne was sitting in someone's quarters. The moving stars in the window indicated it was a spaceship. The bedcovers were twisted together, and the scattered padds, disks, clothing, and containers indicated that the inhabitant wasn't too picky about cleanliness. That meant it wasn't Burgoyne's quarters, because s/he would never be able to live in such a mess.

This time Burgoyne knew that something was wrong. S/he had been on Hermat with a lover. Before that s/he was experimenting with the stasis field on Sharanna's pendant. The chronometric particles must be leaking from the diagnostic unit, because s/he was hallucinating again.

"How about later, when we get off duty?" someone called as the shower turned off.

"What?" Burgoyne tried to snap out of the vision by pure will, but that no longer seemed to work.

A youthful blond head poked around the screen. He looked every inch an ensign, fresh out of Starfleet Academy. "I said, how about tonight? Dinner in the mess?"

Burgoyne didn't know the guy, but it felt familiar. His wide-open eyes were reeling in amazement. Apparently this was his first sexual experience with someone who broke all physical boundaries. Burgoyne was used to being desired because s/he was exotic. It made hir feel special to know that lovers never forgot hir. This lover was obviously still panting with eagerness to find out what other remarkable things s/he could do in bed. He was one of many young ensigns who were exploring the galaxy in their own special way.

"Sure, why not?" Burgoyne felt compelled to say, as s/he did whenever s/he was in that situation. S/he had agreed to have dinner with Sharanna back on Argelius II, and look what happened then. . . .

Burgoyne was back on Hermat, reclining in the baths. S/he could tell it was one of the larger settlements, because of the old frescoed walls and the variety of shallow cold and hot pools stretching into the greenish gloom. It was evening and the trees around the open baths shaded the last lingering light.

When s/he moved, pain shot into hir arms and down hir legs. It wasn't an injury, as s/he soon discovered, but a general stiffness in hir joints and muscles. S/he stopped fighting it and lay back in the soothing warm water.

In the back of hir mind, s/he knew s/he was hallucinating. S/he had just been on a starship, and before that running across Hermat. But it felt so real. S/he really was an aged Hermat who had come back to die among hir own people.

A tumble of prepubescent children poured into the baths. It was one of the child gangs that roamed Hermat. They must have chosen this settlement as their stopping ground for tonight. Some gangs would stay for weeks, while others would move on the next day. It depended on what the kids wanted to do. If it was surfing, they went to the beach. If it was climbing, they went to the mountains. Children grew up quicker on Hermat than anywhere else.

Burgoyne fondly watched the dozen or so young Hermats as they splashed into the baths among the adults. S/he wasn't the only one who indulgently let the young ones disrupt the calm of hir pool. S/he loved to see them rub their shiny wet bodies together, already engaging in the ancient dance that would lead to sex when they were old enough.

Laughter, fun, and sex had long been Burgoyne's motto. S/he'd had a full lifetime of lovers, more than s/he could remember. Even though s/he knew it wasn't really happening, it seemed like a fitting end for an old Starfleet codger to sit in the baths and watch the newest generation play. . . .

The visions kept changing, one after the other endlessly. More lovers in strange places, on planets Burgoyne had never seen, on ships s/he had never heard of. Always more sex, fun, and laughter. Throughout it all, s/he knew that s/he belonged back on *Excalibur.*

But the visions kept coming. Most of them involved relationships with a bewildering variety of aliens, each with their own unique sexual passions. S/he knew that Sharanna had no idea how effective her revenge would be.

Commander Shelby appeared in the door to the diagnostic room. When Burgoyne didn't answer her calls, the computer gave Shelby hir location. "Lieutenant, we were supposed to have a meeting to finalize these maintenance schedules—"

Burgoyne was sitting stock-still in front of the diagnostic unit, staring at the screen.

"Burgoyne?" Shelby asked. But the Hermat didn't respond. Hir eyes were fixed open. Hir arms were rigid and hir head didn't move. Even hir breathing seemed shallow.

The diagram on the screen of the unit showed a cylinder. It took a moment before Shelby realized it was that pretty souvenir Burgoyne had brought back from Argelius II. The filigreed silver casing seemed delicate in the clamp, but the rapidly scrolling readout indicated there was furious activity happening inside the diagnostic unit.

Shelby's hand hit her combadge. "Captain, we have a problem in engineering!"

After too many visions to count, Burgoyne fell into one that was familiar. S/he was back in the windowed house that looked out on distant, barren mountains. Except now, the sky was lit with orange and red neon fire. At first Burgoyne thought it was a battle. Then s/he realized it was a sunset. It looked too lurid to be real, but the colors gradually changed and intensified as the sun disappeared.

Burgoyne went toward the adjoining room to see hir shadowy mate. Her back was facing Burgoyne, but this time when the woman spoke s/he could hear her. "The optimum boiling time is different depending on your elevation."

Now Burgoyne was sure it wasn't Sharanna. The cadence of her voice was different, cool, and detached, whereas Sharanna could barely contain her emotions.

Burgoyne went forward, but s/he somehow knew that s/he couldn't simply put hir arms around this woman. She needed to be wooed carefully.

It wasn't real, but Burgoyne tried to hold on to the moment. Before s/he thought it was boring and stifling, but after that never-ending whirl of visions with one person after the other, it felt safe and comforting. It was easier for hir to stand near this woman and know that s/he didn't have to search for the next lover, and the next one, and the next one. This woman accepted hir for who s/he was, and had chosen to be with hir.

Burgoyne closed hir eyes and took a deep breath, relaxing in the security of love, rejecting the frenetic excitement of variety. S/he felt herself slipping, as if being drawn into another vision, but s/he resisted. S/he wanted to stay right where s/he was. The feeling expanded and lingered for a long time—

"Burgoyne!" Commander Shelby exclaimed.

A hand caught Burgoyne's shoulder as s/he started to slump. S/he was back in the diagnostic room.

"Lieutenant, are you all right?" Shelby asked anxiously.

Burgoyne brushed hir forehead, feeling hir eyeballs scratching against hir lids. "What happened?"

"I found you here when you didn't show up for our meeting this morning."

A medic was on the other side, passing the tricorder over hir skull and chest. "There's no permanent physical damage. Your vital signs are normalizing. But you should get up and move around, Lieutenant. It looks like you've been sitting here for hours."

Burgoyne stumbled as s/he stood up and had to grab on to Shelby's arm to steady hirself. "Thanks."

"We shut off the antiproton beam," Shelby explained, "and encapsulated the stray chronometric particles within a stasis bubble. They should decay in a week or so." She gestured to the mobile stasis unit. "What were you trying to do, Lieutenant?"

Burgoyne glanced at the diagnostic unit, where one of the other engineering assistants was carefully removing the pendant from the clamp. "I wanted to find out how the stasis field worked."

The engineering assistant aimed her tricorder at the cylinder. "It doesn't work anymore. You must have broken it."

Burgoyne took the pendant, almost afraid to look into it again. But it was different now, darkened and inert. It no longer flashed rainbow colors. All that was left of the crystal was a spiky mesh framework. "The particles must have been released. That means the stasis field was powered by them. That's not much use to us."

"Next time work with a partner when you experiment, Lieutenant,"

Shelby told hir with a pat on the arm. "For now, I think we need to reschedule that meeting."

"The lieutenant should go stretch a bit, then rest," the medic agreed, packing up his gear. "Let me know if you have any problems."

Burgoyne thanked them again and quickly retreated, hoping to avoid the chief engineer, who would surely ask too many questions. S/he was still clutching the cylinder in hir fist when s/he reached hir quarters. Part of hir hoped it would flare to life again, but it remained dim.

News of hir nighttime experiment would spread throughout the ship by tomorrow. S/he would get a laugh or two, but it wouldn't be taken seriously. Burgoyne knew s/he couldn't tell anyone what had happened. It was too private.

It also made hir wonder if maybe Commander Shelby wasn't the only one who had snapped hir out of it. Burgoyne was sure that final vision was important. It had gone on for much longer than the others. And hir feelings no longer seemed absurd. That unceasing round of lovers had gotten as monotonous as a driving beat, while the one lone scene of hir standing close to hir partner had felt good.

Maybe it wasn't so outrageous. After all, Burgoyne had always chosen to do the unexpected, and what would be more unexpected than for hir to fall in love?

CALHOUN & SHELBY
A Little Getaway

Peter David

After the destruction of the *Ambassador*-class *U.S.S. Excalibur*, Captain Calhoun was believed killed. When he returned alive and well, he asked Captain Shelby to marry him, which she accepted after belting him. Before he took command of the new *Galaxy*-class *Excalibur*, and before Shelby took over the *Trident*, the two of them went on their honeymoon. "A Little Getaway" is the story of that happy occasion . . .

Peter David

Peter David is still at large.

"We're going to *Xenex?*"

Newlywed Elizabeth Shelby had been looking forward to an increase in the quality and frequency of communication with her longtime love, sparring partner, rival, and commanding officer, Mackenzie Calhoun. They were, after all, husband and wife, married in a ceremony officiated by Jean-Luc Picard that could be called, at best, impromptu, on the bridge of Calhoun's once and future command, the *Excalibur.*

The truth was that every fragment of Shelby's common sense had warned her that marrying Calhoun was folly. But, hell, the man had literally come back from the dead to ask for her hand in marriage. How could any woman, any person, with a fragment of romance in their soul, walk away from a situation such as that?

Very easily if she had any brains, Shelby was starting to think.

Calhoun, after having undergone a debriefing so that Starfleet knew exactly what his whereabouts had been during the time he'd been believed dead, had been given two weeks' time to rest, recuperate, and honeymoon with his brand-new bride. ("During which time, Shelby will no doubt repeatedly debrief him as well," Kat Mueller had deadpanned, a comment that had gotten puzzled looks from some crewmen and guffaws from others.) Calhoun owned a state-of-the-art runabout, which had been moved to the new *Excalibur,* almost in a sort of in memoriam gesture. So it was conveniently there when the happy couple required it.

Crew members had assembled on the holodeck, armed with handfuls of rice to be thrown, a tradition that was incomprehensible to Calhoun, who thought it represented a collective desire that they put more fiber in their diet. Shelby had explained that it represented a hope for fertility, which had sent Calhoun into such spasms of laughter that she wished she'd said that yes, it represented fiber. For his part, Picard had taken the opportunity to make reservations for them at the resort world of Risa, generously offering to pick up the cost as a present to the newlyweds. So Risa was, naturally, where Shelby was anticipating they were going to go.

That anticipation took an abrupt U-turn when she saw the coordinates Calhoun had entered into the nav computer and the intended destination.

"We're going to *Xenex?*" It was the second time she'd said it, because Calhoun had simply nodded the first time.

"That's what I was hoping," said Calhoun. "Well, my love . . . let's fire up the engines and not keep all the nice folks waiting for our depart—"

"Hold it!" Shelby said, standing. "Nothing's getting fired up, Mac, including you on our wedding night tonight, until you explain this. Xenex? Your homeworld?"

"It's the only Xenex I know of."

"Why?" she demanded.

He sighed heavily. "I'm sorry. You're right. I shouldn't have assumed. I mean, it would only add a day to the trip, but it wasn't a given that—"

"Spare me the halfhearted apologies, Calhoun. What's going on?" She leaned against the console, her arms folded, clearly not backing down.

"All right . . . look," said Calhoun. "I know that Picard conducted the ceremony, and in the eyes of the Federation and Starfleet it's all legal, proper, aboveboard . . ."

"But . . . ?" she prompted.

"But . . . I am Xenexian. Before I was Starfleet . . . before I was anything . . . I was, and am, Xenexian."

"I know that, Mac," she said, beginning to have a suspicion what the problem was. "And I know it hasn't always been easy for you, balancing the heritage and upbringing you have with the man that your time in Starfleet has made you become." She reached over and ruffled his hair affectionately. Then she glanced at the view on the monitor. The folks outside were looking impatient. "Okay, so . . . Xenex . . ."

"In the eyes of Xenexian society," said Calhoun, "our marriage wouldn't be considered legal. We would need to be married in a ceremony conducted by the village shaman. Otherwise, I'd feel like . . ." Then he stopped and shook his head. "But this isn't your problem, Eppy. You're looking forward to the honeymoon, and you've taken such a leap of faith in marrying me already. This is my problem, not yours, and if the Federation considers us married, that should be all that matters. . . ."

"But it's not," Shelby said. "What matters to you, Mac, matters to me. That's what being married is all about. You've made it clear it's important

to you, and all the backtracking you're now trying to do, out of consideration for me . . . well, it's sweet because it is being considerate of me, but it's
unnecessary. I feel good about our being married, Mac. No . . . I feel great
about it. And I don't want there to be any impediment to your feeling
great about it as well. And it's one day. One day out of the rest of our married life. Besides, let's face facts: Being married won't be easy. We'll be
spending a good portion of our time apart, in separate commands. I want
our bonds to be as strong as possible, and if that means having a second ceremony on Xenex, I'm all for it."

"Really?"

"Really." She smiled.

A minute later, the runabout lifted off, and the crew members pelted the
vessel with rice as it headed for the forcefield door. It eased through the
field, the atmosphere in the shuttlebay staying neatly intact behind it.

The moment they were gone, Zak Kebron said loudly, "All right. Taking
bets as to how long it will last."

Activity was fast and furious.

It had been many years since Shelby had set foot on Xenex, and it was
every bit as hot and uninviting as she remembered. But Calhoun was grinning ear to ear the moment they disembarked from the runabout, and that
alone was enough to make her smile as well. Then again, they'd had a fes-
tive and very active wedding night, so it seemed natural that he'd been in
an exceedingly good mood. She thought it was sweet the way he kept
reaching over, touching her hand or her shoulder, especially since he'd
never been that much of a touchy-feely person before. When she'd made
an observation about his attitude, he'd simply said, "It helps me to believe
you're actually here." That seemed even sweeter.

"Amazing," Calhoun said, gesturing around at the spaceport where
they'd landed. "None of this was here years ago. Now look how built up
it is."

"Built up" was hardly the phrase Shelby would have used. It was one of
the smallest spaceports she'd ever been to, with exactly two landing fields as
opposed to the typical nine or ten, and no conveniences for the transporting of luggage. But Calhoun seemed impressed by it, and she had to suppose that, for him, it was impressive. He had, after all, walked this world
when he was little more than a savage fighting for his world's freedom, and
even a simple glass of water was considered an amenity. So she supposed it
was all relative.

Calhoun obtained a land skimmer to take them the fairly short distance to his home territory of Calhoun, the location that had provided him the last name he'd adopted for his career in Starfleet. "Mackenzie Calhoun" was a much easier name for non-Xenexians to say than his given name of M'k'n'zy of Calhoun.

Upon arriving in Calhoun, he was greeted boisterously by other Xenexians, who spoke at him in their rapid-fire native tongue. They'd received advance word of Calhoun's survival when he'd previously been believed dead, so naturally there were joyous greetings from all. The Universal Translator handled it all for Shelby, of course, but she was nevertheless struck by how raunchy and racy virtually all of the Xenexian expressions were. "You look well!" for instance, was literally translated as "I wager your genitals have not shrunk!" It wasn't enough to bring a flush of embarrassment to Shelby's cheeks, but it was sufficient to throw her slightly off her stride. Nor did any of the Xenexians make the slightest pretense of doing anything other than openly sizing her up. They looked her up and down as if assessing a potential racehorse, and they were quite vocal in their appraisals. Some dismissed her as "too stringy," which made it sound like they were considering whether she'd make a good meal. Others, however, nodded approvingly, and made candid comments about which parts of her anatomy were the most pleasing.

In short, the Xenexians displayed a total lack of tact. So much so, in fact, that it gave her a new, fuller appreciation for all the strides that Calhoun had made in his time with Starfleet. Her husband might have been a maverick with little regard for rules and regulations, but at least he didn't meet women and say, "Your hips seem more than adequate for childbearing."

D'ndai, Calhoun's brother, was not on Xenex, a discovery that disappointed and frustrated Calhoun. D'ndai was ostensibly in important meetings on Danter and couldn't get away. "He's there so much, one would almost think he was becoming Danteri," grumbled more than one of the Xenexians, who looked to D'ndai for leadership. From Calhoun's grim expression, it seemed to Shelby that possible problems for D'ndai might be arising in the near future if these attitudes among his people continued.

Finally, Calhoun turned to her and said, "This way." Cutting through the throng, shaking hands, assuring them that he'd take the time to continue conversations later, he led her across the city. The buildings were all very simple, built low to the ground, and although Calhoun kept commenting on how living conditions on Xenex had improved, it still looked terribly primitive to her. But Shelby was, first and foremost, a Starfleet officer, and she refused to sit in judgment on the Xenexians.

"Here," Calhoun said finally when they stopped in front of one particular house. It was smaller than the others, and the exterior was covered with various symbols and signs that Shelby couldn't begin to comprehend. Calhoun saw the way she was looking at them, and said by way of explanation, "They're prayer symbols, asking the gods for strength, wisdom, and guidance."

"Ah," said Shelby. "Well, they're very nice. Very striking. Is this the residence of the shaman . . . ?"

"Yes." He nodded. "B'ndri. He has been the shaman here since I was very young. He seemed ancient to me even then, so I can't even begin to guess how he'll look now. But he was always supportive of me, particularly when I took on the responsibilities of warlord. If he hadn't been behind me, I doubt I would have gotten the confidence of the people . . . or perhaps even had confidence in myself."

"I find it hard to picture you without confidence in yourself," Shelby said with a grin.

Calhoun returned the grin, and then knocked on the edge of the front door. There was silence from within for a moment, and then a gravelly voice said, "Come, M'k'n'zy."

Shelby and Calhoun exchanged glances. "How did he know?" she asked.

He shrugged. "He just does." Then he led the way in and she followed, feeling a bit tentative and mentally assuring herself there was no need for her to be that way. She had met any number of planetary dignitaries under a vast array of circumstances. Granted, this had a certain personal involvement, but nevertheless, it shouldn't be anything she couldn't handle.

The moment she entered the small house, she started wondering if she was wrong.

There was exactly one room in the place, and the man she presumed to be the shaman was seated directly in the middle of it. He was wearing long blue robes, with a gray beard dangling from the point of his chin, and his lighter gray hair splayed around his head as if it had exploded there instead of growing upon it in orderly fashion. His eyebrows were so thick that it was difficult to see his eyes beneath them. He was seated cross-legged upon the floor, his hands resting upon his knees. The room itself was devoid of furnishings. If he had possessions, Shelby couldn't see where they were.

Calhoun bowed deeply to him, and Shelby immediately imitated. "I bring greetings, B'ndri," said Calhoun. "It has been a long time."

"Too long, M'k'n'zy," replied B'ndri, "so long that I have come to believe you have forgotten your roots." The problem was, he wasn't looking at Calhoun. He was looking at Shelby.

"Never, B'ndri," Calhoun said.

"You say never. Yet you do not even call yourself M'k'n'zy anymore, do you?" Still he was focused on Shelby. It was disconcerting.

"It was painful to hear offworlders pronounce it," said Calhoun lightly, clearly trying to bring some levity to the proceedings. Unsurprisingly, B'ndri didn't so much as crack a smile. Calhoun cleared his throat loudly and said, "B'ndri, it is with the greatest supplication that I present you my mate, Elizabeth Paula Shelby. Elizabeth, this is the honorable B'ndri."

To play it safe, she bowed again. "A great honor indeed, sir," she said.

He looked her up and down, and then finally stared at Calhoun. "This is one of those who has weakened you."

"What?" said Shelby.

"What?" echoed Calhoun, shaking his head. "Honored one, no. She has been a source of strength, not weakness. I've learned much from her . . ."

"And I from him," Shelby quickly added. "That's why we're so good for each other. We shore up each other's weaknesses . . ."

"The world you represent is the only weakness that M'k'n'zy has had to contend with," B'ndri told her. "He was a great man, a great leader, before he left here."

"And I still am," Calhoun said flatly. She could see that he was becoming more irritated with each passing moment. "Honored one, with all the respect in the world . . . . you seem ready to pass judgment on me, and on Elizabeth, so quickly . . . yet you hardly know us. . . ."

"That," B'ndri said, "is precisely the point, M'k'n'zy. Once, you were someone I knew. Someone I knew better than he knew himself. I look at you now . . . and it is as if the M'k'n'zy I knew is gone. As if his warrior heart has been cut out."

Calhoun looked visibly staggered at that, and it was more than Shelby could take. She kept her voice neutral, polite, but there was undeniable iron in it as well. "Again, with all respect, sir . . . you're wrong."

"Eppy," Calhoun tried to say.

But she'd started talking and wouldn't back off. "This man, whether you call him M'k'n'zy or Mackenzie, has more of a warrior heart than anyone I've ever met. It's what has gotten him through all of the challenges he's had to face, be it adjusting to the world of Starfleet or facing down death itself. He never gives up, never stops believing in himself. It's the thing that most attracts me to him."

"Indeed. You are attracted to it . . . because you yourself do not possess it?"

Shelby was thunderstruck that he would say such a thing, but it was Calhoun who immediately responded. "No, B'ndri. Not at all. Elizabeth has just as strong and determined a heart as me. I couldn't love her, marry her, if she did not."

"So I am to take your choosing to wed this woman as sufficient proof that she is what you say she is. That she is a fit mate?" asked B'ndri. "I am to substitute your judgment for my own? Have you grown so far from our ways, M'k'n'zy, that that is what you would expect of me?"

And Shelby saw the darkening of the scar on Calhoun's face. She knew what it meant, knew that his temper was starting to become inflamed. Obviously he had come into this situation with a set of expectations as to how it would go, and what he was getting instead was so far away from those expectations that he was having trouble keeping himself in check. "B'ndri," Calhoun said with exaggerated attempt at self-control, "your support, your blessing . . . means a great deal to me. But Elizabeth means the world to me, and if you're unable to—"

"Wait," Shelby interrupted, and Calhoun looked at her curiously. She reached over, put a hand on his arm, and said softly, "Don't try to diminish what this means to you. I know you. I can see it in your eyes, in your face. Let me try to make this right."

"But . . ."

"Please." And before he could say anything else, she turned to B'ndri and said, "What would I have to do?"

"Do?" said B'ndri, challenge in his voice.

"You spoke of substituting Mac's . . . M'k'n'zy's," she said, stumbling over the pronunciation as best she could, "judgment for your own. But you can't make a judgment based on nothing. There must be something, some sort of procedure. Questions you can ask, traditions. I know cultures such as yours. They're always steeped in traditions."

"Eppy, you don't know what you're saying," Calhoun told her.

"She speaks accurately enough for one who doesn't know," B'ndri observed, and that comment bolstered her confidence.

"All right, then," Shelby said. "You're the shaman. The wise man. If there are any procedures, any official ways to test worthiness, you would know them."

"I would," he said, "and there are."

"Eppy, for the love of God, this isn't necessary. . . ."

"Yes, it is," she told him. "The shaman claims he knows you better than you know yourself. Well, to some degree, I do, too. You're willing to walk away from this on my behalf, but I know you. It took a lot for you to admit to me that this meant a great deal to you in the first place. Try to diminish it now, and that will only make its absence worse. I won't be responsible for that."

"Eppy, you don't have to prove anything to me."

"Well, maybe I have to prove something to myself," she said. "You came a long way to be a part of my world, Mac. Maybe, before we embark on our wedded life together, I should try to come a little way toward being part of yours." She turned back to the shaman. "I'm sure there's some sort of official words, but let me just say it this way: I desire your blessing on our union, and I desire for you to conduct a ceremony that will join us, in the eyes of the gods of Xenex, as mates. Whatever I need do to prove to you I'm worthy of this blessing, tell me and I'll do."

"Very well," said the shaman. "The tests will begin immediately."

"*Grozit,* no," Calhoun immediately said, and turned to Shelby. "Eppy, listen to me. You don't understand. This is an ancient series of rituals that we almost never do anymore. You won't be able to handle it. This is supposed to be our honeymoon. It's not right that—"

Shelby bristled at that. "What do you mean, 'won't be able to handle it'? I'm a Starfleet officer, Mac, and I'm also your wife. Don't underestimate me, and don't underestimate what I can handle."

"The rituals will take three days," said the shaman.

"See?" Calhoun said quickly. "Three days. We're supposed to be on Risa by tomorrow morning. . . ."

"Then Risa will wait," Shelby said firmly. "Mac . . . you came back from the dead for me. I can do this for you. And don't you dare, ever, tell me there's something I can't handle. It's insulting."

"I'm just trying to protect you."

"I can take care of myself," said Shelby.

★   ★   ★

They were given temporary quarters, and Shelby was marched off for the first of the trials.

Calhoun sat there and waited, worrying. He sat there as the sun crawled across the Xenexian sky and, ever so slowly, set.

Finally he heard footsteps at the door and rose.

Shelby entered. Her face was streaked with dirt. Half of one of her eyebrows was burned off. Her hair was disheveled, her eyes were bloodshot. Her left nostril was caked with blood.

"Eppy," Calhoun said softly, and started toward her.

She put up a hand and whispered, "Piece of cake. No problem."

"Eppy, let's just get out of here. This is—"

"Remember survival training?" she asked, her voice still a whisper. "This . . . doesn't even come close to that. It's . . . it's nice to know . . . I can still handle it. Don't worry about it. Just . . . help me get . . . my clothes off . . . wash me down . . . maybe . . . we can even make the night . . . interesting."

He did as she asked. And once her clothes were off and he'd washed the soil and dirt from her, she promptly fell asleep, curled up naked against him. He held her close, shaking his head. "You're crazy," he said quietly, and resolved to get her out of there first thing next morning.

When he woke up, she was already gone. She'd left behind a note that said, "Don't you even think about interfering."

The day passed slowly. Calhoun thought he was going to go out of his mind with worry.

When the sun set, Shelby staggered in. She was limping. Her other eyebrow was completely gone. She had small red bumps all over her skin. "What the hell . . . ?"

"Insect bites," she said, her voice hoarse. She held up a tube. "They . . . gave me this for them. Clear 'em right up. . . ."

"Eppy, this is insane! The hell with the shaman! The hell with *all* of them! We're leaving *right now!*"

"The only way I'm leaving," she told him, surprising strength in her voice, "is if you pick me up and carry me out of here."

"Not a problem," said Calhoun.

He reached for her, and she promptly backed up, even though her legs were wavering. She leaned against the wall to shore herself up. "Don't touch me," she said.

"Well, those are the words that every husband wants to hear during his honeymoon," he said. "Elizabeth, what are you trying to prove here? That you can be as stubborn and pigheaded as me? Okay. Fine. You've proven it. Now let's go."

"You know what, Calhoun," she rasped out. "Sometimes not everything in the galaxy is about you. Sometimes things get to be about me."

"I got you into this, Eppy! How in the name of all that's holy is this possibly about you?"

"Because maybe I want to prove something to myself instead of you."

"And what would that be?" he demanded, fists on his hips.

"You showed up, years ago, at the Academy. This . . . this . . ." she gestured helplessly. "This guy. This barbarian. There, I said it. Barbarian. And you went and proved that you could be as good as anybody we had at the Academy. Better. Well, maybe what I need to prove is that I can come into your world and prove that I can be as good as any Xenexian woman."

"But you *can't!*" and he immediately regretted saying it as he saw her expression. Quickly he tried to repair the damage. "Eppy . . . it's a different environment. A different culture. Xenexian women . . . particularly in the ancient times that spawned these tests . . . they were bred from birth to withstand all manner of challenges, physical and mental, that simply aren't part of your world. It's ludicrous to expect you to make up for that gap in upbringing simply out of sheer willpower. It's too grotesquely unfair to you. It's not a proper test of the type of woman you are."

"I disagree. I think it's exactly the type of test I need . . . and maybe the type you need as well."

"I don't need a . . ."

She gripped him by the shoulder and said intensely, "Bull. You do. Admit it. You think you're superior to me. That your culture, your upbringing are superior to mine."

"I thought you said not everything in the galaxy is about me."

"I lied. Happy? Admit it."

"No. I don't feel that way."

"Yes, you do. You always have. You think you know better than me about everything. About how to live. About how to think. About rules, about conduct, about . . ."

"Eppy!" He was stunned by the vehemence in her voice. "If you feel this way about me, if you're so convinced I think so little of you, why the hell did you marry me in the first place? Maybe this was a huge mistake!"

"Maybe it was," she said.

They stood there for a long moment, and she started to tremble. He thought she was going to cry, and he reached for her. But she brought her arms up and brushed him away. He stepped back and she fought for control, finally achieving it.

She held up the cream.

"Would you rub this on me, please?" she asked.

He did so and they spoke no more that night.

The next morning she was gone again. This time Calhoun did not simply stay within their quarters. Instead he asked around, trying to determine where she'd been taken, but he was unable to do so. The shaman was gone as well. Presumably he'd gone with her. To make matters worse, the weather had chosen that day to get bad, and within an hour of his awakening, Calhoun was faced with a torrent of rainfall. The people of Xenex were grateful, naturally, for the precipitation, as the rainfall had been light this year. Calhoun was livid. He was more than prepared to try and track Shelby to wherever she was, but the downpour effectively erased everything from spoors to footprints. After a half-hour of coming up empty, a frustrated Calhoun returned to their domicile to wait.

He considered jumping in the runabout, flying out from the local area in ever-widening circles, and tracking her that way. But he thought about the way she had looked at him, the anger, the vituperation in her voice. This had taken on far more aspects than just being a personal challenge to her. She had managed to tie up everything, all her perceptions about the worth of their marriage, into this insane set of trials. He didn't know how much of it was coming from her, and how much might be stemming from things the shaman had said to her. But the bottom line was that Shelby had staked even more importance to this business than Calhoun had, and he suspected that if his marriage was going to survive, he was going to have to let her have her head in this.

Presuming she had a head by the time it was over.

This time she didn't return until the sun set. When she walked in, Calhoun barely recognized her. She was soaked to the skin. Her clothes were torn, and both the clothing and her exposed skin were covered with dirt. She was walking with a pronounced limp, and was holding her left shoulder gingerly. He gaped. " 'Sokay," she managed to say, her voice sounding like something from beyond the grave. "Managed to pop the arm back into the socket."

He moaned softly. He got up and went to her, and again she backed off. "Elizabeth, I'm . . . I'm so sorry about yesterday . . ."

She shook her head and forced a smile. "No . . . it's all right. Just . . . nowhere on my body that doesn't hurt. So just . . . don't touch me . . . okay?"

He helped her out of the tattered clothes as best he could without putting any pressure anywhere on her body. "I'm going back to the runabout," he told her. "The medikit can do a lot for you . . . get rid of the cuts, the bruises, the . . ."

She laughed. It seemed such an odd noise for her to make. She reached up and touched the scar on his face. "What . . . you're the only one . . . allowed to carry scars as . . . badges of honor?"

"Eppy . . ."

"We can do it . . . later. Now . . . let me sleep. Tomorrow morning . . . it ends. He told me. Last test is tomorrow. Said . . . you could be there."

At this point, the only way I'd let you go without me is over my dead body, he thought.

It was a one-mile drop.

Shelby stood there on the edge of the cliff, staring down. Calhoun was next to her, and he looked equally appalled. Nearby, B'ndri calmly repeated the statement he'd just made that had been met with such disbelief by the two Starfleet officers. "You must dive off the cliff," he said.

She looked at him, then at the drop. It didn't look any shorter. There were stiff winds blowing about her, mussing what was left of her hair. "Dive off."

"Yes."

"Of this cliff."

"Yes."

"And she is to survive . . . *how?*" demanded Calhoun.

"If she is worthy," said the shaman, "then the gods will increase the great gusts of wind, and she will be lifted gently back to the top of this cliff."

"I see," said Shelby.

The shaman approached her and said, "If you truly believe . . . if you think you are worthy of our ways, of this man, of—"

She hit him.

She didn't know she was going to do it until she did it. Later she would swear that the fist had moved on its own. That her arm had simply swung up, straightened out, and delivered a right jab into the shaman's face purely of its own volition, and she was simply an innocent bystander.

Whether it was her idea or not, it caught the shaman squarely in the face. He staggered and almost toppled over, but a quick-moving Calhoun came in behind him and caught him.

Shelby opened her mouth, and for her it was like watching herself from outside her own body. She had no clue what she was going to say until she said it.

"*To hell with you!*" she bellowed. "To hell with your tests! To hell with your rituals! To hell with your whole damned planet! This isn't a test of endurance or worthiness! This is unbridled sadism! *Do you think I liked causing an avalanche and then having to dodge it? Do you think running through a maze of fire was my idea of a good time? What part of 'My God, get these damned insects off of me' made you think that I was enjoying my honey-moon?*" She paused to take a breath. "And now—*now*, you want me to jump off a cliff? *You* jump off the goddamn cliff, because I've freakin' *had it!* I must have been out of my mind! I don't have to jump through hoops to prove my love for Mac! And you know what else? I don't care how much the whole stupid official Xenex marriage ceremony means to him anymore!"

"Eppy, I tried to tell you that it—"

"*Shut up! I did this for you! Be grateful!*"

"I'm grateful," he said immediately.

"You hit me!" said B'ndri, touching his nose tenderly.

"Damned right! You're lucky I don't tear your bowels out with my *teeth!*"

"M'k'n'zy," B'ndri said, turning to face Calhoun. "This woman's actions are the ultimate insult. You must sever all ties with her immediately."

"Sever all ties? Honored one," said Calhoun, his voice flooding with re-lief, "if she'd been insane enough to try and throw herself off this cliff, I would have tackled her before she could do it. I'm glad she's called an end to it. It never should have started in the first place. And we're leaving."

"If you do so," B'ndri said with great severity, "if you walk away now . . . you can never return to your people again."

There was dead silence then. The only sound was the whistling of the wind across the cliff.

"What do you mean?" Calhoun asked.

"You will be dead to us. Shunned. You will be a nonperson. You will have shown us, for good and all, that you have thrown in your lot with . . . these," said B'ndri, casting a contemptuous glance at Shelby. "These, who do not even believe in themselves enough to trust the gods to support them. Never again will any of our people—"

"I get it. Dead. Nonperson. Fine. Let's go." Calhoun held out a hand to Shelby. Immediately she took it, and they started to walk away.

They'd gone five paces when B'ndri said, in a grudging voice, "You passed."

Calhoun and Shelby slowly turned and stared at him. "What?" they said in unison.

B'ndri looked pained as he said, "You, M'k'n'zy, have proven your love for your mate is so great that you would sacrifice everything for her, no matter what it may mean to you. No man can do more for his intended than that."

"And what have I proven?" demanded Shelby.

"That you're not stupid enough to walk off a cliff. Come. We will return to the city, where I will perform the marriage ceremony."

"Forget it," said Calhoun. "None of this was worth it. If you think I'm going to accept . . ."

And Shelby spun, grabbed Calhoun by the front of his shirt, and snarled. "You want to get hit in the face, too?"

He was possessed of a sudden urge to laugh. Wisely, he suppressed it.

"After everything I've been through," continued Shelby, "you *don't* get to pull that. You don't get to walk away. We have this ceremony now or I throw *you* off the cliff."

B'ndri looked at the two of them and then said to Shelby, "I'm starting to like you better than I do him."

The marriage ceremony—or, as the Xenexians called it, the ceremony of bonding—was held with great celebration and festivities. The medical supplies on the runabout weren't required; long, lavish, scented baths restored Shelby to full health, easing the sores, the cuts and bruises, and, most important, the itchy bug bites. They didn't regrow her eyebrows or burned-away hair, but that didn't detract from her beauty as she was brought before Calhoun in as elaborate and beautiful a gown as the women of Xenex could muster. Many of them didn't hesitate to tell Shelby that they would never have been able to withstand the types of trials she had been put through, and that they admired her greatly. And the men told Calhoun that he had picked quite a woman to mate, and wanted to know if she was like a wild animal during sex. He assured them that she was.

And after the ceremony, a very lavish honeymoon suite was prepared for them. It was not their wedding night, granted, but for Calhoun it was even more special, because it was in his native land, with the full support and appreciation of his people. He felt a greater connection to them than he had in a very long time, and he owed it all to Elizabeth Paula Shelby.

Which he would have been more than happy to tell her, if she hadn't fallen fast asleep the moment she was horizontal.

"So much for the Xenexian wedding night," said Calhoun with a sigh, and he curled up next to her, held her close, and allowed her soft snoring to lull him to sleep.

THE *STAR TREK: NEW FRONTIER* TIMELINE
compiled by Keith R.A. DeCandido

The following chronicles the major events of the *Star Trek: New Frontier* cast. Citations in italics are movie, novel, or graphic novel titles (see list at the end). Citations in quotation marks are either short stories or episode titles, which have one of the following designations:

TOS = episode of *Star Trek*
TNG = episode of *Star Trek: The Next Generation*
VOY = episode of *Star Trek: Voyager*
NL = short story in *Star Trek: New Frontier: No Limits*
WLB = short story in *Star Trek: Gateways* Book 7: *What Lay Beyond*
TDW = short story in *Star Trek: Tales of the Dominion War* (forthcoming in 2004)

2267

The *U.S.S. Enterprise* encounters a being named Apollo, once worshipped as a god on Earth. Before committing suicide, he impregnates Lieutenant Carolyn Palamas. ("Who Mourns for Adonais?" [TOS], *Being Human)*

2294

Lieutenant M'Ress has an accident with a temporal gateway that sends her forward in time eighty-two years. *(Cold Wars)*

2305

Lieutenant Arex is involved in a shuttle accident near the Argolis Cluster, which propels him forward in time seventy-one years. *(Cold Wars,* "The Road to Edos" [NL])

2340

George and Sheila McHenry—the latter being the great-great-granddaughter of Palamas—give birth to a son, whom they name Marcus. *(Being Human)*

2345

Morgan Primus, a virtually immortal woman who is now married to Charles Lefler, has her first child in centuries of life, named Robin, and determines that she has not inherited her mother's ability to heal all wounds. ("Alice, on the Edge of Night" [NL])

2348

Fourteen-year-old M'k'n'zy of Calhoun kills his first person, and is given command of a strike vessel that marks the beginning of the Xenexian rebellion against Danteri rule. *(Once Burned)*

Eight-year-old Marcus "Mark" McHenry rejects his supposedly imaginary friend "Missy," truly Artemis, a relative of Apollo. *(Being Human)*

2350

Captain Jean-Luc Picard of the *U.S.S. Stargazer* travels to Thallonian space, where he and his crew thwart a coup attempt by General Gerrid Thul. *(The First Virtue)*

Eight-year-old Si Cwan encounters the Black Mass. *(Dark Allies)*

2353

M'k'n'zy, aided knowingly by his brother D'ndai and unknowingly by support from the Thallonian Empire, succeeds in liberating Xenex. M'k'n'zy meets Picard, who convinces him to join Starfleet. *(House of Cards)*

Morgan, Charles, and Robin Lefler are assigned to the Tantalus colony. Robin starts recording log entries on a battered old tricorder. ("Lefler's Logs" [NL])

2354

With D'ndai offworld, M'k'n'zy fulfills a request by Catrine, a widow of the Calhoun clan, to conceive a child (named Xyon) so her line can continue. D'ndai later makes Catrine a bride of Xenex, blocking an attempt by a rival clan to weaken the Calhouns' power through marrying Catrine. *(Martyr,* "A Lady of Xenex" [NL])

The Leflers live on Rimbor for a year. Robin befriends an Andorian named Whis. Morgan starts disappearing for long periods of time. *(Fire on High,* "Lefler's Logs" [NL])

Changing his name to Mackenzie Calhoun, M'k'n'zy enrolls in Starfleet Academy, as does Elizabeth Paula Shelby. The two of them start a relationship that leads to their being engaged. *(Stone and Anvil)*

2355

Morgan continues to disappear, as she is having trouble dealing with the fact that she will outlive her family. Charles Lefler tells Robin that she's been kidnapped. *(Fire on High,* "Lefler's Logs" [NL], "Alice, on the Edge of Night" [NL])

2356

Si Cwan realizes that his best friend Zoran Si Verdin is a spy for his father. ("Turning Point" [NL])

2357

McHenry, Zak Kebron, Soleta, Tania Tobias, Nikolai Rozhenko, and Worf, son of Mogh, enroll in Starfleet Academy. Rozhenko leaves in midyear, but the remainder of the group stay on friendly terms for all four years. ("Heart of Glory" [TNG], *Worf's First Adventure, Line of Fire, Survival,* "Revelations" [NL])

The Leflers are assigned to Utopia Planitia and Starbase 179. Morgan and Charles have been fighting. Then they're assigned to Starbase 212. ("Lefler's Logs" [NL])

2358

Calhoun and Shelby's engagement comes to an end after Calhoun takes the *Kobayashi Maru* test. *(Stone and Anvil)*

2359

Robin Lefler celebrates her second anniversary at Starbase 212; then they are reassigned to Gemaris V. ("Lefler's Logs" [NL])

2360

Lefler is growing more concerned about the rift between her parents. ("Lefler's Logs" [NL])

Dr. Selar is part of a team sent by Starfleet Intelligence to investigate the mysterious outbreak of a disease previously thought to have been eradicated. *(Catalyst of Sorrows)*

2361

Kebron, Soleta, McHenry, Tobias, and Worf graduate Starfleet Academy. Kebron is assigned to the *U.S.S. Ranger.* Worf, Soleta, and Tobias are assigned to the *U.S.S. Aldrin*. ("Conundrum" [TNG], "Waiting for G'Doh" [NL], "Revelations" [NL])

Kebron is assigned to go undercover as a park statue. ("Waiting for G'Doh" [NL])

2362

The *Aldrin* captures a Romulan smuggler named Rajari, who inadvertently reveals to Soleta that he raped her mother and conceived her. Soleta requests a leave of absence from Starfleet. *(House of Cards, The Two-Front War, Requiem,* "Revelations" [NL])

2363

Soleta is captured on Thallon and freed by Ambassador Spock and Si Cwan. Their departure from Thallonian space is complicated by an encounter with Ferengi. *(House of Cards,* "Out of the Frying Pan" [NL])

Following a failed suicide attempt with a phaser rifle, Morgan starts seeing a psychiatrist, Dr. Kevin Pointer. She then attempts to kill herself and Robin both, but finds that she cannot take the life of her only daughter, and instead later fakes her own death. *(Fire on High,* "Alice, on the Edge of Night" [NL], "Lefler's Logs" [NL])

2364

The *U.S.S. Enterprise*-D is launched under the command of Picard, and encounters the entity known as Q. ("Encounter at Farpoint" [TNG])

Lefler, after consoling her father over the apparent death of Morgan, enrolls in Starfleet Academy. ("Lefler's Logs" [NL])

Selar, now the assistant chief medical officer of the *Enterprise,* briefly encounters a female Q. (" 'Q'uandary" [NL])

The *Enterprise* discovers that several outposts along the Romulan Neutral Zone have been attacked. ("The Neutral Zone" [TNG])

2365

Selar is part of an away team that responds to a distress signal from Graves' World. ("The Schizoid Man" [TNG])

Q sends the *Enterprise* to System J25 in the Delta Quadrant, prompting contact with the Borg. ("Q Who" [TNG])

2366

After determining that the Borg were the ones who attacked the Neutral Zone outposts, Shelby is transferred from chief engineer of the *Yosemite* to Starfleet Tactical, soon taking over Borg Tactical. ("All that Glisters . . ." [NL], "The Best of Both Worlds" [TNG])

Assistant chief engineer Katerina Mueller of the *U.S.S. Grissom* creates a sensor probe that can be clandestinely deployed along the Romulan Neutral Zone. Her handling of the subsequent encounter with a Romulan ship leads Captain Norman Kenyon to give her a promotion to night-shift commander. ("Performance Appraisal" [NL])

Shelby is assigned to the *Enterprise* to assist against a Borg cube. Thirty-nine vessels are lost in conflict with the cube at Wolf 359 before the *Enterprise* stops the ship at Earth. Shelby is then assigned to oversee the reconstruction of the fleet. ("The Best of Both Worlds" [TNG]

2367

Shelby is reassigned to the *U.S.S. Chekov* as first officer under Captain Morgan Korsmo. Along with the *Enterprise,* they are involved in a three-way battle among Starfleet, the Borg, and a "planet-killer." The *Chekov* is irreparably damaged. *(Vendetta)*

2368

The *U.S.S. Excalibur,* under the temporary command of Commander William T. Riker, is part of a blockade of the Klingon-Romulan border assembled by Picard during a Klingon civil war. ("Redemption Part 2" [TNG])

Lefler, now an engineer on the *Enterprise,* aids in an attempt to rescue Picard from El-Adrel IV, then helps to rescue the crew from a Ktarian mind-control device. ("Darmok" [TNG], "The Game" [TNG])

Lieutenant Burgoyne 172, a Hermat engineer on the *U.S.S. Livingston,* is assigned to aid a J'naii doctor named Dorvan in stopping a techno-organic probe that has run amok on Damiano. ("Oil and Water" [NL])

McHenry is assigned to help test an experimental navigation system that will enable ships to travel close to the event horizon of a black hole, but only he with his godlike powers can guarantee its successful operation. ("Singularity" [NL])

Calhoun is assigned to the *Grissom* as first officer. He and Mueller start a relationship. *(The Two-Front War, Once Burned)*

Korsmo and Shelby are assigned as commanding officer and first officer of the *Excalibur.* Burgoyne is made assistant chief engineer under Commander Argyle. *(Triangle: Imzadi II,* "Making a Difference" [NL], "Through the Looking Glass" [NL])

2369

The *Excalibur* encounters a Borg scout ship, which removes a portion of the hull, taking three crew members with it. ("Survival Instinct" [VOY], "Making a Difference" [NL])

Kenyon's brother and daughter are killed during a diplomatic mission to Anzibar. Kenyon goes insane, and eventually kills himself, though not before the crew almost mutinies. Calhoun resigns his commission. *(Once Burned)*

Selar is conscripted by the female Q to give aid to her side in the Q-Continuum's civil war. ("The Q and the Grey" [VOY], " 'Q'uandary" [NL])

2370

Calhoun begins doing deep-cover work for Admiral Alynna Nechayev and Starfleet Intelligence. Among the missions are the unintentional rescue of an Orion woman named Vandelia from Zolon Darg and destroying a phased cloaking device that had been turned over to a Romulan commander by Picard. *(House of Cards, Once Burned, Double or Nothing,* "Loose Ends" [NL])

2371

Selar takes leave from the *Enterprise* to fulfill the needs of the *Pon farr.* In the midst, however, her husband, Voltak, dies. *(House of Cards)*

The *Excalibur* rescues Riker, Worf, Alexander Rozhenko, and Deanna Troi from a Romulan ship. *(Triangle: Imzadi II)*

Burgoyne takes shore leave on Argelius II, sharing a drink with Captain Montgomery Scott, having several liaisons, and being given a vision-inducing gem by a spurned lover. *(The Two-Front War,* "Through the Looking Glass" [NL])

2373

A Borg cube attacks Earth. The *Excalibur* is part of the fleet that engages the cube. The ship survives, but Korsmo is killed. *(Star Trek: First Contact, House of Cards,* "Making a Difference" [NL])

The Thallonian Empire collapses, causing chaos in Sector 221G. The royal family is killed, apart from Si Cwan and his sister Kalinda. The latter is kidnapped by Zoran, who has her surgically altered and her memories suppressed, and brings her to the planet Mondor with the new identity of Riella. The *Excalibur* is assigned to patrol the sector, lending humanitarian aid where necessary. At Picard's recommendation, Calhoun is put back in active service and given command. Shelby remains as first officer, with Burgoyne now chief engineer. Soleta, who has returned to active service owing to the dying wishes of her mother, is transferred from Starfleet Academy to be made science officer. Lefler is made operations officer, McHenry conn officer, Kebron chief of security, and Si Cwan is an unofficial Thallonian ambassador. Mueller is made night-shift commander. *(House of Cards, Into the Void, Once Burned, The Quiet Place)*

Calhoun rescues the ship *Cambon* and helps overthrow a repressive government on Nelkar, then rescues Si Cwan and Kebron from capture on Thallon, shortly before that world is destroyed by the Great Bird of the Galaxy. *(Into the Void, The Two-Front War, End Game)*

Xyon, no longer willing to live in his father's shadow, departs Xenex. He wanders for a while, ending up at the Daystrom Institute, where he encounters the experimental ship *Lyla* and its eponymous sentient computer. With Lyla's cooperation, Xyon steals the ship. *(The Quiet Place, Dark Allies)*

2374

The *Excalibur* goes to Zondar to attempt to stop a civil war, then travels to Ahmista, where they find Morgan Primus, to Lefler's shock. The *Excalibur* crew encounter the legendary Prometheans on Ahmista. Selar and Burgoyne conceive a child. *(Martyr, Fire on High)*

As hostilities with the Dominion begin, the *Excalibur* remains on station in Sector 221G. They encounter a world wiped out by the Redeemer virus, prompting Calhoun to travel back in time to prevent the tragedy. However, their traveling back forward toes awry, and they overshoot their destination by eighteen months. *(Once Burned, Double Time)*

2375

The *Excalibur* returns from its time-travel mission at the tail end of the Dominion War. ("Unhappy Returns" [TDW])

The *Excalibur* rescues the *Independence* from an attack by renegade Romulans. Calhoun is then sent undercover to stop Zolon Darg and Gerrid Thul while Riker is given temporary command of the *Excalibur* to track down the Romulans. *(Double or Nothing)*

Xyon and Lyla rescue Kalinda from the Dogs of War, with aid from Si Cwan, Kebron, and Soleta. The *Excalibur* then combats the Redeemers and the Dogs of War around the Black Mass, with Xyon seeming to sacrifice his life to save them all. Selar and Burgoyne's child is born, and named Xyon in his memory. *(The Quiet Place, Dark Allies)*

2376

The *Excalibur* is destroyed by a computer virus implanted during the encounter with the Romulans under Riker's command. McHenry uses his powers to enable everyone to safely get off the ship. Calhoun is believed killed, but survives on the planet Yakaba. Shelby is given command of the *Exeter* and goes on a mission to Makkus, which goes oddly and leads to her relinquishing command. Kebron and McHenry are sent undercover to stop what turn out to be pranks committed by Q. Soleta is reunited with a dying Rajari, and is tricked into performing a posthumous act of vengeance on his behalf on Romulus. Lefler and Morgan travel to Risa and stop a scheme by an old rival of Si Cwan's. After a failed attempt to settle on Vulcan, Burgoyne and Selar come to terms with raising Xyon together on the *Excalibur*. Calhoun escapes Yakaba, and is given command of a new *Excalibur*, with Shelby placed in command of the *Trident*, and both assigned to Sector 221G. Burgoyne is promoted to first officer of the *Excalibur*, with Mueller assigned as Shelby's first officer. *(Dark Allies, Requiem, Renaissance, Restoration, Being Human)*

Arex appears in the present and is escorted by the Department of Temporal Investigations to his homeworld to attend his father's Day of Death. Upon his return to Starfleet, M'Ress appears in the present, and Arex helps her assimilate. They are both assigned to the *Trident*, Arex as chief of security, M'Ress as a science officer. *("The Road to Edos" [NL], Cold Wars)*

Calhoun and Shelby are married in a ceremony officiated by Picard. They then travel to Xenex for their honeymoon. *(Restoration, "A Little Getaway" [NL])*

The *U.S.S. Voyager*, on its way home from being thrust thousands of light-years away into the Delta Quadrant, encounters one of the three *Excalibur* crew members assimilated by the Borg, and helps her completely disconnect from the Collective. *("Survival Instinct" [VOY])*

During the gateways crisis, the *Excalibur* and *Trident* are sent to mediate between Aeron and Markon, feuding worlds now linked by suddenly active gateways. They are successful, though Calhoun and Shelby are forced to leap through a gateway, which seems to put them in the Xenexian afterlife. While they're away, Burgoyne and Mueller aid the *Enterprise*, the *Defiant*, and a dozen other ships in shutting down the gateway network. *(Cold Wars, "Death after Life" [WLB], "The Other Side" [WLB])*

The relatives of Apollo offer to restore the Thallonian Empire to its former glory, and the *Excalibur* and *Trident* are put in the difficult position of trying to stop gods. *(Being Human, Gods Above)*

Eben, a citizen of a world that worships Xant, is apparently given a vision by Xant, after he is the sole survivor of his world after it was accidentally infected with the Redeemer virus. He is determined to spread the *true* word of Xant. ("Redemption" [NL])

Complete list of novels and graphic novels:

Star Trek: The Next Generation: Vendetta by Peter David

Star Trek: The Next Generation: Triangle: Imzadi II by Peter David

Star Trek: The Next Generation: Starfleet Academy #1: Worf's First Adventure by Peter David

Star Trek: The Next Generation: Starfleet Academy #2: Line of Fire by Peter David

Star Trek: The Next Generation: Starfleet Academy #3: Survival by Peter David

Star Trek: New Frontier Book 1: *House of Cards* by Peter David

Star Trek: New Frontier Book 2: *Into the Void* by Peter David

Star Trek: New Frontier Book 3: *The Two-Front War* by Peter David

Star Trek: New Frontier Book 4: *End Game* by Peter David

Star Trek: New Frontier Book 5: *Martyr* by Peter David

Star Trek: New Frontier Book 6: *Fire on High* by Peter David

Star Trek: New Frontier: Captain's Table Book 5: *Once Burned* by Peter David

Star Trek: New Frontier: Double Time (graphic novel) by Peter David, Mike Collins, and David Roach

Star Trek: The Next Generation: Double Helix Book 5: *Double or Nothing* by Peter David

Star Trek: The Next Generation: Double Helix Book 6: *The First Virtue* by Michael Jan Friedman & Christie Golden

Star Trek: New Frontier Book 7: *The Quiet Place* by Peter David

Star Trek: New Frontier Book 8: *Dark Allies* by Peter David

Star Trek: New Frontier Book 9: *Excalibur* Book 1: *Requiem* by Peter David

Star Trek: New Frontier Book 10: *Excalibur* Book 2: *Renaissance* by Peter David

Star Trek: New Frontier Book 11: *Excalibur* Book 3: *Restoration*
by Peter David

Star Trek: New Frontier: Gateways Book 6: *Cold Wars* by Peter David

Star Trek: New Frontier Book 12: *Being Human* by Peter David

Star Trek: New Frontier Book 13: *Gods Above* by Peter David

Star Trek: New Frontier Book 14: *Stone and Anvil* by Peter David

Star Trek The Lost Era: Catalyst of Sorrows by Margaret Wander Bonnano